gatekeepers

BOOKS BY THIS AUTHOR

Comes a Horseman

Germ

Deadfall

gatekeepers

BOOK THREE OF DREAMHOUSE KINGS

ROBERT LIPARULO

THOMAS NELSON
Since 1798

NASHVILLE   DALLAS   MEXICO CITY   RIO DE JANEIRO   BEIJING

Published in Nashville, Tennessee, by Thomas Nelson. Thomas Nelson is a registered trademark of Thomas Nelson, Inc.

Page design by Mandi Cofer
Map design by Doug Cordes

Thomas Nelson, Inc., titles may be purchased in bulk for educational, business, fund-raising, or sales promotional use. For information, please e-mail SpecialMarkets@ThomasNelson.com.

Publisher's Note: This novel is a work of fiction. Names, characters, places, and incidents are either products of the author's imagination or used fictitiously. All characters are fictional, and any similarity to people living or dead is purely coincidental.

Library of Congress Cataloging-in-Publication Data

Liparulo, Robert.
   Gatekeepers / Robert Liparulo.
      p. cm. — (Dreamhouse Kings ; bk. 3)
   Summary: With their mother still missing after going through a Civil
War time portal in their spooky house, and their father in jail under a
false accusation, Xander, David, and their younger sister continue to
try to bring their mother back, now with the help of an old relative who
has turned up unexpectedly.
   ISBN 978-1-59554-498-8 (hardcover)
   [1. Time travel—Fiction. 2. Dwellings—Fiction. 3. Brothers and
sisters—Fiction. 4. Supernatural—Fiction.] I. Title.
PZ7.L6636Gat 2009
[Fic]—dc22

                                    2008042007

Printed in the United States of America
08 09 10 11 QW 6 5 4 3 2 1

TO MY DAUGHTER MELANIE

You may have outgrown my lap,
but never my heart.

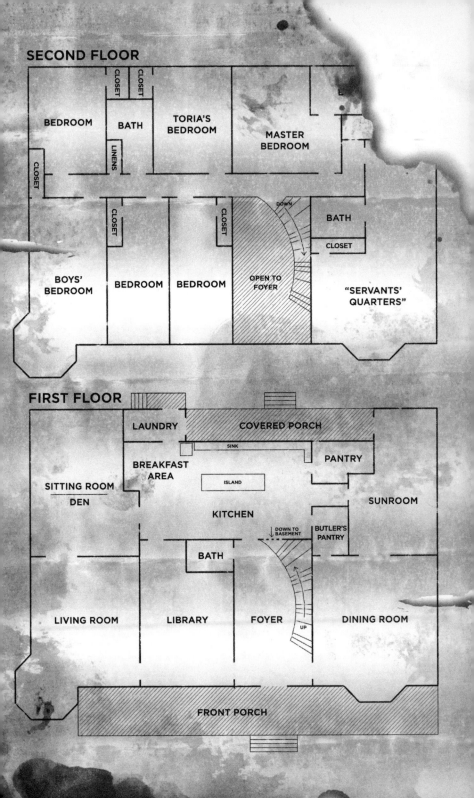

STOP!

READ *HOUSE OF DARK SHADOWS*
AND *WATCHER IN THE WOODS*
BEFORE CONTINUING!

"Who are you really, wanderer?"
and the answer you have to give
no matter how dark and cold
the world around you is:
"Maybe I'm a King."

—WILLIAM STAFFORD, *A STORY THAT COULD BE TRUE*

O, call back yesterday, bid time return.

—WILLIAM SHAKESPEARE, *KING RICHARD II*

CHAPTER

one

TUESDAY, 6:58 P.M.

PINEDALE, CALIFORNIA

Xander's words struck David's heart like a musket ball.

He reeled back, then grabbed the collar of his brother's filthy Confederate coat. His eyes stung, whether from the tears squeezing around them or the sand whipping through the room, he didn't know. He pulled his face to within inches of Xander's.

1

"You . . . you *found* her?" he said. "Xander, you found *Mom*?"

He looked over Xander's shoulder to the portal door, which had slammed shut as soon as Xander stumbled through. The two boys knelt in the center of the antechamber. Wind billowed their hair. It whooshed in under the door, pulling back what belonged to the Civil War world from which Xander had just stepped. The smell of smoke and gunpowder was so strong, David could taste it.

He shook Xander. "Where is she? Why didn't you bring her?"

His heart was going crazy, like a ferret racing around inside his chest, more frantic than ever. Twelve-year-olds didn't have heart attacks, did they?

Xander leaned back and sat on his heels. His bottom lip trembled, and his chest rose and fell as he tried to catch his breath. The wind plucked a leaf from his hair, whirled it through the air, then sucked it under the door.

"Xander!" David said. "Where's Mom?"

Xander lowered his head. "I couldn't . . ." he said. "I couldn't get her. You gotta go over, Dae. You gotta bring her back!"

"*Me?*" A heavy weight pushed on David's chest, smashing the ferret between sternum and spine. He rose, leaped for the door, and tugged on the locked handle.

He wore a gray hat ("It's a *kepi,*" Dad would tell him) and jacket, like Xander's blue ones. They had discovered that it took wearing or holding three items from the antechamber to unlock the portal door. He needed one more.

"Xander, you said you found her!"

Xander shook his head. "I think I saw her going into a tent, but it was at the other end of the camp. I couldn't get to her."

David's mouth dropped open. "That's not *finding* her! I thought I saw her, too, the other day in the World War II world—"

"Dae, listen." Xander pushed himself up and gripped David's shoulders. "She saw the message we left. She saw Bob."

Bob was the cartoon face and family mascot since Dad was a kid, drawn on notes and birthday cards. When David and Xander had been in Ulysses S. Grant's Union camp the night before, Xander had drawn it on a tent. It was their way of letting Mom know they were looking for her.

"She wrote back!" Xander said. "David, she's *there!*"

"But . . ." David didn't know if he wanted to scream or cry or punch his brother. "Why didn't you go get her?"

"Something was happening on the battlefield. They were rounding up all the soldiers and herding us toward the front line. I tried to get to her, but they kept grabbing me, pushing me out of camp. When I broke away"—Xander's face became hard—"they called me a deserter. That quick, I was a deserter. One of them *shot* at me! I barely got back to the portal." He shook his head. "You gotta go! Now! Before she's gone, or the portal changes, or something happens to her."

3

Yes . . . no! David's stomach hurt. His brain was throbbing against his skull. His broken arm started to ache again, and he rubbed the cast. "Xander, I can't. They almost killed me yesterday."

"That's because you were a gray-coat." Xander began taking off his blue jacket. "Wear this one."

"Why can't *you?* Just tell them—"

"I'll never make it," Xander said. "They'll throw me in the stockade for deserting—if they don't shoot me first."

"They'll do the same to me." David hated how whiney his words came out.

"You're just a kid. They'll see that."

"I'm twelve, Xander. Only three years younger than you."

"That's the difference between fighting and not, Dae." He held the jacket open. "I know it was really scary before, but this time you'll be on the right side."

David looked around the small room. He said, "Where's the rifle you took when you went over? The Harper's Ferry musket?"

His brother gazed at his empty hand. He scanned the floor. "I must have dropped it when I fell. I was just trying to stay alive. I didn't notice." He shook the jacket. "Come on."

David shrugged out of the gray coat he was wearing. He tossed it onto the bench and reluctantly slipped into the one Xander held. He pulled the left side over his cast.

Xander buttoned it for him. He said, "The tent I saw her

go into was near the back of the camp, on the other side from where I drew Bob." He lifted the empty sleeve and let it flop down. He smiled. "Looks like you lost your arm in battle."

"See? They'll think I *can* fight, that I *have* fought."

"I was just kidding." He took the gray kepi off David's head and replaced it with the blue one. Then he turned to the bench and hooks, looking for another item.

"Xander, listen," David said. "You don't know what's been happening here. There are two cops downstairs."

Xander froze in his reach for a canteen. "What?" His head pivoted toward the door opposite the portal, as though he could see through it into the hallway beyond, down the stairs, around the corner, and into the foyer. Or like he expected the cops to burst through. "What are they doing here?"

"They're trying to get us out of the house. Taksidian's with them." Just thinking of the creepy guy who was responsible for his broken arm frightened David—but not as much as the thought of getting hauled away when they were so close to rescuing Mom. "Gimme that," he said, waggling his fingers at the canteen.

Xander snatched it off the hook and looped the strap over David's head. "Where's Dad?"

"They put him in handcuffs. He told me to come get you."

"Handcuffs!"

"And one more thing," David said. He closed his eyes, feeling as though the jacket had just gained twenty pounds. "Clayton, that kid who wanted to pound me at school? He came through the portal from the school locker to the linen closet." He opened one eye to see his brother's shocked expression.

"How *long* was I gone?" Xander said. "Where is he now?"

"I pushed him back in. He returned to the school, but he might come back."

"Great." Xander glanced over his shoulder at the hallway door again, then back at David. "Anything else I should know?"

David shook his head. "I guess if I die, I won't have to go to school tomorrow." He smiled weakly.

The school year—seventh grade for David, tenth for Xander—had started just yesterday: two days of classes. Mom had been kidnapped the day before that. David couldn't believe they'd even gone to school under the circumstances, but Dad, who was the new principal, had insisted they keep up normal appearances so they wouldn't attract suspicion.

Lot of good it did, David thought, thinking of the cops downstairs.

"I don't know," Xander said. "Dad would probably figure out a way to get your body there."

David's expression remained grim.

"You'll be fine."

"Don't get taken away," David told his brother. "Don't leave with me over there. Don't leave me alone in this house when I come back. Don't—"

Xander held up his hand to stop him. "I won't leave," he said. "I'll go see what's happening downstairs, but I won't leave. No way, no how. Okay? Besides—" He smiled, but David saw how hard it was for him to do it. "You'll have Mom with you when you come back. Right?"

It was David's turn to smile, and he found it wasn't so hard to do. "Yeah." He turned, took a deep breath, and opened the portal door.

CHAPTER

two

TUESDAY, 7:05 P.M.

David squinted against the bright daylight coming through the portal. A warm breeze touched his face. The odor of gunpowder wafted into his nostrils. It reminded him of his time on the battlefield, and he felt sick again.

"Go," Xander said behind him.

"I am." He stepped through, stumbled, and fell into a bush. He rolled out of it and cracked his cast into a tree. He pulled air through his clenched teeth. Before the portal faded and broke apart like a defective DVD image, he caught a glimpse of Xander looking through it.

David scrambled up to get his bearings and immediately saw the rows of tents across a narrow meadow. Soldiers streamed toward the far hills, beyond which he knew a battle raged. Gun and cannon fire rang out in the distance. His hope for a deserted camp left him as he spotted more soldiers talking in clusters and others moving from one tent to another.

It wasn't the mad dash to the front line Xander had described, and he wondered if time here had skipped one direction or another, like a hiccup, in the five minutes since his brother had left. They hadn't thought of that. Maybe Xander *could* have returned safely. David looked for the portal, any sign of it, but it was gone.

The first time any of them had gone through a portal, Dad had ended up rescuing Xander from a gladiator. He said the items from the antechamber had tugged him toward the portal home. David and Xander had followed the same tugging to get out of the Civil War world the night before. It was as though the items wanted to go home too, and they knew the way. Now, however, the jacket, kepi, and canteen were exerting no unnatural pull. It was like they knew it wasn't time to return.

Get moving, David told himself, but his feet wouldn't obey.

Even this far away from the battle, smoke drifted over him. *Don't get sick, not now, not with Mom waiting.*

Mom. The thought of her unglued his feet. He lurched forward and out of the woods. Approaching the backs of the tents, he tried to remember which one Xander had written on. Had it been two tents from the front or ten? He had no clue. He walked behind the big wedge-shaped structures, peering between them, hoping to spot something he recognized. And he did, but not what he had expected: the Harper's Ferry rifle Xander had dropped. He must be close to where Xander had drawn Bob and, later, where he'd seen Mom.

David picked up the rifle and walked to the front of the tents, coming out in the camp's center aisle. He turned in a circle, but he didn't see the cartoon face. He headed toward the rear of the camp. Four tents along, he saw it—and his heart leapt into his throat. Just as Xander had said, words were scrawled in block letters beside the goofy face: IS THAT YOU? I'M HERE! I'M

Mom! It had to be! Who else knew the face? Who else would write those words?

But what else had she wanted to write? She had obviously been interrupted: "I'M . . . " I'm what? I'm safe? I'm hurt? I'm at this place or that?

Mom, where are you?

Which tent had Xander seen her enter? He remembered it was on the other side of the aisle. Could she still be there? It struck David that he could be in the camp *before* the events

Xander had witnessed—time was *that* weird with the portals; she might not have even entered the tent yet.

Don't start freaking out now, he told himself. *I can do this: find Mom!*

He looked up the aisle one direction, then down the other. Only men—most of them in blue soldier uniforms, some in the bloodied, once-white smocks of surgeons. A soldier was pounding the butt of his rifle against a rock, a blackened metal pot beside him. David had learned that coffee was cherished in Civil War encampments; this was how they ground the beans. Another man sat on the ground, writing on a piece of paper on his thigh. Two men sat on a log, cleaning their rifles. He wanted to ask whether any of them had seen her. He wanted to call out for her. But did he really want to attract attention to himself?

He started for the tents across the aisle, then thought of something. If she knew they were looking for her there, wouldn't she stay close if she could? He returned to the tent bearing Bob's face and threw back the flap. A soldier sat at the edge of a cot, pulling on his boots. Another lay on a different cot, a rag over his face.

The soldier with the boots looked up. "What do you want, boy?"

David backed away, letting the flap fall into place. He moved toward the next tent. He'd check a few on this side, then cross to the other.

"Hey!" It was a man's deep voice. "You, boy!"

David spun to see the bearded officer who had spoken to him yesterday—General Grant. He was limping now. David couldn't remember if he had limped the day before.

As he drew close, the general expertly flipped up the cover of his gun holster with his thumb. He laid his hand on the handle of his pistol and said, "Drop the rifle, son."

"But—" The word squeaked out of David's tight throat.

General Grant's eyes narrowed. "If I pull this pistol on you, boy, I'll use it. Now drop it."

David forced his fingers to open. The gun hit the trampled earth with a thud. He said, "Sir, I—"

"I know you," Grant said. "Last time I saw you, you wore Confederate gray. Now you're wearing blue and carrying a rifle. Where's the soldier who was escorting you to the stockades?"

He meant Xander. They had pretended to be soldier and prisoner to get David off the front lines without getting shot. "I . . . sir . . . he . . ."

The general shook his head. "We better not find him dead, boy." He turned and raised his hand to a passing soldier. "Corporal!"

David dropped to the ground and started to scramble under the edge of the tent. He heard General Grant say, "Oh, no, you don't!" and felt the man grab his heel.

He yanked his foot out of his sneaker, rose, and ran through the tent, jumping over cots and the men sleeping on them. He slid under the tent's back wall as though he were sliding into home plate. His head snagged on the canvas wall. He ducked, and the cloth wall snapped away.

Behind him the general was yelling, "Escaped Rebel!"

David pictured the man pushing through the tent flaps, pistol in hand. He expected to hear a shot any second. Instead, a commotion arose from within the tent: the clamor of soldiers jumping to their feet, going for their weapons, calling out for someone to tell them what was going on.

"Get down, men!" General Grant bellowed. "Out of my way!"

David got his feet under him and ran for the trees. Kicking through the meadow's tall grass, gritting his teeth against the pain of his cast banging against his ribs, he got the feeling of déjà vu: hadn't he run for his life through this very field before?

Yeah, last night!

Only then Xander had been with him. And he'd had both sneakers. Now he was loping along, one shoe on and one shoe off.

He was almost in the woods when the first shot rang out. Though he had been expecting it, the *crack!* of the weapon startled him. His feet did a little dance, and he tumbled over himself. Up again in no time, he plunged into the shadows of the trees. Behind him, another rifle shot cracked. He pushed deeper into the woods, then rammed his shoulder into the trunk of a big oak. He rolled around to the tree's far side and stopped. His breathing came in ragged gulps.

David hadn't bothered to grab the rifle when he'd bolted away from General Grant. He raised his hand to his head and confirmed what he expected: he'd also lost his kepi. But he still wore the blue jacket, which was now applying a pressure like gravity on his body—only in a *sideways* direction, not downward. If the strength of the tug was any indication, the portal was close. He noticed the canteen. It was lifting up on its strap, vibrating slightly, pointing in the same direction the tug indicated.

He craned his neck to peer past the tree. In the field behind the tents, soldiers were gathering around General Grant. The great man himself was pointing toward the woods, pushing at the soldiers and saying, "Get moving! Go!"

Me too, David thought. *I gotta get out of here.*

He pushed off the tree and ran. The canteen strap rotated on his neck until it floated a few inches off his stomach, directly in front of him. It acted like a compass needle, guiding him toward the portal . . . he hoped.

Behind him a voice yelled, "There!"

Someone fired. The musket ball tore past him, ripping through leaves, snapping branches.

David veered left. For a few steps he ignored the jacket's pull and the canteen's shift to his side. Then he turned back, farther than the canteen's bearing. It swung to his other side.

He zigzagged this way, following the tug of antechamber items, but trying to be a difficult target.

Another shot rang out. Bark exploded from a nearby tree.

A hand grabbed the back of his jacket. He yelled and threw his weight into his forward motion. The canteen hit his chest, slid up and over his shoulder. Its strap tightened around the front of his neck. Nobody had grabbed him, he realized—it was the coat, tugging at him to reverse; he had passed the portal. He skidded to a stop, turned, and ran the other way. The canteen shifted sideways. The jacket urged him to plunge into a thicket of heavy bushes. He stopped, trying to understand.

The corner of his eye caught movement toward the encampment. He turned to see a soldier twenty yards away, taking aim. He stumbled back and tumbled into the bushes. The rifle cracked.

CHAPTER

three

The musket ball sailed right over him. David hit the ground hard, flat on his back in a tangle of twigs and leaves. The air whooshed out of his lungs. He tried pulling it back in, but it wouldn't come.

Gotta move! Get up! Go!

Gasping for breath, he scrambled to stand. Not easy with only one good arm and the weight of the cast on the other one. He fell back again. His head smacked the ground—a rock, it was so hard. He realized the light around him was not from the sun. His eyes focused on a lamp mounted to a ceiling.

The antechamber. He was home.

Something struck his leg, a hard kick to it. "Xander?"

But it was the door, closing, dragging his legs with it. He remembered the baseball bat that had broken in two between the door edge and the frame when Mom had been taken. He pulled his legs up quickly, and the door slammed.

He rolled over and pushed himself up on one arm. Foliage fell off him.

"Xander?" he said again, wheezing out the word.

The room was empty. He lowered himself back down, resting his face against the wood planks. He put most of his weight onto the right side of his body, feeling his broken arm throb between his chest and the floor. He closed his eyes and breathed.

Wind hissed into the room, causing the twigs and leaves to flutter, then fly into the air. He watched them zip into the crack under the door. The largest twigs got stuck, and leaves piled up behind them. The twigs cracked and splintered. As they did, they disappeared, along with the leaves, all of it heading back where it had come from—heading back to *when* it had come from.

David stood and stared at the portal door. He didn't expect it to open. He didn't expect anything. His eyes simply needed a place to rest while he came out of a mild daze, as if awaking from a deep sleep. Having brushed that close to death, his emotions should have been raging. Instead, he felt numb. It was as though his mind had said *Enough already!* and flipped a switch. He was thankful for the break.

Slowly, he began to move again. He pulled the canteen's strap over his head and set it on the bench. He dropped his shoulder, allowing the jacket to slide off, and slipped his good arm out of the sleeve. He opened the door and walked into the hallway. He hoped Xander, Dad, and Toria, his nine-year-old sister, had fared better at getting rid of the cops than he had at rescuing Mom.

But when he emerged from the secret doorway on the second floor, he found Xander and Toria hiding in the short hall, peering around the corner toward the grand staircase. Voices drifted up from the foyer.

"I told you," Dad was saying, "you can't search my house. Your warrant or whatever this is limits you to *serving* eviction papers, not *enforcing* them."

"We're not evicting you, sir," a voice said. "We're taking you in for assaulting a police officer."

"Assault? I didn't touch you until you bumped into my hand, trying to come into my house without my permission or the authority to do so. Wait, wait, wait . . . my kids are in the house. You can't take me. It will leave them alone."

"Then call them down," another voice said. "We'll take them with us."

"Kids, stay where you are!" Dad called.

Xander held up his hand and gave David a quiet, "Shhh." Then he looked past David, hope and worry on his face. "Where is she?" he whispered. "Tell me you found her, Dae."

David shook his head. "General Grant recognized me. I had to run, like you did. I didn't even get to the tent you told me about. But, Xander . . ." He gripped his brother's arm. "I saw the message she left."

Love for his mother and disappointment at not finding her welled up from his chest. It dried his mouth and wetted his eyes. So, the emotional numbness had been only temporary, he thought. It was like getting punched in the arm so hard you couldn't feel it for a while.

Xander's sadness showed in his eyes, but he nodded and smiled. *Trying to be the big brother, the brave one,* David thought.

Toria whispered, "Who are you talking about? Mom? What message?"

"I'll tell you later," Xander said. "Now *shhh.*" He looked at David and nodded his head toward the voices. "They've been going at it like that for a while. Dad read the court papers, something about the house being unfit to live in."

"I agree," David said.

Xander scowled at him. "They weren't supposed to get us out of the house, just serve the papers."

"So why don't they just go away, then?"

"Dad asked how much Taksidian paid them to get us out of the house, and that *really* ticked them off. Now they want to take him to jail."

Taksidian's deep voice rolled like thunder up the stairs. "Officers," he said, "Mr. King is correct. You can't take him and leave the children here alone."

Why would Taksidian be pleading their case?

But that wasn't what the man had in mind. The next thing he said was, "Why don't I go get them for you?"

Toria took a step back. Her hand clasped David's.

"Hey," Dad said loudly. "He can't—"

"Sir!" a cop said. "We're handling this. Bill, take Mr. King out to the car."

"No! You can't do this!" Dad yelled.

There was a lot of banging going on down there. David imagined his dad, hands cuffed behind him, getting pulled backward out the door while he kicked out at the cops, at Taksidian. His heels would be striking the floor, hitting the door frame.

Xander started around the corner. David pulled his hand out of Toria's and reached for him. His fingers brushed his brother's shirt, then got a grip on his waistband.

Jerked to a stop, Xander snapped his head around. He was what Mom would have called fightin' mad.

David shook his head. "You'll just make it worse."

"They're taking Dad."

"But you heard him. He wants us to stay here. They'll just take you too. Then where will we be?"

Xander looked from David to Toria. Something in her expression softened his. He flipped a stray strand of hair off her face with his finger and said, "It'll be okay, Toria. Don't worry."

She lowered her head. "First Mom, now Dad."

Below, Taksidian said, "Just give me five minutes."

"Can't let you do that, Mr. Taksidian," the remaining cop said. "It's not your house, sir."

David expected the man to say *Not yet* . . . but what he did say was worse.

"But, Officer Benson," Taksidian said, "there's no place they can hide where I can't find them."

Xander looked over his shoulder at David, his eyes wide.

Outside, Dad was still yelling. David heard their names, but the words were being snatched away by the breeze and the trees and the distance as the cop pulled their father away from the house.

Taksidian wasn't finished. He said, "In the interest of the children's welfare, officer, I can make it worth your while."

"Step outside, sir," Officer Benson said.

David thought the cop sounded angry. Maybe after Dad's accusation of the cops taking money to help Taksidian, this new attempt at a bribe had—finally—grated on the cop's sense of duty.

Slow footsteps echoed downstairs, moving from the foyer to the hollow-sounding planks of the front porch.

"Alexander King, David King, Victoria King," the cop hollered, obviously reading their names. "Last chance to come now." He waited. "We'll return with a court order to remove you by force, if necessary. It's for your own safety."

Silence. Then: "We'll send a car back to wait outside tonight. If you change your minds, go out to the officers. They'll take care of you."

His footsteps took him to the porch. The door closed.

four

TUESDAY, 7:33 P.M.

"Now what?" David said.

Above them, something creaked. Their eyes lifted to the ceiling.

"I'm scared," Toria said.

"Just the house settling," Xander said.

His eyes found David's: Xander didn't believe it, and neither did David.

"What if they do come back to take us out by force?"

David said. "They might board the house up or change the locks."

"I think that'll take some time." Xander licked his lips. "Probably easier now that they arrested Dad. But they can't do anything tonight, no way. I'm more worried about—" He stopped, his eyes dropping to Toria.

"What?" she said. "What are you more worried about?"

"Nothing." He peered around the corner, then walked into the second floor's main hallway and to the top of the stairs.

Toria and David followed him. The foyer was empty, the door was closed.

David thought about how wind always blew into the antechamber after they'd returned from one of the worlds. It pulled everything that belonged to that world back through the door. Something like that had just happened in the foyer. The cops and Taksidian had blown in and taken Dad. But Dad belonged *here*. It wasn't right that they could just take him. The house felt emptier without him—not just one person emptier, but like it had been abandoned for centuries, an ancient tomb.

David felt Toria's hand grab his again. He saw that she also clasped Xander's hand. She looked up at him. "Can you guys sleep in my room tonight? Please?"

David nodded.

Xander said, "Good idea. David, let's go get our stuff. Toria, go clear your floor to make room for us."

They walked hand in hand to Toria's door and released her into her room. Then the boys approached the chair that David had jammed under the linen closet door handle to keep Clayton from coming back through. It was a solid piece of furniture, with spindles that rose from the rear of the seat and ended in a heavy top rail.

David leaned his ear to the door. "I don't hear anything," he whispered.

"How long ago did you send him back?"

"Right before I ran to find you," David said.

"So, what, a half hour?" Xander said. "If he was going to come back tonight, he'd have done it already. He must have gone back to the locker and left. Maybe he'll wake up tomorrow thinking it was a dream."

"Fat chance." David reached for the chair, but Xander stopped him.

His brother glanced back toward Toria's room, then gestured for David to follow him into their room. As soon as they were both inside, he said, "You didn't see Mom?"

David shook his head. "They shot at me again. Xander, they almost got me this time."

"Like they *didn't* before?"

"How are we supposed to get her, when they keep trying to kill us?"

"We gotta find a way. Maybe we're missing something." He moved to his bed and gathered up his pillow and blanket.

David went to his bed. He picked up his pillow and, with one gimp arm, struggled to get the blanket as well.

"Here," Xander said. He tugged off the blanket.

"Thanks. Xander, what you said before, about something worrying you more than the cops coming back . . . ?"

Xander turned, the bedding pressed to his chest with his arms. It made him look like a little kid. "Taksidian," he said. "That guy's not done with us."

"You mean *tonight?*" David closed his eyes. When were they going to get a break? He was exhausted, and he didn't like that being scared was becoming a normal feeling for him.

"I don't know," Xander said. "But I don't think I'm going to get much sleep." He walked into the hall.

At the door, David spotted Xander's mobile phone on the dresser. "Hey," he said, picking it up. "Does Dad have his cell?"

"Usually does."

David flipped the phone open and thumbed a speed-dial number. He listened to the rings on the other end and walked closer to Xander.

"Xan—" Dad's voice said.

Thumps and scratching noises came through to David's ear, then another voice said, "This is Officer Benson. Is this Alexander?"

In the background Dad yelled, "Xander, stay there! Don't—"

David flipped the phone closed. "Oops," he said. "I think the cop just took the phone from Dad."

Xander shrugged. "They would have taken it anyway, at the station. So much for that." He turned away.

"Wait," David said. He pushed the phone into his back pocket. He wanted it close, in case Dad called. He eased the chair away from the linen closet and opened the door enough to peer in. He said, "I should go through."

"Why?"

"Make sure everything's okay."

"That kid knows about the portal," Xander said. "That's not okay."

"We gotta know we can use it, if we have to. You know, *before* we have to."

"What do you think he did, lock it? If he did, and you went through, how would you get back?"

"Taksidian did," David reminded him. "He was in the locker, then went back, without the locker door opening and closing. Must be a way."

"You don't know it," Xander said.

"I can try to figure it out," David said. "If I don't come back in twenty minutes or so, come get me."

Xander scrunched his face. "Go through?"

"No, come to the school and get me out. I don't know," David said. "It may be our only way out, if . . ." He didn't even want to say it. "If Taksidian comes back."

Xander eyed the door up and down as though sizing up an opponent. "All right," he said, dropping the bedding on the floor. "Just there and back. Make sure there's nothing weird."

David opened the door further. He frowned at the interior: shelves of towels and sheets, only enough room to stand in front of them. What if Clayton *had* done something to the locker, something more than locking it? He pictured a fire in it, himself materializing in the flames and unable to get out.

"If you don't want to . . ." Xander said.

David swallowed, feeling the spit slide down his tightened throat. He stepped in and pulled the door closed behind him.

In the darkness, the walls closed in. The floor flexed, buckling under his weight. Metal popped. A scream reached his ears. Had he done that? No . . . not him. Maybe the screech of metal.

The front wall pushed in on him. He cracked his head on the back metal. Something *had* happened to the locker. It was crushed, somehow smaller. If it got any smaller, he'd . . . he'd *implode*, just be crushed with the locker. He elbowed his cast into the side wall and shoved his good arm forward. His hand touched cloth, softness under it.

That scream again—human—followed by sobs, a wretched weeping. Someone sniffed.

David whispered, "Clayton?"

A gasp, more sniffing. "D-D-David?" Fear and panic were in his voice.

David raised his hand. He found a face, wet and gooey. Gross. He wiped it away on his pants. He said, "Clayton, what are you doing in here?"

"You . . . you put me here!"

"I mean, *still?* Why didn't you leave?"

"I . . . I can't!" Clayton said. "I can't get out. And . . . I thought I heard . . . *noises.*"

Could he really not find the little tab on the latch assembly that released the door catch? The kid must have been pretty shaken up, zipping into David's house and back again to the locker. True, it was disorienting, but *that* much? Maybe Clayton thought David had sent him someplace else, like a grave.

David had another thought: he had teleported to a place where another person already was. He remembered what his brother had said when he suggested to Xander that they both go through the locker-linen closet portal at the same time: "In *The Fly,* two life forms ended up all mixed together."

What if he and *Clayton* had melded together?

Oh, man!

But that hadn't happened. They'd wound up in the same tight place, but separate and whole. He hoped. He patted his chest, neck, face. No extra parts. Nothing missing.

Clayton said, "What kind of tricks are you pulling on me! What's happening?"

"Clayton, calm down."

David thought about their location: a locker in a short hallway off the main one. Turning left led to the middle school classrooms. On the right would be the cafeteria's doors. Even the janitor would be gone at this hour—otherwise he would have heard Clayton, got him out, and their secret would be blown.

He said, "I'll get you out of here, but you have to promise never, ever to tell anyone what happened. Not about this locker, not . . . Hey, how did you know to get in the locker anyway?"

Clayton sniffed. "When I was after you. I thought I saw the door close, thought I had you. But when I looked, you were gone. Then I heard your freak brother calling for you. I came back to check it out."

"You can't ever tell anyone, you hear?"

"Are you kidding? You are so busted. I'm going to make sure your—your *coven* fries for this, for this witchcraft . . ."

"Okay," David said. "See ya."

"No, wait! Wait! Get me out of here. I was just kidding, really."

"I can put you back anytime I want to," David said as menacingly as he could. "You understand?"

Clayton started crying again.

David felt sorry for him. A little. He thought of something else, just in case the scare tactic didn't work. He reached behind him.

"Hey," Clayton said. "What are you doing? What's that?"

The flash was blinding in the darkness.

David looked at the picture on Xander's cell phone. Tears and snot covered Clayton's terrified face. He turned it for the bully to see, then hit *save* and shifted the phone to his bad hand. He pushed his arm between Clayton and the locker wall, found the catch, and opened the door.

Clayton spilled out onto the tile floor of the school hallway. He flashed a stunned expression at David, standing in the locker.

David snapped another picture. He said, "Stay quiet and these pictures never make it to the Internet. And remember, snot-face, I can put you back in here."

He reached out, grabbed the edge of the locker door, and pulled it shut.

five

TUESDAY, 8:23 P.M.

The kids stood around the island in the kitchen, staring down at plates of soggy spaghetti. David cut away a chunk and forked it into his mouth. The meat sauce didn't help. It still felt like bloated worms on his tongue.

"I gotta go," Xander said. He pushed aside his plate and picked up Dad's keys.

"Don't do it, Xander," Toria pleaded. Spaghetti sauce

coated her lips and face, as though she had tried to put on lipstick while bouncing on a bed.

"We need to know what's going on," Xander said. "I need to talk to Dad."

"You can't take the car," David said, swallowing hard. His stomach threatened to send the food back up—he didn't know if it was the nasty pasta or the thought of being alone with Toria in the house. "You only have a permit."

Xander rolled his eyes. "Driving without a parent in the car is the least of our worries." He picked up his coat and tugged it on. "Look, just stay down here. If anything makes a noise upstairs, run out the front door."

"That cop said they were sending a car over," David reminded him.

"That's why I can't wait around." Xander headed for the door.

David and Toria rushed around the island to join him.

"Take us with you," Toria said.

Xander stopped. He put his hand on his sister's head. "We already talked about this. Someone needs to stay to keep people out. If they bust me, at least you guys will be here."

"Will you get Dad out?" Toria said.

Xander shook his head. "I just want to talk to him."

"You probably won't even get that close," David said. "It's a *jail*."

"David, I know!" Xander said. His shoulders slumped.

"I have to try." He looked out the window beside the door. "No one's here yet. When I come back, I'll park up the road and cut through the trees. Listen for me knocking on the back door, okay?"

David nodded. He thought about saying *If you come back at all,* but it was nothing Xander didn't already know.

Xander opened the door and slipped out.

David pushed it shut and bolted it. Toria gripped his hand. They watched through the window as Xander reached the 4Runner, climbed in, and drove off.

They turned in the foyer and gazed up to the second floor. David remembered the first day they'd found the house. Toria had gone missing, and then her footsteps had seemed to clomp on for a lot longer than they should have.

"Let's . . . uh . . . " He tried to think of something else. If he heard footsteps now, he would drop over dead. "Let's see what else we got in the kitchen."

"There's a lotta s'ghetti," Toria said.

"Great."

They walked hand in hand toward the kitchen, David focusing on the lighted room ahead of them. He was sure, *sure* he would see shadows moving on the second floor if he looked.

CHAPTER

Six

TUESDAY, 8:30 P.M.

"That's *not* what we agreed," Taksidian told the man standing in front of him. They stood in the parking lot of the cabin-sized building that acted as Pinedale's sheriff's office and jail. "All of them out of the house. That's what I wanted."

He rubbed his sharp nails over the scar on the back of his hand. It was all he could do to keep from wringing the man's neck.

Sheriff Bartlett pushed his fingers up under his hat to

scratch his head. The light from a streetlamp cast itself on the man's displeased features. He said, "What we got here, Mr. Taksidian, is a *favor* that went awry. You spoke to the mayor, who suggested we take immediate action to remove that family from the house. But, sir, those aren't the proper channels. If those kids were really in danger, we got *procedures*. There's a child services office over in—"

"I know," Taksidian said. He brushed his long, kinky hair from his face: he knew his gaunt features, thin lips and unflinching eyes were intimidating, and he wanted the the man to get a clear view of them. "That takes days, even weeks, especially considering the father's position at the school."

The sheriff nodded. "They did a thorough background check before he was hired. The man has an impeccable record. No complaints, no—"

"Sheriff Bartlett," Taksidian said with a heavy sigh. "I'm interested only in the children's safety." An image of their freshly covered graves flashed in his head, and he resisted smiling. "I'm sure once they are out of the house and the proper authorities have an opportunity to investigate, they will find evidence of child endangerment. If not from the parents, then from the house itself."

"The house?" the sheriff said, a puzzled look crossing his face.

"I mean, of course, from the condition of the house," Taksidian said. "It's not fit to live in."

"Look, sir," the sheriff said, puffing out his chest. "I was willing to accommodate a request from the mayor, since it didn't seem like such a big deal . . . with the possibility that you're right about the dangers and all. But those kids didn't *want* to come, and physically removing them—Well, that's a whole 'nother matter. That's a line I won't cross, not without a warrant, sir, no way. The only reason we got the father in there"—he hitched a thumb at the jail—"is he accosted one of my deputies. And quite frankly, I don't blame him. Unless you can get child services down here fast, I can't hold him."

Taksidian pointed a gnarled finger at the man's face. He said, "Listen, the mayor—"

A phone chirped.

Taksidian tightened his lips and gave the sheriff his most piercing glare. Keeping his finger up, he removed a mobile phone from his pocket and flicked it open. "What?"

A child's voice said, "Uh . . . is this Mr. Taksidian?"

"What do you want?"

"A friend of mine . . . from school . . . he gave me your number. You stopped him and his friends on their way home. He said you were asking about that old house outside of town. The haunted one?"

Taksidian turned from the sheriff and stepped away. He spoke quietly into the phone. "I was asking about the family who lives there."

"Well, I thought . . . the house, the family—same thing, you

know?" said the boy on the other end. "He said you offered
. . . uh, money for information?"

Behind him, the sheriff's footsteps crunched over gravel.
He was walking back to the jailhouse.

"Hold on," Taksidian said and lowered the phone.
"Sheriff?" When the man turned to him, he said, "Keep that
man locked up."

Sheriff Bartlett squinted at him. He said, "Mr. Taksidian,
I got my deputies heading over to the house right now. I
don't want anything to happen to those kids." He paused.
"You catch my drift?"

Taksidian glared at him, then turned his back on the man.
Into the phone, he said, "What do you know?"

The boy said, "I know how you can get inside. I mean,
secretly."

CHAPTER

Seven

Ed King sat on the metal cot in the jail cell. His head was lowered into his hands. All he could think about were his kids, left overnight in that house alone.

Overnight? he thought. Who knew how long these yokels were going to keep him locked up? Not for the first time, he wished he could take it all back. He desperately wanted to be in their Pasadena house, his wife and children safe under the roof that had kept the world at bay for years.

His mother had been gone thirty years. What had he been thinking, coming up here to find her? *Bringing his family!* He hadn't even *told* them about the house, the dangers. He had *lied* to get them there.

He slid his fingers onto his head and clutched two fistfuls of hair.

That's when the trouble had started—not when his wife had been kidnapped, but when he had started lying. He had convinced himself that they would have never agreed to moving into the old Victorian—or even to coming to Pinedale—if they had known how dangerous it was. And for what? So he could pursue the crazy dream of finding his mother, a dream—no, a *need*—he had since he was seven years old.

So he'd pretended to know nothing about the house. He'd lied.

He squeezed his eyes closed and tugged at his hair.

What a fool he was.

Now, he'd pulled his whole family into his deceit. He had the kids lying about where their mother was, saying she was in Pasadena, wrapping up the sale of their home. He had taught them to be honest, to live with integrity. Then he had told them to lie, that they *had* to lie.

What a mess he'd made. Everything was spiraling out of control. He had to do something. He had to get them back on track, make everything right again. But what—

Tap . . . tap . . .

He looked around, expecting to see a deputy at the bars. No one stood there.

Tap.

He stood and walked to the bars. There were four cells, two on either side of a short hallway. To his right, a door with a small window led to the sheriff's offices. The tapping came again, and he realized someone was softly rapping on the metal fire door at the other end of the hall, to his left. The knocks took on a pattern, a rhythm he recognized.

Tap . . . tap, tap, tap . . . tap, tap . . . tap, tap.

He smiled. It was the theme from *The Last of the Mohicans,* Xander's favorite movie soundtrack. Every now and then, the boy would play it over and over—in his room, in the car—until the whole family felt as though it was *their* theme, the soundtrack to their lives.

"Xander?" he whispered, then shot a glance to the office door.

The tapping continued.

He noticed a wedge of wood on the floor by the door. He assumed it was used to prop it open when the cells became stuffy.

"Hey!" he yelled, knowing Xander would hear and hoping he'd hide. The tapping stopped. "You, out there, in the office! Hey!" He kept yelling until the office door opened and a deputy stepped in.

"I told you," the man said. "No calls. Not till the sheriff says so, and he just went home, so—"

"Could you turn down the heat?" Mr. King said, tugging at his shirt collar. "I'm burning up." And it was true. He wiped off his forehead and held up his glistening palm.

But the deputy said, "Feels okay to me."

"You want to feel my pits?" he said. "I'm sweating like a fat guy chasing a runaway M&M." He eyed the guy's protruding belly. "Sorry. I'm just telling you—"

"I know, I know," the deputy said. "You're hot." He grabbed the cell door and yanked. It rattled, but didn't open. He went to the fire door, pushed the bar that opened it, and kicked the wedge in place. "Now you're going to get cold," he said.

"I'll yell when I do."

"Don't bother." The deputy went into the office and shut the door.

A few seconds later, Xander's face appeared in the opening. "All clear?" he whispered.

Mr. King waved him in. "How did you know it was safe to knock?"

Xander tiptoed up to the bars. "Movies," he said, as though it were obvious. "The jail cells are always in the back, in a room of their own. That way the deputies don't have to hear the prisoners grumbling or snoring or whatever."

"You were lucky," Mr. King said. "Where are David and Toria?"

"At the house."

"Xander . . ."

"I'll get right back," Xander said. "I told them to stay downstairs, by the door."

Mr. King nodded. "Can you believe this?"

"What are we going to do? Can they just arrest you like that? How long—?"

"It's all garbage," Mr. King said. "I overheard them talking. It's all Taksidian. He got to the mayor. They can't hold me long. First they said we were being evicted, then they said I assaulted one of them."

"But you didn't!"

"Shhh. I know that, and they know that. I think Taksidian just wanted us out for a while so he could plant some evidence in the house . . . or do something to the house that would force us to leave . . . or until he could bribe the right people into issuing a real eviction notice or charge me with child endangerment . . . What are you smiling about?"

"Child endangerment," Xander said. "I think that house fits the bill. And you *did* bring us there."

Mr. King dropped his head.

"Dad, I'm kidding."

Mr. King looked into his son's eyes. He said, "No, you're right. I'm sorry about . . . all of this."

Xander shrugged. "We're in this together now. We can't leave that house until we get Mom . . . and, Dad, I found her!"

"You what? Is she—?"

47

It was Xander's turn to lower his head. "Well, sort of. David and I went into this Civil War world . . . I know we weren't supposed to, but, Dad, I drew Bob on one of the tents. When we checked again, Mom had left a message. She was there!" He frowned. "We couldn't get to her, but we know where she is, and she knows we're looking for her."

His wife's face filled Mr. King's mind. He blinked and saw his son, looking so much like her. He knew he should be angry that Xander and David had broken their promise never to sneak through a portal again. But that was something they could address another time. Right now all he could feel was relief . . . and gratitude. He extended his hand through the bars. Xander squeezed it tightly.

"Xander," he said. "You're doing it, son."

"But . . . but, what now? You're locked up in here. They're trying to take the house. I don't know what to do."

"Be strong and courageous," Mr. King said. He smiled. He'd prayed his children would be exactly that since they were small. "As you have been."

Xander nodded. He looked toward the office door. He said, "So, what . . . hold down the fort till you get home?"

"You got it." He gave Xander's hand a firm clasp, then let go. He said, "You better leave, before the guy out there comes to check on me. Give your brother and sister a hug for me, okay?"

Xander stepped to the fire door.

"Son?"

Halfway through the door, Xander looked back.

"*Ti amo.*"

It was something they said, picked up from the owners of the restaurant where he had proposed to the future Mrs. King. It meant *I love you* in Italian.

"*Ti amo*, Dad," Xander said, and disappeared.

CHAPTER

eight

David heard the knock. He looked through the laundry room to the back door, in the center of which was a decoratively cut window. He didn't see anyone standing there, only shadows from the trees. He wondered if he'd imagined the noise—wanting Xander back so much—or if it had come from somewhere else in the house. He pulled back in.

Toria stared at him with monster eyes.

"No one's there," he whispered. "Didn't you hear—?"

The knock again, a gentle *rap-rap-rap*.

This time a silhouette filled the window. David's heart pounded harder, until he recognized the shape of Xander's shaggy hair.

"What took you so long?" David said, opening the door.

"I came through the woods," his brother said. "There's a cop car out front."

"They showed up right after you left."

They stepped into the kitchen.

"No problems?" Xander said.

"They knocked, but we didn't answer."

"Creaking!" Toria said.

David shrugged. "The house was making some noises. I didn't hear any footsteps."

"I did!" Toria said.

David shook his head. "No, you didn't."

"Did too."

"All right, guys," Xander said. He leaned down to Toria. "This is from Dad." He hugged her.

"You saw him?" David said.

"He said it's all garbage. Taksidian set it up. Dad said it won't stick." Xander looked at David and rolled his head. "I told Dad I'd give you one too."

David hesitated, then smiled. He stepped into his brother's arms.

"Xan-der," David grunted under the crushing pressure. "Not . . . so . . . *tight*." When his brother didn't let up, he brought his foot down on Xander's toes.

"Hey!" Xander hopped away.

"Hey nothing. I got a broken arm, you know."

"Big baby."

David rubbed his arm. "So, what are we supposed to do?"

"Hold down the fort. That's what he said." Xander looked from his brother to his sister. "So that's what we're going to do."

CHAPTER

nine

Sitting in the passenger seat of the police cruiser, Deputy Sam Parsell gazed through the windshield at the house. It was barely visible through the trees. Its lack of color allowed it to blend into the shadows, seeming to become nothing but shadow itself.

"Creepy," he said. He snatched a Styrofoam coffee cup off the dash and took a sip. He grimaced at its taste, something like cold motor oil.

His partner, Deputy Lance Harnett, sat behind the wheel. "Holy cow," Lance said. "Listen to this." He held a magazine closer to the dome light and read: "Authorities in West Virginia are investigating reports of unidentified lights in the sky, which correspond with the claims of a Braxton County woman that a 'monster' attacked her German shepherd and ate it. 'It was horrible,' said Nanci Kalanta. 'I went out to see what Killer was barking at. This *thing* ran out of the woods and gobbled him up. One bite, just like that.' Kalanta described the creature as having six or eight legs, a spiderlike body, and a bulbous head with tiny eyes and a mouth 'the size of a storm drain.'"

Lance pulled the magazine down and gasped at Sam. His mouth seemed as wide as the monster's he had just described; his eyes were big and startled. He said, "Can you believe it?"

Sam slapped the magazine out of his partner's hand. "No, I can't. Stop reading that trash."

Lance picked up the magazine. Flipping through it to find his page, he said, "This ain't no gossip rag. It's the *Midnight Sun*, man." He said it the way another person might have cited the *New York Times*. "It's real. They got interviews and pictures and everything."

"Pictures of the monster?"

"Look," Lance said. He pointed at an image of a backyard cluttered with trash. "That's where the dog *used* to be, and look, you can kind of see where the tree branches are broken."

"Gimme that!" Sam grabbed the publication out of Lance's hands. He jabbed a finger into the cover, right into the fanged mouth of what might have been an orc from the Lord of the Rings movies. "What does that headline say? 'Alien Baby Celebrates Third Birthday.'" He threw the magazine at his partner.

Lance looked injured. He said quietly, "You just don't believe."

"You're right, I don't."

Lance rolled up the magazine and pointed it at Sam. "People used to think gorillas weren't real, either." He shook the magazine. "This here is *science*. It's called *cryptozoology*." He said the word slowly and carefully. "It's the study of creatures we don't know about yet."

"What are they studying, then?" Sam said. He squeezed his eyes shut, mentally kicking himself for opening *that* door.

"Evidence! Eyewitness—"

Sam threw his hands up. "I know, I know. I've heard it already." He looked out at the house. "I can't believe they got us babysitting."

"Well, Sam, them kids are alone in there." Lance's big eyes took in the house, the surrounding woods. "Ain't right."

"Hey, it's their choice. Wouldn't catch me living in a place like that."

Lance turned a big grin on him. "Afraid of *ghosts*?" he said.

"No, I'm not afraid of ghosts. I'd be afraid of rafters falling on me in the middle of the night." Sam opened his door.

"Hey, hey," Lance said, grabbing Sam's arm. "Whatta you doing?"

"I gotta pee," Sam said. "If that's okay with you." He pulled out of Lance's grasp, climbed out, and slammed the door.

Idjut, he thought. He hitched up his pants, adjusted his gun belt, and scoped out the area for a leakworthy spot. The half moon made the house look black and as imposing as an ancient castle. The trees cast deep shadows that shifted as the branches swayed in a light breeze. Mist swirled over the ground, billowing up in the distance. It seemed to glow in the moonlight.

He veered off, away from the front of the house and from where the headlights would catch him if Lance switched them on. As he approached a particularly dark area, a twig snapped somewhere in front of him. He squinted into the shadows.

"Who's there?" he said in his toughest voice.

Something *screeeeeched!*

Sam jumped. His hand dropped to the handle of his pistol.

Screech!

He looked up and saw something moving on the roof of the house. It screeched at him again, and he sighed. It was an old weather vane, mounted to the peak of the gabled roof over the tower. He moved his feet, carefully picking his way over exposed roots and low-lying brambles.

Another twig snapped. He spun toward the sound. It had come from the front of the house on the other side from where he stood.

Animal, he thought. *Had to be.*

He supposed one of the kids could be tromping around, but he and Lance had watched the lights go out more than an hour ago. They had assumed the three inside had gone to bed. He surveyed the front of the house now. No lights.

Something thumped behind him.

Oh, man, he thought, cursing Lance and his talk of ghosts and things that ate German shepherds whole.

CHAPTER

ten

WEDNESDAY, 12:37 A.M.

David woke with a large, warm spider clinging to his face. He brushed at it and realized it was Toria's hand. He lifted it and set it on the pillow between their heads. She mumbled, scratched her nose, and rolled over. She had wiggled toward him until he was teetering on the edge of the mattress. He shifted to his side and gently pushed at her. She didn't budge. He considered joining Xander on the floor, but even a sliver of the bed was better than that.

Bump!

He rose up onto his elbow, listening. Something in the house had made a noise. He heard it again—not a bump this time, but a low creak. Then another.

Footsteps! Or someone trying to walk quietly. His eyes moved to the bedroom door. By the glow of the nightlight he could tell it was still closed. Another creak—out there, somewhere.

"Xander?" he whispered. Louder: "Xander!"

His brother's deep, rhythmic breathing reached him from the floor on the other side of the bed.

He dropped his feet to the floor and stood. Something bumped. He thought about the boxes in the hallway: lots of things to knock into, if you were creeping around in the dark. He went around the bed and knelt in front of Xander. His brother's head was a mass of dark, tangled hair.

David shook him. "Xander, wake up."

Xander shifted in his sleep.

Creak.

David snapped his eyes to the door. He shook his brother harder. "Xander!"

"What?" Xander lifted his head, plopped it back down.

"I hear something," David said. "Someone's moving around out there."

Xander rolled over. He blinked at David, his face like someone in pain. "Someone . . . what?"

"I think someone's in the house."

Xander pushed off his blanket and sat up. He stared at David, listening. "I don't—"

"Shhh," David said.

Ten seconds . . . twenty . . .

Creeeak!

Xander jumped. He got to his feet and pulled David up.

"Where's it coming from?" David whispered.

"In this house, could be anywhere."

"Right outside the door," David whispered. His fear had found its way to his voice.

"I thought maybe . . . upstairs," Xander said.

Great, David thought, *now the house is making each of us hear different things.*

Xander stooped to pick up the toy rifle that had been lying beside him. With a wood stock and metal barrel, it made a sturdy club. He moved to the door.

David grabbed a handful of his brother's T-shirt and followed.

Xander pushed his ear to the wood. He looked back, shook his head.

"Let's go back to bed," David whispered. "Wait till morning."

Xander opened the door.

eleven

WEDNESDAY, 12:41 A.M.

Sam dropped into the passenger seat of the police cruiser and slammed the door. He glared through the windshield at the house.

"Everything come out okay?" Lance said with a snicker.

"There's something going on," Sam said.

Lance followed his partner's gaze to the house. "Whatcha mean?"

"I heard noises. Like someone walking around in the woods."

"The kids," Lance suggested.

Sam didn't speak for a while. He scanned the woods in an arc, starting where Lance's head blocked his view and ending with the passenger-side window. Finally he said, "*Maybe* the kids. But I went up on the porch, checked the door. It was locked. If it was one of the kids, the door wouldn't have been locked."

"Back door, then." Lance's eyes were the size of half-dollars.

Sam could tell he wanted a straightforward explanation for the noises. The guy might get a kick out of reading about boogeymen, but he didn't want to end up in the *Midnight Sun*'s next issue under the headline SHERIFF'S DEPUTY MAULED TO DEATH BY ALIEN DOG-BOY.

"Maybe," Sam said, not believing his own word. All the breaking twigs and thumps had come from the area in front of the house. Kids would have run off when Sam had started exploring, and he'd have heard them making tracks toward the back. "I think I'll—"

Something smacked down on the roof of the cruiser.

Lance screamed. He fumbled for his pistol.

Sam grabbed the man's arm. "Don't," he said. "If the kids are out there . . ." He didn't even want to think of what could happen if Lance started plugging away at the shadows.

"That's no kid," Lance said. "Something landed on the roof."

Sam scowled at him. "What are you thinking? Something *living?*" He shook his head. "A rock maybe."

"It was big," Lance said.

"Well, I don't hear anything now. Nothing's moving up there."

"Waiting."

"Hey," Sam said. "A light just turned on in the house. I can see the windows on either side of the door. Couldn't see them before."

They watched the house, but nothing else happened. No more lights, no movement.

"Turn on the headlights," Sam said.

Lance squeezed his eyes closed and flipped on the headlights. The woods between the end of the road and the house sprang into Sam's vision. The nearest trees seemed to glow in the brightness. Farther trees caught their shadows and appeared to multiply as they approached the house. The lights barely reached the front porch steps.

"Hit your spotlight," Sam said, reaching for the handle on his side of the car. The brighter spots, Sam's and Lance's, came on at once. New shadows snapped into place. Sam's roamed over the right side of the yard—if that's what you'd call the woods in front of the house—Lance's over the left.

"There!" Lance said.

The leaves of a large bush were shaking.

"Wind?" Lance said, hopefully.

"Not the way it's moving back and forth like that."

The shaking stopped.

"Hold the light on it," Sam said. He positioned his own light on the porch and opened the door.

"Wait!" Lance said. "The roof."

Sam stepped out, rising slowly to peer at the roof. A large branch lay over the cruiser's red-and-blue light bar. He looked up. The top of the tree leaned out over the car's hood. He grabbed the branch and showed Lance.

"See?" he said. "Probably just fell. Keep your eyes peeled." He shut the door and headed for the woods. His shadow stretched out in front of him, reaching almost to the house.

CHAPTER

twelve

"Xander!" David said. He was standing at the junction of the second floor's main hallway and the smaller one that went to the room they were using as a Mission Control Center.

Xander was shining a flashlight on the secret door at the end of the short hall.

"It's still latched," Xander said, running his hand over the wall.

"There are lights shining in from outside," David said. The glow flickered in the main hallway, brighter than the dim overhead fixtures.

Xander stepped up beside him and switched off the flashlight. He brushed past David, who once again grabbed hold of his brother's shirt. Xander edged closer to the staircase.

"Is it the cops?" David whispered.

As Xander eased forward, the light caught him, flickering like a fire. He said, "Probably. But what are they doing?"

"Maybe they spotted something," David said, thinking of the creaking floorboards.

They stopped at the top of the stairs. The light was coming through the windows by the doors. Something moved in front of the beams, causing a bobbing shadow. It grew larger and darker. The porch stairs creaked.

"Xander?" David said.

Xander sidestepped behind the wall. They both crouched low. Xander craned his head around the corner; David bent around Xander to see. The shadow took the form of a person: head, shoulders, arms. Footsteps clumped on the porch. The door handle rattled. The person moved to the side window and peered in. He was silhouetted with light radiating from behind.

Xander pulled back behind the wall. He nudged David. "Get Toria," he whispered. "We have to be ready to get out of here."

David looked down the hallway to the chair that they had replaced under the linen closet handle. "The closet?" he said.

"That's the plan," Xander said. "Now, go."

thirteen

WEDNESDAY, 12:52 A.M.

At the window, Sam cupped his hands against the sides of his face. The upstairs lights were on, but he didn't see anyone. The rest of the house was dark. The door was still locked. Probably one of the kids had gone to the bathroom. He turned away from the window.

The cruiser's lights glowed at the end of the road like a four-eyed spider waiting to pounce. Mist snaked slowly from the side of the house, swirling around trees and billowing up against the bushes.

He looked at the big clump of bushes Lance's spot was on. From his perspective it was mostly a shaggy black mass. He went down the steps, treading softly. As he approached the bush, it shook.

He stopped. "Who's there?" He unsnapped his holster and moved closer. "Trinity County Deputy," he announced. "Come out with your hands up."

The bush rattled. Something growled, low and guttural.

Sam stepped back.

A twig cracked, closer to the cruiser—no, no, not a twig. It sounded like something had smacked against glass. He squinted at the car. Had Lance got out? The thing in the bushes growled again.

A loud *crack!* came from the cruiser, and Lance's spotlight blinked out.

What in tarnation?

"Lance?" he called.

A screech made his blood run cold. He swung his head around. That blasted weather vane!

The headlights and his own spot were pointed not at the bush, but at the house. The bush was now illuminated only by the backsplash of light bouncing off the ground and trees. Somehow that made it appear even darker, bigger, and a whole lot scarier than it had looked in only the moonlight.

The leaves rustled. That deep-throated growl reached his ears, getting louder.

He pulled his pistol. "I got a gun," he said. "You hear me?"

Movement drew his eyes to the side of the house. The mist drifted among the trees. Sam's breath froze in his lungs. The clear shape of a man stood rock-solid near the rear of the house.

"Who's that?" Sam said. "Come here . . . slowly."

The figure didn't move.

Sam swung his gun toward it. "I'm not kidding, buddy!"

The bushes shook. The growling continued.

Sam held the gun on the unmoving figure and raised his free hand to shield himself from whatever might rush out of the bushes. He didn't know what to do. He wasn't going to shoot at the figure: Not when the guy wasn't even moving. Not when there were kids around, and he couldn't be absolutely sure the figure wasn't one of them—though the man in the mist seemed a lot bigger, more *solid* than any kid he'd ever seen.

Still . . . should he approach the creepy dude? That would put his back to the bushes—and whatever was in them.

Behind him, he heard the car door open.

"Sam!" Lance said. "Sam, get back here, man! Get out of there!"

That decided it. He took a step back. The ground here was spongy with soft soil and decomposing leaves. He began to tumble, caught himself, and shuffled in reverse.

The car door slammed shut. The trees erupted in flames—that's what Sam thought for a few seconds, until a blue light pushed away the red and he realized Lance had turned on the police flashers. The red light swung around again. Blue. Red. Blue. They flashed against the trees but didn't reach the figure in the mist. To Sam's eyes, they made everything worse, making shadows jump up and fall back. He couldn't tell what was real movement, from which he had to protect himself, and what was merely the dance of light and shadow. He swung his gun between the bushes and the figure and backed away, backed away.

His own shadow became blacker and sharper on the ground as he neared the car. When his heels touched the dirt road, he spun and ran for the passenger door. He hopped in, panting. He scanned the woods through the windshield. He thought the figure was gone, but it was hard to tell, between the darkness way back there and all the lights doing their thing.

"What's going on?" Lance said. He sounded panicked.

Sam looked over at him. The door window behind Lance's frightened face was broken: a dozen cracks fanned out from a small hole in the glass. "What happened?"

"I think someone shot at me! They hit the light!"

"Get us out of here," Sam said. "Come on, start the car!"

Lance cranked on the key. The engine roared. He slammed the shifter into gear, and the cruiser reversed away from the woods.

Sam watched through the windshield, half expecting something to chase them. He held his pistol up, ready. "Did you call it in?" he asked.

"No, I—" Lance grabbed for the radio.

Sam clutched Lance's hand. "Forget it," he said. "Just go, go."

"But—"

"What are we going to say?" Sam said. "That we got scared away?"

"Someone shot at me!"

"That's not a bullet," Sam said. "See the way the glass is crushed around the hole? I've seen it a hundred times. It was a rock."

"Then why are we taking off?" Lance turned the car toward the side of the road and put it in drive.

Sam realized Lance had not seen the figure or heard the growling. He said, "Because I don't know what's going on here, but it ain't no good." He shook his head. "It ain't no good."

"What about the kids?"

"If they're the ones throwing rocks, they don't deserve our protection," Sam said. "If they're inside, they're safe."

"You sure?"

"Sure enough. Go, will ya?"

Lance accelerated, kicking gravel up into the wheel wells, sounding like angry rattlesnakes. He swept the car around and got it pointed away from the house.

Sam turned in his seat to watch the blackness through the

rear window. Lance braked, casting red light on the road behind them and the trees on both sides.

Then the car rounded a bend, and Sam relaxed. He closed his eyes and sighed. He said, "I never did like that house."

fourteen

WEDNESDAY, 1:05 A.M.

Keal watched the police car vanish around a curve. He crunched across the forest floor and stopped next to a bush.

"For Pete's sake, Jesse," he said. "I should never have let you talk me into taking you out of the nursing home. You didn't say anything about throwing rocks at cops."

The bushes laughed, a thin coughing sound. Hiding behind them, the old man said, "I haven't seen people move that fast since someone passed gas in an elevator."

"It's not funny," Keal said, but he laughed a little in spite of himself. He shook his head. "It's one thing for me to fly you across the country because you think the folks in this house are in danger. It's something completely different to attack police officers. I'm just saying, you better know what you're doing."

"Oh, pooh," Jesse said from behind the bushes. "Wasn't us who scared them away. It was the house, this place. We just helped it out a bit. Now, don't just stand there. I got a stick jabbing me in the back."

Keal made his way around the foliage. The shadows here were even darker than the rest of the woods. He couldn't make out anything.

Jesse wheezed in a breath, and Keal moved faster. He was supposed to take care of the old guy. Didn't matter if it were back at Mother of Mercy Nursing Home or here, Jesse was his responsibility.

He said, "You okay?"

"Nothing I'm not used to," Jesse said. "These old lungs don't work the way they did once." His laugh sounded like sobs. "Nothing does. *Owww!* You stepped on me."

"Sorry," Keal said. "Can't see."

He knelt down, running his hands over Jesse's scrawny body. He cupped his hand under Jesse's head. When he lifted it up, a stray beam of moonlight caught the old guy's face. He was smiling.

"Now, that was fun," Jesse said.

"I wasn't laughing, man," Keal said. "That cop pointed his gun at me. I was sure I was a goner. And he was heading right for you."

Jesse growled.

Even watching the old man make the sound, it put goose bumps on Keal's arms and the back of his neck. "That's just freaky," he said.

"It worked," Jesse said. "Did you see that guy hightail it for his car?"

"I'll give you that one. You all right?"

"Just tired," Jesse said. "Not used to being up so long. I feel like . . ." His lids drooped. "Like I could just . . ." His eyes closed, his mouth fell open, and he snorted in some air.

"Yeah, funny . . ." Keal leaned closer. "Jesse?"

Jesse's eyes sprang open. He smiled. "I ain't *that* tired . . . or old. You going to get me off this cold ground or what?"

Keal got his arms under Jesse and lifted him. It was like picking up a scarecrow, the man was so light.

Jesse said, "I gotta admit, I wasn't expecting the gun."

"They're cops, Jesse. What *did* you expect?"

He felt the old man shrug.

Jesse said, "Smooth move, putting out the light, my friend. And with only two throws. You missed your calling. You should have been a pitcher."

It was Keal's turn to shrug. "Spent some time in the minors. I'll tell you about it someday." He crunched over the ground cover, carrying Jesse toward the front of the house. He stopped.

In the distance, mist was billowing up between the trees, glowing in the moonlight. In front of the slowly stirring cloud stood a man, silhouetted against the mist. His shoulders rose and fell as though he were breathing heavily.

"Jesse?" Keal whispered.

Jesse caught his stare and followed it. He let out a deep sigh.

"Who is it?" Keal said quietly.

"One of *them*," the old man said. "I knew it had started again."

"*What* started, and *who* . . . ?" Before Jesse could answer, Keal called out, "Hey! What do you want?"

The dark figure backed into the mist and disappeared.

Keal waited, but the man did not reappear. He heard no sounds from the woods besides the wind and an occasional squeak from the weather vane.

"A watcher," Jesse said.

"Watcher? What's he watching?"

"Us. The house. Everything that happens here."

Keal didn't move.

Jesse said, "Never mind him, Keal. If he was going to do anything, he'd have done it. He's only someone else's eyes."

"*Who* someone else?" Keal moved his attention from the mist to Jesse's face. He was surprised to see not even a hint of concern in the old man's features; only sadness.

"Could be anyone," Jesse said. "This place, what it does, has always attracted . . . *outsiders*, people who don't belong, who want to use it for their own wicked intentions."

Keal could not find the words for all the questions zipping through his brain.

"What'd you think," Jesse said, "that a house like I told you about could possibly exist and *not* draw the likes of him and whoever he answers to?"

Keal looked for the man again. Nothing but trees.

"Let's get on with it," Jesse said.

Unsure, Keal carried Jesse to the porch steps and lowered him. He glanced around, stopping on the windows flanking the doors. He said, "Lights on inside. Someone must be home."

"Well, I should hope so," Jesse said. "I came to see them, not *this* place."

"Those cops'll be back, you know. With an army."

Jesse shook his head. "Not if they're anything like the ones I knew back when. They didn't want anything to do with the house."

"Let's hope they still don't," Keal said, nervously scanning the woods on both sides. "Still, why do you think they were here?"

"Never can tell," Jesse said. "Always something *interesting* happening 'round here."

"I guess so," Keal said. "I should get the car."

They had pulled it behind some bushes around the bend.

"That can wait." Jesse opened his eyes. "We got business to attend to." He raised his eyebrows. "I can use my chair, though."

Keal started to walk off. He stopped. He couldn't keep his eyes from darting around. "Why don't I take you with me?"

"Because then you'll have to carry me *and* the chair." Jesse waved him away. "Go, go. The worst that will happen is someone will watch me sitting here growing older."

"I wish I felt as confident as you sound."

"Keal," Jesse said with a sigh. "You could have been back with the chair by now."

"Okay, okay. Wait here."

"What else am I going to do?"

Keal trotted into the woods. He came back with Jesse's wheelchair, folded up flat. He sprung it open, scooped Jesse off the steps, and eased him into the chair.

Jesse leaned his head back to take in the imposing facade before him. "I thought I was done with you," he whispered to the house.

CHAPTER

fifteen

743 BC

Tiyari Mountains, near Nineveh, Assyrian Empire

Raindrops struck Dagan's face, as biting as lions' teeth. He blinked against the onslaught, determined to reach the cave above him before one of the lightning bolts that cracked through the black sky blasted him off the mountain. He paused in his ascent, lowering his head to breathe without water rushing into his throat. The narrow ledge he had been traversing before spotting the shelter lay twenty meters below. Currents of rain sluiced over it, becoming drops again as the water flowed over the edge into a bottomless ravine. In the space of a thousand heartbeats, the ledge had become impassible.

At least the other boys wouldn't be able to get ahead of him. Not while the storm-god Adad was so angry. Perhaps one of them would try; certainly, the stakes were high enough to make them consider an attempt.

The academy to which they belonged instructed its pupils in the arts of death: stealth, infiltration, and murder. The best of them would graduate into the most elite rank of the great Assyrian war machine, that of Assassin. Every year the academy sent all of its students sixteen years of age on a grueling, five-day trek from Nineveh to Autiyara, equipped with only the clothes on their backs and a blade. The first one to arrive continued his studies. The runner-up became his lifelong servant, sharpening his weapons, cleaning his clothes. The others were consigned to the regular army as front-men, fodder for their enemies' spears.

As he had been since his recruitment into the academy on his eighth birthday, Dagan was the best in his class, and he was ahead of the others now. But Amshi, his dearest friend since the two had endured the initiation rites together eight years before, was not far behind. Always a close second, Amshi was Dagan's only real competition in this latest challenge. The thought of becoming Amshi's servant—of not becoming an assassin himself—made Dagan sick, as though a serpent had made a home in his guts.

But that isn't going to happen, he thought. Not by the war-god Nergal would Dagan allow himself to lose.

He turned his face up into the pounding rain. Beyond the cliff to which he clung, gray clouds roiled, expelled from Adad's mouth like poisonous vomit. Lightning flashed down, momentarily blinding the boy. He pushed himself higher toward the cave, making sure each rock he grabbed was secure. If he fell, his blade would never taste human blood, and that was unacceptable. How could he spend eternity in Irkalla saddled with that kind of shame?

At the lip of the cave, the wind whispered his name. He stopped, listened.

" . . . Dagan . . ."

A million raindrops crashed into the stone cliff, roaring like a crowd welcoming home a triumphant army. Dagan strained to hear . . . he was sure he had heard . . .

" . . . Dagan . . ."

From his perch just outside, he peered into the darkness of the cave, then at the empty air around him. That's when he saw Amshi down on the ledge, squinting through the rain at him. The boy, Dagan's age but much younger looking, gestured back the way they had come, probably to a more accessible shelter.

Dagan shook his head, scowled at his friend, and pulled himself into the cave. He crawled a few feet in and collapsed onto the gritty floor, panting. He was amazed at how good it felt to be out of the incessant pounding. He rose to his hands and knees and went back to the cave's mouth. He stuck his head out, felt the rain like a swarm of insects, and saw the top of Amshi's head. The boy was following, scaling the cliff toward the cave.

Dagan returned to the dry darkness of the cavern. Gritting his teeth, he cursed his friend. He knew full well what Amshi was doing: he had realized the futility of trying to progress along the ledge, and since he had to stop, why not do it where he could keep an eye on Dagan, the only one who posed a threat to his reaching Autiyara first? Amshi would rest well, knowing the competition was not pressing on.

The serpent inside Dagan coiled around his heart.

He moved farther into the cave, found a fissure in the wall, and pressed himself into it. He listened to the storm outside, to water dripping from his hair to the stone floor, to his breathing, growing slower.

His hair had dried by the time he heard Amshi heave himself into the cave. The boy did what Dagan had done: he crumpled to the ground and waited for his breath to return. Then he called, "Dagan?"

Dagan heard him getting to his feet, stepping deeper into the cave.

"Dagan? Where are you? Are you hurt? I found an overhang out of the rain, but this is much better." He drew closer. "Dagan, where——?"

Dagan emerged from the fissure. His arm shot up.

Amshi jumped, caught sight of Dagan, and smiled, a wide boyish grin. Then it vanished as he saw the object Dagan held slicing through the air toward him.

And for the first time, Dagan's blade tasted human blood.

●●●●●●●●

The cramped darkness in which Dagan—now Taksidian—stood reminded him of that initial kill, so long ago. He thought of Amshi—not the playmate who'd laughed when their voices cracked at the onset of manhood, who'd eased the tension of a trying day on the training fields with a whispered joke—he thought of the body he'd left in the cave. It would have decayed, even the skeleton becoming powder after so many millennia.

Taksidian squeezed the hilt of his knife. The weapon had made him the assassin he was, the man he had become. And on more than a few occasions, it had saved his life. It was his friend, more surely than Amshi ever had been. His blade had feasted many times since that first taste. Now it was hungry again.

For the dozenth time, he checked the door. The handle turned, but the door wouldn't open. He tried to quietly shoulder his way through, but whatever held it was strong. He was about to return to the locker in the school when he heard noises beyond the door, in the hallway.

He leaned his ear against the door. Soft footsteps. Quiet voices. Something was going on out there, in the house. He shifted his feet into a more comfortable stance and leaned back against the shelves. He would bide his time in the closet a little longer.

He would await the opportunity for his blade to feast again . . .

Sixteen

WEDNESDAY, 1:16 A.M.

David led Toria into the hallway by the hand. She was half-asleep, mumbling something about going on a ride. Her free hand clutched her "nigh-night," a threadbare baby blanket she always slept with. She stumbled and stopped, seeming ready to doze standing up.

"Come on, Toria," David said.

Xander was on all fours in the hallway, peering around the corner to the foyer below.

David realized the lights were no longer shining through the windows. "Did they leave?" he whispered. He knelt beside his brother and leaned to see the front doors and the windows beside them.

"I don't know. A car left, but I just heard voices out front."

"Where are the policemen?" Toria said. She had plopped down behind the boys and now blinked heavy lids at them.

"I think they were the ones who left," Xander said. "There were red and blue lights flashing through the windows, and now they're gone."

"Why would they leave?" David said. "And if it's not the cops out there, who is it?"

Xander looked at him with raised eyebrows. "Who do you think?"

"Taksidian?" David's chest grew tight. It seemed that no matter how many times something frightened him, he never got used to it.

Footsteps clomped heavily on the porch steps.

Xander backhanded David in the arm. "Come on," he said. "Let's get to the other side of the stairs before they get to the windows."

David reached back for Toria, but she was already rising. They darted past the staircase and the railing that overlooked the foyer. Where the wall started again, opposite Toria's bedroom, they dropped to the floor. Xander looked around the corner and through the railing to the front door.

Toria nudged David. She said, "Why did Xander want us on this side of the stairs? Aren't there more hiding places on the other side? We could go up to the third floor."

"Xander," David said. "Toria doesn't know about the closet."

With all their discussion of the closet-to-locker portal, let alone their use of it, it was difficult to believe it had remained a secret.

Xander smiled at her. "If we have to run, you're in for a big surprise."

"I don't like surprises," she said.

Xander shook his head. "Then you live in the wrong house." He turned his attention back to the front door.

Something banged down on the porch. There was a squeak, somehow different from the weather vane, which had been reaching David's ears every now and then since he'd awakened.

He rose on his knees to see the front door over his brother's head. A shadow moved over the tall, narrow windows. Both he and Xander pulled back.

"I have to go to the bathroom," Toria said.

"Can you hold it?" David said.

She bit her lower lip and shook her head.

"Make it fast, Tor," Xander said.

Bam! Bam! Bam!

David jumped and grabbed Xander's shirt again. "They're *knocking?*" he said.

"Pounding," Xander corrected.

"Taksidian can't expect us to answer."

"David," Toria called quietly. She was standing in front of the bathroom, pointing at the chair in the hallway. "What's *that* doing there?"

Xander swung his head around. "Don't touch it," he said. "It's part of the surprise. Go, if you have to. Hurry."

"And don't flush," David said.

Toria made a face and disappeared into the bathroom.

The pounding on the door continued.

"What if it's the cops?" David said.

"We're still not answering."

The door handle rattled.

Now David's stomach tightened and rolled. It felt like one of the cannonballs he had recently seen.

Somebody spoke, the deep voice of a man. David could hear the rhythm, but he could not make out the words. A second voice, quieter, responded.

Bam! Bam! Bam!

"Hello?" the deep voice called. "Anybody in there?"

David said, "I don't think that's Taksidian."

"I don't care who it is," Xander said. "It's after one in the morning, we're alone, and people are out to get us."

A thump followed by scraping echoed from the door.

"What's that?" David said. His fear was morphing into panic.

"They're trying to break in," Xander said.

The boys scrambled up and headed down the hall. Xander stopped and reversed so quickly, David lost his grip on his brother's T-shirt.

"What——?" he said, then he saw the toy rifle Xander had left on the floor.

Xander snatched it up, hefting it in his hands.

"Wish it was real," David said.

Toria came out of the bathroom.

"We're leaving," Xander told her. He pointed at David. "You go first. Get out of the locker as fast as you can. I'll send Toria next."

Thinking of Clayton's experience, David said, "I can open the door for her from the outside, when I hear her come through."

"Come through?" Looking up at them, Toria's eyes were big and scared. "What locker? Where are we——?"

Xander put his hands on her shoulders and leaned his face close to hers. "The people outside are trying to break in. Just trust us, okay?"

David watched her searching for reassurance in Xander's eyes. She must have seen it: her features softened, and she nodded.

Something banged against the front door—not a knock. But David realized with some relief it wasn't the door crashing open, either.

David and Xander looked at each other, drawing strength from one other.

"Okay," David said. He gripped the closet door handle as

Xander bent to pull the chair away. Under David's hand, the handle moved—all by itself. He lunged at Xander, knocking him away from the chair. The toy rifle clattered away.

Xander hit the wall, and they both went down.

"What are you doing?" Xander said.

"There's someone in the closet!" David said. "Where's the flashlight?" He spotted it on the floor on the far side of the grand staircase. He planted one hand on Xander's chest and pushed himself up. He ran past the foyer and the stairs, certain the door would burst open.

He grabbed the light and ran back. Toria saw him coming and flattened herself against the wall. David dropped to his knees, then flat on his stomach, in front of the chair. He switched on the flashlight and shined it beneath the door: *shoes!* They were black. They shifted apart as their owner adjusted his stance. The right one rose out of the light. A heavy crash rattled the door as the person inside kicked it.

"Xander!" David yelled.

Xander was already leaning over him to brace his arms against the back of the chair, which in turn pressed against the door. The handle shook, and the door rattled under the impact of another kick.

While David watched, the shoes appeared to evaporate. They lost their shape and melded with the blackness around them. A feather-light breeze touched his face . . . was gone . . . then blew out from under the door again. In time with the pulsing breeze, the flashlight beam stuttered. It didn't flick on and off, but seemed to be *consumed* by the draft. Between flickers, the shoes disappeared.

David panned the light back and forth along the empty floor, while Xander continued leaning his weight into the door.

Finally David said, "He's gone."

"You sure?"

"Pretty much." He scooted away and stood.

The front door creaked open.

CHAPTER

Seventeen

WEDNESDAY, 1:23 A.M.

Jim Taksidian stepped out of the locker. The school hallway was dark. The only light came from the moon through the windows. He leaned backward, stretching his spine. He bent, pulled up his right pant leg, and slipped his knife into the sheath strapped there. He straightened and ran his fingers through his long hair, smoothing it and tucking it behind his ears. He turned back to the locker. It looked just like all the others. But of course it wasn't, just as the house wasn't like any other house.

He shut the locker door and touched the little plate riveted to it: 119. Good to know the number, finally.

He walked around the corner and down the hall. His footsteps were silent on the tiled floor. His fingers massaged the heavy scar on the back of his right hand. Even after all these years, it still ached: sometimes it merely throbbed in time with his heartbeat, but occasionally it felt like a white-hot wire pressed into his flesh.

He welcomed the pain. It reminded him of the injury, the last time anyone had spilled his blood. The prince's guards had fought valiantly. They had nearly killed him, in fact. But in the end, it was they—and the prince—who had paid the ferryman. Taksidian had survived, and he had accidentally discovered the portal that brought him to the house. *From assassin to king*, he thought, thinking of the fortune he had amassed since then. *Not a bad trade.*

He pushed through the double doors at the end of the corridor and turned left. He stopped beside the glass exit doors and punched in the code that would reactivate the school's security system, giving him thirty seconds to leave. It never stopped amazing him, what people would tell for the right amount of money. Slipping the janitor two hundred bucks had bought him unimpeded access to the school, day or night.

He pushed through the doors into the central courtyard. The air was crisp, turning his breath into plumes of mist. He gazed up at the half moon, the same one he'd wondered about as a young man, before the rise of the Roman Empire. He strolled across the grass toward the boy waiting for him on a picnic table. The boy was young: not yet a teenager, but close. He had his feet propped on a bicycle, rocking it back and forth.

"Well?" the boy said.

Taksidian scanned the dark windows of the school, the forest beyond, and the parking lot. He slipped a hand into the pocket of his black overcoat and withdrew a wad of cash, peeled off a few bills and held them out. His eyes wandered the sky; watching the boy accepting the money was just so . . . *crass*, like witnessing a dog devour a rabbit.

"Hey," the boy said, "you're short."

Taksidian turned his eyes on him. He stared until all of the boy's confidence had drained away like blood from a slaughtered pig.

The boy lowered his eyes. "I mean . . . it's just . . ."

Taksidian's voice was deep and flat. "The closet door was locked."

"What?" The boy's eyes went wide. "You couldn't get in? How was I to know? It was open before." His tone had risen, panicked now—not for the money, but for what Taksidian might do to him for wasting his time.

Fear was an emotion Taksidian appreciated in others. It had

serviced him well over the years. He ran the thick, sharp fingernail of his index finger over his bottom lip.

The boy stared at it.

Taksidian reached out. His fingernail grazed the boy's skin as he flicked a lock of hair off the boy's forehead. "What scares you?" he asked.

"What do you mean, what scares me?"

Taksidian stared into his eyes. "What haunts your nightmares?"

The boy melted under Taksidian's gaze. He said, "Vampires." He swallowed. "Snakes."

Taksidian leaned close. He whispered, "The deadliest snake in the world is the Inland Taipan. A single bite contains enough venom to kill a hundred full-grown humans. But it's a puppy dog . . . compared to me." He let his breath wash over the boy's face, then he backed away. "As for vampires, they have nightmares about *me*."

He let that sink in, then said, "Do you understand?"

The boy nodded.

"Forget about the Kings and their house. Forget about the locker. Forget about me."

The kid was shivering, but Taksidian was sure it had nothing to do with the cold.

He smiled. "Of course, if you learn anything else, I want to know about it."

The child nodded again.

Taksidian turned away, then spun back around. He leaned over and ran a fingernail along the side of one of the bicycle's tires. "What did you say your name is again?"

"C-C-Clayton."

The tire popped.

Taksidian smiled. "That's so you have plenty of time walking home to think about what I said."

eighteen

WEDNESDAY, 1:23 A.M.

The door downstairs thunked open. Footsteps moved from the porch into the foyer.

David's eyes jumped to Xander, leaning against the closet door. He heard Toria pull in a breath, and he clamped his hand over her mouth before she could scream.

Eeek-eeek. A squeak like the weather vane, but this came from downstairs. The chandelier hanging over the foyer came on.

Someone said, "Shut the door, Keal. Don't want our friend outside to wander in."

A voice smooth as a sports announcer's said, "I thought you said he was only watching."

The other man mumbled something David couldn't make out. The door closed.

The smooth voice called, "Hello? Anyone home?"

"What do we do?" David whispered, so quietly even his own ears didn't hear.

Xander nodded at the linen closet door.

"No," David said, louder. "Taksidian—or someone— just went through. He'll be there."

"Then we have to use one of the doors upstairs, one of the time portals."

Toria pulled David's hand off her mouth. "I don't want to," she whispered. "I don't want to go through a portal."

David couldn't blame her, with all the stories she'd heard from him and Xander.

Xander pushed himself off the closet door and put his face in front of hers. "We have to," he said. "These people want to take us away. Then who will rescue Mom?"

A voice came at them from the foyer. It was fragile and quavery, as though the speaker were sitting on a paint shaker. "I can hear you," the voice said. "I'm not the bad guy. I'm here to help."

Toria's eyebrows shot up, and she smiled.

Xander frowned. "What else would he say? 'Come on down so I can kill you'?"

David heard that same *eeek-eeek* again. He got a crazy vision of a pirate standing in the foyer, his wooden leg squeaking every time he moved. In this house, he wouldn't be surprised if the person downstairs actually turned out to be a pirate.

"I know about the portals," the shaky voice continued.

"See?" Xander said. "Has to be one of Taksidian's men."

"I know that one of you saved a little girl in World War II."

Xander's eyes flashed wide. He gaped at David.

David's lips moved, but they found no words. Finally he said, "How . . . ?"

"Huh?" Toria said. Her face reflected complete bafflement. "What little girl?"

David started for the grand staircase.

"Dae, no!" Xander grabbed his arm.

"Taksidian can't know that," David said. "Only you, me, and Dad."

Xander thought about it. He released David's arm and stood.

David took a step, and his brother grabbed him again.

Xander said, "Be ready to run."

David said, "Straight upstairs, right?"

"Right." Xander gave Toria a firm look.

David walked slowly, willing that ferret in his chest to settle down. He took a deep breath and stepped up to the banister that overlooked the foyer. A big black man stood, staring up at him. He was standing behind an ancient geezer in a wheelchair. The old man was mostly bald, except for a cloud of white hair circling around from one temple to the other. He had a thick silver mustache and eyes so blue David could see them sparkle, even from a floor away.

The old man spotted him and squinted. His lips pushed into a radiant smile.

David felt hope rush through him, as though his blood had warmed by a couple degrees: the man had the kindest face he had ever seen.

"I should have known," the old man said. He shifted in his chair to smile up at the guy standing behind him. "I should have known." He started coughing. It was a wheezy, raggedy sound.

The other man put his hand on the old man's back. He leaned around to watch his face as he coughed. He said, "Jesse? Jesse, you all right?"

The old man—Jesse—fluttered a scrawny hand in the air. When he looked up at David again, his eyes were wet. He said, "I can't tell you how wonderful it is to see you again . . . David."

David took a step back and bumped into his brother.

"And *you!* Xander."

David said, "How do you know us?"

The wrinkles on Jesse's face rippled and hardened in a posture of concentration. He said, "Let's just say that *I* have met *you.*"

Toria stepped up to the banister.

Jesse said, "Oh . . . and who is this?" He wheeled his chair back for a better look. One of the wheels creaked. *Eeek-eeek.*

Toria told him her name.

Xander said, "How do you know David and me, but not our sister?"

"It's a long story, and I hope to have the time to tell it." He glanced around. "Please tell your parents I'm here."

"They—" Xander started, then stopped. "What are you doing breaking into our house?"

"I'm sorry about that," the old man said. "We wanted to call, but information gave us a 626 area code. That's not around here."

"That's our old number," David said. "In Pasadena. We just moved in."

The old man nodded. "Information didn't give a new one. We drove straight from the airport. I . . . I wanted to get here as soon as possible."

Xander said, "So you just barged in?"

Jesse looked up at them sheepishly. "Keal did knock."

"Well, you can just wheel yourself right back—"

David elbowed his brother in the ribs. Hard.

Xander yelped.

David whispered, "There's something about him, Xander, can't you tell? I think he's on our side."

"Dae, they *broke in!*"

The two boys looked over the handrail. Jesse was grinning as though he was the guest of honor at a surprise party.

"Who *are* you?" Xander said.

"Name's Jesse. This is my friend Keal."

Xander leaned against the railing. "I heard, but *who are you?*"

"Unless I've miscalculated . . ." Jesse closed one eye as though he were struggling through a math problem. "I'm your great-great-uncle."

nineteen

WEDNESDAY, 1:27 A.M.

David, Xander, and Toria stared down at the old man. They looked at one another.

"Come on," Xander said. He slapped David's arm, grabbed his sister, and practically carried her down the hallway, out of sight of the intruders.

David's gaze connected with Jesse's. Something about the kindness David saw in the old man's face made him want to return it, however vague and unsupported by action it was. He held up his index finger. He said, "Be right back."

"Take your time," Jesse said.

When David reached Xander and Toria, he said, "I like him."

"You don't know him," Xander whispered. "If we're related, how come we've never met him before? How come we've never even heard of him?"

Toria skewed her face. "How's he *related* to us?"

"It'd be like . . ." Xander closed one eye, thinking, and David thought he looked an awful lot like Jesse at that moment. "Dad's dad's dad's brother. The brother of our great-grandfather."

"Or great-grandmother," David said.

From downstairs, Jesse called, "Great-grand*father*."

Xander grabbed David and Toria's arms. He walked backward down the hall and into the boys' bedroom. "It's too weird," he said. He looked at David. "Why is he showing up now, and how does he know us?"

"Maybe he's on Mom and Dad's Christmas card list," David said.

"Then he would've known Toria too," Xander said.

"What are you saying?" David asked. "He's an imposter? Why?"

"To get in with us," Xander said, as though it were obvious. "A spy. I wouldn't put it past Taksidian."

"If Taksidian sent them," David said, "why would he try to break in through the closet at the very same time?"

Xander's frown said *Good point.* "To scare us, show us how much we need an ally."

"We already knew that," David said.

Dad had told him that in old times when criminals were stoned to death, it didn't always mean having rocks thrown at them. Just as often, a condemned man would lie on his back, and a board was placed on top of him. Then people piled stones on the board until the collected weight crushed him down so firmly, his lungs could not expand and he would suffocate. The King family problems felt like that . . . like being crushed to death.

David said, "We need a *break*, Xander. Ever since we moved in, it's been one bad thing after another. Why can't something good happen for once?"

"Yeah," Toria chimed in. "Why can't Jesse be here to help?"

"Maybe because he broke into our house?" Xander said. "At one thirty in the morning? Hmmm . . . yeah, that's normal."

"Nothing about this house is normal," David said. "When help comes, it'll *have* to be not normal."

"David, you're being—" Xander stopped. He put his hand on David's shoulder. "You're right, we do need help. I just don't want to be . . . I don't know, so desperate for it that we take anything or anyone who comes along."

"Can't we just talk to him?" David said. "Figure out if he's telling the truth?"

Xander nodded. He said, "Okay, but we stay together."

In the hall, Xander picked up the toy rifle. They stopped at the top of the stairs. Keal was kneeling beside Jesse's wheelchair, one hand resting on the old man's shoulder. David noticed for the first time how pale Jesse looked. It made the moles—"age spots," his dad had once told him—on Jesse's hands, face, and scalp stand out all the more.

"All right," Xander told Jesse and Keal. "Go into the dining room, to the far side of the table."

Jesse's brow furrowed. "What about your parents?" He read their expressions. "Aren't they here?"

"That's none of your business," Xander said.

The old man nodded, and Keal wheeled him into the other room. *Eeek-eeek-eeek.* Chairs scraped against the dining room floor.

Xander went down the stairs, David and Toria moving right behind him like parts of a caterpillar. Xander wielded the makeshift club over his head and peered around the corner of the dining room before he walked in.

Jesse and Keal were sitting behind the table. Their hands were folded in front of them on the flat surface as though patiently waiting for dinner.

David brushed past Xander and took the chair opposite Jesse. The old man stared at him intently, but there was nothing mean about it. It was the way Mom and Dad looked at him sometimes—there was love behind it. But it *was* kind of odd to think that this stranger would *love* him.

Toria sat beside David. Her eyes darted between the two men. David figured she was doing what he'd already done: sizing them up, noting how different they were from each other, but somehow a team.

Like us, he thought.

Jesse noted David's broken arm resting on the table. He studied David's face, the black eye and bruised cheek. "You guys look like you've been in a couple scrapes."

When they didn't respond, he cleared his throat. "I can tell you're very capable children, and I am a guest in your house . . ." He looked each of them in the eyes. "But it's not right that I'm here, talking to you without your parents."

"Well, all right, then," Xander said. "See ya."

"No, wait!" David said. He grabbed Xander's T-shirt. "Xander, please."

His brother frowned. He told Jesse, "Don't worry about our parents right now. We want to know more about *you.*"

"Fair enough," Jesse said. "What do you want to know?"

"How did you get in?" Xander said. "The door was locked. Dad just had it rekeyed."

"Oh," Jesse said, "I know a few tricks about this place."

David said, "How did you know about the little girl in World War II?"

"That was you, right?" Jesse said. "The one who saved her?"

David nodded. "There was a tank—"

"And you grabbed her before it ran her over," Jesse said.

David's mouth fell open. "How . . . ?"

He looked at Xander, who was scowling at the old man.

"Two days ago, I woke up and the world was different," Jesse said. "I mean, it had *changed*. You, David—you changed it."

CHAPTER

twenty

"What do you mean, I changed the world?" David said.

Jesse rubbed the silver stubble on his checks. Folds of skin moved under his fingers. He said, "I'll show you." He reached over his shoulder, groping for something on the back of the wheelchair.

Keal reached behind Jesse and produced a manila envelope. He handed it to the old man.

"Thank you, Keal," Jesse said, flipping open the flap. He pulled out a piece of paper and slid it across the table toward David.

It was a photograph showing a farmhouse in the background. In front was a family posing for the camera: a man, a woman, and a little girl.

David gasped. He picked it up and squinted at it. "That's her," he said. He showed it to his brother. "Xander, that's the girl I saved from the tank!"

Xander took the photo, looked at it closely, then handed it back. He slid the chair around from the end of the table and dropped into it.

David said, "The man who took her from me said her name. Marge . . . Mag . . ."

"Marguerite," Jesse said.

"Yeah."

"Marguerite Rousseau." The old man fished into the envelope again. He withdrew another piece of paper and said, "Do you know what smallpox is?"

"Like chicken pox?" David asked.

"Much worse. Blisters and a rash cover the skin, inside the mouth and throat. Very unpleasant. That's the common variety. Then there were the more severe strains. My friend Jeffrey Lewis was much younger than I. He was one of those people who kept you young just by being around, he was so full of energy. He contracted the hemorrhagic form of the disease on a mission trip. His skin turned black from all the bleeding of his organs and muscle tissue." Jesse looked at Toria. "I'm sorry, sweetheart. Let's just say he suffered terribly. Jeffrey died on September 12, 1994."

"Wait a minute," Xander said. "I thought smallpox—"

Jesse held up his hand to stop him. His eyes were wet. "You have to hear this," he said. "Earlier today, I spoke to my friend. I spoke to Jeffrey Lewis."

David jumped as if Jesse had lunged out of his chair at him.

"What?" Xander said. "You talked to a guy who *died* in 1994?"

Jesse nodded. "At the airport in Chicago. Keal made the calls for me."

"Tracked the guy down," the younger man said. "When I made the connection, I put Jesse on."

Jesse said, "I had a wonderful conversation with him. He's retired now. Wanted to tell me all about his grandkids."

"You just said he died," Xander said, obviously irritated.

"He did," Jesse said, "in the world that existed three days ago. In today's world, he never died. He said the worst illness he ever had was a stomach bug years ago. I asked him."

"That's . . . *impossible*," David said.

Jesse said, "In the world you know, it is, but here—"

"Besides," Xander interrupted, "I learned about smallpox. It's been gone for . . . like forever."

Jesse agreed. "The World Health Organization declared it

eradicated on May 8, 1980." He put the envelope and paper on the table and pressed his hand over them as though preventing them from flying away. "A couple of days ago, I had memories I no longer have. I wrote them all down." He tapped his fingers on the paper. "I remembered the world—today's world—still suffering from smallpox. Two million deaths a year. The disease spared no one: children, parents . . . anyone could contract it, and an average of six in ten of those who did died of it." He panned his eyes across the faces of the King children.

"So you had a dream," Xander said.

"It wasn't a dream," Jesse said. "It was a memory."

"You probably remember polio too," Xander said.

Jesse shook his head. "You don't understand. It was a memory, because three days ago, that's the way the world actually was. Smallpox had not been wiped out. *Two* days ago smallpox was gone—and had been gone for thirty years."

"That doesn't make sense," David said.

Jesse smiled. "Three days ago Marguerite Rousseau had died as a child, a casualty of the German war machine. But two days ago, she hadn't died—because *you* saved her. She grew up to perfect the vaccine that eliminated smallpox from our world."

Xander sighed loudly. He leaned back and ran his fingers through his hair. "Like I said, I learned about how we beat smallpox when I was in seventh grade, three years ago. It didn't just change a couple days ago."

"It did and it didn't," Jesse said. He tilted his head toward one shoulder, then the other like a clock's pendulum. "The world changed when David saved Marguerite. That happened for David two days ago; it happened for Marguerite nearly seventy years ago. Everything became different the moment David saved her, the moment in *history* when he saved her."

"I don't get it," Toria said.

"Time travel is tricky business," Jesse said. "Scientists argue about it. Most say it'd be impossible to change history, because the past is the past."

"But you know better," Xander said.

Jesse's head went up and down, slowly.

David pressed his chest into the table's edge. "I still don't get how you knew it was me who saved her and it was at that moment that history changed."

"Some of us have a gift," Jesse said. "We *sense* those changes. When the change occurs, the way things were *before* the change comes to us like a dream or almost-forgotten memory. After a couple of days, even *that*—the dream, the memory—fades. Then we're like everybody else: we don't remember that the world was ever any different. When I woke the other day, smallpox had been eradicated years before. But I had memories that it hadn't been. I knew someone had changed history. That's why I wrote my thoughts down—before they left my mind for good."

He stopped, raising his head to listen to something David didn't hear. Then he did hear it: the house was groaning, a low, steady sound that reminded him of the way the trees around the house creaked in the wind.

Jesse winked at him and said, "This house has old bones too."

David smiled. He hoped that was *all* it was.

Jesse went on. "Right now, I have no recollection of smallpox during the last forty years. I have no memory of Jeffrey Lewis's death. But I have what I wrote." He picked up the page, shook it, and set it down again. "I used a computer to research smallpox. I learned about Marguerite. In her autobiography, she details her childhood in the French village of Ivry-la-Bataille. I have an excerpt here."

"Oh, come on," Xander said. He stood abruptly. "What's the point?"

"Xander," David said, pleading.

"You want someone to read to you, Dae, I'll go get Grimms' fairy tales. It'll mean as much." He pointed toward the ceiling. "Mom is—" His lips clamped shut. He shifted his gaze to Jesse.

The old man cocked his head, waited for Xander to continue. When he didn't, Jesse said, "You might want to stay for this, Xander. Ms. Rousseau writes about your brother."

twenty-one

WEDNESDAY, 1:50 A.M.

Xander blinked at Jesse. "She wrote about David in her autobiography?"

"Published in 1988," Jesse said.

"I wasn't even born yet," David said.

Xander appeared uncertain. Slowly he sat and scooted the chair forward.

Jesse consulted the paper. "Marguerite tells how her town

was destroyed when the German army came through. Her father was a Resistance fighter and died there. Her mother was also killed."

David looked at the lady in the picture. She could have been the woman he'd seen fall in front of the tank. His heart ached for her.

Jesse said, "Her uncle raised her. He told her how she had almost died as well during the attack. Here's what she wrote." He squinted at the page, a shaky finger moving over lines of text. *"The tank was bearing down on me. My uncle was too far away to help. He said that a boy no older than eleven or twelve darted out into the street and scooped me up. This child risked being shot by the Resistance fighters on one side and the Germans on the other. When he grabbed me, the tank was but a meter away. I sometimes think what that boy must have felt at that moment: the heat from the tank blasting his skin; bullets flying around him, sparking off the tank; the smoke of burning buildings and ignited gunpowder stinging his nostrils, burning his lungs. And yet he saved me. My uncle claimed to have never seen this boy before or since. This is very strange, considering Ivry's small community."*

Jesse glanced up.

David blinked. His chest was tight, remembering.

Jesse said, "I think you'll like this next part. *I have often wondered about this child's bravery, and how he seemed to come out of nowhere and then return to nowhere after saving my life. I have come to this conclusion: he was an angel."*

David's breath caught in his lungs, and he grinned. He

swung around to see Xander's stunned face. He said, "An *angel.*"
He turned to Toria. "Did you hear that?"

She said, "You? That was you? Wow!"

Looking at her, David felt as though he had grown two inches taller, with broader shoulders—if not for real, then at least in his sister's eyes. He remembered the shrapnel that had hit his calf, how badly it had stung. He thought of how scared he had been, so close to puking from fear. He could almost feel the flames he had run through to get to the portal that took him home, and how the fire had burned his shirt collar. All of these things seemed to fall away from him now, like heavy rocks he had been carrying. He had saved someone who had gone on to save millions. All that meant, to himself and to the world, was too enormous for his mind to grasp.

Jesse said, "That's how I knew *when* the world had changed. A long time ago, I took to recording my dream-memories in a journal. Sometimes these memories would leave me so suddenly, I had to stop writing in midsentence. I used to read that journal every now and then. It kept me from forgetting what it was all about."

"What *what* was all about?" Xander said.

"This house."

"Can you . . ." David said. "Can you help us?"

Xander stood and grabbed David's arm. "We have to talk."

David smiled apologetically. He followed Xander into the foyer.

"What are you thinking?" Xander whispered.

"You mean, after everything you heard, you're still not ready to trust him?"

Xander rolled his eyes. "He said some people have a gift to know when history changes. Okay, I'll buy that. This house proves that anything's possible. That doesn't mean he's a good guy."

"Xander, *please*."

His brother looked around, thinking. His eyes settled on the upstairs hallway. He whispered, "What would Dad do?"

"He'd say yes to help," David said. "If it meant getting Mom back faster, he'd say yes. You know he would."

Xander nodded. "All right. Let's see where this leads." He pointed at David. "But don't tell them about Mom. Not yet."

"But—" David started, not sure how they were supposed to get help without saying what they needed help doing.

Xander's stern expression made it clear the point was nonnegotiable.

He gave in. "Deal."

They went into the dining room. Toria's head rested on her arms, which were crossed on the table. Her hair covered her face and spilled over the edge like a waterfall. Her back rose and fell gently.

"She's out," Keal whispered. "This one might be faking." He gestured toward Jesse.

The old man was slumped in his chair, his chin on his chest, snoring.

"Faking?" Xander said.

"Yeah, he likes to tease."

David knelt beside the wheelchair to examine Jesse's face. The old man's lids were closed, eyes moving behind them, the way they do when you dream. His mouth was slightly open, and his bottom lip vibrated with every drawn-in breath.

"Jesse?" David whispered. He looked at Xander. "He's *sleeping*."

"Figures," Xander said.

"But we were gonna . . ." David wasn't sure what it was exactly they were going to do. "*Tell* him . . . ask for his help." It sounded lame, not at all the Obi-Wan Kenobi moment his gut told him it was.

He frowned. The pressure to rescue Mom before something happened—to her, to them, to the house—felt like juggling dynamite. He wanted so badly for someone to step in and lend a hand, to snatch the explosives out of the air and give his arms a rest.

"Do *you* know what's going on?" Xander asked Keal.

"With the house? Him and the house? Some."

"What about him and the house?" David said.

"He *built* it," Keal said, as though they should have known. "His father and brother and him."

David swung his head toward Xander. Both of their mouths hung open, both of their brows furrowed tight.

"He should have said that in the first place," Xander said.

"He'd have gotten around to it," Keal said. "This man's head is like a library—especially when it comes to this house. But you can only read one book at a time."

"When did they build it?" David said.

Keal tightened his face, trying to remember. "I think . . . 1932, '33? He was a teenager. About your age, Xander."

"He must know *everything* about the house," Xander said. "All of its secrets."

"I don't know about that," Keal said. "The way he talks, it's like . . . like the house has a life of its own. Your mom and dad know a lot about you, but not everything. And the older you get, the more things you take on that are your own: experiences, dreams, fears. Seems to me this house is like that."

David didn't want to hear that. They needed for the man who built the house to know all about it, to tell everything they needed to know to beat it.

A hint of disappointment must have shown on his face.

Keal said, "But between the building and the living in it, he's gotta know something, don't you think?"

"How long was he here?" Xander said.

"I think something like . . . forty-five, fifty years."

"*In this house?*" David couldn't even imagine being here that long. He studied Jesse's sleeping face. The adventures he must have had.

The house groaned again, and David knew immediately it wasn't simply "old bones." The sound grew louder and deeper, like the start-up of an engine big enough to power a city. Sharp sounds seemed to signal the splintering of wood, the cracking of glass, but he saw nothing like those things.

Jesse startled awake. His eyes darted around. His hair was buffeting around his head. It snapped out and froze, pointing past his face at the foyer. It unfroze and billowed, as if in a strong breeze. His shirt collar started to flap.

David was kneeling beside Jesse's wheelchair, and he didn't feel a thing. He raised his hand and moved it in front of Jesse. Nothing. He touched his own hair: flat on his head as it should have been. Xander's too: shaggy and uncombed, but not moving.

Jesse said, "I have to leave."

"What? No!" David said.

Jesse's hair went limp.

The groaning and cracking faded until the house was silent again.

"What was that?" Toria said. She blinked sleepily.

The old man said, "The house is talking to us."

"What's it saying?" David said.

Jesse looked down at him. He put his hand on David's arm, which David had draped over a wheel of the chair. His eyes were intense, fire blue, like Mom's and Xander's.

Jesse said, "It's hungry."

CHAPTER

twenty-two

Oh, come on! That was the last thing David wanted to hear: *It's hungry.*

Jesse laughed, an airy wheeze. He patted David's arm. "Don't look so scared, son. It's not just an ordinary house, but I can tell you that you're more than an ordinary boy. You and Xander—your family—you're *meant* to be here."

David shook his head. "I don't understand."

"This house, those rooms upstairs," Jesse said. "It's what we do. It's in our blood. Our society has grown away from it, but there was a time when whole families, generation after generation, knew what part they played on life's stage. Hunter, leader, blacksmith . . . we're all gifted to do something very specific. Not everyone finds out what that is, but it's true. In some cases, like ours, it's in our lineage, it's what this *family* is supposed to do."

"What?" David said. "What are we supposed to do?"

Jesse leaned closer. "We're *gatekeepers*, David. The way gatekeepers of old allowed into the city only those people meant to be there . . . so we do here."

"We do *what*?" David said.

"We make sure only those events that are *supposed* to happen get through."

"To where?" David said.

"To the future."

David looked to Xander, but his brother looked as baffled as David felt.

The house groaned mournfully.

Jesse's hair fluttered. "I have to leave," he said again.

"But . . ." David gripped the old man's shoulder. It felt like nothing but bone under the jacket.

"I'll be back tomorrow," Jesse said. "I promise."

"I was hoping . . ." David said. "I was hoping you'd stay. I mean, in the house with us. Sleep here. We have room."

"I wish I could," Jesse said. "But I've been into those other worlds so many times, they think I'm theirs."

"Theirs?" David said.

"The worlds'. Time's." Jesse scanned the ceiling. He said, "I can feel the pull. I can feel it wanting to drag me back into the stream, the stream of Time. That wind blowing my hair? That's it, grabbing at me. If I stay in the house too long, it'll just—"

He snapped his fingers, inches from David's nose, making him flinch.

"*Snatch* me away, just like that."

"But we need your help," David said.

Jesse put his hand on David's head and brushed his hair back. "And you have it," he said. "I'll be here as much as I can, for as long as you want me. But when I feel the pull, I'll have to go away for a while. Not long: few hours, few days—I don't know. That's the way it has to be."

David frowned. "Okay . . . I guess."

Somewhere in the house a door slammed. All of them jumped, and Toria let out a quick scream.

Jesse took his eyes off the foyer entrance to address the children. "Keal and I are going to a motel in town." He frowned. "If you want, if you'll feel safer, I can get a room for you there too. At least until your parents return."

"We can't," Xander said. "We can't leave the house. Not now."

Jesse appeared disappointed. "Well," he said, "I think it's

acting up because I'm here. You'll be okay." He smiled, pushing up the edges of his mustache.

If he says "I think" now, David thought, *I'm outta here. Motel, here I come.*

But Jesse said no more. He nodded at Keal, and the big man stood.

●●●●●●●●

David and Xander watched through the windows on either side of the front door. Jesse sat on the edge of the porch while Keal carried the wheelchair through the woods to the road.

"His hair's doing it again," David said. It was billowing around his head the way it had done in the dining room. It snapped back toward the house, then forward, as though catching in the ebb and flow of a tide.

"Look beside him," Xander said.

Within Jesse's reach was an elm leaf. It was big and dry and papery looking in the porch's light. On his other side was a clump of pine needles. Neither the leaf nor the needles so much as fluttered.

"It's only him," Xander said, "feeling the wind."

David said, "The way his hair is blowing one way and then the opposite, it's like the house is breathing."

"Great," Xander said. "Like it's not creepy enough. Now it talks and breathes."

"And it's hungry," Toria said from her perch on the stairs.

David made sure the door's dead bolt was locked. He said, "What do you think about what he said, our being gate-keepers?"

"I think he's crazy," Xander said. "*I'm* not supposed to be here. We're going to find Mom and get out of here. As soon as I'm old enough, I'm heading back to L.A. to make movies. Maybe I'll make one about this house. That'll be all the gate-keeping *I'll* do." He looked up toward the second floor. "We gotta go get Mom."

"*Now?*"

"She's waiting for us, Dae."

"I can't, Xander," David said. He was whining, and he didn't care. "I'm beat. Let's start again in the morning."

His brother glared at him. "It's not fair," he said. "We *found* her. She was *right there*. I thought all we had to do was get you in there to show her the way home."

"They chased me away," David said.

"I know, I know." Xander slapped his hand on the ball atop the post at the base of the banister. "Then everything hap-pened to keep us from getting back to her! It would have been better if we'd never seen her message."

"No, I'm glad about it," David said. "It's nice to know she's safe, and she knows we're looking . . . More than looking; we're *close*. I don't know how these worlds work. She went in one, came out and back in another, and now she's in an even different one.

But, Xander, she's going to do everything she can to stay in the Civil War world until we get to her. I know it."

Xander nodded, looking at their sister sitting on the stairs.

Toria's eyes were closed. Her head rested in her hands, and it kept drooping to one side, then snapping back up.

"Okay," Xander said. "Tomorrow, for sure."

"For sure," David agreed, already starting to doze off.

CHAPTER

twenty-three

WEDNESDAY, 2:42 A.M.

David and his sister lay shoulder to shoulder in Toria's bed. Xander was on the floor beside it. All three stared at the ceiling. The paint had peeled in spots, and a few water stains marred its surface. David was sure there was more damage to the ceiling than he could see by the dim glow of Toria's Fiona nightlight. But it didn't matter. What had them all unable to sleep, on edge and frazzled, was the clomping around up there. Footsteps pounded, objects clattered. For the ump-teenth time, David lifted his head to make sure the chair was still wedged under the handle of the closed bedroom door.

He rolled onto his side to see Xander and whispered, "We could move into our bedroom."

"Do you really want to go into the hallway?" Xander said.

David didn't answer. After a while he said, "Good thing we didn't go up there to look for the Civil War stuff."

"I've been thinking," Xander said. "What if it's Mom making that noise?"

David listened to the heavy thumps. "That's not Mom," he said. "It's the big man, the one who took her."

"Phemus," Xander said.

"What?"

"There was a poster at school. It shows Odysseus being captured by a Cyclops. The Cyclops is huge and muscular, but a little flabby too. He's naked, except for these animal pelts around his waist. And he's bald."

"Sounds exactly like the big man," David said, amazed. "Does the Cyclops have a beard?"

"Naw, that part's different."

"Plus, the big man has two eyes," David pointed out. "He's not a Cyclops. What's Phay-mus?"

"Phemus," Xander corrected. "The Cyclops's name is Polyphemus. I call him Phemus for short. That's the guy who took Mom."

"Phemus," David said, feeling it on his tongue.

It sounded like something was being dragged through the third-floor hallway.

"I'd like to know what's going on," Xander said.

"You're not thinking about going up there?" David got a cold chill just thinking about it.

"Are you kidding?"

"I don't want anything to do with that hallway when whatever's making those noises is there. Phemus or whoever. I'd rather never know what's going on and live, than find out and die."

"No, *really*?" Xander said.

David rolled away.

Toria's eyes were closed, her mouth slightly parted.

He settled onto his back. A minute later he whispered, "Good night, Xander."

"'Night, Dae."

David's eyes felt heavy in his head, grainy as though sand had gotten in. Every time he blinked, it took more and more effort to open his lids again. Toria's slow, deep breathing lulled him closer to sleep. The noises from the third floor faded—in reality or only in his own ears, he didn't know, and didn't give it much thought.

His eyes closed and stayed that way.

twenty-four

WEDNESDAY, 9:48 A.M.

His mother woke him. Her hand gently shook his shoulder. His eyes fluttered open. There she was, leaning over him. The morning light radiated behind her.

"Mom?" With consciousness came excitement: She was here! She had found her way home!

"David?" she whispered.

"Mom!" He sat up, throwing his arms around her. *I missed you! I love you! Are you all right?* But none of these things came out.

He just wanted to hold her, squeeze her, feel her in his arms.

"David." She pushed him away.

His eyes found her face, longing to see it.

He blinked. The corners of his mouth dropped, as did his heart.

Toria sat in front of him, her face contorted by concern. She said, "Are you all right?"

"I—" Unwilling to let his mother go, he looked around the room. Daylight through the window made everything clear—and it was clear his mother was not there.

"You're crying," Toria said. She brushed her fingers over his cheek.

"I thought . . ." He blinked, wiped his eyes.

"I know. You thought I was Mom," Toria said. "You were dreaming."

He tried to smile but couldn't.

His sister's face brightened.

"What?" he said.

"I want to go," she said.

He took a deep breath and let it out slowly. He shook his head. "Until Dad sorts things out with the police, we can't leave the house. They might grab us and not let us back in."

"No," she said. "I mean, I want to go get her. I want to go over."

He glared at her. "Who? You? You said last night you didn't want to go through a portal."

"I changed my mind. For Mom. You said they chased you out."

David said, "The first time we went to the Civil War, I was wearing Confederate gray." He saw that she didn't understand. "Xander and I—and Mom—were in *Union* territory. They thought I was an enemy soldier."

"Xander too?"

He shook his head. "I guess they thought he was a Union soldier trying to run away. They don't like that much."

"But they don't know *me*," she said, "and I'm a little girl. What are they gonna do?"

"You don't know these worlds, Toria," David said. "It's almost like the people over there *look* for reasons to not like you, to want to hurt you."

"But I have to go, Dae."

"Go where?" Xander said. He put his hand on the bed and lifted himself up to sit beside Toria.

"She wants to go over."

"No way," Xander said. He gave their sister a little push. He squinted at David. "Were you crying?"

Again David wiped his eyes, his face. He said, "That's . . . something else. Toria knows we can't go back, but she thinks she can."

Xander stared into the corner of the room, thinking. He nodded.

"Xander, no," David said.

Xander raised his eyebrows. He said, "Maybe she's right."

"It's too dangerous."

"*We* made it out alive."

"Barely," David reminded him.

"Look at her," his brother said. "Who's going to hurt anything so cute?"

Toria grinned.

"Dad would kill us," David said.

"Not if everything goes all right," Xander said.

"Yes!" David grabbed Xander's arm. "In this case, even if she gets Mom and comes back without a scratch, he'd kill us. You know he would."

twenty-five

WEDNESDAY, 10:30 A.M.

The argument continued in the kitchen.

David dropped bread into the toaster. He said, "It's never gone smoothly for us when we go over. It's always about fighting, running, survival."

"Not all the time," Xander said. He was scrambling eggs in a frying pan. "There was that one peaceful world. Beautiful meadows. Even the animals weren't afraid of me. Dad and I threw rocks into a river."

"That sounds nice," Toria said. She was opening a package of bacon for Xander to fry up.

David watched the coils inside the toaster turn orange. He said, "*One* place where people weren't trying to kill us. One. And we *know* the Civil War world. It's not a peaceful meadow."

Xander scooped the eggs onto a plate and started laying strips of bacon into the pan. The sizzling meat sounded like gale-force rain striking the windows.

The smells reminded David how hungry he was. The night before, he had choked down maybe three bites of clumpy spaghetti, which had sat in his stomach like Play-Doh.

Tongs in hand, Xander watched the bacon. He said, "Crispy or fatty?"

"Crispy," Toria said.

David said, "I don't know about 'fatty,' but I don't like crispy." The toast popped up, and he transferred the slices to a plate. He put more bread in the toaster, levered them down, and began buttering the finished ones. He said, "I can't believe we're doing this."

"Arguing?" Xander said. "Hey, you're the one who won't listen to reason."

"I mean making breakfast," David said. "Like it's just some normal day."

"Maybe it is," Xander said. "For us."

The toast kept tearing under David's butter knife. Every stroke made the bread uglier. He turned away from it.

"Dad told me, 'Time is God's way of preventing everything from happening at once,'" he said. "But it *is* all happening at once: We have to rescue Mom from a world that's trying to kill us. We have to figure out how to get Dad out of jail without letting them arrest us too. We have to watch out for Taksidian and the fifty ways he's trying to capture us, murder us, or otherwise get us out of the house. We should be picking Jesse's brain for everything he knows."

"Picking his brain?" Toria said. "*Eew.*"

"It means learning what he knows, Toria," David said. "My point is, it's too much, all at once."

Xander smiled at him. "Like I said, maybe that's our normal . . . now that we're in this house."

"I wish we'd never laid eyes on it," David said.

Xander flipped the bacon. He said, "I'm not sure we ever had a choice, Dae."

"What do you mean?" David said. "Like it's our *destiny* to be here?"

Xander shrugged. "I'm just saying. With Dad kind of making it happen, and the reason he did going back to when he was a kid. And remember, we were excited about this place . . . attracted to it, even though it was scary. Doesn't all of that feel like destiny to you?"

"What about Hollywood? You said you were going to make movies."

"I am. This is today's destiny. Filmmaking is tomorow's."

147

The second round of toast popped up behind David. He said, "I don't know what destiny feels like, but if this is it, I don't like it. I want to un-destiny this place from my life."

"That's why Toria should go over," Xander said.

David wanted to punch him. "Xander, it's too—"

Xander waved his hand at him. "Never mind, never mind. You know those noises last night, the ones coming from the third floor?"

"Creepy," Toria said.

Xander began using the tongs to pull the bacon from the grease and lay the strips on folded paper towels. "David, you said you'd rather not know what was causing them than go up there and die."

"And you said, 'No, *really?*'" David reminded him. He put the new toast on top of the mangled slices, then cut thin patties of butter from the stick and set them on the edge of the plate. He carried his breakfast contribution into the dining room.

Toria followed with the eggs, and Xander with the bacon.

Xander said, "What if I figured out a way to know what's happening without having to go up there?"

David gave him a puzzled look. "Okaaaay . . . ?"

"A camera," Xander said. A big grin stretched out on his face. "We put one right at the beginning of the hallway, just inside the landing."

David followed Toria back into the kitchen. Xander was

right on him, wanting David to tell him what a brilliant idea it was.

Instead, David said, "Will a camera work up there? Your video camera didn't work when I took it over into that jungle world."

"That was through a portal," Xander said. "Who knows why it went wacky? I've filmed all over the house. It works."

Toria brushed past them, carrying three glasses of OJ. David picked up a stack of plates, and Xander plucked forks out of a drawer.

"So what?" David said. "You start filming when we go to bed, then check it in the morning?"

"That's no good," Xander said. "It doesn't record that long, and I want to know what's happening when it happens, not later."

"So what are you thinking?" David passed out the plates and sat down.

"Security cameras," Xander said. "Those wireless ones that show the camera's perspective on a TV or computer monitor."

Thinking about it, David scooped eggs onto his plate and dropped three strips of bacon beside them.

A forkful of eggs was halfway to his mouth when Toria said, "David . . . ?" She was reaching her hands out to him and Xander.

David set the fork down and clasped his siblings' hands. When no one said anything, David gave Xander's fingers a squeeze.

Xander said, "Heavenly Father, thank You for this food. Please keep Mom safe and bring her home soon."

David stepped in before Xander could close the prayer. He said, "Dad, too."

Xander said, "And make us strong and courageous. Amen." He smiled. "Last night, when I saw Dad in jail, he said that's what we have to be."

"He always says that," David said, nodding. He leaned over his plate and began shoveling scrambled egg into his mouth like coal into a furnace.

"So, anyway," Xander said, "the hardware store sells security camera kits."

"Aren't they expensive?" David said.

"Don't talk with your mouth full," Toria said. "Gross!"

David opened his mouth wide.

Toria lowered her eyes to her plate.

"I've got money," Xander said.

"You do?"

"Mom showed me some cash she'd set aside to buy me a car."

"You're kidding." Everything about that amazed David: that their parents had extra money and that they'd put it into a car for Xander.

It wasn't that they didn't *want* to buy their kids things, but teaching—as Dad had done before accepting the principal's position here in Pinedale—wasn't exactly a high-paying career. And Mom had chosen full-time parenting over juggling a job and kids, so that's what she had done since Xander was born.

They were always pinching pennies for little extras, like David's soccer equipment and Toria's piano lessons.

But a car? *Wow.*

"She was so cool about it," Xander said, remembering. "She wasn't going to tell me until my birthday, but she knew the move was getting me down, and she hoped it would cheer me up."

David nodded. "That's Mom." He folded a piece of bacon into his mouth. "When were you thinking of doing it—putting the camera up there?"

"Right away, now," Xander said. "I don't know how long it'll take to set up, and I definitely want it working before we go to bed, in case whatever went on last night goes on again."

"The hardware store's on the other side of town," Toria said.

She had gone there with Dad the other day to get locks for the third-floor doors—locks the house had shaken off the way a dog shakes off fleas.

"That's a long ride," David said.

Xander's bike was a secondhand three-speed with a loose chain and a wobbly wheel.

"I'll take the car again." Seeing David's frown, he said, "If the cops see me, it doesn't matter whether I'm walking or riding my bike or chasing poodles up Main Street in a Ferrari—they're going to haul me away."

David considered telling Xander that getting a camera wasn't worth leaving the house. It wasn't worth risking being spotted by the police. Then he realized how much time it would take to buy it and then install it . . . time *not* spent finding the Civil War world. As much as David wanted to find Mom, he *didn't* want Toria going over. By the time the camera was ready, and his brother started thinking again about sending their sister over, maybe Dad would be home to nix Xander's stupid plan.

David looked at his brother out of the corner of his eye. He said, "I would feel a lot safer knowing what's happening up there."

Xander nodded. "I'll go in a few minutes." He snapped up a slice of toast, folded it, and stuffed it into his mouth. Chewing while he talked, he said, "Toria, you look for the Civil War world while I'm gone. If you find it, stay in the antechamber. That'll keep it from shifting away."

David pulled in a breath, sucking egg down the wrong pipe. He started to choke and let food fall from his mouth onto the plate, not caring what it looked like. Xander stood and slapped him on the back, hard. Then again. Whatever was in there cleared. David swallowed and breathed.

Toria ran around the table to rub his back. "Are you all right?" she said sweetly.

He nodded, cleared his throat. His eyes had begun to water, and he wiped them. He took a swig of juice.

Xander dropped back into his seat and watched David with big eyes. He said, "Wouldn't it be a trip if you choked to death on eggs, after all the things you've survived lately?"

David glared at him. "It would be *sad*," he said, his voice hoarse.

"For us," Xander said. "You wouldn't care. You'd be gone."

David couldn't help but smile. He said, "I'd care. Just before the lights went out for good, I'd be thinking *Eggs? Eggs? You gotta be kidding!*"

Even Toria laughed. The sound of it reminded David why he'd choked in the first place. He said, "Xander, we can't look for the world while you're gone. It's too dangerous."

Xander frowned. He said, "We should get Mom first, then. That's the most important thing."

"It is," David said. "But what if it takes a while for the world to come back around? What if something keeps Toria from getting Mom? Then we'll be back in bed tonight, wondering what's happening on the third floor. Let's just get that done and be covered."

Toria was still standing next to David, pressing into his arm.

He said, "Toria, I'm all right. Go finish eating."

"I'm not hungry anymore." She was scrunching her nose, looking at the food that had fallen from David's mouth.

David covered the mess with a slice of toast. He said, "Just go sit down, okay?"

"Yeah," Xander said. "I think we can get a camera system up and running pretty fast. Let's do that, then we'll look for the Civil War stuff."

"Too bad we can't put a camera in all the rooms up there . . . in all the *antechambers*," Toria said, leaning back in her chair.

David smiled. He could tell she was still trying to get a handle on that word *antechamber*. He wasn't sure if *he'd* ever heard it before coming here. Now they used it like a thousand times a day. He felt his smile fade. He wished he didn't know it, that they'd never discovered that stupid third floor.

Xander's eyes grew wide, his lips made a perfect O. He said, "Then we could see which items are in the antechambers anytime we wanted to."

David said, "It'd take a week to set up twenty cameras like that."

"But wouldn't that be cool?"

"It'd be cooler," David said, "not to *need* the cameras. Let's get Mom and get gone."

Xander pushed his lips sideways. "I'll just get one extra camera to see if it even works in an antechamber."

"I wish Dad was here," Toria said.

"They took him at about seven thirty last night," Xander said. He wiggled his fingers, calculating. "That's fifteen hours ago. He said he thought it was all a scam, that they didn't dare hold him longer than a day."

"That's nine more hours," David said. He was more than a little upset that the house had made a few hours seem like an eternity, like they were holding on to the ledge of a cliff and their fingers were growing tired. He wished everything would just slow down so they could take a breath, so they could *think.*

"After I put the camera up, we'll go get Mom," Xander told Toria. "If you're still up for it."

David hoped she would drop her face, say something like, *I changed my mind. I'm too scared.*

But she didn't. She puffed out her chest and said, "I can do it!"

"Okay," Xander said. He lifted his glass of juice. "To being strong and courageous."

Toria and David picked up their own glasses and clinked them against Xander's.

Despite his feelings about Toria going over, David joined them. "Strong and courageous!" he said.

CHAPTER

twenty-six

WEDNESDAY, NOON

David sat in the Mission Control Center, his head bowed toward the PSP in his hands. His teeth pushed into his bottom lip as he clicked the buttons that caused his on-screen soccer player to make a bicycle kick for the goal: right past the tender and in! As the crowd roared and a teammate gave him a high five, he glanced up to a computer monitor on a desk in front of him.

Xander's face filled the screen. The camera he'd picked up at the hardware store after breakfast made his eyes appear unnaturally large. The pencil he held in his mouth looked more like a horse's bit. He was squinting over the camera, so it seemed like he was staring at David's hair. Xander looked over his shoulder at the crooked hallway of doors behind him, then wiggled the camera around. He was mounting it above the doorway between the third-floor landing and the hall.

Static flashed on the screen, then a band of snow scrolled from the top of the screen to the bottom.

"We're getting interference!" David called over his shoulder.

"What?" Toria called back from the base of the stairs leading to the third floor. She was roughly midway between David and Xander and was conveying their words back and forth.

"We're getting—" David started.

More static broke Xander's face across the screen.

"Hold on!" David said. He pushed back from the desk and stepped out of the MCC.

They had turned what Mom had called the servants' quarters into their base of operations for her rescue. The room was off a short hallway that jutted back toward the rear of the house from the second floor's main hallway. It was close to the staircase leading to the third level, where twenty doors led into twenty small rooms and, beyond them, twenty portals opened into different times, different "worlds"—all of them on earth, but so unlike the time and places the Kings knew, they might as well have been alien planets.

The staircase itself was hidden behind the wall at the end of the short hallway. One evening David and Xander had spotted the big man—the one Xander dubbed Phemus—in their house. They'd followed him and found a secret door in the wall.

Now, David stepped into the opening of that door. Six feet beyond it was another wall, this one coated in unpainted plaster. Even the unsanded swirls of the trowel that had applied the plaster were still visible. Whoever had built it wasn't concerned about appearances: the wall was nothing more than a barrier to keep people out. Or more likely, David thought, to keep people *in*, to keep them from coming through the portals and into the main part of the house, as Phemus had done when he took Mom. Set in this second wall—not directly in front of the secret door, but off to the side—was another door, covered in metal.

Lot of good the extra security did, David thought.

The metal door was open, and Toria was leaning against its frame.

"What?" she said.

"Just looking," David said.

"What's going on?" Xander called from the floor above.

"We're getting static," David yelled. "I'm wondering if there's anything between the camera and the monitor that's causing it."

He scanned the area between the walls, about the size of a walk-in closet. The backside of the hallway wall was imperfectly finished, like the other one.

David stepped past Toria to the base of the steps that rose straight up to the landing. He could hear Xander fiddling with something, but his brother was out of sight, in the hallway to the left of the landing. He rapped his knuckles against this second wall, but the sound told him nothing about what was inside.

"I can't tell," he said. "There might be wires running through the walls that are interfering."

"Get back to the monitor," Xander said. "I'll fiddle with the camera, see what I can do."

"Get back to the monitor!" Toria yelled into David's ear, trying to be funny. They had told her to yell to the other whatever one of them said. "I'll fiddle—!"

David clamped his hand over her mouth. "I heard," he said. He wiggled a fingertip into his ear, frowning at her. "That hurt."

He went through the secret door into the short hall and returned to the MCC. The room was coming along. Dad had hung a timeline of history near the ceiling; it spanned the length of two walls. Tough guys from Xander's movie posters—*300, Gladiator, Remember the Titans*—stared down at him. They were meant to psych them up to face the dangers of the other worlds. A series of colored index cards was taped to the wall, reflecting the times and places they'd already visited: the Roman Colosseum, the tiger-and-warrior-infested jungle, the French village during World War II, the Civil War, the peaceful world where Dad and Xander had first carved Bob into a tree. David still wanted to add cards that listed the items they had found in the antechambers and link the cards with string. He wondered if he'd ever find the time to do that.

He dropped into the chair in front of the monitor. On the screen, a brief pop of static fluttered across Xander's face. His brother's mouth moved.

"How's that?" Toria yelled.

Now that David knew what Xander had said, he recognized the way his mouth had moved to form the words. If they did this long enough, he might learn to read lips. That'd be sweet.

"Better!" he hollered back to Toria. "But tell him to move it a little to the left!"

She passed it along, and Xander nudged the camera angle the wrong way.

"*My* left! The camera's left!" David yelled. He heard his sister echo the words.

Xander rolled his eyes. He adjusted the camera, raised his eyebrows in question.

"That's good!" David said.

Xander nodded, took the pencil out of his mouth, and made a mark off camera. His head filled the monitor, then it dropped away. The camera was turned sideways, pointing down the hall. David realized Xander had set it on top of the stepladder while he went to get the screws and screwdriver. Xander moved away from the camera and squatted in front of a box.

David picked up the PSP. The game was over, his team's score in the toilet. He turned it off. He'd rather be kicking his ball around outside than doing this.

Xander walked toward the monitor, screws in one hand, the tool in the other. The camera jerked and bounced around, then settled on the image David had seen a minute before: the hallway of doors over Xander's shoulder.

Xander said something. In the few seconds before Toria could relay it, David tried to guess what it was: *Is the dog dead? I'm a raft? Want to fight?*

"Is that right?" Toria yelled.

Oooo . . . not even close.

"Yeah, perfect!" he said.

Xander moved a screw to the mount behind the camera. The screwdriver came into view, then disappeared from the frame.

David smiled at the faces Xander was making as he tried to get the screw into the wall. Xander's tongue appeared in the corner of his mouth, and David outright laughed. He yelled, "Ha-ha-ha!"

"What?" Toria called.

"Pass it along," David said. "Ha-ha-ha!"

He heard her call out to Xander. On the monitor, Xander's eyebrows came together. He moved his mouth, a word David could read: *What?* Toria repeated it. On the monitor, Xander said something else—too long for David even to guess at.

Toria yelled, "He said knock it off or you can put the camera up."

Xander looked down, probably getting another screw. Then his brother was back to twisting his hand over the screwdriver and making funny faces.

David snickered. A burst of static obscured Xander's face, then scattered away. As it did, David's heart turned to stone. He leaned forward and grabbed the side edges of the monitor.

Over Xander's shoulder, the camera showed the hallway running back to the far wall, which had been, until seconds ago, cloaked in shadows. Now light filled that space. Though David could not see it, he knew only one thing could have caused such brightness: way back at the end of the hall, a door had opened. The light flickered, as though something was moving through it, casting a shadow.

The big man stepped into the hallway.

Phemus!

His bald head almost scraped the ceiling. Wiry hair burst from his face and hung down to his powerful chest. Even in the camera's poor resolution, David could make out the scars that crisscrossed his flesh, the smudges of dirt, the glistening sweat. A raggedy pelt hung from his waist. The man swung his head around to squint back into the light, as though debating about pulling the door closed.

David jumped up, sending his chair clattering to the floor behind him. "Xander!" he screamed. He spun, intending to bolt out of the room, but the corner of his eye caught something on the monitor, and he turned back.

The big man reversed a step as *another* man came out of the room. This one was similar to Phemus: a little smaller—still large—with a full head of long, shaggy hair. He peered into Phemus's face as if for instructions.

"Xan—Xander!" David yelled. He stumbled backward, pivoted around, and crashed into Toria, who was running into the room. They both went down. David's cast cracked against the floor beside his sister's head, sending a bolt of pain shooting into his shoulder and neck.

"David!" Toria grunted under him, pushing him off.

David scrambled to get his feet under him. He screamed, "Xander! Get out of there! Xander!"

As he rose, Toria pushed herself into a sitting position. "What are you—" she said, then let loose with her own piercing scream.

She was looking at the monitor. David snapped his head toward it. A third man had emerged from the room. Like the others, he wore only a tattered pelt. But he was shorter, and so skinny his ribs pushed through his skin. He had splotchy hair springing out from his scalp like water from a colander.

He bounced up and down, looking from Phemus to the other man like a pet hungry for attention.

Toria wrapped both of her arms around David's leg. He yanked on it, but her grip was a bear trap.

"Toria, let go!"

On the monitor, Xander was still making faces, cranking on the screwdriver.

"Turn around, Xander!" David screamed. *Can't you hear them! Why can't you hear them?*

He wondered if the house was messing with the sounds, intentionally keeping Xander from hearing the people behind him.

His brother plucked a screw from his lips and brought his hand past the camera's lens. Over his shoulder, the three men turned their heads. They spotted Xander and began lumbering toward him.

CHAPTER

twenty-seven

WEDNESDAY, 12:06 P.M.

David turned, twisting his leg free from Toria's grasp. He stumbled into the hall and darted for the secret door. It was closed. He slammed against the wall beside it. He tapped the edge of the door with his fingers, but it didn't pop out as it usually did.

"They're getting closer!" Toria yelled from the MCC. She ran up behind him. "Hurry, Dae!"

"I am!" He pounded on the door. It wouldn't budge. "Why'd you close it?"

"I didn't!"

This house!

He looked around, didn't see anything he could use to pry open the door or break it down. Then he remembered and ran into the MCC. Propped against the wall, just inside the door, was the toy rifle both he and Xander had used as a club. He snatched it up.

Frantic as he was to get to Xander, he just *had to* glance at the monitor. His brother was still squinting past the lens, messing with screws and the screwdriver. Behind him, the two larger men were trudging shoulder to shoulder toward him. The smaller, animal-like man was hopping up and down behind them, his eyes wild. In a flash, he tried to squeeze between one of the other men and the wall, but the space was too tight. They had crossed half the distance to Xander.

David sprinted into the hallway. Toria was beating her fists against the secret door.

"Move!" David said. He swung the gun's stock into the wall, blasting a divot of wallpaper and plaster from it. "Xander!"

He didn't have time to tear down the whole wall, but he definitely had the energy and determination. He stepped back and rammed the barrel of the rifle into the wall near the latch. The muzzle made a half-inch-deep hole. He had hit a wooden stud.

He pulled back, rammed again. This time the barrel plunged through up to the trigger. David began rotating the stock with both hands as though turning a handle on a butter churn.

The hole in the wall opened up around the barrel. Plaster fell away. When the opening was the diameter of a dinner plate, he pushed the rifle all the way through. It clattered to the floor on the other side.

If this doesn't work, Xander's dead.

David reached his hand through and found the latch. It wouldn't budge. Maybe his pounding had jammed it.

He pulled his arm out and stuck his face to the hole. "Xander!"

"What?"

"Run! Look behind you!"

"What are you—" Then he screamed, a sound that pierced David's heart like a spear.

Metal rattled and crashed. David realized the ladder had fallen.

"Xander!"

David felt the latch again. He forced himself to slow down, to feel it and picture it. He realized that the lever was pushed too far forward. He pulled it backward, then tugged it down. The wall sprang open. He hooked his fingers around it and pulled.

"Toria," he said, "make sure this door doesn't shut again."

His brother's screams continued. David ran through the

169

second doorway and pounded up the stairs. He hit the landing and spun into the hallway.

Xander was ten feet in, blood smeared across his forehead. Phemus clutched his ankle and was dragging him down the hall. The other two men lurched in to grab at him. But Xander had hold of the aluminum stepladder and was wielding it the way a lion tamer uses a chair to hold back the man-eaters. He was flat on his back, hefting the ladder up, shoving the top of it at his attackers.

David ran forward. He grabbed the ladder and pulled. "Xander, let go! I've got better leverage than you!"

"David!" Xander released his grip.

David pulled the ladder back, yelled—because he had to say something, had to release the knot of thoughts pressuring his brain—"Let go of my brother!" and jammed the ladder's top brace into Phemus's face.

Blood sprayed out of the man's nose. He stumbled back, an expression of complete shock on his face.

"Ha!" David screamed, as though he'd scored the winning point in a video game.

The smaller, spastic intruder—David's frenzied mind instantly tagged this guy "Baboon Man"—stretched to grab the leg Phemus had lost.

Xander kicked the hand. It pulled away, then reached out again. Another kick. The hand retreated, reached again.

David reared back with the ladder and heaved it forward

with every bit of energy he had in him. It struck Baboon Man in the side of the skull with a loud *crack!* The man's head snapped sideways, and he reeled away.

The other two—Phemus, bloody from David's first strike, and the one who was almost as large—lunged for Xander.

Xander bent his knees, placed the treads of his sneakers on the carpet, and pushed himself backward, toward the landing.

David jabbed the ladder at the men. It struck Phemus's chest. David may as well have rammed it into a brick wall: the man didn't budge. The shock of hitting him reverberated along the ladder and through David's bones. His broken arm throbbed.

Xander pushed past him on the floor.

"Go!" David yelled. "Go!"

Xander flipped over and clambered on his hands and knees toward the landing. He yelled, "I'm clear, Dae! Get out of there."

David lunged with the ladder.

This time he caught Baboon Man in the chest. The man *oophed!* and stumbled back again.

Phemus grabbed the ladder and ripped it out of David's hands. He flung it into the wall, smashing one of the wall lamps. David witnessed the briefest flash of satisfaction on the man's scruffy face.

David spun and darted for Xander, who was pulling himself up against the door frame. The brothers collided. Their legs tangled, and they fell onto the landing.

The men in the hallway lurched forward, their arms out-stretched. It occurred to David that Xander would already have a zombie movie in mind to describe this later—if there *was* a later. David flung himself down the stairs, bringing Xander with him. They tumbled over the first steps, grunting, groaning. Then David found himself going down backwards, his butt bouncing painfully against each step. He raised his cast for balance, and Xander's forehead flew into it. They both yelped in pain. They reached the bottom, and Xander flipped over David, crashing into the wall.

Above them, the men pushed through the doorway, their eyes huge and insane.

David scrambled up, and he saw Phemus take the lead, lumbering slowly down each step. His girth spanned the width of the stairwell. Baboon Man leaped and pulled him-self up behind Phemus as though he were scaling a wall. His fingers were bent talons, digging into the big man's flesh at the shoulders and on top of his head, trying to propel him-self over.

Xander grabbed David's collar and yanked him through the doorway. Both brothers grabbed for the door at the same time. Swinging the door around, they tripped over each other. Only their iron grips on the door's edge kept them from spilling to the floor.

Through the opening, David saw that Baboon Man—scrawny, scraggly, jittery—had gotten himself completely onto Phemus's shoulder. For a moment he was perched there, squatting like a gargoyle, his wicked grin trembling over his knees. Then he leaped off, a screeching beast of prey. Arms outstretched, mouth impossibly wide, he flew at David.

The door slammed shut. The impact behind it knocked it open again, flinging David into the wall behind him. Air burst out of his lungs. He inhaled, got nothing, inhaled. He slid down the wall.

Xander was pushing on the door, but Baboon Man had collapsed onto the floor, halfway through. He wasn't moving. Just out cold.

David gasped for breath that wouldn't come.

Xander grabbed him. "It's okay, Dae. Just got the wind knocked out of you. It'll come back." He hoisted him up. "Toria!" he called. "Help Dae. Get him out of here."

David felt Toria's small hands hook themselves into his armpits from behind. It was just enough support to keep him on his feet, and he started backpedaling through the secret door. He watched Xander try to push the unconscious Baboon Man out of the way of the door.

The guy groaned, lifted his head, tried to push himself up. Xander kicked him in the head.

Baboon Man's hand shot out and seized Xander's ankle.

"Wait," David wheezed at Toria. "Let go. I'm okay." He pulled free, stooped, and picked up the toy rifle.

Something crashed into the other side of the wall—David

imagined Phemus picking up speed on the stairs and nailing the wall with arms the size of battering rams. Plaster dust filled the small space between the walls as the entire wall at the base of the stairs broke free from the ceiling and fell.

CHAPTER

twenty-eight

The wall tipped over, striking David's head. He crumpled onto his hands and knees. The wall slammed into the hallway wall, angling from the floor like the side of a pup tent.

Xander had ducked, avoiding the wall by inches. Baboon Man squirmed on the ground toward Xander, whose ankle he continued to clasp with that bony, taloned hand. David hammered the rifle butt into the man's skull.

The guy twisted his face toward David. He growled like

a dog and snapped his mouth open and closed. David gave the guy's forehead a quick, hard jab. His head dropped to the floor.

The wall suffered another devastating blow from the staircase side. Chunks of plaster fell—one giving David another firm knock on the head.

"Xander," he said, "we have to get out of here. The whole wall's coming down."

Dust stung his eyes, filled his already aching lungs. He coughed.

Xander yanked his ankle out of the baboon's claw. He helped David stand, gave him a push, and said, "Go!"

Together they staggered through the secret door into the second-floor hallway.

"Toria, shut the door," David said, panting. "It's not going to stop them, but still . . ." He rubbed his head where the wall and the plaster had hit it. Between his arm, his head, and his bruised backside, he felt like he had just climbed out of a clothes dryer.

Toria swung the door shut, and the latch clicked.

A crash came from the other side, and this outer wall, decorated to look like any other in the hallway, buckled toward them. It cracked from floor to ceiling, and the secret door popped open.

Toria screamed. David grabbed her shoulder, Xander grabbed David's, and they backpedaled past the MCC.

"What are they doing?" David said.

Xander said, "When the wall collapsed, it made the door opening too small for Phemus to fit through. Now he has to come *through* the walls."

"What do we do?" Toria said.

Before they could answer, an explosion erupted at the end of the short hallway. The entire wall fell forward, creaking and cracking. Sparks flashed as electrical wiring broke. The lights went out. Sunlight from the foyer and the open MCC door revealed the wall crashing to the floor, followed by the second wall; it landed on top of the first one. A massive dust cloud billowed up, as though a giant hand had slapped a pile of baby powder. It roiled in the hallway, coming at them like a sandstorm.

Xander said, "Run!"

He grabbed Toria's hand, and they ran around the corner into the second floor's main hallway.

David's legs froze. He watched as a figure stirred in the dust cloud. It became more distinct, solidifying into arms, legs, a head. To the left of this silhouette, the other big man stepped out of the haze. He was grinning and taking long, crunching strides toward him.

David's legs broke from the invisible cement that had bound them, and he ran. He called out, "The closet!"

Xander and Toria skidded to a stop at the head of the grand staircase.

"School's in session," Xander said. "We can't—"

"Yes, we can!" David said. "Two of those guys are too big to fit in the locker. The other might be out cold. Who cares if people wonder where we came from?"

The two men trudged around the corner.

Toria screamed, pulled her hand out of Xander's, and bolted down the stairs.

"Wait!" David said. "Toria!"

Xander grabbed for her, but her legs were moving like a race car's pistons; she was almost to the bottom before he took a single step. The brothers threw panicked glances at each other and tore after her.

Toria reached the front door and yanked on it. It didn't open.

David pushed ahead, thumbed the dead bolt, and opened the door. He grabbed his sister's wrist and flung her through the opening. She leaped off the porch. Xander turned in the doorway, and both boys looked up to the top of the stairs.

The hulking men glowered down at them. Their chests rose and fell. Their eyes, dark under heavy brows, blinked, blinked, as though they were unaccustomed to the bright sunlight.

Xander stepped forward into the foyer.

David touched his arm. "Xander?" he whispered.

His brother straightened his spine, squared his shoulders. "You!" he said, pointing at Phemus.

David remembered what Xander had said about the poster he'd seen: Odysseus challenging the Cyclops.

Xander said, "Where's our mother? Bring her back! Just . . ." His voice cracked. His breathing was fast and shallow. His next words were menacingly quiet. "Bring her back."

David was afraid his brother was going to rush the guy. The last time they'd met, when the man had kidnapped Mom, all three of the King men—Dad, Xander, and David—had almost died. And Xander had been armed with a metal bat. No way the outcome of a confrontation now could be any better. In fact, David was sure it would end up much worse.

He stepped closer and shifted the toy rifle to his left hand. He clasped the fingers of his right hand into Xander's waistband. "Xander, let's go," he said. "Come on. This isn't a fair fight. It's not meant to be. We're supposed to lose."

"We're not going to leave," Xander told the man. His words sounded hard as rocks. "We're staying until our mother's back." He started to turn, then said, "The next time I see you, I'll be ready."

Without taking his eyes off Xander, Phemus began descending the stairs. The wood under his bare feet creaked in protest. The other man grinned and trailed a step behind.

"Xander!" David said. He tugged his brother's pants, yanking him back—a step, then two, till they were on the porch. Toria stood in the woods, watching them.

Xander frowned at David. His eyes were red.

As David watched, a thick rivulet of blood from a cut above Xander's eye ran the curve of his brow, skirted the corner of his eye, and ran down his cheek. It would have made a great movie-tough-guy wound.

They looked through the open door. Here in the sunlight, the interior looked dark and gloomy. The sound of the men's plodding footsteps echoed out to them.

Xander gestured with his head. He whispered, "Let's go."

twenty-nine

WEDNESDAY, 12:20 P.M.

David and Xander descended the porch steps. When they reached Toria in the woods, they turned back.

"Think they'll come out for us?" David said.

Xander shook his head. "That house is their leash. It's as far as their master will let them go."

"Taksidian?" David said. He had heard Taksidian talking to Phemus the other day, when Clayton had chased David through the locker into the house.

"Who else?" Xander said. He still looked ready to rumble.

David thought it would be a short brawl if he and the big guy ever did tangle. He pointed at the blood on Xander's face. "What happened?"

Xander touched the cut and grimaced. He looked at his fingers. "The ladder," he said. "When those guys pulled me off, it came down on my head."

The shadows inside the doorway stirred. Phemus filled the opening. He scowled out at the daylight, caught sight of the kids, and glared at them.

"Are you sure about the leash?" Toria said.

"Yeah," Xander said. "I'm starting to figure things—"

The brute stepped onto the porch.

Toria grabbed David's bicep. David gripped Xander's shirt.

"It's okay," Xander said. "That's it. That's as far as he'll come."

The man lumbered to the porch steps and started down. Toria gasped.

"Ow, Toria," David whispered. "Your nails are digging into my skin."

"Get ready to run," Xander said.

"Where to?" David said.

"Follow me. I have an idea."

David nudged Toria. "You hear? Follow Xander. Don't run off like you did down the stairs."

"I got scared," she said.

"No kidding."

They watched the man reach the dirt at the bottom of the steps. He turned back to his . . . *friend* was the word that came to David's mind, but it was a little like thinking of two killer Rottweilers as play-date pals.

"Let's get out of here," Xander said, and took off.

David grabbed Toria's wrist and fell in behind. He looked back over his shoulder to see Phemus swing his arm in a *Come on!* gesture, but the smaller man backed away and disappeared in the gloom. It took Phemus all of three seconds to spot the kids and start after them.

Xander weaved through the trees and bushes, arcing around the side of the house.

The man's feet pounded the ground behind them, snapping twigs and ripping through the low bushes and rotting deadfalls the kids had jumped over.

"He's getting closer," Toria said.

Xander picked up his pace. He said, "I didn't think that guy could move so fast."

"Like you didn't think he could leave the house," David said.

"All right, all right." Xander angled around a thick bush.

"Anything else you think he *can't* do," David said, "so I have a heads-up about what he's *going* to do?"

"We're about to find out," Xander said.

They broke through a thick patch of bushes and stopped in the clearing. It was an oval-shaped meadow about half the size of a football field. Encircled by trees, the ground here was flat and uniformly covered with lush, green grass. The upper branches of the trees bent inward, hanging over the meadow's edges. The sky above was blue and streaked with clouds, as though brushed with white paint.

David and Xander had discovered the place on their second day in the house. Here, the air was peculiar, and their voices became squeaky, as though they were auditioning for the part of Mickey Mouse in a movie. They could also run faster and jump higher.

But Dad had shown them the clearing's real magic: here, they could *fly*. That was the best word David could think of. What else could you call rising above the ground and moving through the air without wings, wires, or equipment of any kind? But it wasn't just a question of taking off, the way birds fly. You had to find currents, like air currents, but they weren't windy. Then you had to step on them, ride them.

Uh-oh, David thought. He whispered, "Xander, Toria can't do it. Remember?"

Xander had forgotten. He said, "Not at all? Toria?"

She gazed at the grass, shook her head.

"No, no," Xander said. "That's okay." His head snapped up. "Shhh."

The sound of clomping feet grew louder.

Xander waved the others closer. He said, "Toria, try." He looked David in the eyes. "David," he said, "*fly*."

thirty

WEDNESDAY, 12:32 P.M.

David dropped the toy rifle. He held his hands open to the ground as though he were mounting a skateboard. He lifted his foot and felt the air with it. Nothing. He moved deeper into the clearing.

Outside the ring of trees and heavy bushes, something crashed.

David's heart revved up. If he couldn't do it . . . if Toria couldn't . . . there was nowhere to hide. They would have to fight the man, which to David's perspective was like taking on Godzilla.

He felt the air with his foot again: searching for an invisible platform. He remembered thinking that Dad's ability to ride the clearing's currents was like standing on an escalator no one could see. With that image in mind, he raised his foot and tried to *stand* on the air. His foot stomped the ground. He tried again. No go. He sighed and looked over at Xander.

His brother was hovering four feet over the grass. His feet slipped one way and then the other. He zipped higher. He smiled; David remembered the clearing had a way of making them giddy and carefree. But they didn't dare laugh now, not with Phemus tromping around so near.

David swung his foot over the grass. Something snagged his ankle. His foot rose. When it reached the height of his chest, his other foot came off the ground as well. He pinwheeled his arms and fell backward. He closed his eyes and pulled his cast in close to his chest, bracing himself for a crash. The impact never came.

He opened his eyes, turned his head. He was flat on his back, five feet off the ground. Using his stomach muscles, he forced his upper body into a vertical inclination. Now he was sitting—and more than fifteen feet in the air. He was drifting, rising like a balloon. He started moving his arms and legs as he would have in water. He shot forward, arched up, spiraled down.

Xander's waving caught his attention. His brother touched his finger to his lips and pointed at Toria. She was hopping up and down, stepping on currents that weren't there and generally throwing a quiet fit. The boys swam to her, converging above her shoulders.

"Toria," Xander whispered.

She snapped her face up, startled to find her brothers hovering directly above her.

"Give us your hands," David said.

She hesitated.

Xander said, "We won't drop you."

The bushes rustled nearby.

Toria raised her arms and closed her eyes.

David gripped her wrist in both of his hands and squeezed.

"Not so hard," she whispered.

He let up, but only a little. The image of his sister falling four stories tightened his stomach and made him want to clamp down even harder.

Xander got his hands around her wrists. They raised their heads, bringing their feet down, and kicked. Nothing happened. They kicked again and drifted up a few inches. Again—and another few inches.

"We have to do better," Xander said. "He'll see us if we take too long."

David nodded and closed his eyes. He imagined lifting his dad's barbells. He kicked and kicked, mentally bringing those barbells up from the bottom of a pool. Kick. Kick.

An insect fluttered onto the top of his head. He jerked his head sideways, but it wouldn't go away.

Better not be a spider, he thought.

"David," Xander whispered.

"I'm trying." Their voices were high-pitched, but either because he was so frightened or he was getting used to it, David hardly noticed.

"Open your eyes."

When he did, leaves hung down around Xander's head. A branch curled behind him, like the backdrop of a school photograph.

David tilted his head. What he had thought was an insect was the forest's canopy, leaning over the edge of the meadow. He looked down. Toria dangled between them. And *way* below her sneakered feet was the ground. It was scary for *him,* and he could fly.

He told Toria, "Don't look down."

Of course she did. She began wiggling around. Her movements jerked David down, up, down, up, like a fishing bobber.

"Toria," David whispered. "Stop it."

She whined.

"You're not making this easy," he said.

She swung her head back to look at David. Her blue eyes

danced in their sockets, reflecting the frightened pace of her heart.

David whispered, "You've got Mom's eyes, you know. So does Xander."

The randomness of his statement caught her off guard, distracting her from her panic just a little bit. She blinked at him, then adjusted her vision to Xander.

Xander smiled. "Guess we better give them back."

Her lips didn't so much as smile as they did not frown.

"Hey," David whispered, "have you heard this one? Birdie, birdie, in the sky, why'd you do that in my eye? Boy, I'm glad that cows don't fly."

Toria started to chuckle, caught herself, and bit her lip. Her feet slowly stopped their midair pedaling.

Below them, Phemus plowed through the bushes and then stumbled into the clearing.

thirty-one

WEDNESDAY, 12:39 P.M.

Leaves and twigs fell off the big man's shoulders. He swiveled his head around, clearly surprised to have lost his prey. From their perspective of almost directly above him, the man didn't look as huge as David knew he was. All he could see were his gleaming dome, planklike shoulders, swinging arms.

Toria took in her brothers' worried expressions and started to bring her gaze down.

David stopped her. "Hey," he said, quieter than a whisper. He shook his head. "Don't."

"I'll be all right," she mouthed, without making a sound.

When she looked, David felt her arm muscles tighten up. She turned her face back to him.

"It's okay," David said.

"Dae," Xander said. "Let's stay directly over him."

David nodded. It was the least likely place the guy would look. Even if he glanced up, the chances of his looking *straight* up were pretty slim.

Especially with that fat neck of his, David thought.

He wasn't about to release his hand from Toria's wrist, so the only way to adjust their position in relation to the man below was to wiggle and kick. It reminded David of people in movies who have their feet and arms tied; mimicking a snake or caterpillar, they somehow managed to escape.

The man spotted something. He walked to it and picked it up: the toy rifle.

David and Xander wiggled and kicked until they were once again directly over his head. If they dropped Toria, David thought, she would land right on the guy. No doubt it would hurt Toria a lot more than it would the brute. David closed his eyes and tightened his grip on her wrists.

"Ow," she whispered. When he peeked, she mouthed, "Not so tight!"

Below her, the man turned in a circle. He examined the toy as though it might tell him where they'd gone. He headed toward the center of the clearing.

The boys kicked and wiggled to stay with him, but he walked too fast. David cast a concerned look at Xander.

Xander stopped wiggling. He whispered, "Toria, grab my wrist. Good. Now grab Dae's."

When she did, they were not only holding her, but she was also holding them.

Xander said, "Trust me?"

The concern etched into her features deepened.

No kidding, David thought. *That's like the last thing I'd want to hear in her position.*

Still, she nodded.

Xander released his right hand. Toria's eyes flashed wide, then she realized their mutual grip was strong and she gave him a little smile. Xander nodded at David, who released his left hand from her wrist.

They used their free hands to paddle through the air. They could move much more quickly and accurately. Again, they stopped directly above the man.

Toria kept her eyes turned up. She looked from brother to brother, at the canopy of leaves around their heads . . . anywhere but down. Then she squinted at Xander, a puzzled expression forming on her face. "Xan—"

Something small fell away from him. Toria squeezed her

eyes closed. It struck her forehead: a bright red splatter that took the shape of a starburst.

Blood.

The cut above Xander's brow was oozing again. At the edge of the wound, a droplet swelled like a tiny balloon. David's eyes grew with it.

Xander realized what had landed on his sister and began swinging his hand around to the cut—too late: another droplet fell. It missed hitting Toria by less than an inch.

It was so small, by the time it passed her sneakers David had lost sight of it. He held his breath, hoping he had miscalculated the drop's trajectory.

But he hadn't: a small dot appeared on the crown of the man's head.

Phemus raised his hand and rubbed the spot. Then he examined his palm. He looked straight up and grinned.

CHAPTER

thirty-two

Staring down at Phemus's upturned face, Toria screamed.

"Shhh," Xander said. "He's down there, we're up here. He can't do anything."

"Well, that means he can," David said.

"Shhh," Xander repeated.

Continuing to watch them, Phemus backed away.

"Do we follow him?" David asked.

"No point now," Xander said.

Phemus bent his right arm way behind his back.

"What's he—"

"Oh, no," David said. "Move! Move!" He began kicking and wiggling and paddling with his left hand.

Phemus hurled the toy rifle at them. It spun round and round like a circular saw. David heard it cutting through the air like the blades of a helicopter: *whoop-whoop-whoop*. It was heading for Toria.

"Pull her, Xander," David said. "Pull!"

They tugged, raising her between them six inches, twelve inches. The rifle smacked into her ankle. It struck so hard, her legs swung out from under her.

Toria threw her head back and screamed. Her eyes were pinched shut, but her tears found their way out, pooling against her lids and the bridge of her nose. She cried— horrible, wrenching sobs.

David couldn't stand it, watching his little sister cry in pain, unable to do anything about it. They couldn't even check her ankle, rub it, do anything to make it feel better.

"Toria," David said. "I'm sorry."

He felt as though her pain was his. He had never experienced this so clearly: not when Phemus had knocked out Dad or when he had sent Xander crashing into the wall while kidnapping Mom or when the lock blew off one of the doors, gouging Dad's hand.

He said, "We'll get out of this, Tor. We will."

She nodded. She straightened her head, so she was looking neither up nor down, and wept quietly. That pulled on David's heart even more than her wailing agony had done. It was like her *spirit* hurt.

David focused on Phemus's movements, and his stomach took a tumble all over again. The big man was approaching the toy rifle. After hitting his sister, it had spun down, landing at the edge of the clearing. Phemus stooped, snatched it up, then squinted at the three King children.

"We have to do something," David said.

"For one thing," Xander said, "let's protect Toria better."

"How?"

"Pull her up between us," Xander said. "If she puts her arms around our shoulders, and we reach across her back and under her arms, she'll be sandwiched between us. We'll get hit before she does."

"That's okay with me," David said. He tried not to think about what that meant, but images came anyway: the barrel of the gun tearing into his side, the stock cracking into his skull.

"Toria," Xander said, "we'll raise you, and you have to climb up our bodies. Get your arms around our shoulders, okay?"

Her eyes followed the path she would take. "But that means letting go of your arms. I can't do that!"

"Try," David said. "Toria, you'll be safer up here with us."

"Move!" Xander yelled.

David caught a glimpse of the rifle spinning toward them. Both he and Xander threw themselves backward. *Whoop-whoop-whoop.* The weapon sailed over their arched chests, right where their heads had been seconds earlier. It sliced into the forest's canopy, then plunged to the meadow.

David and Xander pulled Toria as high as they could. She released her grip on David's arm and quickly grabbed his shoulder, then did the same with Xander. Their heads were nearly touching, their arms wrapped around each other.

Xander surveyed their surroundings. "How about we—*whoa!*"

Whoop-whoop-whoop!

The rifle sailed up. Xander reached out to grab it. There was a *clack-clack* sound, as though he'd stuck his hand into a fan. He yelled and pulled his arm back. David saw a gash running across the back of his hand.

Once again Phemus plucked the weapon off the ground.

David said, "Whatever we're going to do, we better do it now."

Xander drifted into a beam of sunlight. He blinked, turned his face toward it. "Okay, okay, I got it," he said.

Phemus circled below them, hefting the rifle like a ballplayer about to throw a pitch.

"*Now,* Xander!" David said.

"We gotta get out from under the branches," Xander said. He pointed at the sky. "We gotta go higher."

thirty-three

WEDNESDAY, 12:51 P.M.

Hovering over the clearing with his brother and sister, David said, "I thought this was it. As high as we could go."

"We've only done this once before," Xander reminded him. "And we didn't try to go higher than the trees."

They kicked and paddled their way to the edge of the branches and leaves.

Whoop-whoop-whoop!

The rifle snapped through the fine branches, not a foot from David. A twig shot into his cheek. He reeled back, feeling the sting, as though slapped with a riding crop. "Ahh!"

Below, Phemus snatched the rifle out of the air. He moved around, searching for the best angle of attack.

Toria said, "David, you're bleeding."

He touched his face, looked at the blood on his fingers. He said, "That guy's three for three. He got us all."

"Come on," Xander said. He pointed his face toward the open sky beyond the foliage and paddled his injured hand in the air.

They began to rise. Their heads lifted over the branches. David and Xander shared a smile.

Like flipping from one photograph to another, Xander's expression instantly changed to panic. A second later David's did, too, as the firmness of the air that keep them aloft evaporated and they plunged down . . .

. . . below the forest canopy . . .

. . . and still they plummeted . . .

. . . down, down . . .

David had felt the same plummeting roller-coaster feel in his gut when he'd fallen all the way to the meadow and broken his arm. Only that time he'd been at the clearing's edge and was able to slow his fall by grabbing branches. No branches now, only a free fall to earth.

He closed his eyes and squeezed himself closer to his sister.

His mind betrayed him with a gruesome assessment of what was to come: Their legs would shatter. Their organs and bones, their spines and heads, would compact on themselves. They might splatter or simply crumple into skin-bags of what used to be David, Xander, and Toria. At least that way, they'd have separate coffins.

Against all hope, David kicked and paddled. The wind rushed past him. Then he felt it in his stomach: a lurching stop, like an elevator's but stronger.

He allowed one eye to open, then the other. They were ten feet from the ground and starting to rise again. Phemus ran toward them, swinging the rifle like a club.

"Kick," Xander said.

He hadn't needed to say it. David was already moving his legs and feet faster than he ever had.

Phemus hurled the rifle at them. It nicked David's sneaker, one of an old tattered pair he had to put on this morning because he'd lost one of his good Converses in the Civil War world. His little toe flared with pain, as though someone had stomped on it.

"We can't keep doing this," David said. "It's just a matter of time before one of us gets nailed good."

Whoop-whoop-whoop!

All of them heard it, none of them saw it coming. It sailed up from directly below them, this time spinning vertically, like a propeller—and just as deadly. It passed inches in front of them. If they had leaned their heads down to take a look, it would have clobbered them.

Clobbered? David thought. *No . . . it would have killed them.*

"We're fish in a barrel," Xander said.

"Look," Toria said.

David followed her gaze to the tangle of branches and leaves hung over the edge of the clearing. He said, "What?"

"The branches," she said. "See how thick they are over there. We can—"

"Yeah," Xander interrupted. "If we could get on top of them, we'd have some protection."

"Can we fly above them?" David wondered.

"Probably not," said Xander. "But we can *reach* them, and climb up onto them."

The rifle spun by—nowhere close, for a change.

"Let's do it," David said.

They made their way to the heaviest branch and hovered below it.

"Grab hold, Toria," Xander said. "Pull yourself up onto it. We'll give you a boost."

She released her death grip on David's neck and extended a shaking hand to the branch. The boys pushed her up.

None of them heard the rifle coming. It struck Xander's back. He let out a sharp groan, arched backward as though he'd taken a bullet in the chest, and fell.

thirty-four

WEDNESDAY, 12:55 P.M.

Falling, Xander whirled his arms. He scissored his legs. His descent slowed and he started back up, not unlike a bungee jumper. Groaning, alternately reaching for his injury and paddling, Xander returned to the branch.

"You okay?" David said.

"I'll live . . . this time." He groaned, then said, "Toria, you good?"

She peered past the branch and nodded. Her arms clutched

the branch. "I want to hold my ankle, but I'm afraid to let go."

"Don't," David said.

Xander said, "Just remember to watch for that thing coming at you. Duck away from it, move your hands if you have to. But don't fall off."

"I'll get on the branch right behind her," David said. "I'll grab her if it looks like she's in trouble."

"Okay." Xander's face was twisted into a pained grimace.

"You sure you're all right?"

"I said I'll live, not that I'm all right." He grinned, but David could tell it was forced. "Get up there," Xander said. "I'll help."

David grabbed the branch behind Toria and kicked his feet. He floated up. Before he could swing his leg over, the air's firmness faltered and disappeared. Gravity pulled him down. Xander got his hand under David's rump and gave him a shove. He settled onto the branch just before the rifle smacked it directly under him, kicking up a spray of bark. The toy spun off, right over Xander's shoulder.

Xander reeled away from it. He drifted to the next branch, about ten feet away, and scrambled onto it. He held on with one hand and rubbed his back with the other.

Whoop-whoop-whoop!

The rifle flew up between the branches, tore away leaves, then went down again.

"Hey, Xander," David said. "Remember the weird movie title or whatever it was you thought of when the gladiator was spinning his swords at you?"

"Yeah, that's right," Xander said, remembering. "*Pinwheel of Death.*"

"Fits here, huh?"

The next throw came at the branch that Xander occupied, a foot away from his head. Xander released his grip, tucked his arms close to his body, then grabbed the branch again after the rifle's strike. In a deep voice, with precise diction, he said, "In a world where hiding in trees is the only way to survive, three children must learn to outsmart the . . . *Pinwheel of Death.*"

David smiled. Was it the clearing making them feel a little better, or did people in terrifying situations naturally think of things that calmed their fear? Either way, he liked the distraction. He said, "I don't think that's a movie I'd want to see anymore."

Toria saw the next one coming and tucked in perfectly. When the rifle clattered under David, it was he who almost lost his balance and tumbled off. Phemus must have decided he'd found a weak link; he continued targeting David, toss after toss.

Pulling his arms out of the way for what seemed like the hundredth time, David said, "Man, this is getting to me. Doesn't that guy have to go back to his own world sometime?"

Xander thought about it. "I thought Dad said the worlds had to balance out, eventually. Like the way the items in the antechambers pull toward the portal, and whatever we bring back with us gets sucked into its own world again. I kind of thought that worked with people too."

"Then why didn't Mom come back?" Toria said.

They didn't have an answer.

David closed his eyes, listening for the approaching Pinwheel of Death.

When there'd been no attacks for a few minutes, he opened his eyes. Xander looked asleep. Toria was gazing into the leaves farther along the branch, probably pretending she was looking out her bedroom window or . . . anywhere but balancing on a branch fifty feet in the air with some guy trying to knock her off it. He looked down.

"Oh . . . you gotta be kidding!" he said.

Xander raised his head, looked. "No!"

"What's he doing?" Toria said.

"He's flying."

CHAPTER

thirty-five

Phemus hovered two feet off the ground. He wobbled and dropped onto the grass. He prodded at the air with his toes. He hopped up, as though he'd felt something. He went right back down and tried again. It was a bit like watching a body-builder trying to tap dance, but there was nothing funny about it.

"Do you think he can do it?" Toria said.

"He'd better not," Xander said.

"He already did," David said. "If he floats up two feet, it's just a matter of time before he's coming up here."

As they watched, he did do it. Not for long, not very high, but he definitely sailed up for a few seconds.

"See?" David said.

"We're dead," Xander said. His eyes darted to Toria. "Uh . . . I mean . . . we'll figure something out."

"You can say *we're dead*," she said. "I'm not a baby."

"No, really," Xander said. "We'll figure—"

"Here he comes," David said.

The big man hovered five feet over the grass, wobbling, shifting one way, then the other. He grinned up at the kids, then looked down at his feet.

"Go away!" David yelled.

Phemus snapped his gaze up and crashed to the earth, sitting hard. He hoisted himself up, began feeling the air with his foot. He lifted into the air.

"Hey!" Xander said. "Go away!"

"Get out of here!" David screamed.

Toria simply screamed, a long piercing warble.

This time their attempts to distract him didn't hinder his flying at all. He hovered, slid sideways, came back . . . a little higher.

Xander cast a worried glance at David. He whispered, "I'll come over and get you. We'll both get Toria."

"Then what?" David said.

Xander shrugged. "Dodge away."

"Carrying Toria?"

"We have to try."

"Hey," David said. The bushes at the perimeter of the clearing rustled and parted. A man broke through and fell onto the grass. He eyed Phemus, who apparently hadn't heard his approach—then took in the kids.

"Keal!" David said.

"Help!" Toria yelled.

Keal leaped forward like a sprinter coming off the starting line. He ran directly for Phemus.

"The big guy's too high up," Toria said.

"We'll see," David said.

Keal sprang, sailing higher than anyone ever would have expected . . . anyone who didn't know the clearing. He grabbed Phemus's ankles and pulled the big man down. Phemus flashed a surprised expression and crashed to the earth. Keal was on him, landing punch after punch to the ribs, stomach, face. Phemus hammered a monstrous fist into Keal's back.

David knew too well what that fist felt like. His face still hurt. He said, "Phemus is too strong, even for Keal."

"Maybe not when he's away from the house," Xander said. "I get the feeling he *needs* the house . . . or the world he came from. That's why he keeps going back to it."

Hoping Xander was right this time, David yelled, "Get him, Keal!"

"Get him!" Toria echoed.

Keal dodged a blow. He flipped onto his back on the grass and kicked his heel into Phemus's face.

The big man's head snapped back. He rolled onto his stomach, rose onto his hands and knees, and started to stand.

Keal was already up. He kicked the man's head, shifted and kicked his ribs. He swung his right fist down into the back of Phemus's head.

David heard the *crack* and winced. He hoped the noise wasn't Keal's hand breaking.

If it was, Keal showed no sign. He swung his left fist into the side of Phemus's temple, then planted the right one between his shoulder blades. Keal meant business: He didn't pause, he didn't give his opponent a second to recover. He continued to pummel the man. Punch, punch, kick, punch, kick, kick.

Don't wanna ever get Keal mad at me, David thought.

Phemus swung his arm around, knocking Keal's leg out from under him. Keal went down, and Phemus grabbed his foot. He pulled Keal to him and brought a fist down onto his stomach. Keal wheezed out a gust of air, buckled in half. Phemus swung a fist into Keal's head. Keal did what every fighter does when the blows are landing and he can't get away. He dove into his opponent, hugging him, giving him no room to swing.

They rolled in the grass—and lifted off it. David squinted,

and yes, the two men were tumbling in the air, three or four feet off the ground. Rising higher.

Phemus pushed Keal away. Keal did a backward somersault and stood. He almost fell over, caught himself, and looked down at the grass a half dozen feet below him. He wobbled. He turned a stunned face at the kids.

"Keep going, Keal!" Xander yelled.

"Move like you're underwater!" David told him.

Phemus slid through the air. He reached his opponent and clamped his arms around Keal's torso. The silent scream Keal displayed indicated that Phemus was squeezing him. David could only imagine how much pressure those tree-trunk arms could exert.

Keal began punching Phemus's ear. His knees came up into Phemus's gut. They broke away from each other only to embrace again: Keal encircled his muscular left arm around Phemus's neck. He pounded his right fist into the big man's face, again and again.

Phemus landed one blow after another into Keal's stomach and sides. Without pausing in his face-pounding, Keal kicked at Phemus's crotch.

All the while, the men tumbled and rose through the air. They were in the center of the clearing, measured aerially as well as across its breadth and width. It almost seemed staged to David, but the sounds of their blows and grunts, as well as the blood and sweat flying off them, said otherwise.

Phemus reached behind his back, fumbled with something at the small of his back, where the pelt started, and pulled out a black shardlike object.

"Keal!" David yelled. "He has a knife!"

Phemus raise the blade and plunged it down.

Keal grabbed the big man's wrist. He never released his arm from Phemus's neck. Phemus never ceased in slamming his fist into Keal's ribs. Phemus's arm looked like a machine *pumping pumping pumping*.

David threw himself off the branch. He plunged down five feet, ten feet. He felt the resistance in the air and started kicking, swimming with his arms.

"David!" Toria yelled.

He ignored her and continued moving toward the fighting men. He circled them, keeping himself directly behind Phemus. When he saw his chance, he sailed in and grabbed the hand that held the knife. He could see now that it was a chiseled piece of black stone.

Keal saw David, saw him holding the knife hand. He let go of Phemus's wrist, pulled back, and brought his fist into the big man's nose.

David strained against Phemus's hand that was trying to plunge the knife into Keal. He squeezed his eyes closed and concentrated on not letting that happen. He rose up over the men's heads. He kicked, using the motion to help him keep the knife high in the air, high above Keal.

He heard a *crack!* and looked. Xander was hovering behind Phemus, holding the barrel of the toy rifle. He had apparently retrieved it from the ground and batted the stock into the back of the big man's head. He cocked it back for another strike.

Phemus twisted out of Keal's headlock. He lifted his foot, planted it on Keal's sternum, and pushed off. He sailed away, taking David with him and banging into Xander. Xander spun away, twirling like a top. Phemus dropped straight down, wrenching his hand out of David's grasp. The stone knife slid through David's fingers. David gasped and pulled his hands back.

As he fell, Phemus lunged at Keal, stretching his knife toward him. Keal kicked away, but the blade caught his leg, ripping through his pant leg. Phemus continued falling—all the way to the grass, twenty-five feet below. He landed with a grunt and rolled. He hopped up, glaring at the boys and man above him. Then he ran to the edge of the clearing and disappeared into the bushes.

CHAPTER

thirty-six

WEDNESDAY, 1:22 P.M.

Breathing hard, Keal kept his eyes on the spot where Phemus had disappeared. He drifted and bobbed in the air like a ping-pong ball on the surface of a lake.

David drifted to him and reached out to touch his shoulder.

Keal jerked around, raising a fist. Registering David, he smiled.

"Thank you," David said. He noticed red fingerprints

where he'd touched Keal and looked at his palm. Blood covered his hand, glistening.

"I think his blade was obsidian," Keal said. "Sharper than a razor, so it probably doesn't hurt much, does it?"

Watching the slice across his palm open and shut like a mouth as he flexed his hand, David shook his head.

"It'll take forever to heal, though," Keal said. He rubbed the side of his face, then stuck a finger in his mouth to wiggle a tooth. He spat, watching the bloody goop fall to the grass far below. He said, "This is weirdest thing I've ever experienced."

Xander bumped into David. He said, "You ain't seen nothing yet."

Keal studied the boys' faces, perhaps looking for signs of humor. He tightened his lips and nodded. "I'll be right back." He waved his arms and drifted down.

"How's your back?" David asked his brother.

"Hurts. This too." Xander showed him the back of his hand. The purple had taken on hues of blue, black, and red.

David scowled at it. He said, "I think we've been banged up worse in this world than in any of the others."

They watched Keal reach the grass and trudge into the bushes at the clearing.

"It's *because* of those other worlds that we've been attacked in this one," Xander said. "Taksidian wants the house because of them, and he's doing everything he can to get it."

Toria's tiny voice reached them: "Hey, guys?"

They smiled at each other. Xander said, "Be kind of funny to leave her there a while."

David backhanded Xander's shoulder. "Not."

They sailed up to her. David could tell she'd been crying. It must have been scary, watching the fight. David and Xander each rested a hand on the branch, like swimmers at the edge of the pool. Their legs stirred gently, as they would have in water.

"Xander," David said. "Why do you think Taksidian wants it, the house?"

"A house like that," Xander said. "It's pretty special."

"We just want to get Mom and get out," David said. "We don't want it. He must plan on using it for something. What?"

Xander's brow crunched in thought, squeezing out a drop of blood from the cut on his forehead. "He told us he'd been in the house many times. He's probably been doing something here for a long time. He doesn't like that we're here now, keeping him from continuing whatever it is."

"I want down," Toria said.

"Come on," Xander said.

The brothers turned their backs to the branch so she could wrap her arms around their shoulders and swing down between them. They reached across with their free arms, held each other's hand, and pulled themselves together.

Toria giggled. "Group hug," she said.

As they descended, Keal reappeared through the bushes, carrying Jesse. He was limping.

"Where were *you?*" David called. His voice was Mickey Mouse-ish.

Jesse laughed. It was squeaky, but only slightly so, there on the edge of the clearing. "In the woods. We saw the open front door and the collapsed walls on the second floor, knew you were in trouble. I was worried you'd gone the other way, into one of the worlds. Then we heard you yelling."

The children touched down in front of the men. As soon as the boys released Toria, she said, "Owww!" and crumpled to her knees.

"Toria, I forgot about your ankle," David said. He knelt beside her and helped her to sit.

"What is it, child?" Jesse said.

Keal set the old man on the grass beside her. The big man groaned and touched his ribs, his face, his stomach. "Feel like I had it out with the Terminator."

Xander smiled. If you wanted to get on his good side fast, reference a movie.

Toria pulled up her pant leg and slipped off her sneaker and sock. Her ankle looked like Xander's hand. It was black and blue and swollen to the size of a softball.

Keal dropped to his knees in front of her. "Can you move it?"

She turned her foot in a tight circle, making an *Eeeee* sound the whole time.

The man prodded it, watching for her reactions. "It's not broken," he said. "Maybe sprained. Sure is a nasty bruise."

"Keal's a nurse," Jesse said. "A mighty good one too. Better than most doctors I've known."

"A *nurse?*" Xander said. "You?"

Keal looked up. He leaned back to rest on his ankles. "Now why would that surprise you?"

"It's just . . ." Xander said. "You know."

Keal stared at him, said nothing.

Xander said, "I mean, you're big enough to be a linebacker, you got the muscles of a bodybuilder, and you fight like . . . like some kind of special forces commando."

Keal laughed. He settled into a sitting position on the grass and crossed his leg in front of him. He poked his fingers into the tear Phemus's knife had made and ripped the material through the cuff. He flipped the two sides away, revealing a long gash in his shin from knee to ankle.

His dark brown skin made it difficult for David to tell how much it had bled.

Keal poked at the wound and said, "Well, I was an athlete back in the day. I also served my country, and I enjoy keeping physically fit. As for my profession, by the time I ruled out those other occupations, I was a little too old to pursue a medical degree. But I do like helping people."

He glanced at Xander, who nodded.

David said, "You saved our lives."

Keal smiled. "Looked like you were doing a pretty good job of that yourselves."

"Still," Xander said, "we owe you."

"It was a team effort, gentlemen," Keal said. "I appreciate your help too. Let's call it even."

Xander stepped past Keal to hold his good hand out to Jesse. He curled his fingers around the old man's hand and said, "I'm sorry I doubted you. I guess you are on our side."

Jesse nodded. "Quite understandable, Xander. In fact, I consider your caution both admirable and necessary."

Xander smiled and released Jesse's hand, but the old man refused to let go.

Jesse said, "Does this mean, Xander, that you're ready to confide in me? I can help, but I need to know . . . where are your parents? What has been going on around here?"

Xander's smile faded, but he nodded. Jesse gave him back his hand, and Xander straightened. He rubbed his back, grimacing at the pain still there. He said, "We need to get back to the house. I don't want to be away from it too long, and there may be things we need to show you, if you want to know everything."

"The more I know, the more I can help," Jesse said.

"Okay." Xander looked toward the house. "But . . . do you think they're waiting for us, those guys we fought?"

"More than one?" Keal said.

"Three," Xander said. "Two stayed in the house."

"They're gone," Jesse said. "Keal and I went all through it, looking for you. And I'm sure that one you chased out of here is back where he belongs by now. Visitors don't stay long. They can't. Unless . . ."

"Unless?" Xander said.

Jesse waved a hand at him. "That's for another time. First things first."

"But what if they come back?" Toria said.

"They will," David said. "They *attacked* us. They knocked down the walls. They'll be back."

Jesse shook his head. "They can't. Not for a while. They'll have to sort of *recharge*. It's draining, going over. For them and for us. Haven't you noticed that?"

Xander said, "Remember, Dae, how tired I was after the gladiator thing, and you after the jungle world?"

David nodded. "The showers helped." To Jesse, he said, "Does using the portals make you . . . I don't know . . . more emotional?"

"Crying a lot?" Jesse said with a knowing smile.

"Sort of," David said, shrugging shyly.

"I know how you feel," Jesse said, "but it's not the portals. Not really. It's your *humanity*, David. Going over, you see things most people never do. Terrible atrocities, the worst human behavior. Murder, war, innocence lost. You have a big heart for people. Of course, you're part of the King bloodline—you have to."

"What does that mean?"

"You'll find out . . . in time." Jesse winked. "I'm not trying to be mysterious. It's just that there are other things I need to explain first. It's like constructing the first floor of a house before adding the second."

"Are you saying I'm *sensitive*?" David said, not liking it much. "That's why I've been crying?"

"No," Jesse said. "I'm saying it breaks your heart when people die before their time, because they'll never get to be everything they could have been."

"That sounds like David," Toria said. "He's sad when people get hurt on TV."

"Am not," David said.

"Uh-huh."

"It's okay that you do," Jesse said. "You have a keen sense of the preciousness of life and the finality of death—here on earth, anyway. To you, death does not simply end life. It steals away the sunsets you'll never see, the children you'll never hold, the wife you'll never love. It's frightening to almost lose your future, and it's heartbreaking to witness death snuff out other people's tomorrows." He gripped David's shoulder. "You get it? What's making you cry comes from the same place inside that prompted you to save Marguerite's life. You weep for life lost, and you *act* to prevent it."

David rocked up on his knees and wrapped his arms around Jesse's neck. No one had ever so accurately described his desire for himself and others to experience the fullest possible life; or the ache in his chest at the news of death—by accident, murder, war. Even *he* hadn't put it into words. Now that Jesse had, he recognized it as a grand quality. He hoped he could live up to it.

thirty-seven

WEDNESDAY, 1:36 P.M.

Grunting with effort, Xander struggled to stand. When he finally did, he said, "We gotta head back."

David released his embrace on Jesse's neck and rolled back onto the grass.

Jesse peered around the clearing, rising to take in the trees and canopy. He turned to Xander and said, "I'll give you the rest of my time on earth. Just give me a few minutes now. Can you do that?"

Xander sighed. He stepped past Jesse and Keal and sat beside his sister.

Jesse touched David's arm. "Son, would you mind giving me a hand?"

"I don't think I can pick you up," David said.

"The clearing will help," Jesse said.

David rose and stepped behind him. He slipped his hands under Jesse's arms and lifted. The old man was light, impossibly light.

Jesse's legs dangled under him. His feet were canted at odd angles on the ground.

Walking behind him, David guided Jesse toward the center of the meadow.

"Oh," Jesse said, "it's been so long."

As they progressed, the weight bearing down on David's arms—accompanied by a slight throbbing in the broken one—became less noticeable. Before long, he was pretty sure he wasn't assisting Jesse at all. He realized that his hands, positioned in Jesse's armpits, had risen to the level of his eyes, as though the man had grown taller. He saw that Jesse's feet no longer touched the ground, but hovered a few inches above it.

"Thank you, son," Jesse said, his voice comically high. "I can manage from here."

David lowered his hands slowly, and when Jesse didn't come down with them, he backed away.

Jesse waved his hands and turned. The grin on his face lightened David's heart.

David looked back at the others, his own smile bigger than it should have been, considering . . . *everything*. He was glad to see Keal, Toria, even Xander, looking equally pleased.

Jesse drifted up and laughed, a squeaky cartoon hiccup sound. As Dad had done, he zipped forty feet over and twenty feet in the air. Returning, he performed a somersault—perfect but for his legs, which trailed his body loosely like a those of a ventriloquist's puppet. He buzzed around, soaring high, spinning, brushing his fingers along the canopy leaves. After five minutes he came down on the far side of the clearing. Watching his feet skimming the grass, he drifted toward them, laughing continually.

Drawing near, he said, "I haven't walked in a decade. This is as close as I'll ever come again."

thirty-eight

WEDNESDAY, 1:46 P.M.

Xander carried Toria through the woods, toward the house. Behind them, Keal carried Jesse. David walked beside them.

"What you told me before," David said, "about my being part of the King bloodline? You know, so I *have* to be the way I am, that I care for people, love life? Does that have to do with being a gatekeeper?"

Jesse bounced along in Keal's arms, thinking. He said, "I

shouldn't have told you that so soon. I was just excited, seeing you and all."

"But . . . does it mean we're supposed to stay here? Like you did?"

"That's a discussion we should have with your mom and dad," Keal said.

David stopped.

Keal took another two steps and turned to him.

"My mom's gone," David said.

"Gone?" Jesse squinted at him. "What do you mean, son?"

David watched his brother and sister trudging away. He went to a tree, pressed his back to it, and slid down. "The other night, that guy we fought—Xander and I call him Phemus—he came out of a portal and took her." He looked into Jesse's eyes. The story came rushing out.

"He kidnapped my mother. Took her back into one of the worlds with him. We didn't know which. We've been looking, but all this other stuff has been getting in the way. This guy's trying to get us out of the house . . . he sent those—those *things* after us . . . got Dad arrested . . . people—a kid—found out about the house, the portals . . . and . . . and . . ."

His lungs were pumping fast and hard. Tears streamed from his eyes.

Keal stepped back and settled Jesse onto the ground in front of David. Jesse's kind face had morphed into one of supreme sadness. Not shock, just an expression like that David had seen on TV news reporters when they covered the funerals of children. A phrase he'd heard came to mind: *profound grief.*

Jesse reached out and touched David's shoe. "I am so sorry, David."

David sniffed. He wiped the back of his hands across his eyes. "There I go again," he said with an embarrassed smile.

"Kid," Keal said, "if I were you, I'd be bawling like a baby."

From much closer to the house, Xander called: "David? What's up?"

"Go on!" David yelled. "We'll be there in a minute!"

They listened for a response. When it didn't come, Jesse said, "When you're ready, I'd like to hear everything. Start at the beginning."

David closed his eyes, took a deep breath, and started. He told about their drive to Pinedale, house hunting, setting foot in the creepy old Victorian for the first time. He told about discovering that the linen closet was a portal to the locker at school. His voice rose a bit when he recounted their discovery of the ante-chambers, the items within them, and Xander's trip to the Colosseum. He told about his own trip to the jungle world, where tigers and tribesmen tried to kill him.

At this point, David closed his eyes again. He bit his lip, tight-ened his muscles and his resolve, and went on: Waking up to Toria screaming that a man had been in her room. Mom getting taken, and how they'd all been beat up trying to stop Phemus.

"That's when we found out Dad had lied about the house. He had known about the portals and how dangerous it was." David covered his eyes with his hand. "He just wanted to find *his* mother."

Then they had vowed to stay in the house and rescue Mom, despite Dad's dad giving up on finding *Dad's* mother and leaving. He talked about setting up the Mission Control Center ("we call it the MCC"). Dad showing them what they could do in the clearing. Then Taksidian: his seeing David fly and David breaking his arm because of it. David going through the locker portal and finding Taksidian in their house talking to Phemus. Taksidian chasing him back through to the locker and how Xander and he had locked him inside. The doctor accusing Dad of hurting his kids. The town trying to evict them. Xander and he going to the Civil War world.

And then last night's events ("I can't believe it was only last night"): Dad getting arrested, Clayton coming through the locker-to-closet portal, Xander saying he'd found Mom.

"But he *hadn't*," David said. "She'd left a message for us, but when I went back to get her, I got chased away . . . *shot* at . . . *again*."

Jesse aimed watery, sympathetic eyes at David. And David thought that if a twig snapped, or a door burst open, Keal would jump right out of his skin. They sat like that, silent and listening to their own breathing and wind touching the treetops.

Finally Jesse took a deep breath. "You astound me," he said. "Your bravery, your family's determination."

David could offer up only a weak smile. He said, almost desperately, "Can you help?"

Don't say maybe. Don't say maybe. Don't say maybe.

"Yes, I can," Jesse said.

It was what he had needed to hear since the moment the door had slammed shut on the bat and their mother's screams. This time, David's smile was genuine and big.

Jesse patted David's foot. "Let's get on with it, then, shall we?" He looked over his shoulder. "Keal?"

The man snapped out of some daydream, surely involving kidnapped mothers and evil villains. "Yeah, yeah," he said, standing. "On with it."

Worried eyes landed on David, and David understood that Keal was as clueless about what to do—what Jesse *could* do—as he was.

Keal scooped up Jesse. He stood there, waiting for David, who wasn't so sure his own legs would work if he tried to stand. He felt as though he had gone through all the events of the past week in the fifteen minutes it had taken to describe them. But he pushed himself up, and his legs did work. He fell in beside Keal and Jesse, and they walked to the house.

thirty-nine

WEDNESDAY, 2:11 P.M.

They found Xander and Toria sitting on the front porch steps.

"I told them everything," David said.

"I know," Xander said. He looked at Keal and Jesse, trying to read their expressions.

"Jesse said he can help."

"*Can* you?" Xander asked the old man.

"Absolutely."

Xander smiled at that. He rose and headed for the front door, Toria right behind him. David stopped at the bottom.

"What are you going to do?" David asked, though he had a pretty good hunch.

"Get Mom," Xander said.

"You mean you're sending *Toria* to get her," David said. "You can't do that."

"Dae, we agreed. We said today, this morning, remember? It's always been about Toria going over."

"But—" David turned to Jesse. "Toria's never been into another world. She thinks that because she's a little girl, she won't run into the same problems Xander and I did."

Jesse looked up at Xander. "That may not be true, Xander. You've noticed a lot of aggression toward you in those other worlds, right?"

"Have we!" David said. "Everywhere we go someone's trying to kill us. I'm *twelve*. Do I look like a soldier? Do I look like a spy? But General Grant shot at me! And he wasn't the only one—"

Jesse was patting the air in front of him, telling David to calm down.

"You were wearing the wrong colors when we first went over," Xander protested. "And in World War II, you walked into the middle of a firefight."

Jesse waved his hand at Xander. "Boys! Yes, the circumstances you walk into have a lot to do with whether you're in danger. But it's more than that. You may *look* like you belong when you go over, but you don't. The people over there sense that. Like there's something not right about you."

David thought about the hostile looks the soldiers in the Civil War camp had given him—even though they could see he was a child. And the tribesmen who had immediately thrown spears and shot arrows at him; he hadn't threatened them in any way.

He said, "See? Xander, they'll sense that about Toria. You can't let her go. Jesse, tell him!"

Jesse frowned. "David—"

David saw it in his face: he was about to agree with Xander! "Jesse, you just said—"

"David, if she gets in and right back out . . . it *would* be hard for those men over there to mistake her for a soldier."

David's shoulders slumped.

Behind him, Xander said, "Come on, Toria."

"Wait, wait!" David said. "Toria, you heard what Jesse said. Do you still want to go?"

She made a face that said *Not really.* But she nodded.

"Your ankle! How can you go with your ankle like that?"

"I can walk," she said.

"But you can't run. I haven't been in a world where I haven't had to run."

She simply stared at him, a tight little frown bending her lips.

David didn't care about being outvoted. He just didn't want his sister to go. Not there. Not to *any* of the worlds. But what more could he say?

Jesse said, "I'm sorry, David. Maybe the portal won't come around before we get back, but if—"

"Where are you going?"

"To get your daddy out of jail. I have experience with small-town authorities, thinking they can do anything they wish."

"Xander!" David turned to his brother, then back to Jesse. "Tell them to wait. Dad can go get Mom. They don't know him in that world."

"Thing is," Jesse said, "I don't think they should wait. You mother being lost over there, taken against her will, without any way of finding the portal home—getting her out of there quickly is worth the risk. And given Toria's age and how short of a time she should be there . . ." He looked up to her. "Just in and out, right, young lady?"

"Yes, sir," Toria said.

"David," Jesse continued, "if you weigh the possibility of your mother disappearing forever against the possibility of Toria having some trouble, I think you'll agree. What I'm saying is: get her while you can, however you can."

forty

WEDNESDAY, 3:28 P.M.

David stood rigid at the head of the third-floor hallway, his arms crossed over his chest. Jesse's points were hard to argue with, but Toria wasn't *his* sister.

Xander and Toria marched up and down the crooked hall, checking each antechamber for the Civil War items.

Come on, Dad. Where are you?

They'd been up on the third floor over an hour now. How long did it take to get Dad out of jail?

Xander looked his way, and David changed his worried face to an angry scowl.

"This would be faster if you helped," Xander said.

"I don't want it to be faster," David said. "I don't want it at all."

Xander stopped, the handle of an open door in his hand. He said, "Well, don't get any ideas."

"Like what?"

"Like trying to stop her from going over when we find the right portal."

"At least wait until Dad gets home."

"Nice try," Xander said. "You know Dad wouldn't let her go."

"Which should tell you something."

"It does." Xander opened a door, peered inside, closed it. "That Dad is so cautious, we might never find Mom."

David bit his tongue. Xander wasn't going to listen to anything he had to say.

His brother frowned. "Come on, Dae," he said. "When I was mad at Dad for lying to us about the house, you said we had to get along. Work together. You were right. I'm not mad at you for disagreeing with me now, but you're being pigheaded."

"About Toria's life?" David said. "Yeah, I am."

"You heard Jesse. What might happen to Toria is less awful than what might happen to Mom if we don't find her."

"What's worse than death?"

"She's not going to die."

Xander checked the antechamber closest to David, then headed back the other way. He said, "What if it takes days for Jesse to get Dad out, Dae? What if something happens to Mom while we're waiting? Could you live with that?"

Toria was hobbling from door to door, staying off her banged-up ankle as much as she could.

"Toria," David said. "Don't do this."

She walked toward him, making a sad face. "I don't like you and Xander fighting."

"Then don't go. Tell him you changed your mind."

"But Xander's right," she said. "We need to get Mom, Dae. The people over there won't recognize me." She touched his arm. "I'll be careful, and I'll come right back if it gets scary. I promise."

David went to the landing. It looked as though a bomb had gone off at the base of the stairs. The two walls had collapsed into the second-floor hallway. Wires and studs jutted out from where the walls used to stand, and plaster dust covered it all.

"Got it!" Xander said.

The words hit David's gut like a one-two punch.

Toria shut the door she had just opened, looked at Xander standing in the doorway of an antechamber halfway up the hall. She turned back to David, fear on her face.

Both boys called to her at the same moment.

She went toward Xander.

Five minutes later, she wore both jackets, the Union blue over the Confederate gray.

Xander told her, "If you wind up on the Confederate side, switch them. When you get to the Union side, switch back. But you should come out in the woods right near the camp, so no sweat. In camp, take off the jackets and fold them up. Carry them like you're taking them to get cleaned or something. Your kepi too."

He spun around, grabbed the blue hat from a hook, and pulled it down over her head. It covered her eyes, and she pushed it up.

"I think they're back," David said, though he had heard nothing. He ran to the antechamber's hallway door. "Really," he said. "Wait up and see." He called out: "Dad!"

Behind him, the portal door opened.

Toria and Xander stood in front of the portal. Bright sunlight poured through, along with the odor of smoke and gunpowder. Out-of-focus trees and bushes drifted slowly past.

"It looks like the woods by the camp," Xander told her. "Just like I said. Don't lose the clothes. They'll show you where the portal home is. They'll pull you toward it. It's that simple. You ready?"

"Toria," David said.

But she had stepped through.

He ran to the doorway.

She was lying in tall, yellow grass—she must have tumbled when she stepped through. Nothing unusual about that.

He yelled, "Come right back if you don't find Mom right away!"

Toria squinted at him, and stood. "What?" Her voice wavered, as though caught by the wind.

"David!" Xander said.

The door struck him in the back. It always closed on its own after someone went through. It knocked him into the door frame and pushed him as forcefully as the grill of a semi truck.

Xander grabbed his arm and yanked. David spun back into the room, and the door slammed shut.

CHAPTER

forty-one

David sat on the bench, his eyes fixed on the portal door. His fingernails were absently scraping his plaster cast. He had flaked a groove into it and found some cloth gauze encased within. He fingers now flicked at this, tearing an ever-widening hole.

Xander paced. He walked to the portal door, spun, and walked through the opposite doorway into the hall. He marched back through and did it again.

Neither brother had spoken since Toria had left.

Finally David said, "It's been twenty minutes."

"Almost," Xander said, continuing his back-and-forth strolling.

"Longer," David said. "Xander, something must have happened to her."

"Give her a chance, Dae. She'll be back any minute, wait and see. And with Mom." Now he did stop. His face was alive with excitement. He really believed Toria would find Mom and bring her home.

Xander's belief infected David. He allowed himself to *feel* it, to feel that Mom really was on her way. He could almost smell her, that hint of flowers that seemed natural to her. He imagined throwing his arms around her, squeezing her. He would never let her go.

As worried as he was, he smiled back at Xander.

Somewhere in the house, a door slammed.

"Dad!" David said. He jumped off the bench. Both boys ran into the hall and stopped on the landing. "Dad!" David yelled again. "Jesse!"

No reply.

They turned big eyes on each other. "You think," David said, "maybe it's those big guys again, the ones from the other world?"

Xander shook his head. "They'd come from one of the rooms up here. Besides, Jesse said Phemus couldn't come back so soon."

They returned to the antechamber, and David took up his spot on the bench. He swallowed hard and glanced nervously at the open door. Xander walked to the portal door, tried the handle—locked, of course.

Another bang. David jumped.

Xander gave David a puzzled look and went into the hall. "Dad?" he called. He walked away from the antechamber.

David went to the doorway and peered out.

Xander was standing halfway to the landing, listening. "Probably just the house trying to spook us," he said.

"It's working," David said.

"Could be just the wind," Xander said. " I'll go check." But he didn't move, just stood there, as if expecting David to say, "Nah, never mind."

Instead, David said, "Okay."

Xander smiled. He walked to the landing, then tromped down the stairs.

David watched for a few seconds, then he scanned the hallway. All the other doors were closed, as they were supposed to be. He glanced over his shoulder at the portal door Toria had used.

Twenty, twenty-five minutes she'd been gone. That was too long.

He had an idea. Xander would never let him do it, but hey, he was downstairs. Dad would call it *impulsive*—doing something simply because the chance presented itself. It was unplanned, stupid.

Not stupid this time, David thought. *Not when it's been almost a half hour.*

He slipped into the antechamber, plucked a canteen and the gray kepi off their hooks, and picked up a sword from the bench. He opened the portal door—unlocked now that he held the items—and stepped through.

•••••••••

David ran through the woods toward the meadow of dry grass and the Union army camp on the other side. He could not see much activity among the tents: one or two people walking along the center aisle. Most of the soldiers must be at the front lines. He wished he'd had time to research the Civil War, especially the Union side and its encampments and battle policies, before plunging into it again. But they'd hardly had time to grab a few hours' sleep, let alone do homework.

At the edge of the woods, he dropped the sword into the grass. As he tucked the kepi into his waistband, he looked around for landmarks that would help him find the sword again.

That tree, he thought. *Split, as though by lightning.*

He hoped the pull of the kepi and canteen, and the items Toria had brought, would be enough to guide them to the portal home.

He bolted for the tents. Before he reached them, he heard a scream coming from the front of the camp. *Toria.*

He angled that direction through the field. He reached the back of the first tent and stopped.

Toria was crying. Men were laughing.

David's guts felt twisted. He looked around the edge of the tent. Toria was walking slowly away from two soldiers. She was limping, trying to avoid putting weight on her injured ankle. She wore the blue kepi and jacket, and she was heading south, toward the hill over which David knew the battle raged. And she was carrying a rifle!

The gun was longer than she was tall. She had not brought it over with her. The Harper's Ferry rifle David had used on his first venture to this world was still in the antechamber when he left. She kept glancing back over her shoulder.

The two soldiers followed twenty paces behind, laughing and pointing their rifles at her. Both weapons were fitted with long bayonets.

One soldier yelled at her, "Skedaddle, sweetie! Get out there and fight! Else we'll have to shoot you ourselves." He laughed, stopped, and jabbed the bayonet at her, though she was way out of striking distance.

"Everyone fights!" the soldier said. "Even country gals like you. No excuses!" He turned to his compatriot, a big grin on his face.

The other man yelled, "We don't wanna see you coming back

'less it's on a stretcher. You go all the way! Kill you some graybacks, then we'll think about letting you into camp."

The first soldier spotted David running toward him. "Hey, what's this?" he said, and swung the rifle around.

David didn't slow down. He swung his arm cast at the bayonet, knocking it aside. He jumped and shoved his palms into the soldier's chest. The man backpedaled and fell.

"David!" Toria ran to him. She tossed the rifle away and threw her arms around his neck.

"Woo-woo!" the standing soldier said. "Young love!"

"She's my *sister*," David said. "What do you think you're doing? She's a little girl."

The downed man regained his feet. He picked up his rifle but held it vertically, casually. David thought his fury had startled the meanness out of the man, at least for the moment.

The soldier said, "Well, then, we have *two* greenhorns to send to the front, don't we?"

"We're friends with General Grant," David said. "Where is he? General Grant! General Grant!"

"Whoa, young master," the second solder said. "The general is in battle. Young lady, why didn't you say you knew the general?"

"Both of you!" David said. "I'm reporting both of you!" He grabbed Toria's hand and led her past the men into the camp.

He looked back. The soldiers were standing together, whispering. One of them scratched his head.

"You didn't find her?" David said.

"No," Toria said. "I saw Bob. He was drawn on the tent, like Xander said. And the message Mom left. I looked into a tent, and those two saw me. They started pushing me around, and one of them said I should be fighting."

"They're idiots," David said. Then he yelled, "Mom! Mom!"

"I thought we were supposed to be secret?"

"Who cares now? Let's find her and get out of here. I've had enough of this place. Mom!"

Toria took up the call: "Mom!"

The soldiers they'd left were heading for them. Something had them suspicious—maybe it was nothing more than what Jesse had said, that he and Toria weren't supposed to be there, and they sensed it.

David yelled again. "Mrs. King! Gertrude King!"

The soldiers were closing in.

"Ignore them," David told Toria. They continued toward the rear of the camp. With her limp, Toria's gait was more of a skip than a walk.

"Mom!" Toria yelled.

"Mrs. King!"

"You two!" the soldier behind them said. "You stop right there."

David turned to face them.

The one he'd knocked down said, "Doesn't sound like you're looking for General Grant. I don't think you're friends with the man. In fact, I don't think you even know him." He stepped closer, the bayonet five feet from David's chest. "Sammy, I think we got us some spies. Oooo, those gray-backs are getting tricky, sending kids."

The other soldier said, "You know what we do with spies?"

"Shoot on sight," the first man said.

"David?" Toria whispered.

An older woman, wearing a blood-covered smock, ran out from a nearby tent. She stopped between David and the bayonet. She faced the soldiers, put her fists on her hips, and said, "What do you think you're doing?"

"Well, ma'am . . ."

"These are *children!*" She pointed toward the front of the camp. "Go, both of you, before I have you thrown into the stockades!"

The two soldiers looked at each other, then back at the woman. Their shoulders slumped. They turned and walked away like five-year-olds heading for time-out.

As she watched them depart, she pulled off the soiled smock, crumpled it, and dropped it on the ground. Then she spun around.

David said, "Thank y—"

She darted toward them, grabbing the material over their

chests with her fists. She brought her nose to within an inch of Toria's, then did the same to David. Her eyes were huge, bright and blue.

Through gritted teeth, she said, "Did you say *King?*"

forty-two

WEDNESDAY, 4:25 P.M.

Whatever had made the noises that drew him away, Xander hadn't found it. But when he returned to the Civil War antechamber, David was gone. One look at the hooks, with their missing items, told him that David had gone over.

I'll never figure that kid out, he thought.

He swirled his hands lightly against the grain of the portal door. He willed it to open, to admit back to their rightful time and place his brother and sister.

He could not believe what David had done. That . . . that . . . *punk!* And *he* had called Xander stupid! Xander had merely wanted to find Mom, and sending Toria seemed like the best way to do it. How much more stupid was it to go into a world where the people had chased you out with guns—twice?

When David returned, he was going to punch him, punch him hard.

No, he wasn't going to do that.

It was a brave thing to do, going over for Toria like that. What was with that kid? He would stand behind Xander if a shadow crept up the wall. But then he'd plunge into World War II and the Civil War, where you had to be afraid of a lot more than shadows. When the stakes were high, the outcome crucial, he manned up—because that's when bravery mattered.

Xander's mind kept casting images of all the things that could happen to his brother over there—unpretty things that would make a movie R-rated for "graphic violence."

Stop! He'll be fine.

He sat on the bench, put his hands on his knees, then stood again. He walked to the portal door, then into the hall.

Where was Dad?

Xander and David had shared a room their entire lives. They'd shared vacations and friends and baths. But over the past few years they hadn't spent much time hanging out.

David had his soccer and video games. Xander's interests were becoming more adult—or at least more older-teen: a girlfriend, making movies, driving.

But as they had faced a mutual enemy—the move itself, and then the house—Xander realized that David had been growing and maturing too. He had sharp ideas and a witty sense of humor, and generally gave as good as he got. His brother was someone he truly *liked*, not just loved.

So maybe, when he next saw David, he would give the kid a bone-crushing bear hug. *Then* he would punch him. Hard.

Toria, he would hug and spare the punch. He had to keep believing what he had told David: The people over there would see nothing more than a cute little girl. No threat. No one to throw in jail or shoot at. Her going over was much safer than David's.

He lowered his head into his hands.

The portal door burst open. Sunlight blinded Xander. Shadows cut through the radiance and slapped down on the antechamber floor, followed by tumbling, grunting, air rushing out of lungs. Sand and leaves blew in on smoky currents. The door slammed shut.

Toria sprang up at him and threw her arms around his neck. "Oh, Xander," she said. "It was awful! If David hadn't come, I would have . . . I . . . ." She began to weep.

Xander squeezed her. Peering over her shoulder, he saw David lifting himself off the floor.

Then Xander's heart leaped. There was another person on the floor behind David. A woman. She had her hand pressed to her forehead; her hair hung over her face.

He shifted Toria to the bench beside him. When he turned back, the woman flipped her hair away from her face and looked at him.

His hope popped like a balloon. This was worse than not getting anything for Christmas, worse than not passing your driver's test, worse than being rejected by a girl you'd liked all year and finally summoned the courage to ask out.

It wasn't Mom.

The woman was old, a lot older than Mom. She was breathing heavily through her mouth, which had formed into a curious smile. But she had kind, vibrant eyes that somehow looked familiar.

Xander looked from the woman to David and back to the woman. Finally he said, "Who are you?"

"Are you Xander?" she said, pushing a strand of hair off her face.

Hesitantly, he nodded.

"Well," she said, trying to catch her breath. "From what these two told me . . ."

A realization struck Xander like a hammer between the eyes. He knew where he'd seen her before . . .

". . . mostly while running from soldiers . . ." she continued.

Xander gaped at her. If not her, then her features. The shape of her eyes. The top lip thin, the bottom one fuller. He saw them every day, staring back at him from the mirror.

" . . . I guess I'm your grandmother."

Xander blinked. His mouth formed words, but nothing came out. He shot his eyes to his brother, who had rocked back to sit on his heels.

David smiled, nodded.

"But . . ." Xander said. "How?"

"Bob," she said. "That silly cartoon face—Henry, your grandfather, made up when *he* was a kid. You put it on the tent, right?"

"But our grandpa's name was Hank," Toria said.

"Hank is Henry," she said, "like Jack is John."

"You . . ." Xander said. "*You* wrote the message next to it?"

"Yes, I was so—" Her smile faltered. "*Was?* Toria said his name *was* Hank."

Xander frowned with her. He said, "Our grandfather . . . he died last year."

"Oh . . ." She turned her head away. Her shoulders rose and fell. "I suppose . . . I mean, it has been so long. I always thought of him the way he was the last time I saw him—young. I guess all along he was marching toward that date we all have to keep."

She spoke the way Dad did sometimes. Xander had always liked it, describing things in ways he hadn't thought of before. Songwriters were masters at it, poets too. *Marching toward that date we all have to keep*—death. It made it seem less terrible. A little.

"I'm sorry," Xander said.

"And I'm sorry for you," she said. "I knew him for only ten years. You must have known him longer."

"I was fourteen when he . . . kept his date," Xander said. It wasn't quite right, but she knew his meaning. "I'm fifteen now."

"Fifteen," she said, shaking her head. "And you?" She looked at David.

"Twelve."

"I'm nine," Toria chimed.

"My goodness," she said. "I really have missed so much." Worry etched lines in her brow. "Your father, my son, is . . . is he all right?"

"Grandma called him Eddie," David said to Xander, tickled.

She touched David's knee. "Not Grandma. Call me Nana. I always wanted to be Nana."

"Yeah," Xander said. He was thrilled to give her good news. "Dad's really all right. Aunt Beth too. She's married, and you have another grandkid. Her name's Anne. She's thirteen."

"She's a grouch," Toria said.

"Toria!" Xander said.

The woman—*Nana*—smiled. "Let's see," she said.

"Alexander, David, Victoria, Anne. All royal names. My children kept the tradition. I don't suppose your mother has such a name?"

"Everyone calls her G," David said.

"G?"

All three of the King children said, "Definitely not a Gertrude!" and laughed.

"I see. And how is she?"

"She's . . . over there," Xander said, waving his hand at the portal door.

"What?" Nana said. "Looking for *me*?"

"No, she was kidnapped," David said. "Like you were."

"From this house?" Her hand covered her mouth, and her eyes welled up. "Oh . . . oh . . . I'm sorry. My dear children." She rose and hugged Xander's head. She turned to David and gave him a squeeze, then opened her arms to Toria, who came off the bench to be comforted.

As if to herself, Nana said, "This house, this awful house."

forty-three

WEDNESDAY, 4:41 P.M.

David heard Dad's comfortingly familiar voice call from the hallway.

"Hello? Kids, I'm home!"

He knew his brother and sister's wide eyes matched his own.

"Dad!" he said. He scrambled out of the antechamber. He ran to Dad at the beginning of the hall and jumped into his arms. He squeezed, as if trying to meld their bodies together.

Toria and Xander collided into Dad, their arms binding them all together.

"I missed you, Daddy," Toria said. "I was so scared."

"I knew you'd be fine," Dad said. "But from what Jesse told me on the way over, you guys haven't been bored."

Disentangling themselves, the King kids spoke all at once:

"This big man chased us . . ."

"I was putting up a camera when . . ."

"Toria went over . . . I didn't know what to do . . ."

"Hold on, hold on," Dad said. "I want to hear it all, but I—" His words hit a brick wall.

David followed his gaze to Nana, who had stepped out of the antechamber.

Dad's face flashed from puzzlement to shock to joy. He backed away from this last emotion to settle on hopefulness. "Mom?"

"Eddie," she said. "You're not the little boy I've carried around in my head for thirty years. But I see him in there. I would recognize you anywhere."

Dad began walking toward her. She met him halfway, opening her arms.

"Mom," he said. They embraced, and Dad buried his face in her shoulder. He was big, compared to her. His arms seemed to engulf her.

David imagined that the last time they'd hugged, their physical proportions had been reversed, the difference in sizes even more pronounced. She would not have changed much, but Dad had been seven.

The kids smiled at one another. Toria teared up. Xander's rising and falling chest said he, too, was on the brink of losing it. David was doing a pretty good job of holding it in.

Finally Dad lifted his head and backed away a step. He sniffed and ran his palm over his face. He grinned at the kids. His eyes scanned his mother's face, studying every feature. He said, "I've missed you so much."

Her hand caressed his cheek, then she slipped her fingers into his hair, brushing it back—exactly the way he did with his children.

David marveled at this: the little things from your parents you keep with you your whole life. He wondered what mannerisms he had picked up from Mom and Dad. And that they, in turn, had picked up from *their* parents. How far back could it go, these traits?

He looked at Xander. He and his brother had the same-shaped eyes. Xander's were blue, like their mother's. David's were hazel—brownish green, sometimes appearing one color, then the other—like Dad's and, he knew now, like his nana's.

Xander leaned close to him. He whispered, "But it *wasn't* Mom who left the note. We *didn't* find her."

David nodded sadly. "Back to square one," he said.

They approached Dad and Nana at the center of the hall.

"Guys," Dad said. "I'm going to take your grandmother downstairs. Get her something to drink." He raised his eyebrows at her. "Something to eat?"

"Oh, no," she said. "I might need to lie down somewhere, though. I'm a bit . . . no, a *lot* exhausted. I feel so drained. Too much emotion."

Toria hopped up. "She can use my bed!" She walked up to the older woman and took her hand. "I'll get it ready for you, Nana."

Nana smiled at Xander and David. "I want to hear all about you two. We have so much to catch up on, don't we?"

They nodded.

"And we'll have plenty of time to do it, I'm sure."

David gave her a hug. Xander did the same.

"Thank you," she said. "Thank you for finding me, for bringing me *home*."

Dad escorted her down the hallway toward the landing. Toria strolled on her other side, holding her hand.

Nana looked around at the crooked hallway, at the wall sconces and old-fashioned decorations. "It hasn't changed at all," she said. She spotted something on the wall, sending her fingers to her lips.

David moved farther into the hallway to see that she was looking at four parallel furrows in the wallpaper. He and

Xander had discovered them when they'd first found the hallway.

She started weeping again, and David realized what they were: her scratch marks, put there when she was kidnapped.

They heard a sound behind them and looked back to see Keal appear on the landing with Jesse's wheelchair. He looked surprised to see another person up there with them, but he simply nodded and disappeared back down the stairs. A moment later he reappeared with Jesse and eased him into the chair.

"Jesse, Keal," Dad said. "This is my mother."

Jesse's eyes went wide. His jaw dropped open. "Kimberly?" he said.

Her head tilted. "Have we met?"

"I'm Henry's uncle, ma'am," Jesse said.

She stared at him. Slowly, she released Toria's hand and touched his. "It's been a long time, Jesse."

forty-four

WEDNESDAY, 5:00 P.M.

Keal, David, and Xander stood around Jesse's wheelchair in the third-floor hallway. The light from the strange lamps hanging on the walls flickered, flamelike. To David, it made the curving corridor appear to pulse, as if it were feeling the beating of a distant heart.

"Nana's the one who left the message on the tent," he said, hanging his head. "Not Mom."

"I see," Jesse said. "I'm sorry, son. We'll keep looking." He touched David's arm. "Look on the bright side."

"Dad's got *his* mom back?" David said.

"Well, that too . . . but I was thinking about your mother. Since your grandmother survived for so long, there's no reason to think your mom couldn't do the same."

"For thirty years?" David said. He couldn't even imagine that many years, let alone that many years looking for Mom. He'd be forty-two in thirty years.

"For however long it takes," said Jesse. "But I don't think it'll take that long. You've been looking for your mom only a few days, and you found *somebody*. That's a pretty good record." He looked around the hallway, then reached up and smoothed back his hair.

"The wind's not blowing now," David said. "Like it did last night. That was weird."

Jesse nodded. "I have to say, it's a bit frightening being up here, so close to the portals. If I'm up here and Time decides it wants me, I'm not sure I could do anything about it. Remind me to head back downstairs in an hour."

"Why does it want you in the first place?" Xander said.

"There's a balance to everything in the world," Jesse said. "Things need to be where they belong. We don't belong in the past, but if we go back there enough times, or stay long enough, history sort of . . . gets used to us. It starts to *want* us there, because by our continued presence, we made a place for ourselves. Like if you lie on a bed long enough, you get up and the mattress contains a perfect shape of your body."

"You were in this house nearly fifty years," Xander said. "Going through the portals all that time?"

"In and out," Jesse agreed. "Not every day, but a few times a week. It was enough. The past wants me back. That's why I live half a continent away. Just in case its reach is farther than I've imagined."

"Have you felt it where you live?" Xander said.

"Nope," Jesse said. "Either it can't reach that far or it forgot about me."

David looked around the hallway, at all the closed doors, at the wall lights with their carved figures of tigers and fighters and faces. He said, "You talk about it like it's alive."

"In a way, it is," Jesse said. "But in the manner in which a tree is alive. If you hack into it, sap covers the gouge and eventually heals itself. Trees adjust to circumstances, over time leaning toward the sun, for example." He shook his head. "Not alive as a human is alive, as a human is intelligent. Time abides by certain rules, the way the ocean does. A man drowns in the ocean, and we say the ocean took him. Do we mean that it consciously sought out the man and took him away? No. Time is like that: rules, but no reason."

He looked between David and Xander. "Now, while we're

up here, while I can be here, tell me everything you know about these rooms—what you call antechambers—and the portals. Everything you've seen in every world you've visited. That will tell me the best way to help you."

forty-five

WEDNESDAY, 5:37 P.M.

David had just peered into an antechamber and shut the door when Dad stepped into the hallway.

"Nana's going to take a nap in Toria's room," he said, smiling. "That is, if Toria lets her. Your sister's talking up a storm." He took in the activity in the hallway—David, Xander, and even Keal moving from door to door, checking the items behind each. "What's going on?"

"Ed," Jessie said, beckoning from his wheelchair at the far

end of the hall. "When we spoke on the way home from the jail, you didn't tell me about . . . what did you call it, Xander?"

"Peaceful world," Xander said. "You know, Dad. The place you and I went, where we sat by the river and you carved Bob into the tree."

"The only world that's not violent," Dad said. He patted David's back as he headed for Jesse. "Do you know it, Jesse? You want to go there?"

Jesse's eyes closed slowly. "I know it, Ed, but no. I don't ever want to see it again."

Dad stopped. "I don't understand."

"I know." Jesse's eyes opened as slowly as they'd closed. "But you need to. You need to see it for what it is."

"What it is?" Dad said, spreading his hands. "It's one of the nicest places I've ever been. Even the air has a special quality, like . . . I don't know . . . fresh, invigorating. Right, Xander?"

Xander nodded, but his face was tight, concerned. He looked through the door he had just opened, then shut it. He moved slowly to the next door, prompting David to carry on with the search as well. But David could tell that his brother's ears and eyes were still on Jesse and Dad.

"Jesse," Dad said. He squatted down in front of the old man. "What is this about?"

"That world is not what you think it is," Jesse said. "Something terrible happened. I believe it has to do with the man who wants your house."

"Taksidian?"

"Yes, but when I knew him, he went by another name," Jesse said. "I was here when he arrived. Almost immediately, he began breaking in, going through the portals. It was then that history started changing in ways I had never seen before. Terrible, horrendous ways. I don't know why he did it, but he did."

"Hey . . ." Keal said. "You said a picnic basket, parasol, blanket, and funny hat, right?"

"That's it," Xander said.

"Wait," Jesse said, but Keal and Xander had already stepped into the little room.

Dad said, "I've been there, Jesse. There's nothing—"

"You haven't gone over the hill, have you?" Jesse said. "The biggest hill, a few miles from the lush valley?"

"No, but . . . What's over the hill?"

"The reason this house called you back."

"This house *called* me? I came back to find my mother. I—" Dad looked over his shoulder.

David saw frustration and confusion on his face.

Dad swung his attention back to Jesse. "What does it have to do with Taksidian?"

"It's the reason he's here, as well," Jesse said. "The culmination of his work. Look—" His brows pinched in concentration. "So much to tell you," he said, "and I've never been good at putting my thoughts in the best order. Age has made it worse."

"Just tell me what's over there that's got you spooked," Dad said.

David glanced into the antechamber as he walked past. Xander was setting the floppy golf cap—the tam-o'-shanter—on Keal's head.

David drew up next to his father and Jesse. He leaned against the wall, absently rubbing his cast.

"The future," Jesse said.

"But we've never found a future world," Dad said. He waved his arm around, indicating the doors. "They all lead to times in the past."

"Except that one," Jesse said. "It's why you haven't found any other future worlds. It's—"

Xander's yells came from the antechamber: "Keal! No, wait!"

A door slammed. Xander came out of the room so fast he crashed into the wall on the opposite side of the hallway. "He went through!" he said. "Keal opened the door, then he just *went through!*"

"Go get him!" Jesse said, wide eyes on Dad. "Please . . . he doesn't know what he's doing."

Dad sprang up. He rushed to the antechamber and looked in. His head swiveled toward Jesse, then David, then Xander—unsure what to do.

"Dad, I think he *fell*," Xander said.

"Go get him," Jesse pleaded, wheeling himself forward.

"Bring him back. I'll explain later."

Dad nodded. He went into the antechamber, and Xander joined him.

David slipped past Jesse and stepped into the tiny room. Dad had the picnic basket and blanket slung over his shoulders. He picked up a butterfly net. He turned toward the closed portal door and stood staring at it, as if he hoped Keal would burst back through. He reached for the handle.

"Wait," Jesse said from his chair in the doorway. "Take this." He reached under a knitted blanket that covered his lap. His hand returned with a pistol.

"Whoa," David said.

"Jesse!" Dad said. "Where did that come from?"

"A friend overnighted it to me," Jesse said. He held it out.

"I don't want it," Dad said.

"Give it to Keal," Jesse said. "He used to be an Army Ranger." Dad shook his head.

"You may need it," Jesse said. "I hope not, but . . . *please.*"

Dad stepped across the room, hesitated, and took the gun. He said, "You have a lot of explaining to do."

"Bring Keal back," Jesse said, "and I'll tell you everything."

Dad returned to the door and opened it. Hazy daylight flooded the little room. The fragrance of grasses and wildflowers wafted in. A warm breeze. Through the portal, a blurry vision of a meadow drifted by.

"I don't see him," Dad said.

"The portal's moving," Jesse said. "Hurry."

Dad stepped into the light. He dropped away and disappeared.

Xander reached out as if to stop him. He said, "Why the gun, Jesse?"

Jesse turned wide, almost buggy eyes on him. He said nothing.

Xander spun and leaped through the portal.

"Xander—!" David said. He threw a glance at Jesse, who read his expression perfectly.

"Don't even think it about it, son," Jesse said. "They'll be right back."

David grabbed the edge of the door as it closed. "Dad! Xander!"

Wind blew his words back into his face. The door kept closing, pushing his sneakered feet along the hardwood floor. They protested with stuttering squeaks.

"Let it shut," Jesse said.

The door shoved David into the frame. He couldn't hold it open. Pain radiated through his broken arm, spreading into his shoulders. His other arm, his legs, ached under the strain. He was sure that if he pulled away from it now, the door would catch a foot or arm and snap it off, as it had broken the baseball bat days ago. He tucked himself tight and let the door knock him through the portal like a pinball's flipper whacking a steel marble.

CHAPTER

forty-six

David fell into a patch of flowers. He rolled through them into tall grass and stopped. The air was warm and smelled like the perfume counter at the department store in Pasadena. He stared at a sky the color of a knife blade. Pollen, kicked up from his fall, floated past. He rolled over and got to his feet.

Thirty feet down a gently sloping hill, Xander rose from

the grass. He gave David a stunned look, then turned to Dad, who was a little farther down the hill, beside Keal.

Dad spotted his sons. "What are you doing?" he said. Panic strained his voice.

"I—" Xander said. He swung back to David, as if for an answer. When David said nothing, Xander said, "I want to help."

Dad grabbed Keal's arm and started up the hill. He pointed with the butterfly net. "Then catch that thing," he said. "Stop it from disappearing!"

David turned to see what Dad was pointing at: the portal. It shimmered like a heat wave, showing nothing but the door that had slammed shut behind him. As he watched, it broke apart and scattered like dandelion fluff.

"Too late," David said weakly.

"Great," Dad said. "The portal home could be any-where." He cast a hard eye on Keal. "What's the deal? Why'd you go through?"

"I was just looking," Keal said. "I guess I stuck my head in too far. This . . . *wind* pulled me in."

"Here," Dad said. He handed Keal the gun. "Jesse said you know how to use it."

Keal took it and held it up. "A .357 Colt Python." He flipped his wrist, opening the cylinder. "Loaded." He removed a bullet, saw the curious expression on David's face, and said, "I always keep the hammer on an empty chamber.

Safer that way." He dropped the bullet into a shirt pocket. He snapped the cylinder back into place.

Dad squinted at their surroundings. The slope they were on descended a long way before leveling off. Sunlight glimmered on a river down in the valley. To their left and right, trees formed dense woods.

"You think we need it?" Dad said.

Keal shrugged and pushed the weapon into his pants at the small of his back. "Man, I don't know anything about this place, but if Jesse thinks we do, I'm glad to have it."

"All right," Dad said. "Come on." He started walking.

"Where to?" David said, hurrying to reach them.

Dad pointed at a far-off hill, past a swath of woods and several smaller hillocks. "Whatever Jesse's anxious about is over that hill. We have to find the portal home anyway, so we might as well start over there." He looked at David and Xander, giving them a tight smile. "Stay close," he said. "Give a holler if you hear or see anything dangerous."

"Don't worry," David said, "we will."

forty-seven

WEDNESDAY, 5:59 P.M.

Toria sat cross-legged at the foot of the bed, facing her grand-mother, who sat propped with her back against the headboard. Between them was a collection of stuffed animals.

"And this one," Toria said, picking up a bear wearing a stars-and-stripes shirt and holding an American flag on a stick, "sings 'The Star Spangled Banner.'" She wrinkled her nose. "Off-key. It's pretty bad."

She tilted her head, studying Nana's face. She pushed the bear into her lap. Softly, she said, "I'm sorry. You must be very tired."

Nana blinked slowly. "I am, but I'm also very interested in *you*. You remind me so much of my little girl."

Toria giggled. "You mean Aunt Beth. I never thought of her as a little girl, but I guess she was . . . once."

"She was only four when I last saw her." Nana smiled at the memory.

"How can you *take* it?" Toria said. "Being back after so long. I think I would just . . . *explode*."

Nana looked around the room. "Honey, after a while, you learn to adjust quickly, going from world to world."

Toria sat up straight. "World to world? You mean you . . . *bounced around*?"

Nana nodded. "But now I'm home. In a way, it's just another world for me to adjust to. But it's the only world I *want* to be in. It's the only place where *you* are, and everybody else I love."

Toria smiled. "You're supposed to be here."

"It's where I belong," Nana agreed.

Toria squinted at her grandmother's hair. A few strands were standing up, like what happens when you rub a balloon on your head and static electricity builds up. Except the hair standing up on Nana's head was also whipping back and forth.

Toria crawled over an array of stuffed animals and smoothed the hair down. "You're very pretty," she said, leaning back.

"Thank you," Nana said. "You are too. Does your mom have brown hair too, like you children?"

"Her hair's more blonde," Toria said. "She calls it dishwater blonde, but I think that sounds gross. Who'd want dishwater-colored hair? She has pretty hair, cut like this." She snagged her hair at the neckline and bent it in.

"Sounds lovely," Nana said. "I'll bet you—" She stopped. Her eyebrows came together, and she looked upward.

Toria stared at the strange thing going on at the top of Nana's head. Her hair—not a few strands, but most of it—was standing up and swishing back and forth, as though she was nodding her head underwater.

CHAPTER

forty-eight

David, Xander, Dad, and Keal crunched through a beautiful forest of big trees—oaks or elms, David thought, but he didn't know much about trees.

"I can see the end, just ahead," Dad said. "We're almost at the hill Jesse mentioned."

"What's there?" David said.

"Beats me, Dae. Something scary, according to Jesse."

"Then why are we heading for it?"

"We have to know what it is. Just a peek, then we'll get out of here, okay?"

David frowned. "I guess."

"Hey, Keal," Xander said. "If you need someone to help carry that gun . . ."

"I'm fine, Xander," Keal said. "But thanks."

"Dad," Xander said, "in *The Shawshank Redemption*, these big bad guys kicked Tim Robbins's butt. You run into any of that?"

"Shawshank was a prison," Dad said. "I was in jail. There's a difference."

"So . . . *little* bad guys?" Xander said.

"No bad guys, except for the ones who locked me up." Dad stepped past the last tree and into bright sunlight, where he paused. The picnic basket hung from his shoulder by a strap. He pushed it behind him and swung absently at the grass with the butterfly net.

David stopped beside him. He said, "Sorry about coming through after you and Xander."

"Truth be told," Dad said, "I'm glad you're here. At least as long as we don't have to use that gun." He ran his fingers through David's hair and draped his hand over his shoulder.

"How'd Jesse get you out?"

"I wasn't there when he was talking to the police, but I heard some shouting."

Keal came tromping out of the woods. He carried the

folded parasol under his arm like a British lord expecting some weather. He turned his face up to the sun and held it there.

"Are we safe?" David said to his father. "They're not going to evict us or try to grab us again, are they?"

"For now we're okay, Dae. Apparently a few people in power overreacted to unsubstantiated allegations."

"Xander said Taksidian bribed people to get us out of the house and you arrested."

"Yeah, I think so," Dad said.

"So you still have your job?"

"As far as I know."

"Does that mean we have to go back to school?"

Dad laughed and mussed David's hair. "'Fraid so. Hey, Xander! What's taking you so long?"

"Watering a tree," Xander yelled from the woods. "Be right there."

Dad turned around and looked up the tall hill. The climb seemed about a mile.

"It's so beautiful," David said. "And quiet. What can be so terrible out here?"

"That's what we're going to find out."

"I hope nothing," David said. "I hope Jesse was wrong."

"I wouldn't bet against the man," Keal said.

Xander jogged out from the shadow of the trees. He said, "My back teeth were floating."

"Okay, then," Dad said. "Let's go."

David showed Xander a lopsided grin. He said, "This is serious. Couldn't you have said something more . . . gung ho?"

Xander slapped David on the back. In a deep voice he said, "It's an honor to die at your side."

"Uh . . ."

"Not what you had in mind? How about—" Smiling, Xander raised his arm as if holding a sword. "Strong and courageous!"

"That's better," David said. "Strong and courageous!"

CHAPTER

forty-nine

Jesse kept an eye on the portal door from the hallway. He kept the wheelchair's footrest just inside the antechamber to prevent the outer door from closing. After all these years, being here in the house he had built with his father and brother felt somehow *comfortable*. Not pleasing, but comfortable, the way a surgeon must feel in an operating room. Or even a soldier on the battlefield. It was a place he knew well.

Here, and only here, his skills perfectly matched the challenges presented. As he had told the King children about themselves last night—prematurely, he'd realized later—he was *meant* to be here.

The lights in the hallway flickered. Jesse looked at the nearest wall light. It depicted a frowning sun face—a grinning quarter moon was poking its sharply pointed head into the sun's cheek. Light from the bulb behind the faces shone through the eyes and slits in the sun rays; it splashed up the wall to the ceiling. The light blinked out and returned a second later. The other lamps in the hall did the same.

The walls around him creaked, groaned.

Too soon, Jesse thought.

He'd been sure Time would have allowed him to stay longer before it came to claim him.

A door near the end of the hall, several down from his, crashed open. Light radiated out of the antechamber. He knew it emanated from an open portal.

He wheeled the chair back, turned, and shot down the hall toward the landing.

No wind yet. Coming soon.

Should he try to write a note? No time. Besides, sending the Kings into that world had been his most important task. A peaceful world? *Ha!*

Don't get worked up, old man, he told himself. *Not over that.*

He had shined a light on *that* dark charade.

You want to get worked up? Look behind you! Look at the portal, hungry to eat you!

He reached the landing and propelled himself out of the chair. He began crawling, moving quickly down the stairs. He tried to ignore the pain in his stomach and hips as he bounded down each step. He slowed . . . stopped.

Why no wind?

Didn't it know that if it wanted him, it had to come get him? He wasn't about to just waltz right into the portal of his own free will. He may be old, but he wasn't stupid.

A scream reached him: coming from the second floor, just below him. Beyond the collapsed walls.

Toria!

She was screaming over and over, as loud and insistent as a fire alarm.

It dawned on him.

Not me, he thought. *Nana. Kimberly. It's coming for her.*

She'd been lost in history for thirty years, thirty constant years. Of course Time thought she belonged back there.

He thumped down the remaining steps and dragged himself up onto the fallen walls. He pulled his body over the dust and debris.

Toria's screams continued.

"Nana!" the little girl yelled. "No, no, nooooo!"

Jesse reached the main hallway and turned the corner.

Banging, banging punctuated Toria's screams like a pounding drum, trying to keep time with a manic trumpeter.

"I'm coming, girl!" Jesse yelled, but the words were no more than air coming out of his lungs. He had spent his breath on moving from the third floor to the second.

"No! Nana!"

Jesse reached the grand staircase and crawled past. Toria's room was the next one on the right. He was almost there.

He could hear Kimberly now, crying, groaning with effort. Not screaming, no—all of her energy was invested in fighting the pull.

Inside the bedroom, something crashed. Toria screamed again.

His arms were tiring. He reached out, hooked his fingers on the door frame, and pulled himself forward.

Something inside the room screeched like an angry hawk. A bare foot shot out of the bedroom and struck his face. He pulled his head back. Kimberly's feet kicked the floor in front of him. She gripped the bed's footboard, her body stretched from it to the door.

That *screech!* again, and he saw the bed tremble and scrape closer to the door. Kimberly's feet came farther into the hall. They smacked Jesse's face and shoulder. He rolled away, across the hall. He couldn't help her if he was knocked unconscious.

He pulled himself slightly past the door, then arced

around, edging toward her at a less dangerous angle. "Hold on!" he said.

Toria knelt beside the bed, holding on to Nana's arms. She was crying, pulling in great gulps of air and screaming them out. Her face glistened with tears.

"Jesse! Help her!" Toria yelled. "Make it stop!"

Jesse grabbed Kimberly's feet and tried to push them back into the room.

The bed screeched across the floor. It slammed into the open door and stopped.

Kimberly's legs snapped away from Jesse. They bent around the edge of the door frame, toward the smaller hallway and the stairs leading to the third floor. They shook and twisted as though someone were tugging on them.

Jesse threw his arms around her thighs and squeezed. He heard a *crack!* Another. He prayed it wasn't Kimberly's bones giving out under the intense pressure pulling at her.

Crack! Crack!—and the footboard broke apart.

The woman shot out of the room, banged against the door frame, and turned toward the short hallway. Her body bumped over Jesse's head and kept moving. She was completely out of the room now and sliding along the floor on her stomach.

He lunged for her, seizing first one wrist, then the other. She stared at Jesse, her eyes huge and wet. Her hair whipped around like fire in a strong wind.

She said, "I don't want to go back!"

"I got you," he said.

She continued to slide, and Jesse went with her.

Toria bounded out of her room and jumped over him. She flopped on top of her grandmother, hugging her from behind.

"Toria, let go!" Jesse yelled. "Toria! If she goes, you'll go with her!"

Kimberly's eyes grew even wider. "No!" she said. "Toria, get off! Let me go!"

"I won't!" the little girl screamed. "I won't!"

They slid closer to the railing that overlooked the foyer. Jesse thought he could grab a spindle—that might work . . . for a while. As they passed, he released her right wrist and reached for the banister.

His left shoulder flared in white-hot pain. A muscular hand was squeezing his shoulder. He could not see them, but he knew long nails had pierced his flesh. Blood soaked the material of his shirt.

He gritted his teeth, telling his hand to keep its grip on Kimberly's wrist. But the pain was too great and the wind too strong.

She broke free and sailed away, sliding on the floor, taking Toria with her.

"Toria, let go!" Jesse yelled.

Kimberly and Toria reached the end of the hallway and zipped around the corner. He heard their progression toward the portal: thumping over the fallen walls; *bam-bam-bamming* up the stairs.

Toria screamed, then Jesse heard no more.

He grabbed the hand on his shoulder. It was hard as a statue's. The knuckles, the veins, the thick welt of scar tissue.

He rolled over, and the hand pulled away.

A man stood beside him, engulfed by shadows; Jesse saw only long, unruly hair, the hem of a black slicker. A soft patter, like raindrops, drew Jesse's eyes to the floor beside him. A small pool of blood grew bigger as drops fell from the man's fingers. The man leaned closer, and his thin, muscular face dipped into the light.

Jesse's heart clattered against his breastbone. He wheezed in a breath. He said, "*Dagan!* I should have known."

"They call me Taksidian now, old man." His voice was hard and dry, like bones rattling together. He looked up the hall in one direction, then back the other way.

Jesse saw the linen closet door standing open.

The man he had known as Dagan sighed. He said, "You should have stayed away, Jesse."

He reached down with both hands, and Jesse's world went black.

CHAPTER

fifty

"Wait up," David said.

Dad stopped to rest twenty yards from the top of the big hill. He turned around and scanned the valley below them. "God's country," he said.

David glanced over his shoulder. Tall green grass flowed like waves down to the woods they had traversed. A meadow of yellow and purple flowers fanned out from the other side of the trees, like glitter. A hill similar to the one on which they stood rose up on the other side of the meadow, forming a vista worthy of a postcard. The valley sloped to the river far below.

Dad pointed in that direction. "That's where Xander and I threw rocks into the river. And those trees on the other side of the meadow? That's where I carved Bob."

Xander reached David. He put a hand on David's shoulder and leaned over, breathing hard. He said, "It's steeper than it looks."

"You're more of a wimp than you look," David said.

Xander shoved him. David stumbled back and plopped down. He hopped up and scurried toward his brother, intent on sending him rolling down the hill.

"Boys," Dad said. "Not now."

Keal stepped up to them. "Whew," he said, stretching his limbs.

Dad turned and started climbing. David raced to catch up. Behind him, Xander groaned.

David reached the top first. He felt his eyes stretch wide. Dad rose up behind him and gasped.

They stood on the ridge of a hill that immediately plunged into another vast valley. Directly below them, piled up against the hill and stretching out from it for half a mile, were chunks and slabs of broken concrete. They ranged in size from small boulders to pieces that could have once been the sides of whole office buildings. Rebar jutted from the edges like severed arteries. Scattered among the concrete were clumps of metal. David recognized a demolished car and a nearly flattened dumpster. Tires were strewn everywhere. Except for an absence of paper trash, it looked like a thousand-acre dump.

Deeper into the valley, the debris assumed familiar shapes: a roadway, a bridge, the square top of a building. All of it flowed toward a centerpiece of destruction in the distance . . . the remnants of a great city. The skeletal frames of broken sky-scrapers rose up from collapsed ruins, like the popsicle-stick buildings David used to make and then demolish. Smaller buildings dotted the surrounding land like an angry rash.

Vegetation had staked a new claim on the valley. Forests of trees and lush bushes streamed like water through the streets and boulevards, tall grass covered sidewalks and plazas, moss and vines climbed the buildings. It sapped all color but its own from the landscape: everything was shaded in hues of green.

And black, David realized. Many of the remaining struc-tures were charred. The only exceptions were a smattering of elevated freeway sections that glistened white in the sun like the bones of long-dead animals.

Beyond it all, a gray mist did not quite mask an endless body of water: an ocean or sea.

Keal reached the ridge and collapsed onto his knees.

Xander rose up and brought his hand to his mouth. After a long while, he said, "Dad . . . it's Los Angeles."

David's heart skipped a beat.

Dad nodded slowly.

"I don't understand," David said. But he could see that Xander was right. He could see what was left of the U.S. Bank Tower. And the Capitol Records Building. Half of it, anyway. He'd spent his whole life in this valley, traveled its streets, attended its schools, played with children who'd once lived there. It was like standing at the casket of a dear friend.

"We did this, Dae," Dad said. "Mankind. We wiped ourselves out."

"But . . ." David couldn't get his head around it. "When?"

"Sometime in the future," Dad said. "That's what Jesse was trying to tell me. We've never found a portal that leads to the future because *there is no future*. Just this one."

"No future," Xander repeated numbly.

"Do you think the whole world's like this?" David said. "Gone like this?"

"Has to be," Xander said. "Else they'd have rebuilt it, wouldn't they? Wouldn't they have rebuilt the city, Dad?"

"I don't know, Xander."

A sound drew their attention to Keal. His face was buried in his hands. His shoulders rose and fell.

"What do you think happened?" David asked.

"War, probably," Dad said. "By the look of the buildings."

"But when?" David said again. *The future* wasn't enough of an answer.

"Jesse said it's the culmination of Taksidian's work," Dad said. "So I guess during his lifetime."

"That soon?" David whispered.

They stood, letting the seconds become minutes.

Keal sniffed. He wiped his face and got to his feet. "Ain't right," he said.

"Isn't there anything we can do?" David said. His voice had taken on a raspy tone. His throat and mouth felt dry as dust.

Dad put his arm around David's shoulder. "I don't know, Dae."

Xander picked up a rock. Grunting in anger or frustration, he hurled it out over the descending hillside. It dropped into the trash dump, clattering between concrete and metal. Just as the sound of the rock stopped, a howl rose up from the valley, close.

David said, "What was—"

A mournful wail bellowed from somewhere else.

"Hey," Keal said. "Something's moving down there."

Xander stepped forward to look. "An animal." He didn't sound so sure.

More noises kicked up: howls, screams, yips. Something clanged.

Keal's hand went to the gun in his waistband.

At first it looked to David like the shadows were shifting.

Then, from a broken concrete pipe, crawled a creature. It was fish-belly white with bone-thin arms and legs. A large head on a spindly neck, flanked by narrow shoulders. A pelt of shaggy hair clung to its skull. It rose and stood erect.

"Is that . . . a *man*?" David said.

More of the humanlike creatures emerged from the rubble. They crawled and stepped and scurried out of the shadows like individual nightmares conjured too soon. They were pale, hunched over, jittery. But—yes, they were people. Two of them bumped into each other and began fighting. They bit and scratched and rolled out of sight.

"They see us," Keal said.

Faces were turning up to stare at them. A few of them pointed. Several howled and screeched.

They began scurrying up the hill. A handful at first, then dozens and more.

"There's gotta be a hundred," Xander said.

David backed away. "Dad?"

Dad turned in a circle. He looked back the way they'd come, then toward the approaching horde.

Xander started down the hill, heading for the spot where the portal had dropped them into this world. He stopped. "What are you waiting for?" he called. "Let's go!"

"Dad," David said. "We gotta find the portal. Now." The expression on his father's face made him ask, "What?"

Dad looked at Keal. The man held the pistol in one hand.

With the other, he balanced the tam-o'-shanter on his fingers, carefully watching it as though expecting the hat to hop off his hand and scamper away.

Dad said, "You feel it too?"

"Like a magnet," Keal said.

"What?" David said. "Come on, let's go."

The first of the attacking future-humans were more than halfway up the hill. David could see their crazy, bulging eyes and the sparse, broken teeth in their gaping mouths.

Dad frowned. He said. "The portal—"

"Yes!" David yelled. "You know where it is?"

He nodded, and David knew. Even before he noticed the picnic basket quivering and lifting off of Dad's hip, showing the way home, he knew.

Dad pointed at the mob running up the hill at them.

He said, "It's down there."

NOT THE END . . .

WITH SPECIAL THANKS TO . . .

SLADE PEARCE, for *being* David: you rock!

NICHOLAS and LUKE FALLENTINE (again): you guys
are great

BEN and MATTHEW FORD, insightful readers and my
new friends

ANTHONY, my son and most fervent fan

JOEL GOTLER, my wonderful agent

The rest of my family, for letting me be a kid again

LB NORTON, JUDY GITENSTEIN, and AMANDA
BOSTIC, editors extraordinaire

The terrific team at Nelson: ALLEN, JOCELYN, JENNIFER, KATIE, MARK, LISA, BECKY . . .

And my readers, for letting the King family live!

Reading Group Guide

1. Marguerite, the little girl David saved in the French village, grew up to become instrumental in the eradication of small pox. His heroism saved millions of people from contracting the disease. Do you believe that the things we do—whether good or bad—have a domino or ripple effect on many others?

2. Can you think of something you've done that had a direct effect on people beyond the ones with whom you had direct contact?

3. Confused by events and needing advice, Xander drives the family car to the jail to see Dad, even though he doesn't have a driver's license. Do you think it's ever okay to break rules—even laws? If so, was this one of those times? What should Xander have done?

4. Continuing his aggressive efforts to rescue Mom, Xander is willing to send Toria to the Civil War. David thinks she's too young and should not be put in such danger. In such a situation, would you have been more like Xander or David? Why?

5. David says the family needs help, and he's willing to trust Jesse to get it. At first, Xander doesn't trust Jesse. Does trusting people come easy to you? Has there been a time when you trusted someone when you shouldn't have? What happened?

6. There are many theories about time travel affecting the past. Some say it can't happen because then the people who went back in time should never have known about a world without the change (for example, they would have grown up with the change already affecting them). What do you think of the whole concept of time travel? Can you think of reasons that it should not be possible? (Don't think too hard about this one. I did once and my head exploded.)

For more reading group guide questions, be sure to check out
www.DreamhouseKings.com

DREAMHOUSE
KINGS

timescape

ROBERT LIPARULO

BOOK FOUR IN THE DREAMHOUSE KINGS SERIES

COMING
JULY 2009

Sept 1

COLLEGE DOGMATIC THEOLOGY

COLLEGE

DOGMATIC

THEOLOGY

BY

REV. ANTHONY F. ALEXANDER
Priest of the Diocese of Cleveland

DEPARTMENT OF THEOLOGY
John Carroll University

Author of COLLEGE APOLOGETICS,
COLLEGE MORAL THEOLOGY, and
COLLEGE SACRAMENTAL THEOLOGY

HENRY REGNERY COMPANY
CHICAGO, 1962

Nihil Obstat

> Francis D. Costa, S.S.S., S.T.D.
> Censor Deputatus

Imprimatur

> ✠ Edward F. Hoban, S.T.D.
> Archiepiscopus-episcopus Clevelandensis
>
> *November 17, 1961*

To my classmates of the
St. Mary's Seminary, Cleveland,
ordination class of 1945
this book is affectionately dedicated

Contents

Preface

BEFORE ascending into heaven, Our Divine Lord commissioned His Church with the words, "Go, ye, teach all nations." He used the term "nation" without qualification. It meant, not only all races of all ages, but also every intellectual level within those races. Spiritual infants and spiritual adults were to be taught the doctrines of revealed truth.

Holy Mother the Church has been faithful to the responsibility entrusted to her. From the earliest days of her existence she has drawn up catechisms for the instruction of spiritual infants. But she has not neglected spiritual adults. The Church has encouraged her gifted theologians to unfold as much as possible the hidden meaning of the articles of faith so that they could be better appreciated and loved.

The Church has always been astonishingly practical. She wants her teachings to be more than mere exercises in speculative theology. And so she has taken measures that they be accommodated to the intelligence of all levels of people. It is sometimes forgotten that the Church has maintained the equivalent of universities to present her doctrines in a learned fashion to learned persons. The famous Catechetical School of Alexandria of the Second Century was really a university dedicated to the scientific explanation of revealed truth. There is scarcely a university in all Europe that was not founded by the Church. The list includes such famous schools as Oxford, Cambridge, Paris, and Padua.

A school is more than ivy covered walls, finely equipped laboratories, and heavy endowments. A school's curriculum is the greatest single factor that determines its real worth. And a curriculum which excludes theology is one that has been badly crippled. It would be a strange museum which exhibited picture frames but no pictures. Regardless of how ornate a frame might be or how precious are the materials from which it is made, the fact remains that it was never intended to be exhibited by itself. It has meaning only when it encloses a picture. The curriculum of a school must be built around truth that is of absolute value. That absolute truth is, of course, revealed truth or its scientific exposition in theology. The school that emphasises the sciences or the humanities to the exclusion of theology is like a person who is filling his museum with frames but no pictures inside those frames.

We welcome Father Alexander's effort in writing this textbook in dogmatic theology. We are gratified that he as a priest of this diocese has enriched the theological literature available for use in Catholic colleges. The present volume completes the series of four college texts that he set as his goal many years ago. We beg God's blessing on his sincere efforts.

✠ JOHN F. WHEALON
Auxiliary Bishop of Cleveland

December 1, 1962

COLLEGE DOGMATIC THEOLOGY

I

Revelation

§ 1. *Revelation is the noblest body of truths that one can study, for its purpose is superior to the purpose of any natural science.*

In apologetics we prove that God has revealed supernatural truths to men. Theology is the scientific explanation of those truths. Theology is indeed a science for it investigates a particular field of learning through its four causes. Aristotle showed that these are material, efficient, formal, and final. The most important of these causes is the last. A thing's final cause is the purpose for which it was made. Without this final cause, an object is simply meaningless. It lacks a reason for existing. We best understand an object when we grasp why it was made. For example, the final cause of a watch is to measure time. If it fails to do this, it is meaningless, regardless of the precious metals out of which it was made.

Everything has a final cause even though it might not be immediately apparent. Sciences are no exception. The higher the goal which a science enables a person to reach the nobler the science. Natural sciences can at best engender the imperfect, natural happiness that alone can be experienced on earth. For example, the goal of medicine is the natural happiness engendered by good health. The power of these sciences to produce happiness for a person ends when he dies. Their goal is very circumscribed.

The goal of revelation is the supernatural, perfect happiness that one experiences by seeing God face to face in heaven. It lasts for all eternity. St. Paul was constrained to describe the intensity of this happiness in negatives. When we evaluate the dignity of the different sciences on the basis of their final causes, theology is in a class by itself. Its superiority to all others is not one of degree but of kind. It is not relatively but absolutely more noble. In fact, it is impossible for any science to exist which would be nobler than theology.

§ 2. *Theology is the noblest of the sciences by reason of its subject matter.*

All sciences deal with truth. There are several types of truth in existence. The one in question here is logical truth. A person possesses this truth when he knows a thing as it is in itself. For example, if a person judges a thing to be a stone and it is in fact a stone, he possesses logical truth.

In the natural order, truths are scaled in value according to the objects which they represent. Some are more valuable than others. Knowledge of the atomic table is more important than knowledge of the composition of a piece of chalk. Principles that apply to being in general are more valuable than principles that apply to material being. Sciences can be scaled in dignity or nobility according to their subject matter.

Theology is nobler than any other science, for its subject matter is the most noble subject possible. It is God considered as He is in Himself, namely, as the beginning and end of the supernatural order. Theology, therefore, explains truths that cannot be discovered by the natural light of reason. They are so lofty and sublime that man could learn of them only by divine revelation. It is superior to theodicy which considers God only insofar as He is the first cause of finite beings but not as He is in Himself. Theodicy is the natural science. On the score of subject matter, the superiority of theology over the natural sciences is absolute, not relative.

§ 3. *Revelation is nobler than any science by reason of the certitude upon which it rests.*[1]

About four centuries before Christ there existed a school of philosophy known as "skepticism." Its founder, Zeno of Elea (d. 420 B.C.) held that man can never attain complete certitude, but must content himself with probable opinions. The science of epistemology refutes skepticism and proves that man can indeed attain certitude.

A person can come to possess truth either through his own investigation or he can receive it on the authority of others. In either case he must have a basis for accepting what he accepts. The firmer the basis, the greater is his certitude. The less possibility of error there is in the basis, the firmer will that basis be. Human sciences were built up by beings having limited intellects capable of discursive reasoning. This type of reasoning requires a series of judgments. Where judgment is, there also is the possibility of error. Human sciences because they were built up by human intelligences rest upon the basis of limited certitude.

When a person accepts the doctrines of revelation, he does so with the assurance that they rest upon the firmest possible basis for certitude, namely, God's attributes of infinite intelligence and truthfulness. Unlike human sciences, in revelation, not only is there no error, but there is no possibility of error. The study of apologetics proves beyond all reasonable doubt that God has confided the contents of revelation to the Roman Catholic Church and that this Church has been commissioned to teach them to all races until the end of time. Apologetics concludes with the proof that the Catholic Church was given the endowment of infallibility in teaching the truths of revelation. Theology is easily superior to any science on the score of the certitude upon which it rests.

§ 4. *Revelation is nobler than any science by reason of the completeness of its contents.*

A science explores a particular field of learning with a view toward finding truths that will further man's pursuit of happiness. For example, men pursue medicine because it offers the prospect of happiness through health; they study art because they hope to experience happiness through beauty. So long as some of the truths belonging to a science are yet undiscovered and uncorrelated, the power of the science to produce happiness is incomplete.

No human science is complete today, nor will it be completed within the foreseeable future. In fact, the deeper scientists delve into a field of knowledge, the better they realize its vastness and how much research needs to be done. When God had completed His revelation to the Apostles, He had given to man every supernatural truth that man needed to reach the supernatural goal assigned to him. The content of God's public revelation need not be supplemented with private revelations.

The fact that God's revelation to mankind was completed at the time of the Apostles does not preclude the possibility that man might better understand those truths by unfolding the meaning implicitly or virtually contained in them. This is precisely the work of a theologian. He does not add new ideas to the content of faith but explains those already there. The first person to do this on an extensive scale was St. Irenaeus (d. 202 A.D.), the Father of Catholic Theology. It has been said that St. Augustine (d. 430 A.D.) was the Church's greatest creative thinker and that St. Thomas Aquinas (d. 1274 A.D.) has been its greatest constructive thinker. In the past nineteen centuries only thirty theologians have been given the title of "Doctor of the Church."

§ 5. *Although theology is one science, it has several subdivisions.*

The first writer to attempt to compose a systematic exposition of Christian doctrine was probably St. Justin Martyr (*ca.* 110-*ca.* 165 A.D.) Another notable attempt was made by Origen (*ca.* 185-*ca.* 255 A.D.) in his *De Principiis.* In the Middle Ages, Peter Lombard (d. 1160) composed his famous *Book of Sentences* which marked a notable advance over the attempts of the ancient writers. The most successful summary of Christian doctrine ever written is, of course, the *Summa Theologica* of St. Thomas Aquinas.

It has been the custom of modern writers to divide theology into several parts. The truths that all are to know by necessity of precept fall into four categories. They are the points of doctrine that enable a person to pray, worship, act, and believe as he should. Specifically, these embrace the substance of the Lord's Prayer, the Sacraments, the Commandments, and the Creed. These categories seem to be a logical basis for dividing theology into four subdivisions. The branch of theology which equips one to pray as he should is *ascetical* theology; one is taught to worship as he should in *sacramental* theology; to act as he should in *moral* theology; to believe as he should in *dogmatic* theology.

Everyone must have a basis for accepting the statements that he takes on faith. This is true of theology as it is in profane studies. This basis must mature as one's intellectual outlook matures. In theology, this basis is provided by the study of *apologetics*—the rational science that establishes the teaching authority of the Roman Catholic Church to be the rule of faith.

NOTES

1. *S.T.,* I, 1, 5.

II

God

§ 1. *It is possible both for God to reveal His existence to man and for man to receive this revelation.*

The term "God" is the name given to an infinitely perfect being. In this section, we do not presume God's existence, nor do we even inquire whether or not He exists. That question will be taken up later. We merely inquire whether or not an infinitely perfect being could make His existence known to man, and whether or not man could receive this truth if revealed to him. If there is any impossibility in these matters, it can be only in the inability of God to reveal or in the inability of man to receive this revelation. There is no difficulty on either score.

Granted that God exists, it would be possible for Him to reveal Himself to man. The reason for this is obvious. Since God is almighty, He can do anything that does not involve a contradiction. There is nothing contradictory to God's nature in an act whereby He reveals Himself to man. This act is in complete harmony with the divine nature.

It is possible for man to receive the truth of God's existence. The fact that man has a limited mind does not mean that he cannot know of the existence of an infinite being. One need not comprehend a thing to know that it exists. Comprehension demands that he know it exhaustively, that is, that he know everything knowable about it; to know that it exists he must merely know it as a being.

The object of man's intellect is being in general. A being is anything that exists. One cannot even think without knowing beings. We know things, not insofar as they are finite or infinite, but insofar as they are beings. The knowability of God, therefore, is on a par with the knowability of creatures or finite things. It must be concluded: Granted the existence of God, there is nothing on His part or on man's part that would prevent Him from being known with certitude.

§ 2. *The Church solemnly teaches that God has revealed His existence to man.*

To know that God exists is not the same as to know that God has explicitly revealed His existence to man. We will see that direct revelation is not the only way to learn of the existence of a truth of religion. The proposition says that even though man could learn of God's existence by other ways besides revelation, God has as a matter of fact revealed Himself to man.

It is not difficult to guess why God revealed Himself to man. Learning this truth without God's help is an abstract and intricate process. There is danger that many cannot follow it. God spared man the intellectual labor and possibility of error involved. By revealing His existence, He made it possible for all men to learn of His existence quickly, completely and without error. That revelation has been repeated throughout the ages by the voice of the Church. From time to time, the Church has drawn up creeds or short summaries of the truths revealed by God to man. The Apostles' Creed dates from the end of the First Century, the Nicene Creed from the Fourth, the Athanasian Creed from the Fifth, and the Tridentine Creed from the Sixteenth Centuries. There are many others. The first point of every one of these creeds is that God exists. Since these creeds are summaries of revealed truth, it follows that the Church teaches that God explicitly revealed His own existence to man.

The rationalists of the Nineteenth Century denied the possibility of all revelation. Needless to say, they did not rest their opinion on a single solid premise. The Council of the Vatican in 1870 officially taught, "If anyone shall have said that it is not possible nor expedient that through divine revelation man be taught about God and the worship to be given Him: let him be anathema." (D-1807) This same truth is stated in other pronouncements made by the Holy See throughout the ages of her existence.

§ 3. *The Church teaches that God revealed His existence through the writings of both the Old and New Testaments.*

The Church has defined that the books of both the Old and New Testaments in all their parts are writings inspired by God. Biblical inspiration means that God was so present to the human authors that they first understood and then were moved to write down in apt words and with infallible truth only what He ordered them to write. This at least implies that God revealed Himself in both testaments. There are numerous explicit passages repeating the same thing.

The Old Testament is rich in explicit statements on God's existence. In Exodus we read, "God replied (to Moses), 'I am who am.' Then He added, 'This is what you shall tell the Israelites: I AM sent to you.' " (Exod. 3:14) "I, the Lord, am your God . . . bestowing mercy down to the thousandth generation, on the children of those who love me and keep my commandments." (Exod. 20:2-6) In Deuteronomy, "Learn then that I, I alone, am God, and there is no god besides me." (Deut. 32:39) In Isaias, "I am the first, and I am the last, and besides me there is no God." (Isa. 44:6) "I am the Lord, and there is none else: there is no God besides me." (Isa. 45:5) Scores of other passages could be quoted.

The New Testament writings are replete with passages revealing the existence of God. Whenever Christ claimed divinity, He was plainly revealing God's existence to all who heard Him. St. Paul's Epistle to the Hebrews opens with "God who at sundry times and in divers manners spoke in times past to the fathers by the prophets, last of all in these days has spoken to us by His Son." (Heb. 1:1) There is no real distinction between God's essence and His attributes. Whenever He reveals one of His attributes such as Omnipotence, Omniscience, Eternity and the rest, He is revealing His own existence. A person who wishes to make a select list of Scripture passages showing that God has revealed Himself to man experiences a certain difficulty which comes, not from having too few passages to choose from, but from having too many.

§ 4. *All peoples have believed in the existence of a deity.*

Scholars have amassed an astonishing amount of information about ancient civilizations. They have ingeniously gleaned and pieced together isolated fragments of information from such sources as extant literature, papyri fragments, clay tablets, and the like. A striking feature of all ancient cultures is the emphasis placed on religion. Hundreds of papyri found at Oxyrhynchus and Tebtunis in Egypt contain references to the deity of the country.[1] The ruins of pagan temples in Greece, Asia Minor, Sicily, Southern Italy, and North Africa bear eloquent testimony to the fact that the construction of religious edifices brought out the best esthetic and architectural efforts of the people. The best preserved Aztec and Inca ruins are of a religious nature. All pagan religions of pre-Christian times had sacrifices as part of the ritual. A sacrifice is an act showing belief in the existence of a deity.

The pagan religions were practically all polytheistic, but it is interesting to note that each land had a "supreme god."[2] It was Jupiter in Rome, Zeus in Greece, Aturn-Ra in Egypt, Anu in Babylon, El or Baal in Assyria, and Auramazda in Persia.

The many errors of the pagans on the nature of the deity do not alter the fact that they believed in its existence. The fact that the Greek philosophers could not work out a clear, cogent proof for God's existence does not mean that they were not convinced that He exists.

The Jews of the Old Testament believed in God, but the clear notion they had of Him came from revelation, as the quotations in the last section prove. These people certainly could not have received this truth from neighboring peoples, for their neighbors were deeply immersed in the grossest polytheism. Even after the Jews learned of the One, True God, the prophets had to work hard to prevent them from falling into polytheism and the worship of Baal and Astarte. The Jews certainly did not learn monotheism from Greek philosophy. Aristotle who came the closest to formulating a proof for the existence of God died in 322 B.C. The Jews were in possession of this truth hundreds of years before Aristotle. Isaias wrote before 500 B.C. and he was by no means the first person inspired to proclaim God's oneness to man.

§ 5. *The existence of God is not self-evident; it must be demonstrated.*[3]

Now, we consider the evidence for the existence of God apart from that which is furnished by revelation. We ask what the role of unaided reason is in investigating this matter. The existence of God is not self-evident. A self-evident truth is one which must be accepted as soon as it is understood. No other idea is needed to clarify it. For example, it is self-evident that the whole is greater than any of its parts. The mind accepts it as soon as it grasps the relationship and meaning of "whole" and of "part." God is an infinitely perfect being. We could study this idea and never find in it a cogent reason for holding that the concept represents a being outside the mind. This is a way of saying that God's existence is not self-evident.

The pagans who accepted the existence of a supreme being did not have intuitive knowledge of this existence. Even though they were not able to formulate a demonstration, a clear, logical proof of God's existence, they were nevertheless vaguely conscious of the principles and premises of a demonstration. They experienced difficulty in placing each premise in its correct relationship to the other premises and thereby warranting a logical conclusion.

The philosophers who tackled the question of a demonstration of God's existence with the use of unaided reason clearly had the intellectual ability that the task demanded. But a study of pagan Greek philosophy—easily the most profound system of thought left by an ancient people—shows that no philosopher succeeded in the task. Anaxagoras (428 B.C.) spoke of the *Nous* or Mind responsible for the order in the universe and Aristotle spoke of the Supreme Being as Pure Act. While their statements coincided with some of the conclusions of the proofs formulated in a later age, they were not conclusions rigidly drawn from premises assembled in one place.

§ 6. *The Church has defined that the existence of God can be demonstrated by reason unaided by revelation.*

In history, there have appeared persons who believed in the existence of God but who denied that His existence could be demonstrated by reason alone. In the first half of the Nineteenth Century, several such errors made their appearance in spite of the fact that St. Thomas' proofs had been used for centuries. In 1870, the Council of the Vatican was constrained to define, "If anyone shall have said that the one true God, our Creator and our Lord, cannot be known with certitude by those things which have been made, by the natural light of reason; let him be anathema." (D-1806)

There are a number of passages in Sacred Scripture revealing that God's existence can be demonstrated from the existence of things in the physical universe. In the Psalms, we read, "The heavens declare the glory of God, and the firmament proclaims his handiwork." (Ps. 18:2) In Wisdom we read, "For all men were by nature foolish who were in ignorance of God, and who from the good things seen did not succeed in knowing him who is, and from studying the works did not discern the artisan." (Wisdom 13:1) In Romans, "For God has manifested it to them. For since the creation of the world his invisible attributes are clearly seen—his everlasting power also and divinity—being understood through the things that are made." (Rom. 1:20)

There is clear evidence in ancient Christian literature that the Fathers held that God's existence could be known even by the natural light of reason, but this does not mean that all of them formulated demonstrations. The first attempt at a rational demonstration of God's unity in Christian literature appears in the *Apology* of Athenagoras composed about 177 A.D. The proofs for which St. Augustine (d. 430 A.D.) is famous are the metaphysical and the teleological ones which are the fourth and fifth ways in St. Thomas' set, namely, the proofs from degrees of perfection and from the design in the universe.

§ 7. *There are five separate proofs for the existence of God from reason unaided by revelation.*

A proof may be described as the systematic presentation of irrefutable evidence offered in support of a conclusion. The nature of the conclusion will be dictated by the nature of the evidence. A historical conclusion must be based on historical evidence, a scientific conclusion on scientific evidence, a philosophical conclusion on philosophical evidence. It is illogical to offer or to demand scientific evidence for a philosophical conclusion. A proof must have no defects. It must be complete and universally valid. The fact that many persons will not accept it does not necessarily mean that it is invalid. Just as a conclusion is as valid as the evidence for it, so a denial is as valid as the evidence for it.

In the pages that follow, we present five separate and complete philosophical proofs for the existence of God. They are not five phases of one proof, nor does one strengthen the other objectively. Each is in addition to the other so that if there was only one, it alone would be sufficient to prove that God exists. They are the five famous proofs worked out by St. Thomas Aquinas in his *Summa Theologica*.[4]

Philosophy is the branch of human learning which has the "tools" capable of tackling the problem of God's existence by unaided reason. God is the ultimate cause of all created being. Philosophy deals with ultimate causes. Material science is not equipped to give a cogent answer to the question, for material science deals with proximate causes. One can no more answer this inquiry with the principles of science than the sociologist can solve the problems of nuclear physics with the principles of sociology. At times, scientists have tackled the question of God's existence with the principles of science. Their shaky opinions cannot be called "proofs" in any sense of the term. Students have been quick to notice glaring defects in their premises. The result has sometimes been confusion and doubt in a matter in which there need not be even the slightest trace of error, confusion, or doubt.

§ 8. *An understanding of the principles of identity, contradiction, and causality is essential for an understanding of the five proofs for the existence of God.*

The principles listed in the proposition pertain to being in general, that is, to things regardless of whether they are material or non-material, finite or infinite. They are, in fact, self-evident. (1) The principle of identity means that a thing must be itself. This is the most fundamental principle of being and it is clearly self-evident. Chaos would obviously result if anyone denied it and then tried to act according to his denial. (2) The principle of contradiction means that it is impossible for a thing to exist and not to exist at the same time. There is no such thing as a half-way mark between being and non-being, between existence and non-existence. The two are so diametrically opposed to each other that if one is actual the other cannot be actual. (3) The principle of causality means that every effect must have a cause. This is evident from the nature of a cause and of an effect. An effect is something produced by an external cause. Cause and effect are related terms. The idea of one necessarily connotes the idea of the other.

The principles just considered are the ones used to work out the philosophical proofs for the existence of God. While they are self-evident, we cannot conclude that the proofs are self-evident. On the other hand, if one admits the validity of these principles, it is a comparatively easy task to formulate the proofs. Any attack on the proofs is doomed to failure unless it destroys the validity of these principles. And one proves their validity in the very act of trying to destroy them, for rational, coherent thought rests upon them. The alternative to this is to deny the reality of all truth as the sophists and skeptics of Ancient Greece did.

§ 9. *The proof from motion starts with the observation that there is motion in the universe: it concludes to the existence of a first unmoved mover who is God.*

The six premises of this section must not be considered isolated from each other. They are links in a chain supporting the final conclusion. The student must pay careful attention as to how the premises fit together. Each must be considered in its proper place in the proof. (1) The proof from motion starts with the observation that there are things which move in the world about us. Birds fly, a man walks, a leaf falls to the ground, a meteorite hurtles through space. There are untold billions of examples which could be used. (2) But by "motion" we must understand more than movement from place to place. It is better described as the progressive acquiring of a perfection. An object in motion is acquiring something which it did not have. It is unfolding a capability. A tree growing, a man learning, a thing aging, are also examples of things in motion, for they are obviously acquiring what they did not have. (3) An object cannot move and be at rest at the same time and in the same respect, for rest is the absence of motion and motion is the absence of rest. (4) If an object now in motion was once at rest, it received motion from an external source. Since it was at rest, it could not give itself what it did not have. (5) A series of subordinated movers exhibits "received" motion. Lengthening this series does not account for the initial presence of motion. (6) A mover has either received or unreceived perfection. There is no third possibility. The mover that first gave motion can not have had received motion, for then it would be only a link in the series. The only remaining possibility is that this mover is outside the series and has "unreceived" perfection. He is the First Mover. Since this being has unreceived being, he never had a beginning. Since he never had a beginning, he always was. Since he always was, he is necessarily eternal. If he is necessarily eternal, he is infinite. If he is an infinite being, He is God. Therefore, the First Mover unmoved is God.

§ 10. *The proof from causality starts with the observation that there are things which are effects of causes; it concludes to the existence of a first cause uncaused, who is God.*

(1) The starting point of the second proof for the existence of God is the fact that there are things in the world which are evidently the products of efficient causes. In other words, they were made. Only one example is needed to provide the starting point we need. Myriads of examples could be cited. A building,

an auto, a book, a watch, an airplane, a suit, and many others fit into this category. (2) The product or effect used as the starting point for this argument evidently did not cause itself, for a cause is distinct from its effect. A thing must exist before it can act. (3) If a cause was itself an effect, then it was in turn caused by a previously existing cause. The ability of this intermediary cause to bring about an effect is evidently a received ability. And a series of sub-ordinated causes retains its "received" character regardless of how far into the past it extends. The received character of the series shows that the power to bring about an effect was initially communicated to the series from a source or cause distinct from it. (4) In order to be truly outside the series of causes with received ability, the cause that first conferred the power to bring about effects must be an Uncaused Cause, for causes have either received or unreceived ability. There is no third possibility. Since it never had a beginning, it always existed. Since it always existed, it is necessarily eternal. Since it is necessarily eternal, it is infinite. An infinite being is God. Therefore, the First Cause Uncaused is God.

The student is urged to place this proof side by side with the proof from motion to notice how the features peculiar to each of them make for two distinct proofs.

§ 11. *The proof from contingency starts with the observation that there exist things which need not exist; it concludes that there is a necessarily existent being.*

The same object can be used as the starting point for several proofs, but each proof looks at the object from a different point of view. The student should note carefully the different starting points of the proofs from causality and contingency. (1) There are things in the world about us which do indeed exist, but they need not exist. The millions of living plants and animals belong to this class of things. They were born; they live now; they will cease to exist. Generation and corruption are sure signs of their instability. (2) If there was a time when it did not exist, it is not necessary for an object to exist. For example, we can readily show when a certain person or animal was born or when a tree started to grow. Biologists have estimated the length of time that life has been on earth. (3) Things which now exist but which did not exist at one time clearly did not give existence to themselves. It is absurd to say that a thing can act before it exists. Multiplying the number of beings with received existence does not rid the whole series of its received status. (4) Things having a received existence are evidently dependent on an external source for this perfection. They have contingent existence. (5) Where could contingent beings have derived their existence? Only from a being who does not have a received existence, that is, from one who is not dependent on another being. This being must have unreceived or independent existence. He is necessarily existent. Since he derived his existence from no one, he had no beginning. Since he had no beginning, he always was. Since he always was, he is necessarily eternal. Since he is necessarily eternal, he is infinite. And an infinite being is God. Therefore, God is the necessarily existing being.

§ 12. *The proof from degrees of perfection starts with the observation that some things have limited perfection; it concludes to the existence of an unlimitedly perfect being, who is God.*

(1) There are individual objects in the world about us that exhibit the perfections of truth, goodness, life, beauty, and so forth. We see that these objects have limited degrees of these perfections. A flower, for example, has limited beauty, for there are many beautiful things besides this flower. A tree has limited life, for there are many living things besides this tree. The degree of perfection that a particular object has is limited by the degree of the same perfection that other objects have or

might have. (2) The perfections listed above are unlimited in themselves. All the beautiful objects of the past, present, and future do not exhaust the perfection of beauty. If they did, then no other beautiful object could exist in the realm of possibility. Logic prevents one from accepting any other conclusion. (3) Since there can be objects with limited perfection over and above those now in existence, it follows that the source of all perfection is not a being with limited perfection. Individual creatures taken singly or in aggregate can only have perfection to a limited degree. They, therefore, are not the source of the perfection which they exhibit. (4) Since limited beings are not the source of their perfection, we must conclude that this source is a being over and above the created universe. It is a being having unlimited perfection. A being cannot be a mixture of limited and unlimited perfection, for that is a contradiction. The being having unlimited perfection must be unlimited in every perfection such as truth, goodness, beauty, life, or so forth. This infinitely perfect being is only another name for God. Therefore, God exists.

§ 13. *The proof from design starts with the observation that there are things which serve a purpose; it concludes that there must be a being with unacquired intelligence.*

The starting point of this proof for the existence of God is that there are material things in the world about us that serve a purpose. It is not necessary to show the purposefulness of everything that exists. One bona-fide example of purposefulness would be sufficient, although thousands could be cited. Birds have wings to fly; fish have gills to breathe; plants have roots to take in food and moisture; man has eyes to see.

Purposefulness is achieved in a thing by its parts being fitted together in a proper way. If the delicate arrangement of parts is wrecked, the whole thing is useless. The designer of a purposeful object must first conceive the goal of the object and then go about fitting the parts together so that this goal will be attained.

Before the process of designing the object is begun, the purpose is clearly non-material. And so, at that stage, it can be conceived only by a non-material thinking power or intelligence. Material objects cannot design themselves, for they would have to exist before they could act and furthermore only non-material thinking powers can design. A material object which exhibits design and purposefulness evidently received it from an external power that could act intelligently.

The external intelligence which designs a purposeful object has either acquired or unacquired intelligence. There is no intermediary between acquired and unacquired intelligence. The acquired character of intelligence does not explain the initial presence of intelligence. There must exist a being who is unacquired intelligence and whom we call God. Therefore, God exists.

§ 14. *God's essence and his existence are identically the same.*

Essence is that which makes a thing what it is. It gives an object its special nature, its peculiar set of properties, and sets it apart from other classes of things. For example, a tree is different from an animal because its essence is different and not because it has a different size and shape. The properties of both objects are different because properties necessarily flow from essences. Taken by itself, an essence is only in the realm of possibility. Every material or non-material creature must be in the realm of possibility before it can exist in the realm of actuality. The vast majority of individual essences will forever remain in the realm of mere possibility.

An essence is lifted out of the realm of possibility into that of actuality when it is combined with the perfection known as existence. Every actual creature is a compound of essence and existence regardless of its material or non-material character.

And every compound of essence and existence implies the pre-existence of a compounding agent who annexed the latter to the former. Essence and existence cannot combine themselves, for this implies action and an essence must have existence before it can act.

We have proved that God is in the realm of actuality. He indeed has essence and existence. The conclusion to each of the five ways of St. Thomas was that no agent could have existed before God, for He is necessarily eternal. Therefore, there was no previously existing agent that could have made the combination of essence and existence in God. These two things are in God but not in combination. The two must be one and the same. A creature is an essence with existence. In God, however, essence is existence. It is His nature to exist.

§ 15. *God is an infinitely perfect being.*

The truth that God is an infinitely perfect being is contained in the creeds drawn up by or authorized by the Church since ancient times. Her perfectly uniform teaching is in sharp contrast to the confusion of pagan philosophers on the subject. We read in Sacred Scripture that God revealed His infinite perfection in the Old Testament. "O Lord God, Creator of all things, dreadful and strong, just and merciful, who alone art the good King, who alone art gracious, who alone are just, and almighty, and eternal." (2 Mach. 1:24-25) Just as a prism breaks a single beam of light into a whole spectrum of color, so this passage shows that the many attributes are only different ways of saying that God is infinitely perfect.

Reason unaided by revelation laboriously but certainly arrives at the same conclusion set forth in the proposition. All five proofs for God's existence proceed from the existence of a received perfection to the existence of an unreceived perfection. These perfections are not abstract notions but objective realities. Motion or thought do not exist by themselves. It is always a *being* which moves or which thinks. Received perfection is always a being, for unless it have being it cannot exist. We saw that received being necessitates the existence of one with unreceived being. The notion of the "unreceived" was brought out by the adjectives "First, Necessary, Unlimited, and Unacquired." An unreceived being is an unlimited being; an unlimited being is an infinite being. Perfection cannot exist apart from being and being cannot exist apart from perfection. When we say that God is an infinite being, we must infer that He has all the perfection that being can have. It is contradictory to say that a being can be finite and infinite. It is equally contradictory for a perfection to be finite and infinite. Since God is an infinite being, He must be an infinitely perfect being. This conclusion of reason is in complete harmony with the revelation made by God to man.

§ 16. *There can be only one God.*

Consider the uniqueness of God. The term "unique" is sometimes used to describe a rare or an unusual object. In its technical sense a being is "unique" when only one of its kind is possible and, therefore, applied to God it means that it is absolutely impossible for there to be two Gods. When the creeds drawn up by the authority of the Church or when passages in Sacred Scripture speak of "One God," the term "one" must be interpreted in the sense of unique as set forth here. The justification for this interpretation lies in the fact that these sources use the term "one" in combination with "infinite" or its equivalent.

The content of revelation on God's uniqueness needs no corroboration from unaided reason, but reason on its own arrives at the same conclusion. In the last consideration we saw that God is an infinitely perfect being. The term "infinite perfection" means a great deal more than the sum-total of all *actually existing* finite perfection. It means the actual possession of all *possible* perfection. An infinite being knows of no limitation in any respect. If there were two Gods then neither of them could have all possible perfection, for what one would have the other would not have and would clearly be limited by what it lacked. In other words, the perfection that one of the "gods" possessed would necessarily be subtracted from the perfection of the other, thereby leaving the latter with less than all possible perfection.

In ancient times, the Manicheans held that there are two supreme principles in existence, namely, one is that of good and the other is that of evil. Pressed to its logical conclusion, this opinion would have one hold that there are two supreme beings or "gods." It was based on an erroneous notion of the nature of God and a false notion of the meaning of evil. Many writers, especially St. Augustine, were quick to point out its glaring inconsistencies. The Church condemned it in its original form and in its rejuvenated form known as Albigensianism. (D-428-30)

§ 17. *God is a spirit devoid of composition of any kind.*

This proposition contains two notions. It states that God is a spirit and that He is devoid of composition. There are spirits in existence which are not devoid of composition, for composition does not necessarily imply matter in a thing's makeup. In 1870, the Vatican Council taught, "The ... Church believes and confesses that there is one, true, living God ... who, although He is one, singular, *altogether simple* and unchangeable spiritual substance, must be proclaimed distinct in reality and essence from the world." (D-1782) God's spiritual nature was impressed upon the minds of the Jews in the Old Dispensation by the repeated prohibitions against any attempt to fashion any image whatsoever as a likeness of Him. (Lev. 26:1; Deut. 5:8)

God's spiritual nature flows from the fact that He is infinitely perfect. A being that has all possible perfection has no limits. It cannot be divided, for there is no such thing as a part of infinity. An obvious feature of material things is that they can be divided into parts. If they have parts they can be measured. If they can be measured they are not infinite. But since God is infinite, He cannot have parts and so He must be a spirit.

The proposition states that God is a special spirit, namely, one who lacks all composition. A spirit such as an angel or a soul does have composition, for it is a compound of essence and existence. Such a compound implies the existence of a previously existing compounding agent. We proved that there is absolutely nothing prior to God which could have united essence and existence. In Him, the two things are identically the same. In Him, there is not essence with existence as is the case with creatures. In God, His essence is His existence.

§ 18. *God is absolutely immutable; there is no possibility of change in him.*

Immutability in God simply means that He cannot undergo change of any kind. He cannot gain or lose anything. God's complete unchangeableness was taught by the Church on many occasions. In 649 A.D. the Council of the Lateran defined, "If anyone does not confess properly and truly in accord with the holy fathers that . . . God is . . . *immutable* . . . let him be condemned." (D-254) An Old Testament passage referring to this truth reads as follows, "Of old you established the earth, and the heavens are the work of your hands. They shall perish, but you remain though all of them grow old like a garment. Like clothing you change them, and they are changed, but you are the same, and your years have no end." (Ps. 101:26-28)

Reason unaided by revelation shows that God must be immutable. It flows from the fact that He is infinite in every respect. It was seen that God is all possible perfection. Now for

God to change, He must either gain or lose in the process. And both of these are clear signs of imperfection. If He gained in the change, it would show imperfection in the past, for there clearly was room for improvement. If He lost in the change, it would show imperfection in the future. God cannot gain, for He already is all possible perfection. He cannot lose, for there are no parts in an infinitely perfect being. If He could lose any perfection, He would have to lose all of His perfection, and this is obviously impossible, for it is His nature to exist.

§ 19. *God is necessarily eternal, for an infinite being can have no beginning nor end.*

Eternity is used to describe a being that has no beginning nor end. Complete accuracy demands that God be said to be "necessarily" eternal, for the term "necessarily" adds a new and important notion to the discussion. The Fourth Lateran Council in 1215 A.D. defined against the Albigensians, "We believe and we confess simply that the true God is ... eternal." (D-428) There are a number of Scriptural passages referring to God's eternity. One such quotation reads, "Before the mountains were begotten and the earth and the world brought forth, from everlasting to everlasting you are God." (Ps. 89:2)

All five proofs for the existence of God show that He is a being with unreceived perfection. From the fact that God is unreceived perfection it was concluded that He is infinite in every respect. A being that is infinite must be necessarily eternal and as such it must have no beginning and no end. God's eternity must not be conceived as an endless series of centuries, for this implies a past and a future. God has no past or future, for the passage of time implies change and God is changeless. With Him, everything is the present. This was nicely brought out in the Old Testament passage where it is recorded that God described Himself to Moses by saying, "I am who am." (Exod. 3:14)

Ancient philosophers raised the interesting question: Whether or not the world could be eternal. It is certainly true that from all eternity God had the power to create the world. If God did use this power from all eternity, the world could be said to be eternal. But even in this case, the world would still be a contingent being having a received existence. It would in no sense have the same type of eternity that God has. He has unreceived existence. This is precisely why the proposition describes Him as being necessarily, not contingently, eternal.

§ 20. *God is omnipotent, that is, He can confer actual existence on anything that now can only possibly exist.*

In 543 A.D. Pope Vigilius approved a number of condemnations of Origenist opinions. One of the statements he approved reads, "If anyone says or holds that the power of God is limited, and that He has accomplished as much as He has comprehended: let him be anathema." (D-210) Statements affirming the omnipotence of God have been made on scores of occasions by the Holy See. Sacred Scripture has many passages on the same theme. "I am God the Almighty. Walk in my presence and be perfect." (Gen. 17:1) Those passages that tell us that God created the universe implicitly tell us that He is omnipotent, for only an infinitely powerful being can create.

Omnipotence simply means that there is nothing which is possible that God cannot make actual. He can confer the perfection of existence on any nature. This is merely a refinement of the already established fact that God is infinitely perfect and must remain so.

In this discussion, it is well that the student grasp the ideas represented by the words. There are some things that God cannot do simply because the capability to do them represents imperfection, not perfection. God, for example, could not create another God, for He cannot exhaust His infinite power. He cannot destroy Himself nor make Himself less than He actually is, for it is His nature to exist as an infinitely perfect being. He cannot commit sin, for sin is the absence of goodness or perfection. God cannot make nothingness, that is, the absence of being, for creation is a positive act looking to a positive effect. A contradictory thing such as a squared circle is nothingness. It cannot be made actual for it is not possible. The inability to give actual existence to contradictory things is in no way a limitation of God's power.

§ 21. *God is omniscient, that is, He knows all things past, present, future, and possible.*

The omniscience of God was repeated by the Church at the Vatican Council in these words, "God protects and governs by His providence all things which He created, reaching from end to end mightily and ordering all things sweetly. For all things are naked and open to His eyes, even those which by the free action of creatures are in the future." (D-1784) In the Old Testament, we read that God is the one who "tells the number of the stars; he calls each by name. Great is our Lord, and mighty in power; to his wisdom there is no limit." (Ps. 146:4-5) The student should compare these clear statements with the vague, halting conclusions of the pagan philosophers on God's nature and attributes.

God's omniscience can be proved by reason even without revelation. The proof for God's existence from design showed that God is unacquired intelligence. His power to know, His intellect, is infinitely perfect. It cannot be improved upon. He knows all things knowable. These fall into four categories: all things past, present, future, and possible. For every one thing that is lifted out of the realm of the possible into that of the actual, there are millions of things that will always remain in the realm of the possible. God knows everything possible because He knows Himself perfectly.

God's knowledge would be imperfect if He could lose sight

of even the smallest possible thing. When humans think, they can be conscious of only one thing or detail at a time. This is impossible with God. He knows every actual or possible object with the same complete clarity and utter exhaustiveness that He could give it if it were the only thing in existence. And he knows all these things, not consecutively, but at once. The Scripture passages on God's omniscience are in reality only feeble understatements accommodated to man's feeble powers of comprehension.

§ 22. *God is omnipresent, that is, all of God is everywhere at once.*

The omnipresence or immensity of God appears in official documents drawn up under the authority of the Church as early as the Athanasian Creed formulated in the Fifth Century. Sacred Scripture beautifully proclaims it, "Am I, think ye, a God at hand, saith the Lord, and not a God afar off? Shall a man be hid in secret places and I not see him, saith the Lord? Do not I fill heaven and earth, saith the Lord?" (Jer. 23:23-24) Again, "Where can I go from your spirit? From your presence where can I flee? If I go up to the heavens, you are there; if I sink to the nether world, you are present there. If I take the wings of the dawn, if I settle at the farthest limits of the sea, even there your hand shall guide me, and your right hand hold me fast." (Ps. 138:7-10) We recall how St. John Chrysostom proclaimed God's omnipresence to those who sent him into exile in the Caucasus. He told them that they could separate him from friends but could never separate him from the omnipresent God.

God is omnipresent simply because He is an infinite being. In trying to grasp this divine attribute, we must not try to imagine God in terms of material bigness or size. Since God is a spirit, He does not occupy space, but this does not prevent Him from being everywhere. The fact that He is non-material indicates that He has no parts and so is indivisible. We cannot say that one part of God is in one place while part of Him is in another.

God cannot move from place to place, for motion implies change and change implies imperfection. The only acceptable conclusion to the premises set down above is that all of God is everywhere at once. There is some danger that the student will try to imagine God's omnipresence in terms of things with which he is familiar. It is better for him to try to grasp the meaning of the idea divorced from material parallels and examples.

§ 23. *Atheism is the error which denies the existence of a personal God.*

A person is a substance endowed with intellect and free will. Keep in mind that a substance is anything that exists by itself. God is clearly a substance, for He exists by Himself and of Himself. Theism and atheism are contradictory positions. If one holds one position, he must reject the other. No compromise is possible between them. "If anyone shall have denied the one true God, Creator and Lord of visible and invisible things: let him be anathema." (D-1801) In every statement by which the Church proclaimed God's existence, she condemns atheism. Sacred Scripture says "The fool says in his heart 'There is no God.'" (Ps. 13:1)

The five ways by which St. Thomas demonstrated God's existence clearly established that God is infinitely intelligent and infinitely powerful. A personal God does and must exist. So long as those five proofs remain valid, atheism is doomed as a position tenable on philosophical grounds. We shall not allow atheists to ignore these proofs and then try to construct other seemingly plausible arguments against God's existence. Attacks on St. Thomas' proofs necessitate attacks on the principles he used in constructing them, namely, the principles of identity, contradiction and causality. We saw that these principles are self-evident. One proves their validity in the very act of denying them. They cannot be denied without at the same time denying all existence and the validity of all knowledge. Some attacks consist of just such denials. This is indeed a strange position to take in view of the fact that those who hold it evidently think that they possess valid knowledge. Many attacks on St. Thomas' five ways are really denials that man can acquire certitude, and as such they pertain to the field of epistemology, not theology or theodicy.

§ 24. *Agnosticism and pantheism are variations of atheism.*

The Church has anathematized anyone holding either of the positions named in the proposition. Agnosticism is the error that denies that man can ever acquire certain knowledge of God's existence. Those who profess it are quick to state that they do not deny God's existence, but merely hold that man must ever be ignorant of God's existence. But there is no middle position between theism or atheism. The proofs for God's existence are either valid or invalid. If one does not accept them, he equivalently rejects them. When agnostics equivalently reject those proofs, they do exactly what atheists do. They merit the same label. It will not do to try to find shelter in an imaginary third position of affected ignorance.

Pantheism is the error which holds that everything in existence is God. Against it the Vatican Council stated, "If anyone shall say that the one and the same thing is the substance or essence of God and of all things: let him be anathema." (D-1803) Pantheism is atheism because it denies the existence of a personal God. It is shot through with a number of contradictions. Pantheists are either ignorant of St. Thomas' five proofs or they deliberately blind themselves to their probative force. In each proof, it was shown that a series of received perfections does not account for the initial presence of this perfection.

There is no intermediary between a received and an unreceived perfection. There must exist a Being Who is unreceived or infinite perfection, and Whom we call God. God as the cause of all perfection must be distinct from the effects He has caused. Cause and effect are on essentially different planes. Pantheism says that the received is the same as the unreceived, the finite is the same as the infinite, the clearly material is the same as the patently spiritual. In short, pantheism would have us believe that both sides of a contradiction are essentially the same. This is repugnant to common sense.

§ 25. *Most atheists are impelled by moral motives rather than by intellectual reasons to deny the existence of God.*

There is a logical connection between premises and conclusion, but there is no logical connection between motive and opinion. While there is no logical reason why one should hold atheism, there can be illogical motives. When a person refuses to accept the True God as the Lord of the universe, he must substitute a false god in His place. This false god is the individual himself. He proceeds to call into being an imaginary universe of which he is the center and in which his will is supreme. Within this little universe, the creature recognizes no other law, no other sovereign higher than himself. His will must always be done, and his desires must never be frustrated.

This artificial universe obviously conflicts with the true universe where the will of the True God is supreme. The two cannot coexist. What must be done? The individual decrees that his private universe must be preserved and the other must be destroyed. The True God cannot literally be destroyed, and so, the atheist sets about to destroy Him figuratively. He does this by trying to ignore God so completely that *he lives as though there is no God.* He thereby becomes a practical atheist.

But notice that he has not arrived at this state of affairs by intellectual reasoning. He has driven himself into this impos-

sible position by moral motives. He knows that the thought of
God the supreme judge would be disturbing to his life addicted
to immoral practices. He cannot have God and immorality at
the same time. He makes a choice. He thinks he can quiet his
conscience by convincing himself that he has nothing to fear
in the way of retribution. How could he do this? By convincing himself that there is no God. Agnosticism and pantheism
are feeble efforts at trying to give plausibility to his impossible
position.

NOTES

1. Grenfell-Hunt, *Select Payri* (Cambridge: Harvard University Press, 1931).
2. *Studies in Comparative Religion,* 5 vols. (London: Catholic Truth Society, 1925).
3. *S.T.*, I, 2, 1.
4. *S.T.*, I, 2, 3.

III

The Blessed Trinity

§ 1. *The Church solemnly teaches that in God there is One Nature in Three Persons.*

God's revelation to man was delivered in both written and spoken form, namely, Sacred Scripture and Sacred Tradition. These fonts were confided to Holy Mother Church as is cogently proved in apologetics. The private interpretation of the Bible as advocated by Luther has caused confusion and error. We need the shelter of the Church's teaching authority. And the Church has been most solicitous in clearly stating the doctrines of faith that must be accepted by all.

From all eternity there were certain truths so profound that they were known to God alone. No man or angel could discover them by his own unaided powers. They are called supernatural truths or mysteries. Created intellects could learn of their existence only by divine revelation. The most profound of these truths is the Blessed Trinity, that is, the truth that in God there is one Nature in three Persons. In the fullness of time, God confided this truth to His Church and the Church has proclaimed it to all nations.

The dogma of the Blessed Trinity appears in the very beginning of the Apostles' Creed drawn up about 100 A.D. and still used today. Every Creed since the first one has repeated it. The first general council, the Council of Nicea (325 A.D.), was preoccupied with Arian attacks on it. Another general council repeated the dogma in explicit language. In 553 A.D. the Council of Constantinople defined, "If anyone does not confess that there is one nature or substance of the Father and of the Son and of the Holy Spirit, and one power and one might, and that the Trinity is consubstantial, one Godhead being worshipped in three subsistences or persons, let such a one be anathema." (D-213)

§ 2. *The existence of the Blessed Trinity was not formally revealed to the people of the Old Dispensation.*

There is good reason why God did not reveal the existence of the Blessed Trinity to the people of the Old Law. There are a number of indications in God's dealings with men showing that He accommodated His revelation to the ability of the people to receive it profitably. We read in the New Testament that the people often had to be prepared for a particular revelation. An examination of conditions among the Jews of the Old Testament seems to warrant the conclusion that they were not yet prepared to be told about the Blessed Trinity.

When God chose to reveal Himself to the Jews about 1100 B.C. the whole world was immersed in polytheism. The Jews were ringed with peoples practicing idolatry. These peoples fashioned gods of stone, metal, and wood and placed them in truly magnificent temples. This made a great impression on the Jews. But God set the Jews apart and revealed to them a religion of monotheism. It was no easy matter to get them to accept belief in One God who could not be seen because He was a pure Spirit. The doctrine of the One, True God was the cornerstone of Judaism. The Jews did not easily get used to this truth and there was always danger of their lapsing into idolatry. While the Jews were still getting used to the idea of One God, it was of little use to reveal to them the existence of three Persons in God and so God withheld this truth from them.

A number of the Fathers held that certain Old Testament passages hinted at the Trinity. These are the ones usually quoted: "Let us make mankind in our own image and like-ness." (Gen. 1:26) "Indeed! the man has become like one of us." (Gen. 3:22) "Let us go down, and there confuse their language." (Gen. 11:7) A comparison between these passages and those that will now be quoted and discussed shows that the Old Testament passages are indeed vague hints of the existence of the Trinity.

§ 3. *A first gospel passage revealing the existence of Three Persons in One God is Luke 1:35.*[1]

The passage we examine here records the episode in which the Blessed Virgin Mary is told that she is to be the Mother of Jesus Christ. The Archangel Gabriel said to her, "The Holy Spirit shall come upon thee and the power of the Most High shall overshadow thee; and therefore the Holy One to be born shall be called the Son of God." (Luke 1:35) Several things are to be noticed about this passage. (1) This passage refers to God, for it contains reference to the "Most High" and to "God." To the Jews, these two terms were synonymous. Given the Old Testament revelation on God, the passage refers to a single divine Nature. (2) Careful examination shows that the quoted text tells us that there are three distinct Persons in God. It opens by telling us of the Holy Spirit and then goes on to say that the Holy One is the Son of God. The passage shows that the Holy Spirit is distinct from the Son of God. The use of the term "Son of God" clearly presupposes the existence of a "Father," who is distinct from the Son. (3) The passage infers the existence of a Unity and of a Trinity. The "One" and the "Three" can not refer to the same thing in the same way, for that would be a contradiction. Since there can be no contradictions in Sacred Scripture, the "One" refers to God's Nature; and the "Three" refers to the number of Persons in God.

Some authors question the conclusion that the Gospel passage discussed here pertains to the Blessed Trinity. But there are enough who do hold that it does warrant the conclusion that it is a solidly probable interpretation. The proof of God's revelation of the Trinity does not rest solely on this passage or solely on those examined in this chapter. One not discussed here is the last verse of St. Paul's *Second Epistle to the Corinthians*. It reads, "The grace of our Lord Jesus Christ, and the charity of God, and the fellowship of the Holy Spirit be with you all." (II Cor. 13-13)

§ 4. *A second gospel passage revealing the existence of Three Persons in One God is John 14:16.*

Jesus Christ revealed the existence of the Blessed Trinity on many occasions throughout His public ministry. The words He used on some of those occasions are contained in the Gospels. The meaning of individual passages on the Trinity must not be interpreted isolated from the others. They are like one image captured in many mirrors.

At the Last Supper, Christ spoke these words of comfort to the Apostles, "I will ask the Father and He will give you another Advocate to dwell with you forever, the Spirit of truth." (John 14:16) (1) This passage speaks of God. It must be seen in the light of the many texts scattered throughout the Gospels in which Christ explicitly claims divinity, saying that He is God the Son. Christ ties those texts into this one by His use of the first person singular "I." (2) In the passage we are considering, there is a clear distinction of the Three Persons of the Blessed Trinity. Christ says, "I will ask the Father." On many other occasions, He uses the expression "My Father." He thereby indicates that He Himself is the Son. The two are not the same. They must be distinct. Christ then says "And He (the Father) will give you another Advocate." The Father and the Advocate are clearly not the same Person. They too are distinct. All that remains is for Christ to bring out the distinction between Himself and the Advocate. He does this by saying that the Father will give "another Advocate," meaning an Advocate other than Christ Himself. The passage closes by Christ naming Who the new Advocate is. It is the "Spirit of Truth" or the Holy Spirit.

§ 5. *A third gospel passage revealing the existence of Three Persons in One God is Matthew 28:19.*[2]

The passages we have selected to prove the existence of the Blessed Trinity span the whole earthly life of Jesus Christ. The Annunciation marked its beginning; the Ascension marked its end. The Archangel revealed that there are Three Persons in God on the first occasion; Christ Himself revealed it on the last one.

When Christ was about to ascend into heaven, He commissioned the Apostles with the words; "Go, therefore, and make disciples of all nations, baptizing them in the name of the Father, and of the Son, and of the Holy Spirit." (Matt. 28:19) (1) There is evidence throughout the Gospels showing that the proper nouns used in this passage refer to God. The passage shows that the Persons mentioned are a unity. But in order for a thing to be a unity, it must have one nature. The passage uses the phrase "in the name of." Notice that the term "name" is singular in number. And yet it refers to all Three Persons in exactly the same way. It denotes that the term "name" refers to one Nature. (2) The proper terms "Father," "Son," and "Holy Spirit" are set down in parallel fashion. The use of the conjunction "and" together with the article in the genitive singular case in the Greek proves that the three names refer to three distinct things which must not be confounded in the mind of the reader. (3) The possessive singular used with each of the Persons refers back to the singular noun "name." The conclusion is that the singular nature of God pertains to each of the Persons equally. It is difficult to imagine a briefer yet clearer statement on the Blessed Trinity than the passage of St. Matthew's Gospel which we have just examined.

§ 6. *In Trinitarian discussions, the term "Father" refers to the first Person of the Blessed Trinity and not to the Godhead as such.*

As far back as the Ante-Nicene age, we find that people sometimes used the term "Father" as meaning the Godhead. An example of this usage is the modern expression "The Fatherhood of God and the brotherhood of man." While this expression is perfectly acceptable in certain contexts, it must not be so exclusively interpreted as to make it always synonymous with the Godhead, thereby leaving no room for distinct Persons in the Trinity. Our task here is to show that the term is the name given to the first of the distinct Persons.

An article in the Creed of the Council of Toledo drawn up in 447 A.D. and approved by the Church reads, "If anyone says that God the Father is the same Person as the Son or the Paraclete, let him be anathema." (D-22) The Athanasian Creed of the Fifth Century says " . . . there is one Person of the Father, another of the Son, and another of the Holy Spirit." (D-39) The Church brands as heresy the interpretation of "Father" in a way that would deny the existence of other Persons of the Trinity.

Sacred Scripture reveals the distinction between God the Father and God the Son. Christ often said "My Father, Who is in heaven," thereby distinguishing Himself from the Father. St. Peter wrote, "For he (Jesus) received from God the Father honor and glory, when from out the majestic glory a voice came down to him, speaking thus, 'This is my beloved Son.' " (II Peter 1:17) St. Paul wrote, "Blessed be the God and Father

of Our Lord Jesus Christ." (II Cor. 1:3) And again in writing
to the Ephesians he said, "I bend my knees to the Father of
Our Lord Jesus Christ." (Eph. 3:14) Early heresies occasioned
a tremendous amount of writing on the Trinity. Scores of men
who were both brilliant writers and first class thinkers busied
themselves with explaining the speculative aspects of this mystery. Their writings show that the existence of the Father as a
distinct Person of the Trinity was a universally accepted truth.

§ 7. *The term "Son of God" used in connection with the
Blessed Trinity refers to the Second of the three distinct Persons.*

The purpose of this consideration is not to prove the divinity
of Christ. That will be done in a later chapter. Our task here
is to show that the term "Son of God" or "God the Son" refers
to a distinct Person of the Trinity. Some critics have raised the
question of the possible figurative interpretation of this term.
They point out that it was often used by the Jews to refer to a
pious person or to the Messias, but not strictly to a Person of
the Trinity.

Since the divinity of the Son was attacked at an early date,
it is not surprising to find early dogmatic pronouncements on
this point. In 382 A.D., the Council of Rome declared, "We
anathematize those also who follow the error of Sabellius saying that the same One is Father as well as Son." (D-60) In 561
A.D., the Council of Braga in Spain declared against the Priscillian heretics, "If anyone does not confess that the Father
and the Son and the Holy Spirit are three Persons of one substance—but says there is only one and a solitary person—let him
be anathema." (D-231)

Scripture distinguishes the Son from the other Persons of
the Trinity. At Christ's baptism, God the Father said, "This
is My beloved Son." (Matt. 3:17) At Christ's trial before the
Sanhedrin, the high priest said to Him, " 'I adjure thee by the

living God that thou tell us whether thou art the Christ, the Son of God.' Jesus said to him, 'Thou hast said it.'" (Matt. 26:63) At Caesarea Philippi, Christ confirmed Peter in saying, "Thou art the Christ, the Son of the living God." (Matt. 16:16) These and a whole host of similar passages from the Gospels are thrown into sharper focus by the reaction of the Jews to Christ's statement at Jerusalem. "The Jews were the most anxious to put him (Jesus) to death; because he not only broke the Sabbath, but also called God his own Father, making himself equal to God." (John 5:18) We believe that these quotations are sufficient to bring out the distinction between Father and Son as Persons of the Blessed Trinity.

§ 8. *The Church teaches the existence of a Person of the Blessed Trinity called God the Holy Spirit.*

We read that in the Old Testament God was often referred to as a spirit. He, of course, is a spirit, but this must not be interpreted as a denial of the existence of a distinct Person of the Blessed Trinity, namely, God the Holy Spirit. The Church set forth her official teaching at an early date and she repeated it whenever the situation required. The Council of Rome in 382 A.D. made these declarations, "If anyone does not say that the Holy Spirit, just as the Son, is truly and properly of the Father, of divine substance, and is not true God, he is a heretic." (D-74) "If anyone says that the Holy Spirit is a creature, or was made by the Son, he is a heretic." (D-76) "If anyone does not say that the Holy Spirit ought to be adored by every creature just as the Son and Father, he is a heretic." (D-80)

Sacred Scripture reveals that the Holy Spirit is a distinct Person of the Blessed Trinity. In St. John's Gospel we read that Christ said, "And I will ask the Father and he will give you another Advocate to dwell with you forever, the Spirit of truth." (John 14:16) The term "Advocate" as referring to the Holy Spirit occurs five times in the New Testament. This passage distinguishes between the Father and the Holy Spirit, and the Son and the Holy Spirit. This distinct character is again seen in a number of passages from the Acts of the Apostles and the Epistles. We quote some of them. "Take heed to yourselves and to the whole flock in which the Holy Spirit has placed you as bishops to rule." (Acts 20:28) "The Holy Spirit said, 'Set apart for me Saul and Barnabas.'" (Acts 13:2) Christ Himself said, "Unless a man be born again of water and the Spirit, he cannot enter into the kingdom of God." (John 3:5) The Greek language does not use the article indiscriminately. When we read "the" Holy Spirit we must interpret it as referring to a distinct Person in God.

§ 9. *The Apostolic Fathers contain clear evidence of the belief of early Christians in the Blessed Trinity.*

The passages from the works of ancient ecclesiastical writers that could be cited in connection with the Trinity would literally fill many volumes as Lebreton has shown. We confine ourselves to the most ancient extant extra-Scriptural writings, namely, the Apostolic Fathers composed between 60 A.D. and 155 A.D. Their authors were not speculative theologians but merely echoed the belief of the early Church spread throughout the Empire. They testify that belief in the Blessed Trinity was firm and universal.

(1) Corinth: The *Didache* (60-100 A.D.) states "If thou hast neither, pour water three times on the head in the name of the Father, Son, and Holy Spirit." (Ch. 7) This shows that as many adults as were baptized professed their faith in the Blessed Trinity. St. Augustine (d. 430) said that it was easier to find heretics who did not baptize than it was to find heretics who did not invoke the names of the Persons of the Trinity when they did.

(2) Rome: In the *First Letter of Clement of Rome* (96-98 A.D.) we read, "... for as God lives and as the Lord Jesus Christ

lives and the Holy Spirit (lives) ...." (Ch. 58) In the same writing we also read, "Or have we not one God, and one Christ, and one Spirit." (Ch. 46) St. Basil the Great (d. 379) quotes this very passage to prove the belief of the earliest Christians in the Trinity (M.P.G. 29-201).

(3) Syria: St. Ignatius of Antioch (d. 107) in his epistle to the Magnesians said, " . . . in the flesh and in the spirit, in faith and love, in the Son, and the Father, and the Spirit." (Ch. 13) Again, "You (Christians) are as stones of the temple of the Father, made ready for the building of God our Father, carried up to the heights by the engine of Jesus Christ, that is the cross, and using as a rope the Holy Spirit." (Ch. 9)

(4) Asia Minor: In the *Martyrdom of St. Polycarp* (d. 155) we read that the heroic bishop said at his trial, "I glory Thee (God) through the everlasting and heavenly high priest, Jesus Christ, thy beloved Child, through whom be glory to Thee, and with him and the Holy Spirit, both now and for the ages to come." (Chap. 14)

(5) While St. Justin Martyr (d. 165) was not one of the Apostolic Fathers, his writings have a number of fine passages on the Trinity.[3]

§ 10. *The first attempts to explain the Trinity in theological terms were made as early as the end of the Second Century.*

In the Second Century there began to appear a number of Christian writings that showed marked differences from those of the Apostolic Fathers. They were the works put out by the writers known as the Apologists. These were men of considerable literary and philosophical talent as their writings plainly show. They were not content merely to repeat the teachings received from the Apostolic Age. It was their objective to defend Christian doctrine from the attacks of a number of sneering but cultured enemies such as Celsus, Fronto, and Porphory. Being philosophers, the apologists wanted to explain Christian doctrines as clearly as possible. It was in the pursuit of this goal that they began to speculate on the meaning of the different mysteries of faith. The first truth to engage their minds was the Blessed Trinity.

The writings of Clement of Alexandria (d. 211), Tertullian (d. 220), St. Irenaeus (d. 202), and Origen (d. 255) contain a measure of speculation on this mystery. St. Irenaeus' theology on this doctrine is the firmest and richest we find in the works of the Ante-Nicene Fathers. It was the desire of these men to transmit to readers a more profound understanding of the Mystery and to refute the Trinitarian heresies of Modalism and Monarchianism which had already appeared.

While these Ante-Nicene writers all accepted the truth of the Trinity, they were not always able to give us a clear speculative explanation of it. But this is easily understandable. They were gravely handicapped by the lack of precise and universally accepted theological terms. The words "substance," "nature," "persons," and "hypostasis" had not yet become technical terms representing fixed and definite ideas. Many heretics were conscious of the lack of precise Trinitarian terminology, and deliberately used it to trap unsuspecting persons into accepting their views. A great deal of the effort of orthodox writers went into the fixing of the meaning of terms, and this in turn greatly facilitated the exposition of error.

§ 11. *Modalism was the Trinitarian heresy which held that Father, Son, and Holy Spirit are only three names for the same God.*

There are traces of Modalism in writings composed as early as the middle of the Second Century. One reason for this error was a misguided zeal to defend the unity of God against polytheists. But in doing this some fell into the error of denying a Trinity of Persons in God. Modalism oversimplified the explanation of the Trinity to the point that it was no longer to be looked upon as a mystery. The heretics thought it impossible logically to maintain the unity of God and the divinity of three distinct Persons. Modalism[4] held that there is one Nature and one Person in God, but that the Nature could be seen from three points of view. It said that God in His role of Creator is called Father, in His role of Redeemer is called Son, and in His role of Sanctifier is called Holy Spirit.

On the surface, Modalism could be said to have maintained the divinity of Father, Son, and Holy Spirit. But deeper probings show that it attached special meanings to these names. They were not names for three distinct Persons. Modalism was also known by the names of monarchianism, patripassianism, and Sabellianism. All these errors identified Person and Nature in God. Tertullian (d. 220) refuted modalism as propounded by Praxeas, and St. Hippolytus (d. 235) refuted it as taught by Noetus. In about 260 A.D., Pope St. Dionysius formally condemned modalism. He said, "For the latter (Sabellius) blasphemes when he says that the Son himself is the Father and the reverse: the former indeed (tritheists) in a certain measure proclaim three gods, when they divide the sacred unity into three different substances." (D-48) Notice how the statement of the Sovereign Pontiff avoids the errors of modalism and tritheism by making a clear distinction between nature and persons in God.

§ 12. *Arianism was the heresy which denied that the Word or the Son is truly God.*

After Modalism, the proponents of anti-Trinitarian opinions tried a new avenue of attack on this dogma. For many years before the appearance of Arianism, there existed an opinion labeled Subordinationism. This error held that the Son is truly God, but he is inferior to the Father. This is a contradiction, for if the Son is God, he cannot be inferior to the Father. If he is inferior to the Father he cannot be God, but must be a creature. The Arians saw the contradiction and set out to resolve it. Arianism can be summarized in these points. (a) God the Father is true God, but He cannot communicate His substance. (b) The Son is a sort of a demiurge or intermediary between the Father and the universe, but He does not possess necessary existence. (c) The Son is in fact, a creature and the terms "begotten" and "engendered" when applied to the Son must be taken to mean "created." (d) The Son is the most perfect creature that God could create. (e) The Son is fallible but as a matter of fact he never fell or erred.

The first evidence of Arianism as such can be traced to Lucian and Paul of Samosata in Syria in the last half of the Third Century. It derives its name from Arius, a man from Libya who first began to propagate his error at Alexandria in Egypt in about 313 A.D. There eventually developed a number of groups of Arians such as the Anomeans, the Homoeans, and the Semi-Arians. These made considerable strides in winning adherents from among the pseudo-intelligentia of the Fourth Century. The bitterest enemies of Arianism were St. Athanasius (d. 373) in the East and St. Hilary of Poitiers (d. 368) in the West. In 325 A.D., The Council of Nicea pronounced Arianism anathema. The condemnation was repeated by name against all refinements of Arianism at the Council of Rome in 382 A.D. One of the statements this council issued reads, "If anyone does not say that the Son of God is true God just as His Father is true God and He is all-powerful and omniscient and equal to the Father, he is a heretic." (D-70)

§ 13. *The Pneumatomachi were heretics that denied the Divinity of the Holy Spirit.*

The Pneumatomachi is a generic name given to all the heretics who denied the divinity of the Third Person of the Blessed Trinity. The Arians in denying the divinity of the Son were committed to a course of reasoning which *a fortiori* denied the divinity of the Holy Spirit. They considered the Holy Spirit to be a creature of the Son. We have evidence in the writings of St. Athanasius dating from the middle of the Fourth Century of a group that maintained the divinity of the Son against Arianism but who denied the divinity of the Holy Spirit. They represented the Holy Spirit as a creature who differed only in degree from the angels. In Egypt, they were called the Tropicists because of the metaphorical way in which they explained Scripture passages opposed to their views. In Constantinople, they were called Macedonians and Marathonians after two bishops whose names became associated with the error.

In general, the same orthodox writers who fought Arianism also fought these new groups of heretics. And in the forefront of the fight again was St. Athanasius. Toward the middle of the Fourth Century, the pseudo-intellectuals of the entire world seemed to be gathered against the doctrine of the Blessed Trinity; the Empire and its minions, heretical bishops, philosophers, and learned men. St. Athanasius seemed alone in his resistance, but a historian has said that as long as such a man remained the fight was far from lost. He was a power in himself. The Council of Rome held in 382 A.D. (quoted in the last section also) condemned the Pneumatomachi saying, "If anyone does not say that the Holy Spirit, just as the Son, is truly and properly of the Father, of divine substance, and is not true God, he is a heretic." (D-74)

§ 14. *For an understanding of the Blessed Trinity, it is necessary to have a clear notion of the meaning of "nature."*

In studying the Blessed Trinity, we encounter several terms that must be precisely defined and understood. We saw the confusion that was caused by the vagueness of terms in the works of certain ante-Nicene writers. Heretics deliberately took advantage of this vagueness to hide and to propagate their errors.

Let us examine three of the terms. (1) An *essence* is the sum-total of those notes that a thing *must* have to be what it is. It makes a thing specifically different from other things. A tree is essentially different from a stone, for considered as an individual it has the notes that a stone does not have and can never have. An essence embraces all the notes of a species which distinguish it from any other species. (2) A *substance* is an essence that exists by itself. Notice that substance has what essence does not have, namely, the perfection of independent existence. This term is used to differentiate things that can exist by themselves from those things which cannot exist by themselves and which are called accidents. Motion, for example, is an accident, for it cannot exist by itself. It must inhere in a substance, that is, in a thing that moves. (3) A *nature* is an essence insofar as it is a principle of action. The term "nature" embraces a note over and above "essence," but it does not add anything to the objective reality of an essence. Man has an essence, but when it acts we call it human nature to distinguish his manner of acting from the manner of acting of animals and so forth.

When applied to God, the terms essence, substance, and nature are synonyms. His substance is His essence or nature for in God there are no accidents. In 1215 A.D., the Lateran Council taught this truth in these words: "Firmly we believe and confess simply that the true God is one essence, substance, or nature entirely simple." (D-428)

§ 15. *A person is a substance subsisting in an intellectual nature.*

A great deal of the literature produced by early Christian writers concerned itself with fixing the exact meaning of terms. A number of Trinitarian heresies confused "nature" and "person." Modalism and Tritheism held they were synonymous. The definition above is the one of Boethius. (1) A person is a distinct being, that is, it is a substance, for it can exist by itself. It is not an accident, for accidents must inhere in substances, and do not subsist by themselves. Color, for example, is an accident, for it must adhere in a substance. (2) A person has an intellectual nature. An essence's mode of action determines its nature. We saw that in objective reality essence and nature are the same. For example, a human being has an essence. That essence in action is called a nature. The distinct feature of a person's essence is that it is capable of the non-material activities of thinking and choosing. Without these capabilities a substance would remain a mere substance. It would not rate the new label of "person." (3) A person must have subsistence. Subsistence is that perfection which enables an essence actually to exist. Without subsistence an essence is only in the realm of possibility and not actuality. There are in existence subsisting natures which lack intelligence. These cannot be called persons. They are called supposites. In summary, therefore, we see that a person is a distinct being, it has intellection, and it subsists. Each of these three notes is absolutely indispensable for an accurate understanding of the meaning of "person."

§ 16. *The generation of the Son and the spiration of the Holy Spirit is analogous to self-knowledge and self-love in the intellectual life of man.*

From a study of rational psychology, we learn that a rational soul can understand and can love. The other labels that we give to the functions of the intellect such as judgment, reasoning, and remembering are reducible to understanding. Intellection and volition are the activities possible only to non-material substances regardless of what kind of spiritual beings they might be. St. Augustine seized upon these functions of non-material beings to explain the fecundity of the inner life of God in the generation of the Son and the procession of the Holy Spirit.

A thinking agent in contemplating himself conceives an idea of himself. In a sense, he duplicates himself by his self-consciousness, but he suffers no loss in the duplication. Two natures are distinguishable in this process. One is the real, substantial nature of the thinking agent; the other is the logical, accidental nature of the thinking agent embodied in the idea he has of himself.

After a thinking agent has known himself, he can love himself. Notice that he cannot love himself with his will until he first knows himself with his intellect. Three elements are distinguishable in this act of love, namely, the agent, his self-knowledge, and then his self-love. Of these three elements, the agent is a real and substantial being; the idea conceived in the act of understanding is an accidental being; the love following upon the act of understanding is also an accidental being. The generation of the Son and the procession of the Holy Spirit is analogous to the process described here. We shall now show the new and important differences that must be noted when it is applied to the Blessed Trinity.

§ 17. *God the Father is the unbegotten and unproceeding Person of the Blessed Trinity.*

The purpose of this number is not to show that the Father is God, but to show that He alone of the three divine Persons is unbegotten and unproceeding. In 675 A.D., the Council of Toledo taught against Priscillian heretics, "We confess and believe the holy and ineffable Trinity, the Father, and the Son, and the Holy Spirit, one God naturally, to be one substance, one nature, and also of one majesty and power. And we profess that the Father, indeed, is not begotten, not created but unbegotten." (D-275)

There are a number of adjectives used to describe the First Person of the Blessed Trinity which must be carefully understood. He is called "Father," "Principle," "Unbegotten," and "Ungenerated." (1) The term "Father" is used when referring to this Person in relationship to His Son. But this does not mean that the Father is in any way superior to the Son, nor that the Son is in any way inferior to the Father. (2) The Father is the First Principle of the Blessed Trinity, but Principle here must not be taken to mean that the Father is a cause and the other Persons are effects. (3) The Father among the three Persons is the Unbegotten and Unproceeding, but this does not mean that He is prior to the other Persons, that He was in existence before them. (4) The term "Ungenerated" as applied to the Father does not mean that His role in the Blessed Trinity is active while that of the others are passive in the sense that creatures are active or passive. It was because they did not grasp the meaning of these terms in a way applicable only to God that the Arians were led to say that only the Father is God while the other Persons are creatures.

§ 18. *The Second Person of the Blessed Trinity is the only-begotten Son of God the Father.*

The Church solemnly teaches that God has revealed that the Son or Word is the only-begotten of God the Father. In 382 A.D., the Church taught, "If anyone does not say that the Son was begotten of the Father, that is, of the divine substance of Him Himself, he is a heretic." (D-69) Theologians explain this generation in this way: the Father contemplates Himself, and in doing so, begets an image of Himself. This image of necessity is a perfect image of the Father. Now to be perfect, It must have all that the Father has in the real order, not in only the logical order. In the real order, the Father is an infinitely perfect spirit necessarily existing from all eternity. The Image of the Father, then, has the same essence and substance as the Father and It too must be an infinitely perfect spirit.

The Image is the Word or God the Son. The Father is not the Son, for the Father begot the Son and the Son was begotten by the Father. They are truly distinct. But in order for them to be truly distinct, each must subsist distinct from the other. Since each has the note of subsistence along with the divine nature, it follows that each is a Divine Person, for a person is an intellectual nature which subsists.

In generating the Son, the Father does not lose His nature nor does His nature suffer any diminution. In being generated, the Son does not receive in time a nature that He did not have before having been begotten, for He was necessarily begotten from all eternity. The paternity of the Father and the filiation of the Son do not indicate any superiority and inferiority in the real order.

§ 19. *The Father and Son love each other; the love that proceeds from both the Father and Son is God the Holy Spirit.*

In 675 A.D., the same Council of Toledo that was quoted above taught, "We believe also that the Holy Spirit, who is the third person of the Trinity, is God, one and equal with God the Father and the Son, of one substance, also of one nature; that He is the Spirit of both, not, however, begotten nor created but proceeding from both." (D-277) Love is the tendency of an intellectual being toward a thing seen as good. Father and Son see each other as being infinitely perfect and so tend toward each other with a complete or adequate love. A love is adequate when it is commensurate with the perfection toward which it tends. It is incomplete if it falls short of the degree that the good should be loved but is not loved. In humans, love is an accident. God has no accidents. The love that exists between Father and Son must be commensurate with God's nature. It would fall short of this if this love was not the very essence, substance, and nature of God. This love must also be an infinitely perfect substance. It is, in fact, called God the Holy Spirit.

Since the Love proceeds from both Father and Son, It must be distinct from both of them. To be distinct from the Father and Son in the real as opposed to the logical order, the love that proceeds from both of them must subsist. This love, therefore, has all the notes necessary for a person, namely, it is an intellectual nature with subsistence. God the Holy Spirit proceeds from the Father and the Son, but proceeds from them as from one principle. Between the Father and Son and the Holy Spirit there is an active and passive spiration, but the passive spiration does not imply any inferiority of the Holy Spirit to the Father and Son.

§ 20. *In God, all things are one except where there is opposition of relation.*

This proposition embodies the so-called fundamental law of the Blessed Trinity. It was approved by the Council of Florence in 1439 A.D. Reason and revelation teach us that there is only one God. A real unity is constituted by a unity or oneness of essence. In a discussion of the Blessed Trinity, God's essential unity must be maintained.

Revelation teaches us that in God there is a Trinity of Persons Who are equal in every respect. It cannot be proved that the Unity and Trinity of God involves a contradiction, for we do not say that there is at once one God and three Gods. We must hold that in God there is one essence in three divine Persons. The distinction of a nature and a person is of paramount importance. The proposition must be interpreted in the light of that distinction.

The Father differs from the Son only because there is a perfect opposition of relation between active and passive generation. Father and Son differ from the Holy Spirit only because there is a perfect opposition of relation between active and passive spiration. Where no such perfect relative opposition intervenes, everything in God is perfectly one and indistinct. All the divine attributes such as omnipotence, omniscience, omnipresence, eternity, and so forth, are really identical with the divine essence. Each attribute must be equally predicated of each of the three Persons, for each possesses the totality of the divine essence.

NOTES

1. Pohle-Preuss, *The Divine Trinity* (St. Louis: Herder, 1943), p. 25.

2. I *Apology*, 61-2.

3. Parente. *Dictionary of Dogmatic Theology* (Milwaukee: Bruce, 1951), p. 190.

4. Klein, *The Doctrine of the Blessed Trinity* (New York: Kenedy, 1940), p. 201.

IV

Creation and Angels

§ 1. *The Church solemnly teaches that God created all things from nothing.*

From ancient times, man has speculated on the origin of the universe. All of the pagan religions of pre-Christian times had elaborate cosmogonies. In the first centuries of the Christian era, the Gnostics and Manichaeans held that matter is eternal and evil. In the Fourth Century, the Church condemned Priscillianism, a heresy that held a pantheistic opinion on the origin of created spirits.

While many errors on the origin of the universe resulted from an abuse of theological principles, many were propounded by philosophers. The neo-platonists of ancient times held that matter is eternal and uncreated. Spinoza (1631-1677) identified all things with God thereby holding the error of pantheism. The same opinion was again put forth by certain philosophers in the Eighteenth and Nineteenth Centuries and it was again condemned by the Church.

The creation of the universe by God is one of the first doctrines taught by the Church. The Apostles' Creed, drawn up in about 100 A.D. reads, "I believe in God, the Father Almighty, *Creator of heaven and earth.*" (D-6) The Council of Braga in 561 A.D. condemned the Manichaean and Priscillian errors.

53

(D-235) And the Vatican Council in 1870 A.D. condemned the modern versions of pantheism. The exact words of the decrees read as follows: "If anyone does not confess that the whole world and all things which are contained in it, both spiritual and material, as regards their substance have been produced by God from nothing, let him be anathema." (D-1805) "If anyone shall say that one and the same thing is the substance or essence of God and of all things: let him be anathema." (D-1803) "If anyone shall say that finite things, both corporeal or spiritual, or at least spiritual, have emanated from the divine substance: let him be anathema." (D-1804)

§ 2. *The creation of the universe by God was revealed in Sacred Scripture.*

The Old Testament contains revelation of the creation of the universe. We must confine ourselves to the quotation of only a few of the passages. In Genesis, we read, "In the beginning God created the heavens and the earth." (Gen. 1:1) Of the things that make up the universe, the Psalmist wrote, "Let them praise the name of the Lord, for He commanded and they were created." (Ps. 148:5) A splendid verse on this subject is this one, "I beseech thee, my son, look upon heaven and earth, and all that is in them; and consider that God made them out of nothing." (II Mach. 7:28) These three passages span the thousand years before Christ during which the different books of the Old Testament were being composed. The revealed truth on creation was perfectly uniform throughout the period.

The New Testament revelation is in harmony with the passages already quoted. St. John expressed the completeness of the creation of the universe by God. He wrote, "All things were made through him (God); and without him was made nothing that has been made." (John 1:3) This verse from the first chapter of St. John's Gospel takes on added significance when we recall that the chapter summarizes the relationship between God and the universe.

Some rationalistic critics who deny the need or possibility of revelation, would have people believe that the doctrines of the Old and New Testaments were taken from pagans. But this opinion is untenable for no pagan thinker of pre-Christian times held these beliefs on creation. Greek philosophy either held that matter was eternal or that it was not distinct from God. The Jews were not influenced by Greek speculation, nor were they given to philosophical speculations of their own. It is impossible to give a human source as the font of the truth concerning creation. Its uniformity and firmness point to its being revealed by God Himself.

§ 3. *The creation of the universe by God was defended by Christian writers from the most ancient times.*

The literature on the creation of the universe produced by the Ante-Nicene writers is in perfect agreement with both Old and New Testament writings. This literature continues it and re-echoes it. A new feature of these writings is worth mentioning here. These works are apologetical in character, having been composed for the most part by men who form the group known as the Apologists and who tried to explain revealed truth in terms of philosophical principles. The creation of the universe by God was defended by St. Justin Martyr, Tertullian, Clement of Alexandria, and others who wrote before 325 A.D. Its most elaborate exposition is found in the five books of the *Adversus Haereses* composed by St. Irenaeus (d. 202). He met the opinions of the Gnostics head on and did not hesitate to use philosophy to refute their errors. Gnosticism held a dualism of good and evil, thereby denying the creation of the universe by God. St. Irenaeus was quick to point out that denial of creation by God leads to atheism. He proposed this dilemma: if one confuses God with the world, he falls into pantheism which is a form of atheism; if he holds that matter is necessarily eternal, he must hold that God is not an infinitely perfect being, and so, not God at all. He then invites the Gnostics to hang themselves on either horn of the dilemma.

The Ante-Nicene writers who defended the doctrine discussed here hailed from widely separated parts of the world. Yet they held the same truth. What was the cause of this uniformity? It was the fact that they received it from a common source—the teaching authority of the Church. It illustrates in a practical way the unity of doctrines taught by the Church throughout the ancient world.

§ 4. *The creation of the universe by God can be proved by reason unaided by Divine Revelation.*

The term "creation" as used in this chapter means bringing something into existence out of nothing. More philosophically, it means the act of lifting a substantial being out of the realm of pure possibility into the realm of actuality. We touched on this point when examining the five proofs of St. Thomas for the existence of God. In the third proof we saw that there are things in existence which indeed exist but which need not exist. Living things fall into this group. Since they did not exist at one time but do exist now, it is obvious that they have "received" existence. An aggregate of things with received existence owes its existence to someone having unreceived existence. A being having unreceived existence is necessarily eternal. Since it is necessarily eternal, it is infinite. And the infinite being is God.

An infinitely perfect being can have no equal. It is a contradiction to say that there are two infinite beings, or two beings with unreceived existence. The only possible explanation for the existence of finite beings is that they have received their existence and so they must be dependent on God for it. God is a completely simple being in whom essence and existence are identified. It is a manifest contradiction to say as pantheists do, that God is at once unreceived and received, spirit and matter, infinite and finite.

§ 5. *The Church solemnly teaches that God freely created the universe in time.*

The Vatican Council defined, "If anyone shall have said that God created not by a volition free from all necessity, but as necessarily as He necessarily loves Himself: let him be anathema." (D-1805) Even reason shows that God freely created the universe. If God could be compelled to create, the compulsion would have to come from within Him or from a force external to Him. Both of these avenues are out of the question. It certainly could not come from a higher, external being, for God is infinitely perfect and cannot have an equal nor a peer. It could not come from a force within God Himself, for a force that could compel God to act would have to have the perfection that God Himself has. Such a force would have to be equal to God. This is impossible, for God is infinite. Reason and revelation tell us that God was free to create or not to create.

Did God create the universe in time or in eternity? Reason says that God could have created the universe from all eternity, but revelation says that *de facto* He created it in time. Philosophy proves that God could have created the universe at anytime that He had the power to do so. Since He had this power from all eternity, He could have created from all eternity. Notice that such a universe would still be a contingent being completely dependent on God. In no sense would it be equal to God. Reason cannot definitely say what actually did happen, but revelation can and has. St. Thomas says that faith, not reason, tells us that the universe is not eternal but was created in time.[1] In 1215 A.D. the IV Lateran Council taught that God "by His own omnipotent power from the beginning of time created each creature in the same way from nothing, spiritual and corporal." (D-428) We shall see on a later page that this does not mean that God created all that he actually has created at one instant. It means that He began in time to exercise His power to create.

§ 6. *After God creates a thing, His infinite power is needed to keep it in existence.*

A thing has either received or unreceived existence. God has unreceived existence; all creatures have received existence. There is no third possibility. In the act of creation, God conferred actuality on a thing that was only possible. After creating the universe, God did not leave it alone to exist without Him or without His power. We must not imagine that God could withdraw Himself from His creatures after giving them their initial impetus, then allow them to subsist. This matter is not like giving a car an initial push down a hill and then letting its momentum sustain it in motion. If God would withdraw His sustaining power from the universe, it would revert back to the status of a non-existent being. Just as infinite power was needed to create the universe, so infinite power is needed to sustain it in existence.

If a thing could exist without God's sustaining power, it would exist independently of God. A being that exists independently of God would have to be equal to God, that is, it would have necessary, not contingent, existence. We have already proved that this type of existence is absolutely impossible for creatures. It must be concluded that God's infinite power is constantly needed to sustain the universe in existence.

The size of a creature does not make it more or less dependent on God. The mightiest star in the firmament does not have a firmer grip on existence than does a grain of sand. They are both equally contingent on God. The story goes that some people once asked St. Augustine why God does not manifest

His infinite power today. The learned bishop of Hippo told them that God does indeed manifest His infinite power to men every day and that all they need to do is to open their eyes to see it in the persistence of the material universe.

§ 7. *God's providence extends to each and every one of His creatures.*

God's providence is the way that He governs creatures so that they will fulfill the purpose for which they were created. The truth of the proposition rests on the relationship between God and His creatures. He is necessary; they are contingent. God is infinitely intelligent. He does nothing without a purpose, that is, without assigning a creature its specific goal. Nothing can slip out of God's control, for He knows all things and He sustains them in existence. Only God, the Creator, can assign a creature its goal and no one can substitute another goal in the place of this one. God's will, insofar as the purpose of creatures is concerned, cannot be frustrated.

An examination of creatures gives added proof to the conclusions just drawn. Every creature of the material universe exhibits design. The design of even the smallest atoms is fantastically complex and uniform. Design means the intelligent arrangement of parts. And this arrangement is a sure sign of purposefulness. The laws of nature govern the manner of acting of material things so that without creatures there would be no such laws. The laws of nature are contingent on the will of the Creator and He impresses them upon things so that they will be directed toward their assigned goal.

The fact that God's purpose in creating is infallibly attained must not be interpreted as favoring human determinism or fatalism. It is not a contradiction for a thing to have a primary or ultimate as well as a secondary or intermediary goal. The first does not depend on the free choice of rational creatures;

the second one might depend on such a choice. The former can never be rejected; the latter might leave room for alternatives but neither militates against the all-embracing character of God's providence.

§ 8. *One purpose of creation is God's external glory.*

The truth stated in this proposition was taught by the Vatican Council. It said, "This only, true God by His goodness and omnipotent power, not to increase His happiness, and not to add to it, but to manifest His perfection . . . fashioned each creature out of nothing." (D-1783) "If anyone shall have denied that the world was created to the glory of God: let him be anathema." (D-1805)

God has been infinitely happy from all eternity. Nothing could be added to Him to make Him happier than He already is. He certainly has nothing to gain from the universe. It would be blasphemy to hold that God created intelligent creatures in order to experience the happiness of having persons to praise and applaud Him. Vainglory is completely out of the question as a motive for creation. It is an anthropomorphic expression to say that God is glad when people are good.

The universe manifests God's glory in the sense that His attributes are reflected in it and are stamped on it. A beautiful musical composition, for example, must reflect the talent of its composer; an intricate piece of machinery reflects the engineering skill of its designer. The very existence of the creatural universe must reflect God's attributes of power, beauty, intelligence, and so forth. They could not exist without doing so and they do so even when no rational creature sees them.

There is a very practical side to what has been said here. The objects in creation should be used to elevate one to contemplate God's greatness. St. Francis of Assisi saw God's beauty reflected in the beauty of a flower. St. Jerome saw His power in the violence of a storm. St. Augustine saw His intelligence reflected in the structure of an insect.

§ 9. *Another motive that impelled God to create was to lavish benefits on His creatures.*

Every intelligent agent must have a final cause or purpose for performing an act. A deliberate act presupposes a desire; every desire must have an object that occasions it. The object of a desire is always a thing seen as good. Happiness is caused by possessing a good thing. What has been said here applies to all intelligences regardless of their classification. It applies to God as well as to angels and men.

There are some points of difference between the ways that uncreated intelligence and created intelligences act. This is due to their essentially different natures. Created natures are imperfect and so they can receive perfection and can communicate it to others. By either operation they seek happiness, for everyone seeks happiness by every one of his deliberate and free acts. This remains true even when a finite nature commits sin.

When God acts, He too must have a final cause. But since nothing existed outside of God before the act of creation, it follows that the final cause for creation must reside in God Himself. The good that impelled God to act must have been His own attribute of infinite goodness. Since God is infinitely perfect, He cannot receive goodness. He can only communicate it. God's own goodness impelled Him to create such intelligent creatures as angels and men.

We have seen that happiness is engendered by the possession of a good thing. We must conclude that God created rational creatures in order that they might have the happiness that only He can bestow. The existence of creatures does not give God a happiness greater than He had before they were created, for

He was always an infinitely perfect being incapable of any improvement.

§ 10. *All of God's dealings with creatures are stamped with the mark of His love.*

God's providence extends to each and every one of His creatures. All things were created for a definite reason. While each can have a secondary goal in creation, they all have the same ultimate goal: God Himself. In the last section, we saw that love impelled God to create intelligent agents. Here we see that God continues to deal with them in a loving manner.

Nothing can happen to us by chance, for nothing takes place without God's knowledge and permission. Everything in existence must act according to its nature. This is true of God as well as of rational and non-rational creatures. Reason as well as revelation tells us that God is infinite goodness or love. A final cause for creation had to be God's desire to bestow benefits on creatures. This is only another way of saying that love impelled God to create.

There is a very practical aspect to what has been said here. It is the key to the understanding of the purpose of the events in which we have a part. Even the most insignificant events have a definite purpose in God's plan for us. Since the ultimate goal is love, all intermediate steps toward that goal must be stamped with love. These steps are all the things that happen to us during our lifetime. God sends them to us to help us toward the ultimate goal that He has assigned to us. While some allow us to move forward slowly, others permit us to be catapulted toward our goal. This also applies to those events which are sometimes labeled misfortunes such as disgrace, disease, disappointment, and the rest. The crosses that God sends are proof of His love. Each of them has been exactly measured. In God's dealings with the people on earth there is no such thing as punishment merely to avenge wrongs. Everything is stamped with His love. But this fact does not destroy free will, nor does it leave room for a fatalistic view of life.

§ 11. *The Church teaches that God has revealed the existence of pure spirits called angels.*

A pure spirit is a non-material substance that was never intended to be substantially united with a material body. The existence of pure spirits or angels was taught on a number of occasions by the Church. In 1215 A.D., the Fourth Lateran Council taught, " (God) who by His own omnipotent power . . . created each creature from nothing, *spiritual* and corporeal, namely, angelic and mundane." (D-428) These words were repeated verbatim by the Vatican Council in 1870 A.D.

The New Testament contains evidence attesting to the existence of angels. We read, "Then the devil left him; and behold angels came and ministered to him." (Matt. 4:11) Again, Christ said, "See that you do not despise one of these little ones; for I tell you, their angels in heaven always behold the face of my Father in heaven." (Matt. 18:10) Next, "Amen, amen, I say to you, you shall see heaven opened, and the angels of God ascending and descending upon the Son of Man." (John 1:51) Finally, St. Paul wrote this of Christ, " (He) having become so much superior to the angels as he has inherited a more excellent name than they. For to which of the angels has he ever said . . . ." (Heb. 1:4)

The doctrine of the existence of angels appears very early in Christian literature. St. Ignatius of Antioch (d. 107) wrote to the Trallians, "Though I am in bonds and can understand heavenly things, and the places of the *angels* and the gatherings of *principalities* . . ." (Trall. V) An early writing that seems to contain evidence of the existence of angels is *Pastor Hermae* composed *ca.* 150 A.D. Some deny that this writing has any reference to angels. Origen wrote a great deal about angels. From the middle of the Second Centry, the Gnostic heretics propounded certain errors on the nature and role of pure spirits. Apart from materialists who denied the existence of any spiritual substances, no heretics denied the existence of angels. St. Thomas Aquinas (d. 1274) devoted fourteen questions to the angels in his *Summa Theologica*.

§ 12. *Since an angel is a created spiritual substance, it is naturally immortal.*

Real things fall into one of two categories. They are either possible or actual beings. An essence must be possible before it can be lifted into the realm of actuality. Nothingness can never have the perfection of existence. Actual things have both essence and existence. In God, the two are identically the same, for it is His essence to exist. He is completely devoid of composition. All actual creatures exhibit composition regardless of whether they are material or non-material. A spiritual substance such as an angel is a compound of essence with existence. A material substance is a double compound, for it is essence and existence as well as matter and form.

A combination or compound indicates the pre-existence of a compounding agent that effected the union. In studying the chapter on God's existence, we saw that a possible being can receive the perfection of existence only from the Being that has the fullness of existence, namely, God. Since there is no room for an intermediate cause between God and angels insofar as their creation is concerned, it follows that only God could have created the angels.

A living thing is destroyed or killed when it is broken down into its component parts, when the compound is dissolved. In the case of material things, physical means either internal or external to the object can be used to separate matter and form. Angels, however, are spiritual beings. They cannot be destroyed by physical causes, for these causes cannot separate essence from existence. God could separate these two by withdrawing the perfection of existence thereby annihilating it. Natural or finite causes that are internal or external to the angels cannot bring this about. Hence, we must conclude that angels are naturally immortal.

§ 13. *An angel is a person having an intellectual nature.*

The term "angel" is derived from a Green noun meaning "a messenger," but in Christian literature it has always been used to denote pure created spirits. God never intended these spirits to be substantially united to a body. Disembodied human souls clearly do not measure up to this definition because they were once joined to bodies.

An angel is a person; it is a subsisting nature endowed with intellect and free will. The student should here review the difference between substance and accident as well as the difference between a supposite and a person as discussed in the last chapter.

Angels have intellects. To better understand the power of their intellects, we should compare them with those of humans. Man has a rational intellect; he acquires knowledge in a discursive manner. He abstracts an idea from a phantasm. This is simple conception. The human mind then compares two ideas in judgment and then can compare two judgments in reasoning. The process is a slow one and the possibility of mistaken judgments is great. Angels have intuitive knowledge. They directly grasp the essence of a thing without any preliminary labor of abstraction. In grasping an essence they instantaneously see the conclusions that could be drawn from it. In one act, angels grasp principles and conclusions without any intermediary steps or judgments. And since intuitive knowledge leaves no room for judgment, neither does it leave room for error or falsehood in the intellects of angels.

Angels do not know the free future unless it be revealed to them by God, in spite of their wonderful intellects. They know only those things that take place in a cause and effect sequence. Only God knows the free future, for He alone sees events in themselves and not only as effects of past causes.

§ 14. *Angels have free will.*

When God creates anything, He must assign it a goal, a purpose for existing. This is true of inorganic objects, plants, animals, and intellectual natures. When God gives a creature a goal to reach, He always gives it the means or equipment that will enable it to reach that goal. Inorganic things and plants are able to tend to their goal by virtue of the laws of nature implanted in them. Animals have a measure of cognition, that is, senses and instinct which enable them to reach their goal. Men and angels are much higher creatures and so they have much more wonderful powers to enable them to tend toward their goal.

The goal toward which all things tend must be a good grasped according to the thing's cognitive powers. If an object's cognitive powers are material, as is the case with sensitive creatures or animals, then its striving power must also be material. There must be a balance between these two powers. We saw that angels are non-material substances having non-material thinking powers. Therefore, they must have non-material striving powers to be able to tend toward the object presented by the intellect. This striving power is called the will.

Since angels have an intellectual nature, they have a notion of goodness as such. With this notion they can recognize what objects have a greater or a lesser degree of goodness. Only the object which is infinitely good compels an individual creature to choose it. If an object is recognized as imperfect, an intelligent creature is not compelled to choose it. It is at liberty to reject it. This is only another way of saying that angels have free will. St. Thomas writes that wherever there is an intellect there must also be a free-will, for all things were made for a goal. The intellect grasps this goal in a non-material way; the will must tend toward it in the manner that the intellect presents it, also in a non-material fashion.

§ 15. *Each angel is specifically different from every other angel.*

This proposition must be interpreted to mean that not only is each angel an individual but each angel is a distinct species. The human beings on earth are different individuals but they all belong to the same species. St. Thomas gives the philosophical reasons why each angel must be considered a species in itself. The individuals in the classes of beings lower than angels are grouped into the same species because of the matter with which they are substantially united. Disembodied souls of humans are of the same species because of their relationship to matter. But angels are pure spirits. Their Creator never intended that they should ever be united to a body. Man's body accounts for his individuality within the species. Each angel is a species for they have no material element that could gather a number of them into a species.

All angels are not on a par with each other. What accounts for some being on a higher plane and some being on a lower plane? Some approach more closely than others the unique intellectual nature of God. God contains the whole plenitude of intellectual knowledge, in the divine essence, by which He knows all things. The higher an angel is, the fewer the ideas are needed to grasp the whole mass of intelligible things it knows. The fewer ideas an angel has, the more universal these ideas must be. The intellect having these universal ideas sees more things and to a more profound degree than an intellect needing many ideas to grasp the same truth. The intellectual capacity of some angels is greater than that of others, accounting for some angels being on a higher plane than others. When God created the angels, He filled their intellects with infused ideas. It follows that each angel cannot advance to a plane higher than the one on which it was created.

§ 16. *God assigned to the angels the supernatural goal of seeing Him face to face.*

Every creature of God has a goal toward which it is inclined. God has given it the means with which it could pursue this goal. In higher types of creatures, these means are their cognitive powers. The more perfect a creature is, the higher or more perfect the goal assigned to it and the more perfect the powers given it for reaching this goal. There must always be a balance between goal and powers. Angels have completely non-material natures. Their powers of intellect and will are non-material powers. The goal of the intellect is the Supreme Being; the goal of the will is the Supreme Good. These two goals are the single being called God.

Angels, seen as creatures, are natural beings. With their natural powers they can at best see God in a natural way. But God in His infinite love wanted angels to have the higher happiness of seeing Him in a supernatural way, of seeing Him with the same immediacy with which He sees Himself. To make this possible, the angels had to be elevated to a supernatural plane by the reception of sanctifying grace. St. Thomas thought that the angels were created in grace, that there was no interval of time between their creation and their reception of grace.

Did God confer the same degree of grace on all the angels? Probably not. Some theologians propose the theory that the different degree of the natural gifts of the angels is also an indication of the difference in the degree of their supernatural gifts. They argue that God did not give some angels greater natural gifts to be directed toward a natural end. It would seem difficult to explain this inequality of intellectual power if it was not also an indication of the inequality in the degree of sanctifying grace that God gave the angels.

§ 17. *Although the angels were created in grace, it was possible for them to sin.*

Although the angels were created in grace, they still retained their free will. Before they reached their assigned goal, they could use this free will either to choose to have God or to choose to have themselves in place of God. When one chooses himself as the supreme good, he clearly rejects God as his supreme good. The malice of serious sin lies in this perverted use of free will.

Happiness is natural only to God. It cannot be separated from His nature. As far as creatures are concerned, happiness is not indispensable to their make-up. It can be separated from them. It is their goal. Whenever there is a goal assigned to an agent and he is given the means to reach that goal, it follows that he cannot reach the goal unless he uses the means. In the case of the angels, it meant that they had to use their free wills in order to reach their supernatural goal. The wills of the angels could be necessitated only in the presence of the universal good or God. They would then have in fact reached their goal. But before this, their wills were not necessitated and they were free to reject God; they could commit sin.

St. Thomas teaches that the angels who chose God reached their goal and received their supernatural happiness immediately after having made their choice, which was one meritorious act. He bases his opinion on the parallel between angels and saints. Humans in grace receive their happiness immediately after death unless they have venial sin or temporal punishment due to sin. But venial sin and temporal punishment due to sin were impossible in good angels. And so they reached their goal after their first meritorious act.

The good angels cannot now advance in merit or happiness, for only wayfarers can make this advance. An agent who now possesses his goal cannot advance toward it. Since the angels had reached their goal after a single will-act, they were no longer wayfarers. Therefore, they could not merit more grace than that in which they had been created by God.

§ 18. *The angels who sinned immediately became devils.*

Every rational creature has free will and any creature with free-will and still a wayfarer can commit sin unless it be confirmed in grace. The angels were no exception. Immediately after they were created, the angels were presented with the mutually exclusive alternatives of choosing God as their supernatural goal or rejecting Him. Those who chose God were immediately rewarded with the face to face vision of God in heaven. The angels who became devils fell at this time. If they had not fallen then, they could not have fallen afterwards.

What sin did the fallen angels or devils commit? It could have been only a sin that requires intellect and will for commission, since they had no bodies. Every sin is a forbidden choice, and a choice presupposes alternatives. What were the alternatives before the angels? In the last analysis, a person tempted to serious sin must choose between God as His ultimate goal or himself in place of God as His ultimate goal. If he chooses the latter, He automatically rejects the former. The angels who fell made the perverted choice called the sin of pride.

A person who commits a mortal sin of pride figuratively creates a new universe in his own mind and places himself over it as its lord and master. By disregarding God's commandments, he refuses to recognize God's dominion over him. While humans on earth must observe all Ten Commandments in order to preserve the correct relationship between themselves and God, the angels were required to observe only the First Commandment. It was this commandment that the devils chose to break by preferring themselves to God as the ultimate goal of their existence. This is what it meant when it is said that the devils wanted to be as God.

§ 19. *The fall of the angels had a profound effect on their intellects and wills.*

The sin of the fallen angels was a true sin, causing them to be stripped of the sanctifying grace they needed to see God in heaven. However, it left them with a complete angelic nature having intellect and will. Before their fall, the devils had two kinds of knowledge: the knowledge that comes with grace and the knowledge that comes with nature. When they lost grace, they either completely lost the first kind of knowledge or had it diminished. But they retained the knowledge that is natural to them as pure spirits. They still had intuitive intellects capable of holding an enormous amount of knowledge. As pure spirits, the devils were simple and indivisible. Nothing proper to their nature could be taken away without destroying that nature. Since the angels are by nature intellectual beings, they must retain the knowledge proper to their nature which they had even before their fall.

Previously, we showed that all intellectual beings must have free will. The fallen angels are no exception to this. While the devils indeed have free wills, there is a fixity in their choice. These positions are not at all contradictory. From the moment of their perverted choice and from thence forward forever, the devils freely and without compulsion choose to continue their rejection of God in a fixed and adamant fashion. It can even be said that God's mercy extends even to the devils, for mercy is God's readiness to forgive any truly repented sin. The devils can not avail themselves of this mercy because they now freely choose not to repent of their sin but to remain forever in their obstinate attachment to the forbidden object that entails rejection of God.

§ 20. *It is the ordinary teaching of the Church that every Christian on earth has been given a Guardian Angel.*

A revealed truth is either solemnly defined or it is taught by the ordinary *magisterium* of the Church. The solemn definition is made by the pope alone or with the bishops gathered in a general council. The ordinary *magisterium* of the Church means the teaching authority of the bishops taken as a group although scattered throughout the world. While the Church has not solemnly defined the existence of Guardian Angels, it is taught universally by her ordinary *magisterium*. Therefore, it is a matter of faith. All Catholics must believe it and commit serious sin if they refuse to do so.

There are several Scripture passages quoted by theologians to show the existence of Guardian Angels. Christ said, "See that you do not despise one of these little ones; for I tell you, *their* angels in heaven always behold the face of My Father in heaven." (Matt. 18:10) "Are they not all ministering spirits, sent for service, for the sake of those who shall inherit salvation?" (Heb. 1:14)

Belief in the existence of Guardian Angels is solidly embedded in Sacred Tradition. St. Basil the Great (d. 369 A.D.) wrote, "Every one of the faithful has an angel standing at his side as educator and guide, directing his life."[2] St. Jerome (d. 420 A.D.) said, "How great is the value of the soul that every single person has from birth received an angel for his protection!"[3] St. Thomas Aquinas (d. 1274 A.D.) devotes eight articles to the existence and functions of Guardian Angels in his *Summa Theologica*. In these articles he quotes or refers to writings on this subject by St. Jerome, St. Augustine, St. Gregory the Great, St. John Chrysostom, St. John Damascene, Origen, and Pseudo-Dionysius. The dates and native lands of these men in themselves show how universally the truth has been held. It is only an opinion that each and every human being has a Guardian Angel regardless of whether or not he is a Christian or a non-Christian.

§ 21. *The Biblical account of the creation of the universe must be interpreted in accordance with the general purpose of Sacred Scripture.*[4]

The Church has solemnly defined that the Bible in all its parts is a writing inspired by God and as such contains no errors. It is heresy to deny what she has defined. God revealed the truths of supernatural religion to us in both written and unwritten form. Together, they contain the doctrines that all must believe and the precepts that all must observe to reach the goal assigned to them by God. The Bible (Sacred Scripture) contains the truths that God delivered to us in written form. The human authors inspired by God sought primarily to convey clear ideas to their readers. They, therefore, used expressions and idioms familiar to the people. They never intended to use technical terms, nor a strictly scientific vocabulary. The account of the creation of the universe found in the Bible must be understood in the light of these principles. The Church never said that the Bible was to be looked upon as a textbook of history or science.

Some "scientists" have tried to interpret the biblical account of creation according to modern geological and anthropological theories. When the biblical accounts did not coincide with their theories, they pronounced the biblical account erroneous. There is another side to this picture. While we do not question the ability of some of these critics, we do question some of their motives. Many of them have fastened on apparent discrepancies between "science" and the Bible in order to heap ridicule on the Bible and to justify their opinion that it is a puerile writing unworthy of the credence of learned people. Their ultimate aim is to try to destroy the faith of the people in the existence and even in the possibility of supernatural revelation and religion.

§ 22. *Sacred Scripture contains nothing concerning the general order that God followed in creating the universe.*

The universe is a great deal more than the earth inhabited by humans. It includes all the firmament made up of billions of celestial bodies. The account of creation was set down in the Book of Genesis. On the first day, God created night and day; on the second, He created the firmament; on the third, He separated the land from the sea and created plant life; on the fourth, He created the sun and moon; on the fifth, He created the fishes for the sea and the birds for the air; on the sixth day, He created man; on the seventh day, He rested. This description is brief indeed.

The Church has made no solemn pronouncement on the content of Genesis as it pertains to creation other than saying that it is a writing inspired by God and contains no error. The account of creation leaves out many details of interest to astronomers, geologists, and biologists. It has many terms such as "day" and "God rested" whose meaning has not been fixed. The Church allows exegetes a considerable latitude in interpreting these verses.

The student must never confuse the incontestable fact that God created the universe with the other question of the order He followed in creating its different parts. The two are not the same. In fact, they must be kept distinct. The fact that the latter is uncertain in no way casts doubt on the former. The verses of Genesis have at times been abused by certain materialists and monists who have seized upon their indefinite character and then have tried to conclude that the Bible is in error. In many cases, these critics have tried to confound the fact of creation and the order of creation. Some of their tactics seem to be an attempt to pave the way for the acceptance by all of their conclusion that matter is eternal and uncreated—a conclusion that can be proved to be utterly false.

NOTES

1. *S.T.*, I, 46, 2.
2. *Adv. Eunomium.* 3, 1.
3. *Com. In Matt.*, 18, 10.
4. Ott, *Fundamentals of Catholic Dogma* (St. Louis: Herder, 1954), p. 90.

V

Creation and Fall of Man

§ 1. *The Church teaches that God has revealed that man is a creature composed of body and soul.*

We shall prove that reason without revelation shows that in man a material body is substantially united with a spiritual soul. A person unfamiliar with philosophical studies would experience some difficulty in making this inquiry by himself. Yet it is of paramount importance that an individual realize as soon as possible that he does have an immortal soul. The easiest and surest way for him to acquire this knowledge is by having it revealed to him by God. This is precisely what has taken place. The Fourth Lateran Council in 1215 A.D. taught: "God . . . Creator of all visible and invisible things . . . created each creature from nothing, spiritual and corporeal . . . the human constituted . . . of the spirit and the body." (D-428)

The teaching of Sacred Scripture is explicit on the make-up of a human being. Christ Himself made a clear distinction between man's body and his immortal soul when He said, "And do not be afraid of those who kill the body but cannot kill the soul. But rather be afraid of him who is able to destroy (meaning to damn) both soul and body in hell." (Matt. 10:28) Again "What does it profit a man, if he gain the whole world, but suffer the loss of his own soul? Or what will a man give in exchange for his soul?" (Matt. 16:25,26)

Christian writers from earliest times were emphatic that man has both a body and a soul. The apologists of the Second and Third Centuries could not use the argument from Scripture very effectively against the pagan writers. They were compelled to formulate philosophical argument to defend their position. The oldest extant writing devoted exclusively to the proof of the existence of the soul is Tertullian's *De Anima* composed about 210 A.D. While its philosophical arguments lacked the cogency of later works on the subject, it was a significant start on the solution of this difficult problem.

§ 2. *Man is endowed with a non-material cognitive power called the intellect.*[1]

This argument is a philosophical one. Even though the intellect cannot be seen with the eye, its existence and non-material character can be established from its mode of operation. When we prove its non-material mode of operation, we also prove its non-material nature, for everything must act according to its nature. In knowledge, there is a union of the object known and the subject that knows. The object known does not change because of the fact that someone knows it, but the subject that knows is affected by the fact that it knows the object.

Non-materiality is the root of all knowing. Animals have only material senses and so they can be aware of only material beings. The less material a thing's knowing power is, the greater is the range of objects it can know. The object of man's knowing power is not merely material beings but being in general. It can know things that are infinite or finite, actual or possible. Since being in general is the widest possible range of things, it follows that man's thinking power must be devoid of anything that will limit the kinds of beings it can know. Materiality is the only thing that can so limit cognition. We must conclude that man's intellect is not material but non-material. However, the fact that the object of man's intellect is being in general does not mean that it can know being exhaustively.

An examination of the nature of man's ideas also shows that he has a non-material thinking power called the intellect. There must be a balance between the ideas and the power that conceives them. Since the ideas are natures grasped without the individuating notes that the natures have in objective reality, it follows that they are universal and so non-material. Non-material ideas can be conceived only by a non-material cognitive power called the intellect.

§ 3. *Man is endowed with a non-material appetitive power called the will.*

Every purposeful action is an inclination toward a goal. This is true of every class of things regardless of their inorganic, vegetative, sensitive, or intellectual nature. Scores of examples could be given illustrating this. A stone falls to the ground, not by chance but by design; the roots of a tree grow in the direction of moisture; a hungry animal searches for food; man seeks happiness.

A thing seeks its goal with the cognitive power it has. If its cognitive power is material, its goal also must be material, for cognitive power and goal must be on the same plane. Inorganic objects and plants have no cognitive powers, and so they seek their goal blindly in accordance with the tendencies implanted in them by their Creator. Animals strive after things in accordance with their sense knowledge. They have instinct; they can see, hear, taste, smell, and feel. The objects of these senses are material things. Therefore, animals can seek only material goods.

Man's cognitive power is his non-material intellect. Its common object is being in general which is non-material. Its proper object are the natures of sensible things insofar as they are universalized or non-material. Knowing a thing is different from striving to possess it, but the manner that one strives to possess follows upon the manner that he knows it. Since the object of the intellect is non-material, the object of the will or appetitive power must also be non-material. The object of the first is non-material being; the object of the second is non-material good.

A power must be proportioned to its object. Since man has the power to strive to possess the non-material good known with his intellect, it follows that he has a non-material striving power distinct from his intellect. We call it the will.

§ 4. *The will is free in its operation from any internal or external compulsion.*

Any compulsion exerted on the will would have to come from within it or from without. If it can be proved that both of these are to be ruled out, then the will must be pronounced free in its operation.

The will is capable of either elicited or sanctioned acts. An elicited act is a choice or desire made by the will but one which does not overflow into external or physical action. Physical force cannot compel this kind of act. Being a force external to the act it must also be beyond the reach of the will that elicited the act. Force cannot control an elicited act because it cannot control its cause or source. A sanctioned act is one which is performed by the body under the direction of the will. Walking, looking, eating, and so forth are sanctioned acts. These acts can be compelled, but the compulsion does not strip the will from being internally free. In forcing one to act, an external agent compels the act of the body, but it does not, and cannot, compel the will to subscribe to it.

There is nothing internal to the will that necessitates it to act in a certain way thereby taking away its freedom. The basis for holding that the will is internally free is the fact that the intellect which guides the will is undetermined in the presence of an imperfect good. If the intellect can be compelled to judge a thing to be imperfectly good, the will is not compelled to choose it. In judging the degree of goodness exhibited by an object, the intellect sees it in comparison with perfect goodness. While the intellect is judging the comparative worth of imperfect objects, nothing can make it settle on any particular one. The intellect does not determine which alternative will be selected as the final one. It is the will that steps in, stops further consideration, and makes a final choice. There is nothing in the nature of the judgment that compels the will to choose. It remains internally free.

§ 5. *Man's intellect and will inhere in a non-material substance called the soul.*

In 1312 A.D., the Council of Vienne in France taught, "Whoever shall obstinately presume to assert, define, or hold that the rational and intellective soul is not the form of the human body in itself and essentially must be regarded as a heretic." (D-481)

Although we cannot see the intellect and will with the eyes of the body, we can prove their existence and non-material nature. We know these things from a study of their mode of operation. From the effects, we have learned a great deal about the causes. We press this investigation farther and learn of the existence and nature of the substance in which these powers inhere, the soul.

The intellect must receive help from the will and the will must receive help from the intellect in order to be able to act. The will is a blind power which must be given a target or goal to reach. This goal must be supplied by the intellect, for one cannot choose what he does not know. On the other hand, the intellect is not an appetitive power. It must be driven to enrich its store of knowledge by the will. If the intellect and will inhered in separated substances in man, then neither would be able to receive from the other the help that it must receive in order to be able to act. But experience clearly shows that both of them do act and that they act as a unity. A person does not say "My intellect thinks" or "My will chooses." He says "I think" and "I want." This unity could be achieved only if these two powers inhered in the same substratum.

This substratum must be a substance, a being that can exist by itself, since thought is impossible without a substantial being which thinks. Without this substance there would be no way by which a person could tie together by memory the experiences of a lifetime. Intellect and will are non-material powers and the substance in which they are rooted must be on the same plane. Therefore, that substance, must also be non-material. It makes little difference what name is given to it. The name by which it is most commonly known is the soul.

§ 6. *Since man's soul is a non-material substance, that is, a spirit, it is naturally immortal.*

A perfection that a being can have is either essential or accidental. An essential perfection flows from an object's essence so that the essence could not exist without this perfection. It is one of its properties just as it is fire's property to be hot. An accidental perfection is one that is added to a nature and is over and above the essence, just as color is the accident of a dog. From revelation we learn that man's soul is immortal; from philosophy, we learn that it is naturally and not accidentally immortal. The soul could not exist without this perfection.

The root of the soul's immortality is its spirituality. Any living object that has matter as part of its make-up can be killed or destroyed. Material things are composed of matter and form. Physical means can be used to separate the matter from the form. The soul also exhibits composition but it is a composition of essence and existence, not matter and form. The soul is completely devoid of material parts, for it is a non-material substance.

The cause of death to living material objects can be internal or external to those objects. But neither type of destructive cause can have any effect on the soul. No external cause can destroy it, for such a cause would have to be physical and so ineffective on a substance having no parts. No internal cause could destroy the soul, for a created being cannot separate its own essence from its own existence. It must be concluded that man's soul is naturally, not accidentally, immortal. Gold could annihilate the soul by withdrawing from its essence the perfection of existence. There are a number of solid reasons for holding that He will never do this.

§ 7. *Every human soul is immediately created by God.*

All limited things have received perfection. They are contingent beings which owe their existence to the Being with Unreceived Perfection, who is God. This fact is enough to prove that the soul of man was created, for it is a limited perfection.

There is a feature of the origin of man's soul that is not shared with created objects of a material nature such as plants and animals. While the life principles of plants and animals multiply according to laws implanted by God, each human soul is immediately created. In the case of lower living things, God has placed an intermediate material cause that accounts for the production of the living thing. But there is no such intermediary cause between God and the soul. The reason for this is simple. It is owing to the soul's spiritual nature. Created agents cannot act on pure potentiality, for then they would be able to create. They can bring about effects only with the use of instruments. There is no room for the use of instruments in the production of non-material substances. Spirits can come into existence only by the immediate creative act of God.

When are human souls created? The Church has anathemized Origenists who held that souls exist before they are infused into the body.[2] While the Church has made no other official pronouncement on the subject, the more probable opinion is that the soul is created at the moment of conception. In practice, this is the opinion that must be followed in cases of morality touching upon the observance of the Fifth Commandment.

§ 8. *God can confer on man gifts that are over and above what is necessary for human nature.*

A creature is said to be perfect when it has all the notes needed to constitute it as a complete nature. In essence, man is a rational animal, for he has a body and a soul. He is a composition of matter and form, of essence and existence. All things having composition must be creatural. As creatures they are limited in every respect. We can conclude therefore that a thing can be a perfect nature and yet be limited.

The very fact that a thing is limited implies that there is in it capacity for improvement. It can be given new powers in addition to those which it already has. The efficiency of already existing powers can be increased. Any benefit that a thing receives over and above what it must have to be a complete nature is a gift. A gift, then, is defined as an unearned benefit which can improve the receiver's existence or efficiency. God, the Creator, can confer gifts on creatures, for He has the power to give them and they, as creatures with limited existences, have the capacity to receive them.

The gift we discuss here is called a praeternatural gift. It is a created gift but one which is proper to a higher order of creatures. For example, a tree has the power to grow but a stone does not. If the stone received the power to grow, it would have received a created gift that properly belonged to a higher order of things. To a stone, the power to grow would be a praeternatural gift. A parallel of this example could be applied to man. He has a rational nature constituted by the substantial union of body and soul. Both body and soul have limited powers. There is nothing contradictory about the conclusion that God could endow either body or soul with gifts that are proper to angels. Although these gifts would be natural to angels, they would be praeternatural to man.

§ 9. *God can confer and man can receive a gift that surpasses all created natures.*

While a gift is an unearned benefit, it need not be a substance, that is, something that can exist by itself. A gift is anything which improves existence or efficiency. There are scores of examples of things that are not substances and yet answer this description. Knowledge, for example, improves the mind yet it is not a substance; health improves the efficiency of a sick body, but it cannot exist by itself. Although a gift can be a substance, it can also be a quality which is an accident unable to exist apart from substance.

Can man receive a gift or unearned benefit from God that will enable him to act in a fashion superior to any creature? At the very outset, it must be said that such a gift cannot be a substance. God alone is the uncreated substance, for He is an infinite being and cannot have an equal. If man could receive such a gift, it must be a quality. It is not contradictory for man to receive such a gift. Since man is a limited being there is room for improvement and the process of improvement does not destroy man's nature but elevates it. It is possible for God to confer such a gift, for it does not necessitate a new being equal to God, nor is man absorbed into God thereby losing his individuality.

A human being could not discover the existence of a supernatural gift by his own ingenuity or powers of investigation. Unaided reason can discover only those gifts of God that are necessary to man's nature. The quality we have discussed is over and above all created natures. It is completely supernatural and could only be learned by God's revelation.

§ 10. *The Church has not defined the manner of the production of the body of the first man.*

In 1950, the papal encyclical *Humani Generis* allowed all men of science great latitude in their research on the manner of production of the body of the first human being. God could have immediately created the body of the first human, or He could have infused a rational soul into the body of a highly evolved brute. Special creationists hold the first position, while evolutionists hold the second. The question probably cannot be answered with the information now available to scientists. The similarity of bodily structure existing between man and high type brutes is in itself no proof that God *de facto* infused the soul of the first man into an animal. If it was proof, evolution of man would not be still labeled a "theory," that is, an unproved proposition.

In the Book of Genesis, we read that God said, "Let us make mankind in our image and likeness . . . In the image of God he created him." (Gen: 1:26,27) The Church has never said that this verse must be interpreted to mean that God immediately created the body of the first man, otherwise the encyclical cited above would not have allowed the latitude it does. The Fathers who wrote on this subject looked upon the production of the body of the first man as being a great deal more than a biological question. In fact, to them it was primarily a theological matter. The vast majority of them held that God did not infuse a soul into a primate brute, but created Adam's body immediately. They argued that the superior dignity of man would lead one to suspect that immediate creation of the body was indicated and was more appropriate.[3]

§ 11. *The Church teaches that all humans have Adam and Eve as their common parents.*

While the Church has not defined whether or not the body of Adam was immediately created by God, she has officially taught that Adam and Eve are the proto-parents of all the humans on earth. We shall see that this is primarily a theological and not a scientific question. In 418 A.D., Pope Zozimus approved a canon of the Council of Carthage which indirectly stated that Adam was the first man. (D-101) In 1459 A.D., Pope Pius II condemned this statement, "God created another world than this one, and that in its time many other men and women existed and that consequently Adam was not the first man." (D-717C)

The evidence in Scripture on the proto-parenthood of Adam and Eve is clear. We find it in both Testaments. In Genesis we read, "And the man called his wife Eve because she was the mother of all the living." (Gen. 3:20) The accidental differences between the races do not erase the fact that all human beings are essentially the same, for they all have the same human nature.

Sacred Tradition is also explicit on the point of doctrine discussed here. Scores of texts from Christian writers dating from the First Century could be quoted here. Clement's First Epistle to the Corinthians written about 96 A.D. says, "Jealousy has estranged wives from husbands, and made of no effect the saying of our father Adam, 'This is now bone of my bone and flesh of my flesh.'" (I Clem. VI-3).

There is a cogent indirect proof for the unity of the human race. The Church has defined that all persons on earth must be baptized to have original sin removed. It is also a doctrine of faith that all persons receive this sin from Adam. Since original sin is transmitted by generation, it follows that Adam and Eve must be the proto-parents of all people on earth.

§ 12. *It is an opinion of theologians that Adam and Eve were endowed with the praeternatural gift of infused knowledge.*

While the Church has not formally defined the doctrine embodied in this proposition, it is a doctrine held by the vast majority of theologians. Denial of it by a Catholic is sinful. As early as the Fifth Century, St. Cyril of Alexandria wrote, "Adam, the head of the race was perfect in knowledge immediately from the first moment of his existence."[4]

Humans on earth today conceive ideas by a complex process of knowledge. They have no ideas when they are born. All their knowledge must be acquired. They first see sensible material objects and then abstract non-material notions from percepts of these objects. It is believed our first parents were spared this effort. God infused ideas into their minds. He "poured" these notions into their intellects without any effort on their part. Infused knowledge is natural to angels, but not to man. This is why it was a praeternatural gift to Adam and Eve.

How much knowledge did Adam and Eve receive from God? St. Thomas says that they did not see Him face to face; this would have rendered them incapable of sinning.[5] But he claims they did have "perfect" knowledge. This does not mean that it was infinite. In this context "perfect" means that they were given all the knowledge they needed to pursue the goal assigned them by God. We shall see that God gave them a supernatural goal. Adam and Eve were enlightened to grasp the nature of this goal. Since one must use proportionate means to reach a goal, it follows that God also infused the knowledge that our first parents needed to move toward this goal.

§ 13. *It is almost a defined doctrine that Adam and Eve were endowed with freedom from inclination to sin due to concupiscence.*

The basis for this proposition is drawn from a statement of the Council of Trent. The Council first quotes St. Paul's Epistle to the Romans 6:12 as saying that because of Adam sin entered into the world. It then goes on to explain the exact meaning of "sin" as used by the Apostle. "This concupiscence, which at times the Apostle calls 'sin' the holy Synod declares that the Catholic Church has never understood to be called sin, as truly and properly sin in those born again, but because it is from sin and inclines to sin. But if anyone is of the contrary opinion, let him be anathema." (D-792) The teaching of the Fathers is in harmony with this. St. Augustine wrote that before the fall there was "in our first parent undisturbed love of God."[6]

How can the freedom from inclination to sin be described? It does not mean that our first parents lacked human emotions; these are part of man's natural equipment. They were capable of sorrow, fear, love, joy, hatred, and the rest. Emotions are morally indifferent. They receive their coloring from the object to which they are directed by the will. When they get out of control, they can distort judgment and facilitate the commission of sin. In Adam and Eve, the emotions were under the complete control of the will.

Freedom from this inclination to sin in our first parents is called integrity. The inclination to sin that comes from the body is called sensuality or the attraction to inordinate pleasure. The inclination to sin that comes from the soul is the temptation to pride. There was nothing in Adam and Eve that could becloud their judgment. The acts of our first parents while they had integrity were cold, calculated, dispassionate choices.

§ 14. *The Church solemnly teaches that Adam was given the praeternatural gift of bodily immortality.*

In 418 A.D., the Council of Carthage in a canon approved by Pope Zozimus anathematized those who deny that Adam possessed bodily immortality before the fall. The Council of Trent repeated, "If anyone does not confess that the first man Adam, when he had transgressed the commandment of God in Paradise, immediately lost his holiness . . . and that he incurred . . . the death with which God had previously threatened him . . .

let him be anathema." (D-788) The Council is not only referring to spiritual death but also to loss of bodily immortality.

The Scripture passages most often quoted in official pronouncements of the Church as proving the praeternatural gift
of immortality is one from St. Paul's Epistle to the Romans.
It reads, "As through one man sin entered into the world and
through sin death, and thus death has passed unto all men because all have sinned." (Rom. 5:12) The Fathers who quote
and comment on this passage use it to show that since Adam's
sin caused death, it must be inferred that he had been originally placed in a state of deathlessness or bodily immortality.

There are several types of immortality. Which kind did
Adam and Eve have? As humans composed of matter and form
they did not have natural immortality, for physical means
could be used to separate body and soul. Thus, it was not the
type of immortality which the angels have. They could have
had only one other kind: that immortality which is praeternatural to their nature and which could be separated from their
essence. It must have been a gift, for they could exist without it.
With his characteristic cogency of expression, St. Augustine
conceived the immortality of our first parents as the possibility
of not dying, rather than the impossibility of dying.[7]

§ 15. *Theologians commonly hold that our first parents were
endowed with impassibility, that is, freedom from suffering.*

The capacity of a human being to endure suffering must not
be considered isolated from other gifts. St. Thomas shows that
the full meaning of suffering can be grasped only when studied
in conjunction with death. This capacity is an early warning
system that alerts one to the presence of elements that can cause
bodily harm and which might bring about death. The application of this to the impassibility of Adam and Eve is obvious.
The Angelic Doctor said that if Adam and Eve had been able
to suffer they would also have been able to die.[8] It has already

been proved that they enjoyed bodily immortality. From this theologians argue to the needlessness of the capacity to suffer in our first parents before the fall.

We know that in our present state we can endure, not only physical pain, but also mental anguish. Were our first parents free from this latter type of suffering in the state of innocence? We have reason to conclude that they were. Apart from the mental suffering or worry occasioned by the fear of pain and death, all purely mental suffering is in some way related to sin. Before the fall there was no sin, so this major cause of suffering was non-existent. And if there was no cause, there could be no effect.

A human being as such has the capacity to suffer simply because he is a mortal being. The freedom from physical suffering given to Adam and Eve was a gift over and above their complete human natures. It was a praeternatural gift. St. Augustine again describes it in terms similar to those cited in the previous example. Impassibility is not the impossibility of suffering but rather the possibility of never having to suffer.

§ 16. *Man is obliged to move toward the goal God has assigned him.*

God is infinitely intelligent. He must have a reason for everything He does. Here we consider created things in their relationship to their Creator. Just as God must have a reason for creating, so creatures must have a purpose for existing. These two things coincide perfectly with regard to the purpose of creation which is to manifest God's attributes and His glory.

God has assigned each creature a goal. This is true of both rational and irrational creatures. Irrational creatures are obedient to immutable laws so that they necessarily attain the goal assigned by God. They lack intellectual natures and cannot choose or reject their goal but must move toward it blindly.

We learn a great deal about the type of goal assigned any

creature by studying the nature of its God-given powers, since all powers must be subordinated to the task of moving toward the ultimate goal. Man has a rational nature. It was proved that man's intellect and will are non-material powers. Since they are man's highest powers, it follows that the goal assigned to man by God must be in harmony with these powers. We have seen the superiority of man's cognitive powers over those of animals and how the appetitive power follows the cognitive power. Reason even without the aid of revelation indicates that man's ultimate goal must be a non-material being that man can know his intellect and choose with his will.

§ 17. *God Himself is the goal man has been assigned.*

Every one of man's powers has an object. For example, the object of his eyes is light or color; the object of his hearing is resonance; that of taste is things as they are savory, and so forth. The intellect and will also have objects. The object of the intellect is truth, the non-material natures of things. The object of the will is things insofar as they are good.

While truth and goodness are the objects of the intellect and will, there is a scale of truth and goodness in existence. Some things are more important and more valuable than others. Knowledge of general principles is more valuable than knowledge of a singular application of that principle. Goods of the mind possess greater dignity than do those of the body.

The higher a truth or good man seeks to possess the more he ennobles his intellect and will by putting them to better use. Now, he puts his intellect to its highest possible use when he uses it to know the highest truth. He puts his will to its highest possible use when he uses it to pursue the highest good.

The highest truth and goodness must be the highest being. This is obviously God Who alone is the infinitely perfect Being. Since God can have no equal, He is the primary or highest object of man's non-material powers. He is the ultimate goal of man's life on earth. Man's life is purposeful, that is, it makes sense only when he moves toward this goal. He does this when he practices religion. Notice that nothing has been said as to the means that must be taken in attaining this goal. They will be discussed later. It is our task here only to prove that man has an inescapable duty to press toward the goal that God has assigned him.

§ 18. *The fact that man has an inescapable desire to be happy proves that God must be his goal.*

All men seek happiness by every one of their deliberate and free acts. This desire is part of man's natural equipment. He is born with it and never outgrows it. He does not acquire it by education or training. Every person of every age and race has always had the inescapable desire to be happy. Even when a person submits to pain he indirectly is seeking happiness.

Man is never fully satisfied with partial happiness but is ever seeking perfect and complete happiness. Happiness is produced by possessing desirable things of either the material order such as health or of the non-material order such as knowledge. Partial goods can at best produce partial happiness. And happiness is partial if it satisfies a person in one respect but does not satisfy him in another. For example, wealth produces only partial happiness because there are many things that man wants but cannot buy. It is also partial if it must end. Experience clearly shows that man is always driving toward perfect happiness, toward the possession of the perfect good that will satisfy him in all respects and for an unending period.

God does nothing in vain. For example, God would act in vain if he created teeth to chew food but did not create food, or lungs to inhale air but did not create air. Applying this to the present discussion, it must be said that since man was given the craving to be perfectly happy, there must exist the perfect good that man can possess and thereby experience the perfect happiness he craves.

God Himself is the perfect good, for He is an infinitely perfect being. When man strives for perfect happiness, he is implicitly striving to possess God. God, then, is the ultimate goal of man's life. "For Thyself Thou hast created us, O God, and our hearts are not at rest until they rest in Thee." (St. Augustine)

§ 19. *God could have assigned man the goal of seeing Him by the natural light of reason.*

God is an essentially supernatural being. Man considered merely as creature is an essentially natural being. Creator and creature, therefore, are beings on two different planes. The difference is one of kind, not merely of degree. We saw that God is the goal that man must reach by his activity during his earthly life. Since man was given an intellect and will with which to carry on his pursuit, it follows that he can possess God by seeing Him with his intellect and enjoying Him with his will. Seeing God by the natural light of reason would be possible only after death, since it would produce the perfect natural happiness man obviously does not experience during life before death.

A person who would see God by the natural light of reason after death could not see God as He is. Natural cognitive and appetitive powers cannot behold a supernatural being. Man would see God in a heavily veiled fashion, but even this would engender an ecstacy of love, joy, and happiness far surpassing any happiness he could experience on earth. It would be complete and unending.

It is difficult for us to imagine what it means to see God even by the natural light of reason. For example: An art critic is very impressed by a masterpiece of a Renaissance painter. He admires the composition and arrangement of figures. But he does not see the actual painting. He sees only the sketch of that picture made by an amateur artist. Enough of the genius of the original artist has come through to make the original recognized as being of superlative worth. The person who would see God by the natural light of reason would experience a happiness far superior to any happiness that could result from the possession of the finite goods of earth.

§ 20. *God could, and actually did, assign to all men the goal of seeing Him face to face.*

The very fact that man's powers of soul (his intellect and will) are limited indicates that their capacity can be increased. Man can receive praeternatural gifts, or benefits that are natural to angels. He can also receive gifts that exceed all created objects, provided these gifts be qualities and not substances. The greatest natural happiness that a person might receive is to see God by the natural light of reason, in a heavily veiled fashion. But God could so elevate the powers of our soul to enable us to see Him face to face. In this case, we would see God as He sees Himself, without any hindrances to obstruct vision. The soul would not know God exhaustively, but while the extensiveness of this vision would be limited, one would see God with the same directness with which God sees Himself.

To see God face to face produces a happiness like the happiness that is proper to God. The soul then knows and loves God with a directness similar to that with which God knows and loves Himself. Using again the previous example, the critic would not see the masterpiece of art reproduced in a sketch or photograph but would see the real thing under the most favorable conditions possible. This supernatural happiness far outstrips the happiness produced by seeing God by the natural light of reason. In fact, God with His infinite power could not give a created being a goal or happiness greater than seeing Him face to face. Reason can prove that a supernatural goal for man is possible, for it involves no contradiction. But reason cannot prove that it is the one actually assigned to us. We are assured of this assignment by the clear voice of the teaching authority of the Church.[9]

§ 21. *The Church teaches that God assigned Adam and Eve a supernatural goal and endowed them with the sanctifying grace needed to reach it.*

This truth is deduced from defined doctrines and therefore is theologically certain. The Council of Trent taught that our first parents lost sanctifying grace by their transgression. It said, "If anyone does not confess that the first man Adam, when he had transgressed the commandment of God in Paradise, immediately lost his holiness and the justice in which he had been established . . . let him be anathema." (D-788) The terms "holiness" and "justice" indicate the presence of sanctifying grace.

In the Epistle to the Romans, St. Paul wrote, "As through one man sin entered into the world and through sin death . . ." (Rom. 5:12) The Apostle does not qualify the type of death caused by Adam's sin. In the Gospels, a person lacking sanctifying grace, or justification, is often called dead. The implication is that our first parents were endowed with grace.

St. Augustine's writings on the doctrine we discuss are especially important, for he is called the "Doctor of Grace and Original Sin." He wrote, "God . . . fashioned their nature (Adam and Eve) and endowed them with grace . . . (but) as soon as they disobeyed the Divine Command, they forfeited divine grace."[10] (*De Civ. Dei* 13:3)

St. Thomas asked at what instant of their lives Adam and Eve were given grace?[11] He answers that our first parents were not first created and then endowed with grace. They were endowed with it from the first moment of their existence. The Angelic Doctor proves his conclusion from the fact that God never intended man for anything but a supernatural goal. Since the means must be proportioned to the end, the all-just God must have given Adam and Eve the means (grace) needed to reach the goal at the same time, from the first moment of their existence.

§ 22. *God entrusted Adam with the title to the grace that He wished to bestow on all the members of the human race.*

It is theologically certain that God bestowed on Adam the sanctifying grace that He wished Adam and his children to receive. In this context, the children of Adam are not only those immediate begotten by Adam, but all the members of the human race. The truth embodied in the proposition is labeled certain because it was deduced from dogmas defined by the Church. In 529 A.D., the II Council of Orange taught, "If anyone asserts that Adam's transgression injured him alone and not his descendants, or declares that certainly death of the body only, which is the punishment of sin, but not sin also, which is the death of the soul, passed through one man into the whole human race, he will do an injustice to God, contradicting the Apostle who says, 'Through one man sin entered in the world, and through sin death, and thus death passed into all men.' " (D-175) Obviously a person can lose only what he possesses. Since Adam caused all to lose grace, he in a sense possessed the grace of all men.

In what sense did Adam have the grace of all men? A careful distinction must be made between controlling an object and holding the title to that same object. A thief, for example, controls an object, but he does not hold title to it. A title is the lawful basis for laying claim to it. One may receive title to a thing long before he actually takes possession of it, but not vice versa. The proposition does not mean that God actually conferred on Adam the sum-total of the grace that He wished the human race to have; this would force the acceptance of several improbable positions. A far more likely interpretation is God entrusted Adam with the title to grace he wished to give to each individual. In this case, the members of the human race would indeed receive grace immediately from God, but they would have to receive the necessary title to this grace through Adam.

§ 23. *After endowing Adam and Eve with supernatural and praeternatural gifts, God placed them on probation.*

It is theologically certain that God subjected Adam and Eve to a test of obedience. Although the Church has not defined the precise character of certain accidental details involved, the essentials of the trial are very clear. Sacred Scripture supplies several vital notes. We read in Genesis, "And the Lord God commanded the man (Adam) thus, 'From every tree in the garden you may eat; but from the tree of the knowledge of good and evil you must not eat; for the day you eat of it, you must die.' " (Gen. 2:16 ff) Analysis of this passage shows that it involved a true probation. (1) God issued a command and not a mere exhortation or directive. The use of the imperative in the Hebrew and in the Vulgate which is translated "must" in English is sufficient to indicate this. (2) Although Adam and Eve had been endowed with sanctifying grace and had a right to actual grace that would enable them to keep it, they also had free will. At the moment they received God's command, they were faced with two alternatives. One was God's love and friendship; the other was a seriously forbidden object described to us as the fruit of the knowledge of good and evil. Now, an object is "seriously forbidden" when it cannot be co-possessed with love of God. If Adam chose God, he necessarily had to reject this object; if he chose this object, he would have had to reject God. (3) Every serious command carries with it a penalty for those who disobey it. God spelled out for Adam and Eve the sanction placed on the disobedience of His command, thus completing the details of their probation.

§ 24. *God cautioned Adam and Eve that disobedience of His command would entail loss of the gifts He had given them.*

The truth embodied in this proposition can be deduced from many pronouncements made by the Church. (D-788) In Genesis, we read that God warned Adam and Eve that "death" would be the penalty for any transgression of his command. "But from the tree of the knowledge of good and evil you must not eat; for the day you eat of it, you must die." (Gen: 2:17) And again, "The woman (Eve) answered the serpent, 'Of the fruit of all the trees in the garden we may eat; but of the fruit of the tree in the middle of the garden, God said: You shall not eat. Neither shall you touch it, lest you die.'" (Gen. 3:2) (1) Both passages refer to death without qualification. In a number of places in Scripture, a person lacking sanctifying grace (justification) is said to be "dead." Besides this meaning, the term is also commonly accepted as meaning the loss of vitality on the part of a body that was once alive. (2) The passages quoted show that Adam and Eve would suffer death as soon as they sinned, meaning punishment would be inflicted immediately after the transgression. The Book of Genesis records that after Adam and Eve had disobeyed God they were driven from Paradise while yet physically alive only to die later. The point that must be noted here is that the term "death" used to describe the penalty for disobeying God could be taken in several ways. It meant the loss of the soul's supernatural life and also the body's loss of natural life. We shall see that these deaths were really very much related to each other. They must not be studied as different penalties. Both are to be considered as a single death.

§ 25. *The Church solemnly teaches that Adam and Eve disobeyed God's command and thereby committed original sin.*

The doctrine of the reality of original sin appears in documents issued or approved by the Holy See as early as the first decades of the Fifth Century. She at least implicitly repeats it whenever she teaches the necessity of Baptism. In the Sixteenth Century, the Council of Trent again taught it in these words, "If anyone does not confess that the first man, Adam, when he had transgressed the commandment of God in Paradise, immediately lost his holiness and the justice in which he had been established, and that he incurred through the offense of that prevarication the wrath and indignation of God and hence the death with which God had previously threatened him . . . let him be anathema." (D-788) The holy council teaches in this definition that the penalty was incurred immediately after the sin was committed and that it was a mortal sin in the theological sense because it stripped Adam of sanctifying grace.

The fall of our first parents is recorded in Scripture. "She (Eve) took of its fruit and ate it, and also gave some to her husband, and he ate." (Gen. 3:6) After saying that through one man sin entered into the world, St. Paul identifies this "one man" as being Adam (Rom. 5:13)

The doctrine of original sin explicitly appears in Christian literature as early as the Second Century in the writings of St. Theophilus of Antioch. Great impetus was given to the speculation and explanation of the subject by several heresies of the Fourth and Fifth Centuries, especially Pelagianism, which denied the need of actual and sanctifying grace. It was against these heresies that St. Augustine composed no less than sixteen major works. The premise for these particular writings was the reality of original sin.

§ 26. *By their commission of original sin Adam and Eve lost sanctifying grace for themselves and for their descendants.*

Adam was in a singular position when he committed original sin. He held the title to the grace God wished to confer on every member of the human race. The Church has defined that Adam sinned. We now consider the effects of this sin on all men except the Blessed Virgin Mary. In 418 A.D., Pope Zosimus taught, "By His (Christ's) death that bond of death introduced into all of us by Adam and transmitted to every soul, that bond contracted by propagation is broken, in which no one of our children is held not guilty until he is freed through Baptism." (D-109a) Earlier in this chapter, we quoted the teaching of the II Council of Orange confirmed by Pope Boniface II on the same subject.

Several things are to be noticed about this statement. (1) The Council repeats at least implicitly that the term "death" is to be interpreted to mean loss of sanctifying grace for our first parents as well as for all their descendants. (2) Although the individual members of the human race did not themselves reject God, the sin they received from Adam and Eve was a true sin. Every attempt to interpret it figuratively must be avoided. It was the cause for man's loss of the sanctifying grace needed to reach his supernatural goal. (3) After Adam and Eve had committed original sin and made it impossible for us to reach our supernatural goal, God did not change the goal that He had originally assigned to all men. If man had an option as to which goal he must strive after, then original sin would have been a mere privation. But this was not the case. God still wanted us to reach a supernatural goal. Anything that prevents this from being attained is a sin and original sin certainly answers to this description.

§ 27. *The loss of sanctifying grace by Adam's sin entailed the added loss of the praeternatural gifts that God wished all men to have.*

Pronouncements of the Church imply that the supernatural and praeternatural gifts given to our first parents were so tied together that loss of the former meant loss of the latter. The II Council of Orange gives us information on the extent of the harm wrought by original sin. "If anyone says that by the offense of Adam's transgression not the whole man, that is according to body and soul, was changed for the worse, but believes that while the liberty of the soul endures without harm, the body only is exposed to corruption, he is deceived by the error of Pelagius and resists the Scripture." (D-174) In 418 A.D., the Council of Carthage taught the loss of immortality because of original sin. (D-101) In 1547 A.D., the Council of Trent repeated that the same sin caused man to lose integrity of will and knowledge. (D-788)

St. Thomas gives the rational explanation for the loss of the praeternatural gifts.[12] Man received praeternatural gifts to help him to be orientated toward supernatural life. Nothing exists without a purpose. When Adam and Eve lost supernatural life, they lost the opportunity to reach their supernatural goal. They thereby stripped the praeternatural gifts of their meaning and purpose, for there is no such thing as a praeternatural goal.

The Church says that original sin caused the death of our first parents. It caused the death of the supernatural life of the soul and at the same moment caused the physical death of the body. Concerning the latter death, St. Augustine said that Adam's body started to die as soon as he sinned. The process of dying merely reached its final stage when his soul left the body. In this respect the two deaths were simultaneously caused by original sin.

§ 28. *Although original sin stripped man of the gifts that God wished him to have, it still left him with a complete human nature.*

A thing is complete when it has all the notes necessary to constitute its essence. A human being is constituted by the substantial union of body and soul. The fact that one person has less intellectual ability than another does not make him less a person than the other. While original sin stripped the members of the human race of supernatural and praeternatural gifts and left them with a strong inclination to sin, it nevertheless left them with a complete human nature. Certain leaders of the Protestant revolt denied the existence of free will in man after his fall. Luther held that it rendered man incapable of good work. Calvin held that a person is predestined to heaven or to hell in spite of any effort on his part. Against these pernicious errors, the Council of Trent in 1547 A.D. defined, "If anyone shall say that after the sin of Adam, man's free will was lost or destroyed . . . let him be anathema." (D-815)

There are few doctrines for which more passages could be cited in Sacred Scripture than that of free will. Without it, God's injunction to obey the Ten Commandments, to practice virtue, and to repent of sin would be utterly meaningless.

Reason, even without revelation, can prove that man today has a free will. It was established that free will is natural to a rational person. It is impossible for man to be without it.

§ 29. *The punishment meted out by God for the commission of original sin was perfectly just.*

Original sin is the cause of the horrible deaths that humans undergo, the terrible sufferings, the darkened intellect, and the wayward will he must cope with. One might be tempted to think that man's punishment is out of proportion with the sin responsible for it. He might even look upon the devastation as an act of revenge visited by God upon an ungrateful people. Some argue that God inflicts punishment on innocent people who had nothing to do with the commission of original sin.

The fundamental error in this line of thinking is that it forgets that God is infinitely perfect and so must be all-just. It is absolutely impossible for Him to mete out punishment that is greater than the sin deserves. God cannot perpetrate even the smallest injustice. The magnitude of an offense is measured by the dignity of the one offended. Original sin was a mortal sin aimed at God. St. Thomas teaches that it was an act of infinite malice.[13] All the suffering of the entire human race could not atone for it. It took an act of infinite worth to atone for the indignity it represented.

This whole subject is matter for fruitful meditation. The immense number of mortal sins daily flung at God tends to deaden the horror with which we should regard even one such sin. Physical suffering makes a great impression on us. Imagine for a moment the pain caused by all physical ailments such as cancer, the suffering of starvation, the miseries of war. Multiply them by all the generations of people who have endured them, then remember what was their cause. We will then have a little better appreciation of the malice of even one mortal sin. We should not judge things by their external appearances but should try to grasp the inner natures.

§ 30. *After Adam and Eve had committed original sin, God promised that He would give man a second opportunity to reach his supernatural goal.*

We read in Genesis that God addressed Satan, the tempter of our first parents, in these words, "I will put enmity between you and the woman, between your seed and her seed; he shall crush your head, and you shall lie in wait for his heel." (Gen. 3:15) This passage is known as the *protoevangelium,* or the prediction of the coming of the Messianic kingdom. In 1909, the Pontifical Biblical Commission ordered that this passage be interpreted as referring to the promise of the coming of a future restorer. (D-2123) A number of the Fathers dating from the Second Century have explained it in this way so that the directive of the commission was not arbitrary nor hasty. The earliest Christian writer who comments on it seems to have been St. Irenaeus (d. 202 A.D.).[14]

Scholars and theologians explain the passage quoted in this

way: God says that there will be an irreconcilable opposition between the followers of Satan and the children of Eve. Satan had succeeded in getting Adam and Eve to commit the sin that would prevent the human race from reaching their supernatural goal. The seed of Eve would completely overthrow the work of Satan. This must mean that the members of the human race would in some way receive a second opportunity to reach the goal that God assigned them before the Fall. It is a promise made by God to man. The person promised is called the Messias.

§ 31. *Old Testament prophecies predicted the manner in which the Messias would redeem the members of the human race.*

The phrase "to redeem" means "to buy back." In this discussion, it means to win back the opportunity and means needed to reach the supernatural goal assigned to us by God. The *protoevangelium* promised that the members of the human race would be redeemed but it did not state how this would be accomplished. Later revelation supplied this information.

In the Old Dispensation, God revealed the tenets of the religion known as Judaism. It was a divine and true religion. One of the distinct features of Judaism was that it was a religion of preparation for the coming of the Messias. It derived its efficacy from the work of the Messias.

We can reconstruct an outline of the life and character of the Messias from Old Testament prophecies. He was to be born of a Virgin Mother[15] of the root of Jesse and line of David[16] in Bethlehem of Juda.[17] He would rule as a king[18] in a kingdom extending to the ends of the earth.[19] He would inaugurate a reign of peace;[20] he would be a mighty teacher[21] and would hold a priestly office.[22] The Old Testament writings show that the Messias would fulfill his mission by suffering. He would meekly[23] submit to be mocked,[24] ridiculed,[25] and finally crucified.[26] It seems to be a reasonable conclusion from the study of the Old Testament that the Messias was to fulfill His mission of redemption by the act that climaxed his stay on earth, namely, his death.

Reliable studies have been made showing how the Jews under the influence of their leaders and teachers drifted away from the notion of a suffering Messias to that of a temporal one. The latter notion was deeply engrained in their national and religious life when in the fullness of time the Messias did come.[27]

NOTES

1. Phillips, *Modern Thomistic Philosophy* (London: Burns-Oates and Washburn, 1939), I, 252 ff.
2. D-203.
3. *S.T.*, I, 91, 2.
4. *Com. In Joannem*, 1, 9.
5. *S.T.*, I, 94, 1.
6. *De Civ. Dei*, 14, 10.
7. *De Gen. ad Litt*, 5, 25.
8. *S.T.*, I, 97, 2.
9. Pius XII, *Humani Generis*, D. 3018.
10. *De Civ. Dei*, 13, 3.
11. *S.T.*, I, 95, 1.
12. *S.T.*, I-II, 85, 3-5.
13. *S.T.*, III, 1, 2.
14. *Adv. Haer.* 3, 22, 3.
15. Isaias, 7:14.
16. Jeremias 23:5.
17. Mich. 5:2.
18. Ps. 2:6.
19. Ps. 2:8.
20. Ps. 71:4.
21. Isaias, 42:1.
22. Ps. 109:4.
23. Isaias 53:7.
24. Isaias 50:6.
25. Ps. 21:8.
26. Ps. 21:17.
27. Lebreton, *The History of the Primitive Church* (New York: MacMillan, 1952), I, 55 ff.

VI

Jesus Christ

§ 1. *Jesus Christ is the Messias promised by God to mankind after the fall of Adam and Eve.*

In the Hebrew language, the one promised by God is called the "Messias." In Greek, the name given this same person is "Christ." In English, these words mean "the annointed one." In 1907 A.D., Pope St. Pius X repeated the traditional teaching of the Church in condemning the error of Modernism which denied that the Messias is identified with God the Son. (D-2030)

New testament writings explicitly tell us that Jesus is the Messias whose coming was promised and foretold in the Old Testament. At Jacob's well the Samaritan woman said to Jesus, " 'I know that Messias is coming (who is called Christ), and when he comes he will tell us all things.' Jesus said to her, 'I who speak with thee am he.' " (John 4:25-26) When St. John the Baptist had heard of Jesus' deeds he wondered if he was not the Messias and sent his disciples to ask, " 'Art thou he who is to come, or shall we look for another?' And Jesus answering said to them, 'Go and report to John what you have heard and seen.' " (Matt. 11:2-4)

St. Paul was the most persistent of the Apostles in calling

attention to the fact that Jesus was the Messias. His missionary efforts followed a pattern. He would go to a city having a Jewish synagogue and mingle with the people. When invited to speak he used the opportunity to prove that Christ was the Messias promised to the people of the Old Testament. "But Saul grew all the stronger and confounded the Jews who were living in Damascus, proving that this (Jesus) is the Christ." (Acts 9:22)

§ 2. *The Roman Catholic Church has always taught that Jesus Christ is God the Son made man.*

The Church usually makes a solemn doctrinal pronouncement when that doctrine is attacked by heresy. This is well illustrated by her teaching on the divinity of Christ. (1) In 325 A.D., the Council of Nicea against Arian heretics taught, "We believe in . . . our one Lord Jesus Christ the Son of God, the only begotten of the Father, that is of the substance of the Father, God of God, light of light, true God of true God . . . who for our salvation came down, and became incarnate and was made man." (D-54) (2) In 431 A.D., St. Cyril of Alexandria wrote against the Nestorians, "If anyone dares to say that Christ is a man inspired by God, and not rather that He is truly God, as a son by nature, as the Word was made flesh and has shared similarly with us in blood and flesh, let him be anathema." (D-117) (3) In 1208 A.D., the profession of faith for the Waldensian heretics was made to read, "We confess that the Incarnation of the Divinity took place neither in the Father, nor in the Holy Spirit, but in the Son only; so that He who was in the Divinity the Son of God the Father, true God from the Father, was in the humanity the son of man, true man from a mother." (D-422) (4) In 1564 A.D., the Council of Trent, included in its profession of faith, "I believe . . . in one Lord Jesus Christ, the only-begotten Son of God, and born of the Father before all ages, God of God, light of light, true God of true God, begotten not made, consubstantial with the Father . . . who for us and for our salvation descended from heaven, and became incarnate . . . and was made man." (D-994) (5) In 1907 A.D., the Holy Office condemned the heresy of Modernists who held that "the divinity of Jesus Christ is not proved from the Gospels; but is a dogma which the Christian conscience has deduced from the notion of the Messias." (D-2027)

§ 3. *Christ used clear and unequivocal language in proclaiming His Divinity.*

In the twenty-sixth chapter of St. Matthew's Gospel, we read the account of Christ's religious trial before the Sanhedrin. Caiphas sought a charge against Christ that would make the death penalty seem justified. An accusation of blasphemy would certainly fit his needs. The high priest addressed Christ saying, " 'I adjure (put you under oath) thee by the living God that thou tell us whether thou art the Christ, the Son of God.' Jesus said to him, 'Thou hast said it. Nevertheless, I say to you, hereafter you shall see the Son of Man sitting at the right hand of the Power and coming upon the clouds of heaven.' " (Matt. 26:63-64)

In the tenth chapter of St. John's Gospel, we read that on Solomon's Porch in the Temple, the rabbis and doctors demanded that Christ tell them whether or not He claimed to be the Christ. Jesus answered them, "I tell you and you do not believe." (John 10:25) When the rabbis heard this answer, they took up stones to throw at Him giving as their reason, "Not for a good work do we stone thee, but for blasphemy, and because thou, being a man, makest thyself God." (John 10:33)

In the ninth chapter of St. John's Gospel, we read the account of Christ restoring sight to the blind man. "Jesus heard that they (the pharisees) had turned him (the blind man) out, and when he had found him, said to him, 'Dost thou believe in the Son of God?' He answered and said, 'Who is he,

Lord, that I may believe in him?' And Jesus said to him, 'Thou hast both seen him, and he it is who speaks with thee.' " (John 9:35 ff)

§ 4. *Christ's Divinity is repeatedly proclaimed in the New Testament.*

The contemporaries of Christ whose testimonies we cite here left extant writings. They either knew Christ personally or lived at the time when Christ walked the earth. They do not always quote Christ but their statements reflect Christ's claim as they understood it. There is perfect harmony between these statements and those made by Christ in His own behalf.

St. Peter was one of the Twelve Apostles, having been with Jesus from the beginning of His public ministry. When Christ and His apostles were nearing the town of Caesarea Philippi, Christ asked them who they thought He really was. Peter answered with his celebrated profession of faith saying, "Thou art the Christ, the Son of the living God." (Matt. 16:16) In reply to this confession, Christ confirmed its correctness with the words, "Blessed art thou, Simon Bar-Jona, for flesh and blood has not revealed this to thee, but My Father in heaven." (Matt. 16:17)

St. John the Evangelist wrote to refute the Corinthian heretics who denied Christ's divinity. The theme of his whole Gospel is that Christ is God. He summarizes what he has written in these terms, "But these are written that you may believe that Jesus is the Christ, the Son of God, and that believing you may have life in His Name." (John 20:31)

One is struck by the Christo-centric character of St. Paul's epistles. In these fourteen short letters, the Apostle uses the name "Jesus" or "Christ" or "the Lord" or "Son of God" for a total of 639 times.[1] His greatest Christological reference reads, "Have this mind in you which was also in Christ Jesus, who though he was by nature God, did not consider being equal to God a thing to be clung to, but emptied himself, taking the nature of a slave and being made like unto men." (Phil. 2:5-7) The fact of Christ's two natures, one divine and one human, could not be set down in more explicit fashion.

§ 5. *Christ's enemies who were His contemporaries understood His claim to divinity in the literal sense.*

In the eighteenth and nineteenth chapters of St. John's Gospel, the civil trial of Christ befose the Roman governor, Pontius Pilate, is recorded. During the trial, Pilate sought to ascertain what charges were preferred against Christ. He asked the crowd what crime Jesus had committed that would justify the death penalty they demanded. The people, coached by their leaders, shouted, "We have a law, and according to that law he must die, because he has made himself Son of God." (John 19:7) The demand of the people was not based on an isolated statement of Christ but on the fact that he had repeatedly made it throughout His public ministry.

It is interesting to compare the quotations of the people milling around the cross after Christ had been crucified. St. Luke quotes the people, "He saved others; let him save himself, if he is the Christ, the chosen one of God." (Luke 23:35) St. Matthew records their remarks, "He saved others, himself he cannot save! If he is the King of Israel, let him come down now from the cross, and we will believe him. He trusted in God; let him deliver him now, if he wants him; for he said, 'I am the Son of God.' " (Matt. 27:42-43) St. Mark records the reaction of the centurion guarding Christ. Seeing the earthquake, he said, "Truly this man was the Son of God." (Mark 15:39) The centurion is repeating with a measure of reverence the statements that he had been hearing the people sneeringly utter. He is quoting them as they were quoting Christ in His claim to be God. Note also people's use of "Christ" and

"Son of God" synonymously. It is another indication that Jesus used them in this way when referring to Himself.

§ 6. *Christ's divinity was professed by Christians from earliest times.*

The evidence cited here dates from about 100 A.D. It shows that the belief of the people was identical with the evidence on Christ's claim to divinity found in New Testament writings. It was not a gradual sublimation of the notion of Messias as Modernists hold.

The oldest extra-Scriptural writings today are those the Apostolic Fathers composed in widely separated places of the Christian world in the century after Christ's death. Nine of the fourteen writings were composed before 110 A.D. Every one of these works refers to the divinity of Christ with a casualness that indicates that the readers were well acquainted with Christian belief on this matter. With a Christo-centric approach reminiscent of St. Paul, St. Ignatius of Antioch (d. 107) first states that Christ is God and then repeats the name "Jesus Christ" no less than 137 times in his seven very brief extant epistles.[2]

There is an extremely interesting note in a letter of Pliny the Younger, the governor of the province of Bithynia to the Emperor Trajan, composed about 112 A.D. Pliny tells the emperor that he is alarmed at the rapid spread of Christianity beyond the city and its country districts. He then adds that when the Christians are put on trial the only thing he can discover is this, "They declared their guilt or error as simply this: On a fixed day they used to meet before dawn and sing hymns to Christ, as though he were God."[3] (*Bk. X-Ep.* 96)

Archeologists have proved that early Christians used the fish to symbolize their belief in the divinity of Christ. The letters that make up the Greek word for fish were used as an acrostic. Each letter stands for a word. The letters I X T H U S stand for "Jesus Christ, Son of God, Savior." The oldest extant picture of this symbol dates from about 125 A.D. It can still be seen in the crypt of Lucina in the Catacombs of Callixtus at Rome. The famous inscription of Abercius made about 165 A.D. at Hieropolis in Phrygia also alludes to the divinity of Christ under the symbol of the fish.[4]

§ 7. *The writers of the Second and Third Centuries defended the divinity of Christ.*

The Apostolic Fathers were not given to speculation, but transmitted doctrine as they received it. In the Second Century, Christianity was attacked by pagans of intellectual ability and literary skill. Fronto, Porphory, Celsus and others struck hard at Christian practices and doctrines. One of their prime targets was the divinity of Christ which they looked upon as the fundamental article of faith. But they triggered counter-attacks by a group of writers who composed works of an apologetical nature. The most prominent of these were St. Justin (d. 160), St. Irenaeus (d. 202), Clement of Alexandria (d. 211), Origen (d. 255) and above all Tertullian (d. 220). The attacks of the pagans forced these writers to fortify their positions with philosophical arguments. These writers not only had to set forth what Christians believed but also why they believed them.

The Ante-Nicene writers insisted on the divinity of Christ. *St. Justin* "His (God's) Son alone is properly called Son; the Logos, who alone was with him and was begotten before the works, when at first he created and arranged all things by him, is called Christ."[5] St. Irenaeus, "No one else, therefore is called God or Lord except He who is the God and Lord of all, and His Son Jesus Christ."[6] *Clement of Alexandria* holds that the Logos is the Savior of the human race and the founder of a new life which begins with faith, proceeds to knowledge and leads through charity to immortality and deification. Christ as the

incarnate Logos is God and man.[7] *Origen,* "Jesus Christ who
was begotten from the Father before all creatures . . . emptied
Himself in recent days, became man . . . and having become
man, He nevertheless remained what He was, namely, God."[8]
Tertullian, "We see plainly the two-fold state, which is not
confounded, but conjoined in one person—Jesus, God and man
. . . so that the property of each nature is so wholly preserved
that the Spirit on the one hand did all its own things in Jesus
such as miracles, and mighty deeds and wonders; and the flesh,
on the other hand, exhibited the affections which belong to
it."[9]

§ 8. *Christ usually combined the working of miracles with His
instruction of the people.*

It is very revealing to notice what Christ did when an occasion
to teach presented itself. He taught at such diverse places as
at the sea-shore, on the mountain-side, in private homes, in a
wheat field, on a public road, in the synagogue, and in the
Temple. His audience varied greatly in number and in intellectual ability. But it would be a serious mistake to think that
His instruction periods were haphazard in procedure. There
is evidence that they were carefully planned and followed a
definite pattern.

The format of the instruction periods is seen from these
Gospel passages. "And Jesus was going about . . . teaching in
their synagogues, and preaching the gospel of the kingdom,
and curing every kind of disease and infirmity." (Matt. 9:35)
"And when the Sabbath had come, he began to teach in the
synagogue. And many, when they heard him, were astonished
at his doctrine, saying, 'Where did he get all this?' and 'What
mean such miracles wrought by his hands.' " (Mark 6:2) "And
coming down with them, he took his stand on a level stretch,
with a crowd of his disciples, and a great multitude of people
. . . who came to listen to him and to be healed of their dis-

eases." (Luke 6:17-18) "This man (Nicodemus) came to Jesus at night, and said to him, 'Rabbi, we know that thou hast come a teacher from God, for no one can work these signs that thou workest unless God is with him.' " (John 3:2)

These passages—one from each of the Evangelists—show that Christ made it a practice to combine the working of miracles with the preaching of truth. These are linked together too regularly for it to be mere coincidence. We are led to suspect that there is a connection between them and that they must not be isolated from each other. We will presently see the real connection.

§ 9. *Christ wanted His miracles to be looked upon as proof that what He taught was true.*

The purpose of Christ's miracles was not merely to impress people with His power but to instill faith in them. Faith is not merely a blind confidence in someone or something. It is not a synonym for hope. It includes the acceptance of a statement as true on the authority of the one who makes it. Faith is a synonym for believing. Christ told the people many things that they could not comprehend. He told them that He had to atone for the sins of the world; that He had the power to forgive sin; that those who believed in Him would never see death; that He would give His flesh to eat and His blood to drink. These ideas simply staggered the minds of His listeners. While some found them too much to accept, others sought a basis for accepting them. "From this time many of his disciples turned back and no longer went about with him." (John 6:67)

Christ wanted His miracles to be looked upon as His credentials. They were the "signs" that the people demanded to see. When people had enough good will to appraise correctly the purpose of miracles, Christ rarely refused to work them. "Then Jesus answered and said to her, 'O woman, great is thy *faith*. Let it be done to thee as thou wilt.' And her daughter was healed from that moment." (Matt. 15:28) "While he was yet speaking, there came one from the house of the ruler of the synagogue, saying to him, 'Thy daughter is dead' . . . But Jesus on hearing this word answered the father of the girl, 'Do not be afraid; only have *faith* and she shall be saved.' " (Luke 8:49-50) "And Jesus addressed him, saying, 'What wouldst thou have me do for thee?' And the blind man said to him, 'Rabboni, that I may see.' And Jesus said to him, 'Go thy way, thy *faith* has saved thee.' " (Mark 10:51-52) Commenting on the miracle of changing water into wine at Cana, St. John wrote, "This first of his signs Jesus worked at Cana of Galilee; and he manifested his glory, and his disciples *believed* in him." (John 2:11) This then is the connection between miracles and teaching. Christ wanted to drive home by means of miracles the truth of what He taught.

§ 10. *Christ was especially anxious to have people accept the truth that He was God.*

We include here Gospel passages to prove that Christ wanted people to accept Him, not merely as a wonder-worker or a religious leader or a teacher, but as God. Once the people looked upon Him as divine, it would be easy to get them to grasp the meaning and authority of the Church He would found and the sacraments He would institute. (1) To the person freed from the demoniacal power, Christ said, " 'Go home to thy relatives, and tell them all that the Lord has done for thee' . . . And he departed, and began to publish in Decapolis all that Jesus had done for him." (Mark 5:19-20) Notice that "Lord" and "Jesus" refer to the same person. (2) Christ struck at the incredulity of the Jews with these two statements, "If I do not perform the works of my Father, do not believe me. But if I do perform them, and if you are not willing to believe me, believe the works, that you may know and believe that the Father is in me and I in the Father." (John 10:37) Again, "Do you believe that I am in the Father and the Father in me? Other-wise believe because of the works themselves." (John 14:11-12) (3) For the sake of emphasis, we quote again the splendid passage tying miracles to the acceptance of Christ as God. "Many other signs also Jesus worked in the sight of his dis-ciples, which are not written in this work. But these are writ-ten that you may *believe* that Jesus is the Christ, the *Son of God*." (John 20:30-31)

We now see the pattern of the periods that Christ devoted to instruction. He taught all who were willing to listen to Him. Before or after a lesson, Christ often worked miracles. The purpose of the miracles was to drive home to people that what He had just taught was true. The truth that Christ was espec-ially anxious to impress on people and get them to accept was the fact that He was really God.

§ 11. *Christ appealed to His miracles and prophecies as proof that He was divine.*

The proofs for the divinity of Christ from reason are fully con-sidered in apologetics. A study of the dogmatic aspects of the Incarnation presumes that the student is acquainted with the cogency of those proofs. In apologetics, Christ's miracles and prophecies are examined from a philosophical point of view. The conclusions to those inquiries is that only one with infinite power and knowledge can work them. In the course of that study, no appeal is made to authority. Here we merely cite those Gospel passages which show that Christ wanted His mir-acles to be looked upon as proof of His divinity. First, "If I do not perform the works of my Father, do not believe me. But if I do perform them, and if you are not willing to believe me, believe the works, that you may know and believe that the Father is in me and I in the Father." (John 10:37-38) To the person freed from demoniacal power, Christ said, " 'Go home to thy relatives, and tell them all that the Lord has done for thee.' And he (the cured man) departed, and began to publish in Decapolis all that Jesus had done for him." (Mark 5:19-20) Notice that "Lord" and "Jesus" refer to the same person. Finally, St. John summarizes the theme and purpose of his Gospel with this verse, "Many other signs also Jesus worked in the sight of his disciples, which are not written in this book. But these are written that you may believe that Jesus is the Christ, the Son of God, and that believing you may have life in his name." (John 20:30-31)

Beside the explicit appeal made to miracles shown in the above passages, there are numerous episodes in the Gospels which show Christ usually combined miracles with teaching. The juxtaposition of the two shows that the purpose of the miracles was to drive home to His listeners the truth of what He taught.

§ 12. *A study of Christ's miracles shows His dominion over all categories of creatures.*

There are five levels of creatures in existence. They are pure spirits, rational, sensitive, vegetative, and inorganic beings. An examination of the miracles recorded in the Gospels shows that Christ had dominion over all creation. Since Christ claimed to be divine, it was most appropriate that He should show mastery of all things contingent on Him.

About forty miracles are recorded in detail in the Gospels. (1) Christ showed His mastery over inanimate objects by stilling the storm on the Lake of Gennesareth, by multiplying loaves and fishes at Capharnaum, and by changing water into wine at Cana. (2) He proved His dominion over vegetative or plant life by causing the barren fig tree to wither. (3) He worked several miracles to show that He was Lord to the animal kingdom. The two miraculous catches of fish as well as the fish caught with the shekel prove this. (4) The many instances when Christ freed persons victims of demonical possessions shows that He was master of pure spirits such as devils. There are six miracles of Christ dealing with devils. Perhaps the most spectacular of these was the one worked at Gerasa.

(5) Twenty-six of the miracles described in detail in the Gospels were worked on or involved humans. This is not surprising for they best fitted into the purpose of miracles. The persons who benefitted by them were almost forced to think of the one who worked them. It is difficult to see how the healed lepers and paralytics, the blind persons who received their sight, the dead who were brought back to life, and others could ever forget the part that Christ played in their lives. The intensely personal nature of the miracles on humans was far more effective and lasting than some that could have been spectacular but would have soon been forgotten. Christ worked a great many more miracles that are recorded without details in the Gospels. The Evangelists often cluster many of them in a single verse. "In that very hour He (Jesus) cured many of diseases, afflictions, and evil spirits, and to many who were blind he granted sight." (Luke 7:21) Notice how they too pertain to the last group of miracles considered.

§ 13. *The greatest miracle by which Christ proved His divinity was His own resurrection from the dead.*

Attacks on the reality of Christ's resurrection from the dead have proceeded along two paths. The first denies that Christ really died on the cross; the second denies that He really arose from the dead. Critics refuse to accept the fact that Christ arose from the dead simply because they deny the possibility of miracles. They freely admit that their denials are based on philosophical and not historical grounds.

The Gospels plainly show that Christ died on the cross and all attempts to interpret the account in figurative fashion have failed. "But when they (the soldiers) came to Jesus, and saw that he was already dead, they did not break his legs; but one of the soldiers opened his side with a lance, and immediately there came out blood and water." (John 19:33-34) Again, "And he (Joseph of Arimathea) went in boldly to Pilate and asked for the body of Jesus. But Pilate wondered whether he had already died. And sending for the centurion, he asked him whether he was already dead. And when he learned from the centurion that he was, he granted the body to Joseph." (Mark 15:43-46)

There are in all twelve different apparitions of Christ after His resurrection recorded in the New Testament. One of the most celebrated is the one in which Thomas played a part. "Now Thomas . . . was not with them when Jesus came. The other disciples therefore said to him, 'We have seen the Lord.' But he said to them, 'Unless I see in his hands the print of the nails, and put my finger into the place of the nails, and put my hand into his side, I will not believe.' And after eight days, . . . He (Christ) said to Thomas, 'Bring here thy finger, and see my hands; and bring here thy hand, and put it into my side; and be not unbelieving, but believing.' Thomas answered and said to him, 'My Lord and My God.' " (John 20:24-28) There is a reason why this particular apparition is cited. It is because it appears in St. John's Gospel. It is probable that the Evangelist composed his Gospel to refute among others, the Docetist heretics of the First Century who denied that Christ had a real body and, therefore, denied the reality of the resurrection.

§ 14. *After Christ's ascension, the Apostles emphasized that His miracles and especially resurrection proved His divinity.*

The people who listened to the Apostles were far from being a credulous lot. The Apostles had to present two sets of credentials, one to prove that they had been authorized by God to preach, the other to prove that Christ was really God. It is the second of these that interests us here.

The importance of being a witness to Christ's resurrection

is seen by the fact that it was decided that Judas's successor had to be one who was well-acquainted with the resurrection. "(Peter said) ' . . . Of these men (candidates) . . . one must become a witness with us of his resurrection.' " (Acts 1:21-22) The Acts of the Apostles contains several examples of the catechesis delivered by the Apostles after Christ's ascension. All of them were built around Christ.

In The Acts, St. Peter and St. Paul refer to Christ's resurrection no less than eight times. They also make frequent reference to it in their epistles. "For I delivered to you first of all, what I also received, that Christ died for our sins according to the Scriptures, and that he was buried, and that he rose again the third day, according to the Scriptures, and that he appeared to Cephas, and after that to the Eleven. Then he was seen by more than five hundred brethren at one time, many of whom are with us still, but some have fallen asleep. After that he was seen by James, then by all the apostles. And last of all, as by one born out of due time, he was seen also by me." (I Cor. 15:3-8) The dogma of the resurrection of Christ and consequently of our own resurrection is one of the pivots of the theology of St. Paul.[10] His emphasis on Christ's resurrection was interestingly noted in the ancient Christian art found in the catacombs. St. Paul is often pictured in murals with a phoenix at his feet. In ancient times the phoenix (a bird) was used as a symbol of resurrection and immortality.[11]

§ 15. *A miracle is an act exceeding the manner of acting of all created agents and so attributable only to God.*

In the succeeding discussions we will examine a miracle from a philosophical point of view to ascertain whether or not the works of Christ really prove that He was God. Critics have precluded all discussion of this question saying that miracles are impossible and that the acts ascribed to Christ must be attributed to a variety of natural causes.

The proposition shows that there is nothing vague or indefinite about a miracle. It is entirely possible, for it in no way involves a contradiction in God or in the subject in which it is worked. The distinct feature of a miracle is that it can be worked only by a being having infinite power. Created agents, even though they might be such beings as angels, cannot work one.

Philosophy, the study that investigates ultimate causes, is the branch of learning that can tell us whether or not an act is a miracle. An act that can be attributed only to God must be traced to the ultimate cause of the creation of all things. Natural science deals with proximate causes and is incompetent to give us the answer we seek.

We list the three types of miracles possible. (1) An absolute miracle transcends the powers of created agents in every respect. An example of such an act would be bringing something into existence out of nothing. (2) A substantial miracle is an effect which never occurs in creatures unless God directly brings it about. An example of this would be the act of giving sight to a person born blind. (3) A modal miracle is an effect which does occur in nature, but which does not occur in this way unless God intervenes. An example of this kind of miracle is the instantaneous cure of a disease that always requires a long time and treatment to bring about the cure. The instantaneous cure of tuberculosis or leprosy would exemplify this act.

§ 16. *Only a being with infinite power can create, that is, can lift a possible being into the realm of actuality.*

Real natures are either actual or possible. Nothing can become actual if it was not previously possible. In both instances the nature is the same except that an actual nature has evidently received the distinct perfection called existence. The process by which existence was added to a possible nature is called creation. (1) A nature that has only possibility cannot create itself. We saw that in creation actuality is annexed to possibility. A possible being clearly cannot give itself something that it still does not have, namely, existence. (2) An actual creature cannot impart to another a part of its perfection of existence, for existence as such lacks parts and cannot be divided. There can be no existence apart from essence just as there can be no motion apart from something which moves. (3) An actual creature cannot give its whole existence to a purely possible nature. The reason for this is quite simple. Only an actual being can perform the act of giving. An actual being clearly cannot keep its existence and at the same time give it completely to a possible being so that the latter can be made actually existent. The conclusion of these three points is that finite actual creatures cannot create.

Finite things distinct from God have been brought into existence. Since creatures could not be responsible for this phenomenon, it follows an infinite being did create. Creation is the most universal of all effects. Therefore, it owes its existence to the most universal of all causes, the First Cause of God. The same power that conferred existence on the universe as a whole is required to confer existence on any part of that universe regardless of how large or how small that part may be. The power to create is so proper to God that He cannot transmit it to another, for there can be only one infinite being.

§ 17. *Jesus Christ probably worked miracles of creation. This would prove that He was God.*

Writers point to Christ's multiplication of the loaves and fishes as being miracles of creation. "His disciples came to him, saying, 'This is a desert place and the hour is already late; send the crowds away, so that they may go into the villages and buy themselves food.' But Jesus said to them, 'They do not need to go away; you yourselves give them some food.' They answered him, 'We have here only five loaves and two fishes,' He said to them, 'Bring them here to me.' And when he had ordered the crowd to recline on the grass, he took the five loaves and two fishes, and looking up to heaven, blessed and broke the loaves, and gave them to his disciples, and the disciples gave them to the crowds. And all ate and were satisfied; and they gathered up what was left over, twelve baskets full of fragments. Now the number of those who had eaten was five thousand men, without counting women and children." (Matt. 14:15-21)

Several things must be said or noticed about the passage just quoted. (1) There was never any doubt as to the textual integrity of this or the passage recording the other multiplication of loaves and fishes. (Mark 8:1-9) It appears without variance in all critical editions of the Greek New Testament. (2) Notice how Christ skillfully draws the people into the desert, lets them exhaust their food supplies, and thereby makes them dependent on Him for relief from hunger. He is consciously setting the stage for a miracle. (3) Christ selects a miracle designed to reach every single person who made up His audience and one which forced them to contemplate the source or cause of the food with which they filled their stomachs. (4) How many miracles did Christ work on this occasion? Some scholars say one, others say many. The probative force of the miracle is in no way weakened if one holds either position. Those who say that many miracles were worked see new amounts of food created in a series of acts.

§ 18. *Only an agent with the power to create can immediately change one substance into another substance.*

Material objects are composed of what philosophers call prime matter and substantial form. Prime matter gives a thing its size and bulk. It is the undetermined principle of matter and so is the same in all things. A stone and a tree, for example, have the same prime matter. Substantial form gives a material object its distinct nature and makes it what it is. It is the source of an object's distinct properties and sets it apart from other things. A stone and a tree have different substantial forms.

Matter and form do not exist independently of each other, but unite immediately to make up a single complete material being. The word "immediately" as used here means that no intermediary holds matter and form together. A unit is an individual, not a composite of several previously subsisting things.

What would be necessary to change one substance into another substance? It would necessitate the changing of the substantial form that is united to the prime matter. Since the two principles are united immediately, it could be done only by an agent that can act immediately. To be able to act immediately means the power to act on things that are purely potential, for there is no intermediary between an actual object and a potential one. Such a being would have to be able to confer existence on possible beings. In other words, it would have to have the power to create. For this reason, it must be said that the power capable of bringing about immediate substantial change must be God alone. He cannot communicate this power to another; it is an infinite power proper to Him. Now we will show that many of Christ's miracles were ones of immediate substantial change. Their probative force is on a par with miracles of creation, for they too show that Christ had the infinite power that only God can have.

§ 19. *Christ worked miracles of immediate substantial change to prove that He was God.*

It is difficult to pin down exactly how many of the thirty-five or more miracles described in detail in the Gospels were ones of immediate substantial change. But this difficulty in no way weakens the probative force of them. There are a number of miracles that certainly fall into the category we consider here.

The substantial form of a dead body is clearly different from that of a living one. Each exhibits a different set of properties. In order to bring a dead person back to life it is necessary to have the power to replace one substantial form that calls for lack of immanent activity with a form that does call for immanent activity. Since forms are immediately joined to prime matter, only a being capable of creation or immediate action can bring the dead back to life. Jesus did precisely this. "And it came to pass soon afterwards, that he went to a town called Naim . . . And as he drew near the gate of the town, behold, a dead man was being carried out . . . And he went up and touched the stretcher . . . And he said, 'Young man, I say to thee, arise.' And he who was dead, sat up, and began to speak." (Luke 7:11-15) The Evangelists also record the resurrection of Lazarus by Christ, the daughter of Jairus, Himself, and others. (Matt. 11:5)

Infinite power is required to create an object regardless of its size. It takes the same power to create a grain of sand as it does to create a constellation. The same is true of immediate substantial change. It was the power used by Christ to bring the dead back to life. It was also the power used to give sight and hearing to those congenitally blind and deaf, and to change water into wine. "And as they were leaving Jericho, a great crowd followed Him. And behold, two blind men sitting by the wayside heard that Jesus was passing by, and cried out, saying, 'Lord, Son of David, have mercy on us!' . . . Then Jesus stopped, and called them, and said, 'What will you have me do for you?' They said to him, 'Lord, that our eyes be opened.' And Jesus, moved with compassion for them, touched their eyes; and at once they received their sight." (Matt. 20:29-34) Christ restored sight to the blind at Capharnaum, Bethsaida, and Jerusalem beside those at Jericho.

§ 20. *A modal miracle can be performed only by God, for He alone is the author of the laws of nature.*

A modal miracle is one in which an effect is brought about after suspending the laws of nature which are necessary for the production of the effect. For example, a person has a disease such as tuberculosis or fever or an affliction such as a broken leg or arm. The ravages of these diseases and these handicapped conditions can be corrected by medical science or even by the passage of time. Time-consuming steps and treatments leading to cure are dictated by the laws of nature. The reason why there is such a thing as medical science is because there are such things as laws of nature.

Who laid down the laws of nature? What is their purpose? The purpose of the laws will tell us a great deal about their author. It has been proved that God created the universe and gave it a definite purpose. The physical laws which nature obeys were embedded in things to insure that physical objects will move toward the goal for which they were created. Since God created all things in the universe, it follows that He is the author of the laws that govern them. From this it must be concluded that He alone can suspend the working of these laws to allow for the production of effects without them. To hold that a being other than God could suspend the working of the laws of nature would be tantamount to assigning to this being an existence equal to God and independent of God. Such a conclusion would be completely erroneous, for God alone is necessarily existent.

Science deals with the laws of nature. It can tell us whether or not a given phenomenon is a modal miracle. But science deals with proximate causes. It is completely incompetent to pronounce on the possibility of miracles. This is the province of philosophy; and philosophy tells us in no uncertain terms that miracles are possible regardless of whether they be of the absolute, substantial, or modal variety.

§ 21. *Christ worked modal miracles to prove that He was the author of the laws of nature and, therefore, was God.*

Earlier we saw how Christ's miracles showed His dominion over all levels of creatures. Now we complete the proofs showing that Christ worked all three types of miracles. It is difficult to determine exactly which of Christ's miracles were absolute and which were of substantial change. It is also difficult to show which miracles are of substantial change and which are modal. In either case, their probative force is the same.

While there are some miracles recorded in the Gospels that cannot be definitely classified as modal miracles, there are some that can. An example is the cure of the Centurion's servant who was at the point of death. Christ wanted to go down to cure him, but the Centurion said to Christ, " 'But say the word, and my servant will be healed' . . . Now when Jesus heard this, he marvelled, and turning to the crowd that followed him, said, 'Amen I say to you, not even in Israel have I found such great faith.' And when the messengers returned to the house, they found the servant in good health who had been ill." (Luke 7:1-10) Another modal miracle is the one by which Christ cured the lepers. "And as he was entering a certain village, there met him ten lepers, who stood afar off and lifted up their voice, saying, 'Jesus, have pity on us.' And when he saw them he said, 'Go show yourselves to the priests.' And it came to pass as they were on their way, that they were made clean. But one of them, seeing that he was made clean, returned, with a loud voice glorifying God, and he fell on his face at his feet, giving thanks." (Luke 17:12 ff)

The category of Christ's modal miracles includes such works as relieving the fever of Peter's mother-in-law, the two great catches of fish, the stilling of the storm over the lake, healing the woman suffering from an issue of blood, healing of the ear of Malchus, and a number of others. In every case, the phenomenon could not be explained by the ordinary working of the laws of nature. In each, Christ as God suspended the laws of nature and brought about the effect by His own divine power.

§ 22. *A prophecy can be made only with the unlimited knowledge proper to God.*

A prophecy is the prediction of a definite, free future event whose occurrence cannot be foreseen by the natural prevision of created intellects. There are two notes about a prophecy that must be understood. (1) A prophecy must be the foretelling of a definite future event. This means that the event or events must be pinpointed by details. The prediction must include such things as the time, persons, place, and other circumstances that will accompany the phenomenon. The person must give out the prediction as a certainty and not merely as a probability. Vague descriptions that could fit a number of different events are not prophecies. (2) The event predicted in a prophecy must take place because someone freely chose to perform it. Predictions fulfilled by conspiracy between the "prophet" and "performer" are clearly not freely performed in the sense needed for a prophecy. The cleavage between the two should be such that the person who performs it does not know of the prophecy or does not know that he fulfills it.

There are two types of intellects in existence, the received and unreceived. Creatures have the first; God, the second. In the light of the two notes of a prophecy defined above, there are literally hundreds of different events that could occur at the time, place, and circumstances needed for a prophecy. A created intellect, not knowing all things, must have a basis for selecting the one that he does select, otherwise he is guessing. If he is guessing, his selection does not involve a definite event which will surely occur. If he does have a basis for his prevision, then his selection is made by prevision. In either case the prediction is not a true prophecy.

One who makes a true prophecy does not see the future in the light of the past, but sees it as it is in itself. We have just seen that created intellects, those in humans, angels, or devils, are too limited to be able to do this. Only God who is un-received intelligence and who knows all things can make a true prophecy.

§ 23. *Christ predicted the manner of His own passion and death in order to prove His divinity.*

There is not space to quote the wealth of details accompanying Jesus' prophecies of His passion and death. An inspection of the Gospels will convince the reader of Christ's efforts to elimi-nate all vagueness from His listeners' minds when making the prediction. "And as Jesus was going up to Jerusalem, he took the twelve disciples aside by themselves, and said to them, 'Be-hold, we are going up to Jerusalem, and the Son of Man will be betrayed to the chief priests and the scribes; and they will con-demn him to death, and will deliver Him to the Gentiles to be mocked and scourged and crucified; and on the third day he will rise again.' " (Matt. 20:17-19) The fact that Christ refers to His passion and death on several different occasions proves that He had a fixed event in mind. The words quoted are clear, simple, and unmistakable. Our Lord even predicts in them that He will be put on trial twice. His foretelling of His resur-rection was completely beyond any human prevision, for what human can predict a miracle of God?

The fulfillment of Christ's prophecy is amply demonstrated from the Gospels. "Then the soldiers of the procurator (Pi-late) took Jesus into the praetorium, and gathered together about him the whole cohort. And they stripped him and put on him a scarlet cloak; and plaiting a crown of thorns, they put it on his head, and a reed into his right hand; and bending the knee before him they mocked him, saying, 'Hail, King of the Jews!' And they spat on him, and took the reed and kept strik-ing him on the head. And when they had mocked him, they took the cloak off him and put his own garments on him and led him away to crucify him." (Matt. 27:27-31) It is almost certain that the soldiers whose actions fulfilled Christ's prophecy never knew of the prophecy. They were Gentile soldiers from the garrison at Caesarea on the coast who moved into Jerusalem during the Passover time to guard against the possibility of Jewish rebellion. Pilate showed his ignorance of what Christ had said by the very fact that he asked both Christ and the Jews for data on which he could base a judgment about Christ.

§ 24. *Christ prophecied events in which Peter, Mary Magdalene, and Judas would have a part.*

Christ predicted that on the night He would be arrested by the agents of the Sanhedrin, Peter would first deny Him three times and then a cock would crow. The curious detail of the cock crowing completely eliminates collusion or prevision from the prophecy. And yet the event came to pass. "And after a little while the bystanders came up and said to Peter, 'Surely thou art one of them, for even thy speech betrays thee.' Then he began to curse and to swear that he did not know the man. And at that moment a cock crowed. And Peter remembered the word that Jesus had said, 'Before a cock crows, thou wilt deny me three times.' And he went out and wept bitterly." (Matt. 26:73-75)

On the night of the Last Supper Christ made another prediction besides the one noted. He prophecied that Judas Iscariot would betray Him by pointing Him out to those seeking to arrest Him. Just as there was the detail about the cock in the first, so there is a detail in the second that rules out collusion and prevision. It was the detail that Christ's betrayer would dip his hand in the dish at the same time that Christ did. The Evangelist describes the dramatic betrayal of Christ by Judas. "Now his betrayer had given them a sign, saying, 'Whomever I kiss, that is he; lay hold of him.' And he went straight up to

Jesus and said, 'Hail Rabbi!' and kissed him. And Jesus said to him, 'Friend, for what purpose hast thou come?' Then they came forward and set hands on Jesus and took him." (Matt. 26:48-50)

When Christ was in the house of Simon the leper, Mary Magdalene poured precious ointment on His head as He was at table. Christ predicted that this simple act of kindness performed by a little known penitent in this obscure place of a subjugated land would be told throughout the world in every age. (Matt. 26:6-13) The very magnitude of the task required to fulfill this prediction shows that no created intelligence could foretell it. There is nothing vague, nor indefinite about it. The fact that this event is reproduced in all Gospel manuscripts in every language and of every age is proof that the prophecy has been fulfilled. The force of the prophecy will be projected into the future until the end of time.

§ 25. *Christ prophecied the complete destruction of Jerusalem and the massacre of its inhabitants by Gentile armies.*

Christ gave out details of the prophecy of the destruction of Jerusalem at different times depending on the occasion. The admiration of the Temple building by the Apostles evoked the prophecy that it would be utterly destroyed. His last sight of Jerusalem moved Him to tears as He predicted the terrible siege to which it would be subjected. "And when he drew near and saw the city, he wept over it saying, 'If thou (Jerusalem) hadst known, in this thy day, even thou, the things that are for thy peace! But now they are hidden from thy eyes. For days will come upon thee when thy enemies will throw up a rampart about thee, and surround thee and shut thee in on every side, and will dash thee to the ground and thy children within thee, and will not leave in thee one stone upon another.' " (Luke 19:42-44) Christ is not predicting a rebellion by the Jews against Rome. It could be said that this could have been seen by prevision. But Christ said something much more specific. It was the destruction of a city, an event that could not be seen by prevision.

The fulfillment of Christ's prophecy was first recorded by Josephus, a Jewish writer (37 A.D.–95 A.D.) who actually witnessed the destruction of Jerusalem by the Roman armies in 70 A.D. His narrative extant today fills several books. He writes that about forty years after Christ's death the Jews rebelled against Roman rule. The Emperor Vespasian dispatched his son Titus with picked forces to crush Jerusalem. Josephus then describes the horrible seige and massacre of the population estimated as several hundreds of thousands of peoples. As a conclusion, he wrote, "Titus, on entering the city, was amazed at its strength. . . . And when, at a later period, he demolished the rest of the city and razed the walls, he left these towers as a memorial of his attendant fortune."[12] The triumphal arch commemorating Titus's victory at Jerusalem still stands in Rome. In history, the city of Jerusalem has been captured by invading forces no less than nineteen times. It is not mere coincidence that the only capture that is widely remembered is the one that fulfilled Christ's prophecy.

§ 26. *Christ prophecied that His followers would be persecuted because they bore His name.*

Christ predicted that His followers would undergo both red and white persecution. White persecution means that they would be ridiculed, hated, insulted, discriminated against, and denied freedom of worship simply because they professed membership in Christ's true church. Red persecution means that Christ's followers would actually shed their blood out of love for Him. Christ includes both types of persecution in one Gospel passage. "These thing I have spoken to you that you may not be scandalized (meaning taken unawares) . They will expel you from the synagogues. Yes, the hour is coming for everyone who kills you to think that he is offering worship to God." (John 16:1-2) Since no time limit was placed on the fulfillment of this prediction, it follows that Christ prophecied that His followers would be persecuted in every age. The very magnitude of the persecution of Catholics extending to all lands and in all ages is proof in itself that the prophecy could not have been made by prevision.

Historical evidence that Catholics have been subjected to both red and white persecution for their faith in Christ fills many volumes of authentic narrative.[13] It has been impossible to write a definitive history of the ten Roman persecutions which ended in 313 A.D. let alone the many which have been carried on since then. But the ancient ones set the pattern for the persecutions conducted since those times. The apologists, especially Tertullian (d. 220 A.D.), proved that the only reason Christians were persecuted was because of their faith and that persecution stopped as soon as they apostatized. He proved that Christians were persecuted for bearing Christ's name. Jews have always been persecuted but primarily for racial and economic, not religious reasons. The fact that Christ's followers are persecuted because they bear Christ's name makes this a very specific prophecy. It is not at all a case of many different events fitting a vague guess on the part of one claiming to be a prophet.

§ 27. *The concept of a nature does not include the concept of a person.*

A nature consists of the sum-total of notes that constitute things into a particular class distinguished from other classes. It includes the proximate genus and specific difference that are the basis for gathering similar things into a special group. For example, man has human nature. He is a rational animal; he has the ability to think in common with angels, but he has animality which places him in a class by himself distinct from angels. A nature as such is common to every individual of a species actual or possible. A nature as such does not exist outside of the mind.

Before a nature can exist in objective reality (outside the mind of a thinking object), it must receive two new perfections: subsistence and existence. For example, man does not exist as man. He exists as this particular man. Now *this* man has more than the notes of a rational animal in common with other individuals of the species. He has notes such as size, height, color, talents, and so forth which are not common to others but are peculiar to him. We call them individuating notes or accidents. It is impossible for a being to exist in objective reality without both essential and accidental notes. It is the perfection of subsistence that binds these two sets of notes together.

A being that has received the perfection of subsistence has been constituted as an individual nature, but one that is as yet only possible. No individual can be actual unless it was previously possible. In order for a possible individual to be an actual individual, it must receive the new perfection called existence. What had been said of the notions of nature, subsistence, and existence is true of every creature regardless of the class to which it may belong. When existence is added to a non-rational subsisting being such as a stone, a plant, or an animal, the result is what philosophers call "supposite." When it is added to a rational subsisting being, the result is a *person*.

§ 28. *A person is defined as an individual substance with a rational nature.*

The definition set down is the one of Boethius. Each of the terms has a precise meaning. We intimated in the previous consideration what they are. (1) A nature is the sum-total of those notes that are necessary to constitute a thing in a species. It embraces the proximate genus and specific difference that separates one class of things from another. (2) A person must be a rational being, that is, one having intellect and will enabling him to think and to choose. (3) A person must be a substance, that is, a being that can exist *by* itself although not necessarily *of* itself. It is not an accident, (something that cannot exist by itself). A tree or a stone is a substance for either can exist by itself. But color, size, motion, shape are accidents, for they cannot exist by themselves but only inherent in substances. (4) The term "individual" is extremely important to the definition of a person. It means that the being is autonomous and incommunicable. In this case, the term "incommunicable" means that the thing cannot give anything of itself to another and still retain its own individuality. An individual embodies not only a nature but also those accidents that might accompany a nature when it receives the perfections of subsistence and existence.

A person is the ultimate subject of all the actions of the rational being. It is neither a part of another being, nor under its control. It is an independent whole. For example, we do not say that a man's eyes see, or that his ears hear, or that his tongue speaks. We say that *he* sees, *he* hears, and *he* speaks. The actions do not proceed from a part and are not performed by a part. They proceed from the independent whole being or individual through the part such as the eyes. Actions of a pattern must not be attributed to part of the being but to the whole.

§ 29. *In Jesus Christ, there are two distinct natures united in one person.*

In Jesus Christ, the nature of God and the nature of man are united. As God, He is infinitely perfect; as man, He shares the same human nature common to every human being on earth. But in Christ these two natures are really and objectively distinct. The term "distinct" as used here does not mean that they are physically separated so as to constitute two different individuals. It means that each nature has all the notes essential to constitute it as a distinct nature. Christ has all the notes of the nature proper to God and all the notes of the nature proper to man. The distinctness of natures results from the fact that none of the notes needed for Christ to be God is needed for Him to be man. He is, therefore, true God and true man.

Jesus Christ is only one Person. Keep in mind that a person is an individual substance subsisting in a rational nature. When God the Son assumed human nature the result was a single individual or whole. Christ's human nature was not one half of His Person and His divine nature was not the other half. He is not half God and half man. A person is not an aggregate of parts that exist by themselves. Christ is one incommunicable rational substance having two natures. Christ used the pronoun "I" hundreds of times. It had the same meaning then that it has today. It denoted a single individual and not an aggregate of persons.

It is a principle of philosophy that actions are performed not by the nature but by the supposite and if it is a rational substance, by the person. The application of this to Christ has important implications to be discussed in the next chapter. When Christ acted, He acted as an individual or unit. He did not act at times only as a man and at others only as God. He always acted as the God-man.

§ 30. *The Church solemnly teaches that only the second Person of the Blessed Trinity, God the Son, became man.*

Some ancient heresies maintained that all three Persons of the Blessed Trinity assumed human nature. The official teaching of the Church on the doctrine stated above is very explicit. In 675 A.D., the Council of Toledo, in a statement approved by Pope Adeodatus, said, "We do not say that the Virgin Mary gave birth to the unity of the Trinity, but only to the Son, who alone assumed our nature in the unity of His Person." (D-284)

There are many passages in Sacred Scripture which show

that only God the Son assumed human nature. St. John wrote, "And the Word was made flesh and dwelt among us. And we saw his glory—glory as of the only-begotten of the Father." (John 1:14) This verse states that it was the Word, that is, God the Son, alone that took on human nature, for it makes a clear distinction between God the Father and God the Son. All passages that tell us that Christ is God also teach us that only God the Son assumed human nature.

The incarnation of the Word does not necessitate the incarnation of the other two Persons of the Blessed Trinity. The key to understanding lies in the explanation of the Blessed Trinity. In God, there is one Nature in three distinct Persons. The distinction between the Persons is objective and not a fictitious or mental one. It is heretical to deny this objective distinction. Revelation tells us that in the Incarnation, the union that resulted was a hypostatic union. Human nature was immediately united to the distinct subsistence of the Word. The act of union was produced by the three Persons, whereas the term of the union was proper to the Son; that is to say, the human nature was assumed by the Godhead precisely as possessed in a relatively incommunicable way by the Son of God.

Heretics held that the incarnation of one Person of the Blessed Trinity necessitates the incarnation of all three Persons. Patripassionism was an error that held that God the Father suffered on Calvary. But this heresy is really a variation of Modalism and Monarchianism which denied a real distinction of Persons in the Blessed Trinity. It will be recalled that the heresy held that Father, Son, and Holy Spirit are really three names for the same God. They identified nature and person and concluded that God is one nature and one person.

§ 31. *Christ's human nature was transmitted to Him from Adam.*

It is one thing to say that Christ had a human nature and another thing to say that He derived it from Adam. The

Adamic origin of Christ's human nature was denied by the Docetists who held that Christ had only a phantom body. Other heretics held that Christ brought His human nature with Him from heaven and did not derive it from His Blessed Mother. Valentinius, a Gnostic of the Second Century, held that Christ merely passed through the virginal womb of His Mother, rather than deriving His Body from her body.

The Church has defined that Christ derived His human nature from Adam. In 451 A.D., the Council of Chalcedon taught, "We teach that He (Christ) is perfect God and perfect man . . . and as touching His manhood, He was for us and for our salvation born of Mary, the Virgin, Mother of God." (D-148) Sacred Scripture is clear on the Adamic origin of Christ's human nature. It was to bring out this fact that St. Matthew and St. Luke include Christ's genealogy. The archangel said to Mary, "Behold, thou shalt conceive in thy womb and shalt bring forth a son . . . He . . . shall be called the Son of the Most High; and the Lord God will give him the throne of David his father." (Luke 1:31-32) St. Paul said of Christ that He was made of the seed of David according to the flesh. (Rom. 1:3; see also Gal. 4:4)

The importance of determining the Adamic origin of Christ's human nature has notable consequences touching upon His role as Mediator between God and man in the redemption of the human race.

§ 32. *At the incarnation, God the Son assumed a complete and perfect human nature.*

The Church teaches, "We believe and confess that Our Lord Jesus Christ, the Son of God, is God and man. He is God begotten of the substance of the Father before time, and he is man born of the substance of his mother in time; perfect God and perfect Man." (D-40) The human nature of Christ had all the notes of our nature. Christ had a body like ours and a soul like ours. This soul was endowed with an intellect and a will. We get a clearer notion of this matter by noting the Christological heresies that the Church has anathematized.

(1) Docetism, an error that first appeared before 100 A.D. but which recurred in later times, held that Christ did not assume a human nature at all. He assumed what seemed to be or what appeared to be a human nature. The error said that Christ had only a phantom body. (2) Monophysitism, an error which still persists in Egypt and Ethiopia, holds that Christ is one nature and one person. It is subdivided into three groups: Eutychianism held that God the Son indeed assumed a human nature but that it was completely absorbed into the divine nature. Appollinarianism held that Christ's human nature consisted of a body and a sensitive or animal soul but lacked an intellectual soul. The divine intellect took over the function of the human intellect. Monothelism held that in Christ there is no human will but that its function is taken over by the divine will. (2) Nestorianism holds that God the Son did not assume a human nature that resulted in a union of two natures in one Person. It held that the human nature subsists in one Person and that the divine nature subsisted in one Person. It held that in Christ there are two natures and two persons. They are morally, not hypostatically united. This moral union of two persons, is called Jesus Christ. There are scores of other errors that have splintered off from these listed here. They have all been condemned by name as heretical at different times in history by the Church.

§ 33. *Christ's two natures were hypostatically united at the moment He was conceived.*

The expression "hypostatic union" used in Christological works means that the union of the human and divine natures in Christ exists in one Person. The Church solemnly teaches that these two natures were united at the moment of Our

Lord's conception by His Blessed Mother. In 543 A.D., Pope Vigilius taught: "If anyone says and holds that the soul of the Lord pre-existed, and was united to God the Word before His incarnation and birth from the Virgin, let him be anathema." (D-204) "If anyone says or holds that the body of Our Lord Jesus Christ was first formed in the womb of the holy Virgin, and that after this God, the Word, and the soul, since it had pre-existed, were united to it, let him be anathema." (D-205)

The Church's teaching on the fact of the Incarnation is well-anchored on Scriptural evidence. In St. Paul's Epistle to the Philippians we read, "Have this mind in you which was also in Christ Jesus, who though he was by nature God, did not consider being equal to God a thing to be clung to, but emptied himself, taking the nature of a slave and being made like unto men. And appearing in the form of man, he humbled himself, becoming obedient to death, even to the death on a cross." (Phil. 2:5)

There are many patristic writings on the subject we are discussing here. St. Ignatius (d. 107 A.D.) had this clear passage, "There is only one physician both carnal and spiritual, both born and unborn, God became Man, true life in death, sprung both from Mary and from God, first subject to suffering, and then incapable of it—Jesus Christ Our Lord."[14] "He was really of the line of David according to the flesh, and the Son of God by the will and power of God; was really born of a Virgin and baptized by John."[15]

§ 34. *The divine and human natures of Jesus Christ once united will never be separated.*

In 675 A.D., the Council of Toledo in Spain taught, "In this Son of God, we believe there are two natures, one of divinity, the other of humanity, which the one Person of Christ so united to Himself that the divinity can never be separated from the humanity, nor the humanity from the divinity." (D-

283) The statement of the Church does not qualify the length of time during which the natures would stay united. They will stay united for all eternity. Not even during the three days that Christ's body was in the tomb were they separated. Certain heretics like Marcellus of Ancyra held that Christ would eventually put aside His human nature. St. Paul provides Scriptural basis for this doctrine. He writes, "Jesus Christ is the same yesterday and today, yes, and forever." (Heb. 13:8)

The Fourth and Fifth Centuries saw the bitter Christological disputes between heretics and those who defended the Church's traditional teaching. A noted defender of the faith, St. Cyril of Alexander (d. 444 A.D.), wrote, "We defend always the absolutely indissoluble union (hypostatic union) believing that the same is both the only Son and the first born; the only Son, as Word of God the Father and emanating from His substance; the first born, inasmuch as He has become man."[16] (*Adv. Nest.* 4-60) The fact that he says the union is *absolutely* indissoluble means that it is everlasting.

St. Thomas says that the grace of union whereby God the Son was united to a human nature is greater than the grace of adoption whereby others are sanctified. The first is ordained for a personal union whereas the second for a union of sanctification. The union of sanctification is broken only by sin. Since the personal union of divine and human nature is greater than the other and since it is impossible for Christ to sin, it follows that there is nothing to make God revoke His eternal decree for His Son to stay united with the human nature assumed at the Incarnation. The two natures were not separated even while Christ's body was entombed between Good Friday and Easter.[17]

§ 35. *Christ's human nature always had the fullness of grace.*

While the doctrine stated in this proposition has not been formally defined by the Church, it has been taught by her. It would be seriously sinful for anyone to deny it, for there is almost unanimous agreement among theologians on this point. The principal font of this doctrine is Sacred Scripture as explained by Sacred Tradition. St. John wrote, "And the Word was made flesh, and dwelt among us. And we saw his glory— glory as of the only-begotten of the Father—full of grace and of truth . . . and of his fullness we have all received." (John 1:14-16) [18]

The "fullness of grace" means that Christ's human nature had all the grace that a creature could possibly have in the present order of Providence. The degree of sanctity that a creature can have depends on its capacity to receive and on its proximity to the source of the grace. The only limitation that Christ's human nature could have in the reception of grace was that limitation arising from the fact that it is a creature, for all creatures are essentially limited. The other limitation possible in men, moral fault, was out of the question in Christ. Christ's human nature was in the closest proximity possible to the source of grace, His divine nature. No union of natures can ever be closer than two that are hypostatically united in one Person.

When did Christ receive the fullness of grace? The conditions discussed above prevailed from the first moment of Christ's conception. It was from that instant that we must date the full sanctification of Christ's human nature. The expression "Jesus advanced in wisdom and age and grace" (Luke 2:52) does not mean that Christ's human nature received more grace. It means that externally, to those observing His actions and His manner of living, He showed the effects of the fullness of grace with increasing frequency and power.

§ 36. *Christ's human soul enjoyed the Beatific Vision from the first moment of its existence.*

This proposition is theologically certain; no one may willfully refuse to accept it without being guilty of serious sin. It is drawn from pronouncements made by the Church and more specifically from the ones teaching us that Christ's human nature possessed the fullness of grace from the very beginning of its existence, or His conception.

The Scriptural passage in St. John's Gospel (John 1:14) used to show the existence of this "fullness of grace" in Christ rules out any qualification or limitation of this "fullness." St. Thomas shows that in itself the term is capable of a double interpretation.[19] Both are applicable to Christ. (1) In the previous section we saw that it meant that Christ's human nature received all the grace a human nature can receive. It was as *extensive* as it could be. The reason for this conclusion was given there. (2) The term "fullness of grace" also means that Christ experienced the complete realization and fruition of the power of grace. It was as *intensive* as it could be. Christ's human soul enjoyed all the benefits grace could bestow upon it. This statement could not be made if Christ was denied the ultimate and, therefore, the primary benefit of grace which enables one to see God face to face, to behold the Beatific Vision. Christ's human soul enjoyed this vision from the first moment of its existence.

Therefore, Christ's human soul possessed beatific knowledge. Christ's human intellect's capacity for knowledge was completely filled. When the Gospel speaks of Christ's "growing in knowledge" it refers to experimental knowledge, that is, to the knowledge of actually experiencing something.

§ 37. *In His human nature, Christ was capable of suffering.*

The most ancient heresy that denied that Christ was capable of physical suffering was Docetism. Its denial of the reality of Christ's body left no room for suffering. The Monophysites who denied the duality of natures in Christ were forced by their own premises to conclude that Christ as God suffered. The Creed of the Council of Toledo in 400 A.D. said, "If anyone says or believes that the man Jesus Christ was a man incapable of suffering, let him be anathema." (D-27) The creed of St. Leo IX in 1053 said that Christ has a divine and a human nature. In His humanity "for us and for our salvation (Christ) suffered in the true passion of the body and was buried." (D-344) In 1441, the Council of Florence taught that, "It firmly believes, professes, and proclaims that the Son of God in the assumed humanity was truly born of the Virgin, truly suffered, truly died and was buried." (D-709)

The Gospels are replete with instances showing that Christ could and did undergo bodily suffering. We read that after fasting forty days He was hungry; at Jacob's well He asked the woman for a drink of water because He was thirsty. The narrative of His passion and death leaves no room to doubt that Christ was capable of suffering pain.

How could Christ have enjoyed happiness and suffered pain at the same time? One explanation is that good objects cause joy and bad ones cause sorrow. It is possible for both good and bad causes simultaneously to have their effects on an individual. Theologians illustrate this by the simultaneous joy and torments that the early Christian martyrs experienced while they were being tortured in diverse ways.

§ 38. *Christ was not only free from original and actual sin, but was also free from the inclination and from the capability of committing sin.*

There is nothing about human nature that connotes the idea of past, present, or future sin. Christ possessed a perfect and complete human nature, but one to which the notion of sin was not, and could not, be attached. Theodore of Mopsuestia (350—428 A.D.) held that Christ was born with the inclination to sin but gradually freed Himself from it. The Second Council of Constantinople in 553 A.D. branded his opinion heretical. (D-224)

Christ's soul possessed the fullness of grace from the first moment of its existence. This is reason enough to conclude that Christ's soul was never stained with original, mortal, or venial sin. There is a definite relationship between sin and the inclination to sin. In Christ, there was no sin nor a capability of sinning. This fact removes from Him any inclination to sin.

The Evangelists record that Christ was tempted by the devil. Satan presented certain enticements to Christ. But this does not mean that those enticements, which could influence a person with a fallen nature, had any influence on Him. They remained completely external to Him. At no time did they make any impression on Christ to cause Him to ponder their apparent value.

Basically, sin represents a forbidden choice. A mortal sin is the rejection of God in favor of a seriously forbidden object. A venial sin is deliberately choosing something not referable to God, something not conducive to the Last End. One who sins deliberately blinds himself to the true value of things. In Christ the ontological impossibility of sinning comes from His divine personality. For God to sin is a contradiction in terms.

§ 39. *We are to give Jesus Christ, that is, to God the Son made Man, divine honor and worship.*

The Council of Constantinople in 553 defined, "If anyone ... does not adore with one worship God the Word incarnate with His own flesh, just as the Church of God has accepted from the beginning, let such a one be anathema." (D-221) This definition has strong Scriptural evidence to support it. St. Thomas the Apostle, putting his finger into Christ's hands and side adored Him saying, "My Lord and my God." (John 20:29) And Christ accepted this act of adoration. St. Paul wrote, " ... at the name of Jesus every knee should bend of those in heaven, on earth and under the earth." (Phil. 2:10) The "bending of the knee" to which St. Paul refers means to adore.

The proposition does not mean that in the Incarnation,

Christ's human nature was absorbed into His divine nature as the Monophysites thought. Christ's two natures are truly distinct even though they are hypostatically united. The one Person in whom this union took place will exist forever. The two natures will never be separated. The theologian studying the properties of Christ's human nature considers it by itself, that is, isolated from Christ's divine nature. But this separate examination will never be true in objective reality. We can never adore an idea or a figment of the imagination which Christ's human nature isolated from His Person would now be. We adore an objectively real being, namely, the God-man. Hence, the truth of the proposition.

What has been said of the adoration of Christ's sacred humanity applies also to each of Its parts. This is the theological doctrine that forms the solid basis for devotion to the Sacred Heart, the Precious Blood, the Five Wounds, and others. The adoration that must be given to these is not dulia or hyperdulia but latria, that is, the adoration reserved for God alone.

NOTES

1. Prat, *The Theology of St. Paul* (London: Burns-Oates, 1942), I, 208 ff.
2. *The Apostolic Fathers,* trans. by Lake (Cambridge: Harvard University Press), I, 172-277.
3. *Letters,* Bk. X, Ep. 96.
4. Cayre, *Manual of Patrology* (Tournai, Desclee & Co., 1936), I, 154.
5. II *Apology,* 6.
6. *Adv. Haer.,* 3, 6, 2.
7. Quasten, *Patrology* (Westminster: Newman, 1960), II, 133.
8. *De Principiis,* 1, 21.
9. *Adv. Prax,* 27.
10. Prat, *Op. cit.,* I, 133.
11. Grossi-Conti, *I Monumenti Cristiani* (Rome: Gregorian Univ. Press, 1923), p. 135.
12. *Jewish Wars,* Bk. VI, 403.
13. Allard, *Ten Lectures on the Martyrs* (New York, Benziger, 1907).
14. *Ad Eph.,* 7, 2.
15. *Ad Smyr,* 1, 1.
16. *Adv. Nest.,* 4, 60.
17. *S.T.,* III, 50, 2.
18. Pius XII, *Mystici Corporis* (Washington, D.C.. N.C.W.C., 1943), p. 21.

VII

Redemption

§ 1. *Redemption is the act of ransoming or liberating another.*

The phrase "to redeem" is derived from a Latin verb meaning "to buy back." An analysis of the idea reveals that four distinct elements are implied in it. (1) It presupposes the existence of a person who at one time possessed definite rights and dignities. The term "right" means that one has title to things that he needs to reach an assigned goal. If he is given a duty, he must also be given the means to fulfill it. (2) The person who is to be redeemed has in some way lost the rights or means that he must use to reach the goal or to fulfill the duty assigned to him. The rights may have been taken from him or he may have destroyed them. The fact remains that he does not now control them and, therefore, he cannot use them. He has been harmed and impoverished by their loss. (3) The key element of redemption is the performance of an act that restores to the harmed person the rights that he has lost. He can again use them as a means to pursue the end or duty assigned to him. (4) The act of redemption does not imply that the person to whom lost rights have been returned must actually make use of them. The redemption is completed when the title to the benefits has been returned. The fact that one refuses to make use of that title or refuses to accept it does not destroy the objective efficacy of the redemptive act.

The elements described here can be illustrated by the following example. In the Middle Ages, Christians were captured by Moors. They lost their freedom and were enslaved. When a ransom was paid for their release, the captives regained their freedom and were allowed to return to their homes. The paying of the ransom completed the redemption and its value was not nullified even in the cases of some who refused to return to Christianity and chose to remain among the Moors.

§ 2. *As it refers to mankind, redemption is the act that enables men to reach the supernatural goal assigned to them by God.*

All the elements of redemption seen in the last section are distinguishable in this proposition. (1) It is impossible for God to do anything without a purpose. When He created man, He had to give him a goal and the means needed to reach it. The goal in question was the supernatural happiness of seeing God face to face in heaven. The means needed to reach it was sanctifying grace. (2) It is defined doctrine that our first parents committed the sin whereby they lost for themselves and for the members of the human race the grace that is the indispensable means to the goal. Like any mortal sin, the sin of Adam and Eve was an act of rejecting God in favor of a seriously forbidden object. Man was clearly reduced to an impoverished state, for although he still was required to seek the supernatural goal, he had stripped himself of the grace needed to reach it. (3) The act by which mankind could be redeemed had to be of such value that it could restore to all men the grace that had been lost. The act of atonement had to be objectively complete. (4) An act of redemption can be complete and adequate even though some men do not avail themselves of its benefits. Even after man was redeemed, he still had free will and the choice to accept or reject the title to grace that had been restored to him. Redemption does not mean that all men automatically are rendered free from original sin and endowed with sanctifying grace. They are not subjectively redeemed without taking any further means of sanctification. It is important that we draw a distinction between objective and subjective redemption. Failure to receive the latter does not lessen the value of the former.

§ 3. *Fallen man could not by his own proper efforts recover the sanctifying grace that had been lost by original sin.*

Original sin is a true sin, not only for Adam and Eve, but also for all the members of the human race. It stripped the souls of all of justification as effectively as a mortal sin does for the individual who commits it. In order to better grasp the harm caused by original sin, we should try to realize the greatness of the state of Adam and Eve while in grace. We are all familiar with the phenomenon of life. A living thing is far more perfect than an inorganic object such as a stone. All life on earth is in itself natural life regardless of whether it be found in plants, animals, or humans. Sanctifying grace is also life, but it is a new kind of life, a life essentially superior to all life of earth. This is precisely why it is called supernatural life. It is difficult for us to grasp the superiority of this new kind of life to the life with which we are born. Since the superiority is one of kind, and not of degree, we can say that supernatural life of grace is as superior to natural life as natural life is superior to death.

The members of the human race lost the title to sanctifying grace by the commission of original sin. The sin left them with merely natural powers. A person can do only that which he has power to do. Natural powers can never bring about a supernatural effect regardless of how many people pool their natural efforts. The application of this to the present discussion is obvious. The redemption of mankind after original sin means making it possible for man to regain supernatural life or sanctifying grace. It can be accomplished only by supernaturalized powers. No act of atonement performed by a natural individual or a group of such individuals could be of sufficient worth to repair the harm to mankind caused by original sin. There would always be an essential disproportion between the cause and desired effect. In other words, this cause could never bring about the effect.

§ 4. *After man fell into sin, only God could decide whether or not the members of the human race should be redeemed.*

The sanctifying grace in which man was created established a bond of love between God and man. Its presence was a title to all the helps that man needed to maintain this bond. But man abused his free will, committed original sin, and reduced himself to the status of an enemy of God. When a person breaks this bond of love by sin, he completely divests himself, not only of grace, but also of any future right to be forgiven. He retains no basis on which to make even a request that he be given a second opportunity to receive God's love. In fact, he makes himself liable to a punishment commensurate with the gravity of the crime.

The initiative for repairing the broken bond of friendship must come from the offended, not from the offending. The offended party must make the decision either to extend mercy or not to extend mercy. If the decision is not to extend mercy, he does the offending party no injustice whatsoever, for the offender has no basis to demand forgiveness. If the decision is to extend mercy, he must then decide whether to forgive the guilty party completely without exacting reparation or to exact reparation. If the decision is to exact reparation, then the one offended must lay down conditions that must be met for fulfilling this act of reparation. Two possible sets of conditions can be laid down. According to the first, God could demand that only partial reparation be made. According to the second,

He could demand that full and complete reparation in justice be made. God could empower man as man to make partial reparation. We shall soon see why man as man could not make full reparation for original sin.

§ 5. *Only a person who is God-man can completely atone for sin.*

The magnitude of an offense is measured by the dignity of the person who is offended. Dignity is annexed to the possession of legitimate authority or power. It is the quality that bids us to recognize a superior's position of authority. God possesses infinite dignity, for He is the Creator and Lord of the universe. His authority is infinite, for not only is it not superseded by that of another, but it cannot be. Sin was an offense against God. It insulted Him in that it was a complete rejection of His commands and therefore, of His love. In a sense, sin was an offense of infinite malice.

Atonement is the act of repairing the wrong done to another. The value of an act of atonement is measured by the position of the person who performs it. A human being is a finite person with limited powers. Any act of atonement that he performs can at best be of limited worth, for there must be a balance between cause and effect. Regardless of how many human persons make acts of atonement, the aggregate worth of these acts is still limited.

The infinite malice of sin could be atoned for only by an act of infinite worth. Who could perform such an act? Since a person with a human nature sinned, such a person must atone. Since God alone can perform an act of infinite worth, it follows that only a Person who is God-man can completely and adequately atone for the offense to God inherent in sin. In the last chapter we saw that Jesus Christ is a Person who answers this description.

Theologians speculate whether or not God the Son would have assumed human nature if Adam and Eve had not sinned.

St. Thomas said that in divine revelation, Christ's incarnation is closely associated with His redemptive act. While recognizing that there are other opinions on the subject, he says that he is of the opinion that although God the Son could have assumed human nature if Adam had not sinned, He would not have done so.[1]

§ 6. *Any act of atonement on the part of a Person who is God-man is of infinite value.*

The value of an act of atonement is measured by the rank of the one performing it. Although human beings can indeed perform such acts, they are of only finite or limited value. There are many degrees of finite value. When the act of atonement is performed by a Person, Who is God-man, the situation is greatly changed. In this case, it is not human nature or the divine nature that atones. Keep in mind that nature as such does not exist in actual reality. A rational nature must receive the perfection of subsistence and then also receive the perfection of existence to become the actually real thing known as a person. It is a principle of philosophy that concrete actions must not be attributed to the nature but to the person.

Jesus Christ is not a person who is half God and half man. A person is a single, subsisting individual with a rational nature. Christ is precisely a single, subsisting individual with two distinct natures. Because of the presence of an infinitely perfect divine nature in Christ, each act of this Person is the exercise of infinite power, for God must act according to His nature. Creation, for example, is an act of infinite power, but the thing created is a finite creature, for creatures can never be infinite. The cause of the act is infinite, but its product or effect can be finite. We shall soon examine the act by which Christ atoned for man's sin. We should keep in mind that He could have chosen one far less painful and still have redeemed mankind adequately.

§ 7. *The divine will and the human will of Christ freely chose to redeem the members of the human race.*

It is a truth of faith that there are two wills in Christ, a human will and a divine will. This is the express teaching of the Third Council of Constantinople, 680 A.D., "And the two natural wills are not opposed as the godless heretics have said; but the human will is compliant, and not opposing or contrary; as a matter of fact it is obedient to his divine and omnipotent will." (D-291) Freedom from compulsion or necessity is one of the conditions for a meritorious act; and since Christ merited our salvation by His passion and death, He was necessarily free in regard to these actions. Theologians are free to discuss how Christ's human will could be free since it was impeccable. It is simply unthinkable that Christ disobey the command of the Father to die for the sins of the world. Yet we know He was in fact free.

Because Christ is a divine Person we say that God died for us. However, He saved mankind by means of His human nature. He suffered and died as man. He redeemed us by means of the acts of His human will, namely, His human love for the Father and His obedience.

Since there is only one divine nature, there is only one divine will; therefore, the divine will of the Father and the divine will of Christ are one and the same. It is only in a hypothetical (conditional) sense that we say that it is necessary for God to redeem mankind. God had freely promised to do this. Thus He owed it to Himself to keep His promise. It is clear that this is not a matter of compulsion. It is the result of a completely free choice of God.

§ 8. *Christ was motivated by love in choosing to redeem mankind.*

In 1459 A.D., Pope Pius II condemned the error of those who held that Christ did not suffer and die to redeem the members of the human race because of His love for them. (D-717d) A person acts out of love when the motive that impels him to act is the desire to confer a temporal or spiritual benefit on the other. In many examples of love, the desire to bestow a benefit on another co-exists with the desire to receive a benefit as well. The more one forgets self, the more altruistic the love is.

We can consider Christ's death in relationship to His heavenly Father, to the members of the human race, and to Himself. (1) In its relationship to God the Father, Christ's death was an act of love, for it was an act of atonement. St. Thomas shows that it means that "one offers something which the offended one loves equally or even more than he detested the offense."[2] Christ gave more to His heavenly Father than was necessary to compensate for the offense of the whole human race. (2) Redemption is the effect of Christ's death as it pertains to man. Two things must be noticed here. Original sin had enslaved mankind, for "everyone who commits sin is a slave of sin." (John 8:34) To be redeemed means to be bought back with a price. "Christ made satisfaction, not by giving money . . . but by giving what was the greatest price—Himself." Our Lord paid this price in the most intensive way possible, for He Himself said, "Greater love than this no one has, that one lay down his life for his friends." (John 15:13) (3) Christ's act of love was completely selfless. As God, He was infinitely perfect. It was absolutely impossible to add anything to Him to make Him greater. As man, He already was experiencing the greatest degree of happiness that a creature could experience. His human intellect and will already enjoyed the Beatific Vision. It is impossible for anyone to experience a joy and happiness greater than this one of seeing God face to face.

§ 9. *Christ freely accepted the mandate to redeem mankind by suffering and dying.*

St. Thomas lists a number of reasons why it was appropriate that Christ's redemptive act should culminate in His death.[3] (1) The whole human race was sentenced to death because of original sin. It is a fitting way of satisfying for another to submit oneself to the penalty deserved by that other. (2) Christ died to prove to all that He had really assumed human nature and human flesh. If Christ had not died then people would have been tempted to accept the Docetist heresy that He had only a phantom body. (3) By dying, Christ delivered us from the fear of death. He destroyed the power of him who had ruled the empire of death. He invited all men to look upon death as not being the end of life but the beginning of its real fruition. He wished to instill the spirit of St. Paul's expression in which he desires to die in order that he might be with Christ. (Phil. 1:23) (4) Ever since the loss of the praeternatural gifts, death is a punishment for original sin. Christ did not contract the taint of sin. When He decided to die, He decided to undergo the penalty reserved for sin. He thereby wanted to give us the example that we should die to sin, that is, to loosen the power of sin over us. "Know for certain that thou must lead a dying life; and the more thou dost learn to die to thyself the more thou dost begin to live in Christ." (*Thomas à Kempis*) (5) By dying, Christ prepared the way for a glorious resurrection and thereby proved that He had completely triumphed over death. In this way He could instill in us a hope of a resurrection. "If Christ is preached as arisen from the dead, how do some among you say that there is no resurrection of the dead?" (I Cor. 15:12) We have already seen that Christ did not have to go so far as to die in order to redeem mankind. Any act of atonement on Christ's part would have been as efficacious as the passion and death that He actually endured.

§ 10. *Crucifixion was the most disgraceful way that the ancients could put a person to death.*

In ancient times, capital punishment was inflicted in different ways for different crimes. Penal codes followed in the Roman empire prescribed such executions as beheading, throwing to wild animals, burning at the stake, stoning, putting on the rack, stabbing, shooting with arrows, being thrown into quick lime, being gored by bulls, drowning, suffocating, being sewed up in a sack with poisonous reptiles, and others. A measure of disgrace and ridicule was attached to each type of execution, for many of the executions were conducted in public. The disgrace was designed to intensify the harshness of the death penalty, for internal pain was combined with external suffering. We know that St. Paul suffered the speedy death of beheading because he was a Roman citizen.

The most disgraceful way that pagan barbarism could invent to execute a person was to crucify him. Pagan writers cannot find words to express adequately the horrors of crucifixion. Cicero said, "For a Roman citizen to be bound is a misdemeanor; for him to be struck is a crime; for him to be killed is almost parricide; what must I say when he is hung on the cross? There is no epithet whatever that may fittingly describe a thing so infamous."[4] The person nailed to a cross was lifted up to the full view of the people so that he could be a better target for jeers, insults, and curses of the milling mob, and a better mark for those who stood off to throw stones at. Death came very slowly. Persons hung on the cross for several hours. There are on record authenticated cases of crucified persons hanging on the cross for several days before death. When the executioners wanted to hasten death, they often would break the legs of the crucified person.

§ 11. *In His passion and death, Jesus Christ endured every type of suffering.*

Every kind of punishment was inflicted on Christ. His sufferings were extensively complete. (1) All peoples participated in inflicting pains on Christ. The world was divided into Jews and Gentiles. The Jews pressured the Gentile Pilate and his soldiers into executing Christ. Then too, Christ suffered from rulers and subjects, from friends and enemies. (2) Our Lord endured internal pains. He was abandoned by friends, namely, the Apostles and the beneficiaries of His miracles. He suffered in His reputation by the accusation of being a blasphemer and a seducer; in His majesty from mockeries and insults. He was arrayed as a king but then buffeted as a slave; addressed as one knowing things and then slapped as if He were ignorant of the identity of His assailant; in His emotions by sadness and fear; in His mind by the thought of man's past sins and future rejections. (3) Our Lord suffered in all parts of His body. The extremities of His body, that is, His hands and feet, were pierced with nails; His head was crowned with thorns; His face was slapped and spit upon. He was scourged about His whole torso. Persons about to be crucified were subjected to one of two kinds of beatings.[5] A lesser one called *verberatio* was administered with rods; a greater one called *flagellatio* was administered with a leather whip having five or six tails tipped with metal so that it could tear flesh. The person was bent over a short stump or pillar and tied. His neck, back, hips, legs, and arms were so viciously beaten that he was soon reduced to a bleeding mass of flesh. No one knew or cared how many times the condemned person was struck. Our Lord underwent the *flagellatio*, not the *verberatio*. (4) Our Lord suffered in all of His bodily senses. "In touch, by being nailed and scourged; in taste, by being given vinegar and gall to drink after He said, 'I thirst'; in smell, by being fastened to the gibbet in a place reeking with the stench of corpses, for Calvary was the execution place of Jerusalem and the bodies of the dead were left to be eaten by the dogs and vultures; in hearing, by being tormented by the cries of blasphemers; in sight, by beholding the tears of His Mother and of the disciple whom He loved."[6]

§ 12. *In His passion and death, Jesus Christ endured pain greater than could be endured by any other person with a human nature.*

In His passion and death, Jesus endured both internal and external suffering. He suffered in His body and in His soul.

St. Thomas traces the superlative intensity of Christ's sufferings to four causes. (1) The sources of pain were the greatest. As regards His bodily suffering, it was caused by crucifixion which we have already seen was the most painful and disgraceful way pagans could put a person to death. As regards His spiritual pain, that is, the pain endured in His soul, it was caused by sin which is by its very nature the agent causing the greatest spiritual pain. (2) Christ had a greater capacity for pain than any other human being could have. Since His body was miraculously formed and free from the effects of sin, it was sounder than those of others. The sounder a body is, the greater must be the blow that destroys its life. Since the capacity of His mind for truth was completely filled, He could see the ugliness of sin with unusual clarity. This unusual clarity was translated into unusual suffering. For example, when vandals disfigure a painting of the masters, an art critic feels the loss more keenly than does an amateur artist. (3) When a human suffers, his thoughts and hopes can soften the pain he endures in his body. In Christ, each of His powers suffered independently so there was no possibility of, for example, the soul mitigating the suffering of the body. (4) Christ voluntarily accepted suffering in proportion to the magnitude of the good that He foresaw would be derived from it. He saw that His suffering would be the cause of the greatest possible good that could be bestowed upon men, namely, the grace that would enable them to see God face to face. He willingly accepted the greatest degree of suffering than any human being could accept.

§ 13. *Christ's passion and death was the most appropriate way of redeeming the members of the human race.*

In a previous section, it was pointed out that there were several avenues by which God could have restored man to his lost dignity. Christ chose that it should be done by a horrible passion and death. There are several reasons which prove the wisdom of this choice. (1) Humans are inclined to return the love of those who have loved them. The greater the love they have received, the more disposed they are to return love of the same intensity. By dying on the cross, Christ demonstrated the greatest love that one can have for another. He thereby furnished man with the greatest possible motive for returning to Christ the most intense love of which he was capable and by it to receive the greatest benefit from Christ's redemptive act. (2) Men admire excellence and are inclined to imitate those who show examples of it. During His passion and death, Christ gave the greatest examples of obedience, meekness, mercy, love, and perseverence that He could give and man could receive. A person who imitates these virtues is moved to receive, to increase, or to keep sanctity. And the permanence of this good example is obvious. When one imitates the saints, he is really imitating the example of Christ reflected in the saints. (3) In specific torments which He suffered, Christ pointed out in a special way the three great enemies of man's spiritual life. These enemies are the world, the flesh, and the devil, that is, the inordinate attachment to temporal goods, sensuality, and pride. By being stripped of His garments, Christ wished to teach us to remain detached from earthly goods and honors; by the terrible scourging, He underscored the heinousness of sins of sensuality in general and impurity in particular; by His crowning of thorns He called attention to the malice of sins of pride. Figuratively speaking, the intellect is looked upon as residing in the head. Pride is loosely called a sin of the intellect.

§ 14. *Christ's death on the cross had all the notes of a true sacrifice.*

The Council of Trent in 1562 A.D. defined, "If anyone says that blasphemy is cast upon the most holy sacrifice of Christ consummated on the cross through the sacrifice of the Mass, or that by it He is disparaged: let him be anathema." (D-951) Sacred Scripture states that Christ's death on the cross was a sacrifice. "Walk in love, as Christ also loved us and delivered himself up for us an offering and a sacrifice to God to ascend in fragrant odor." (Eph. 5:2)

In a sacrifice, a gift is offered to God and is then destroyed in recognition of God's sovereignty over the universe. The act has four elements, namely, a victim, a priest, the destruction, and the purpose. (1) On Calvary, the *victim* was Christ Himself. St. Paul wrote, "How much more will the blood of Christ, who through the Holy Spirit offered *himself* unblemished unto God . . . " (Heb. 9:14) (2) In a sacrifice, a priest offers a gift in the name of the people. On Calvary, Christ was the priest who offered Himself. The Council of Ephesus in 431 A.D. taught, "If anyone says that the Word of God Himself was not made our High-priest . . . when He was made flesh . . . let him be anathema." (D-122) (3) Although any act of Christ could have redeemed mankind, He chose to accomplish our redemption by undergoing a passion and death. The victim was truly destroyed for Christ could do no more than give His life. "Christ, our passover, has been sacrificed." (I Cor. 5:7) "If anyone says . . . that He (Christ) offered the oblation (i.e. Himself) for Himself and not rather for us alone . . . let him be anathema." (D-122) (4) The action of Calvary appeased God's justice and redeemed mankind. It clearly recognized God's supreme dominion over the universe. Christ died to satisfy for the unlimited offence against God's majesty wrought by the sin of Adam and Eve. Such an act of atonement necessarily implies recognition of the existence of a Being who is Lord and Master of all things. "For it has pleased God the Father that in him (Christ) all his fullness should dwell, and that through him he (Christ) should reconcile to himself all things, whether on the earth or in the heavens, making peace through the blood of his cross." (Col. 1:19, 20)

§ 15. *Christ's death on the cross was a vicarious atonement for all the sins of mankind.*

The Council of Trent teaches, "Jesus Christ, who when we were enemies, for the exceeding charity wherewith he loved us, merited justification for us by His most holy passion on the wood of the cross, and made satisfaction for us to God the Father." (D-799) In this statement the word "us" means the members of the human race. The fact that it is used without qualification can be interpreted to mean that atonement was made not only for all men but also for every sin that men would or could commit. In 1658 A.D., the Church condemned as heresy the tenet of Jansenism that Christ died only for those who are saved.

Atonement means offering an offended party something that he loves to counter-balance the insult that he has sustained. It is adequate atonement if the thing offered is of equal value, that is, if it fully satisfies the insult. It is vicarious atonement if the offering is made by someone other than the one who offered the insult. In the case we discuss, it is offered by the sinless Christ in behalf of sinful mankind. Christ Himself said, "I lay down my life for my sheep." (John 10:15) "The Son of Man has not come to be served but to serve, and to give his life as a ransom for many." (Matt. 20:28) "We have an advocate with the Father, Jesus Christ the just; and he is a propitiation for our sins, not for ours only but also for those of the whole world." (John 2:2)

The first letter of Pope St. Clement to the Corinthians written about 96 A.D. has this beautiful passage, "For the sake of the love which He had for us Our Lord Jesus Christ, according to the will of the Father has given His blood for us, His flesh for our flesh, and His soul for our souls."[7]

As has been shown above, the infinite value of Christ's act of atonement is a consequence of the fact that it was performed by a Person in whom a divine and a human nature are hypo-statically united. In the order of atonement, an act of God is an infinite act.

§ 16. *Insofar as it affects man, the fruit of Christ's redemptive act is potentially unlimited but actually limited.*

The effect of Christ's death on the cross can be seen from several points of view. Intrinsically, it is of infinite value. We have seen that it is an act of atonement to God. Where there is no limit to the capacity of the one who receives its value, that value is boundless. This was seen in the last section. But Christ's act can also be seen from another point of view, namely, as a redemptive act which confers benefits on man.

Human beings are creatures and as creatures have limited capacities. We can make a distinction between possible and actual humans. The fruits of the redemption are limited in that the capacities of actually living human beings are limited. Actual humans are those who have lived, do now live, or will live in the future. A potential human being is one who could but who never will be lifted out of the realm of the possible into that of the actual. A moment's reflection reveals that possible humans far outnumber the actual ones. For every human who is there are millions who could be.

There is an endless number of possible individuals but not an infinite number of them. The term "endless" must be used to describe a series of individuals to which some can always be added. There can be no such thing as an infinite series, for a series denotes parts or links. An infinite being can have no parts. An infinite number is a contradiction. The term "un-limited" used in the proposition must be taken in the sense of endless, not infinite. With the explanation of these terms, it should be easy to see why we say that the fruits of Christ's death seen as a redemptive act are potentially unlimited but actually limited. They would be able to fill up the capacities of an end-less number of individuals but as a matter of fact only a limited number of possible individuals will enter that select number of actual individuals.

§ 17. *After His death on the cross, Jesus Christ descended into hell.*

The Lateran Council of 1215 A.D. repeated what already had been contained in many creeds, "Although He (Jesus) accord-ing to divinity is immortal and impassible, the very same Christ according to His humanity was made passible and mortal, who, for the salvation of the human race, having suffered on the wood of the cross and died, descended into hell." (D-429) The term "hell" has had a variety of meanings in Christian litera-ture. Its meaning today is quite specific. In ages past, the term was used to denote the state of any person excluded from heaven regardless of the reason for the exclusion. It meant both permanent or temporary exclusion; exclusion due to personal fault or without personal fault.

St. Thomas says that Christ could have descended into hell in two ways,[8] namely, in essence and in effect. A teacher, for ex-ample, is present in a classroom in essence when he is bodily there. An author of a textbook used by students is present in the classroom, not in essence, but in effect. Christ was present to some in hell through His essence and was present to others in hell through His effect on them. He was present to the damned in effect, for He accentuated their shame; He was pres-ent to those in Purgatory—hell used in the wide sense—by giv-ing them hope of going to heaven; He was present to those about to receive grace by shedding upon them the light of ever-lasting glory. It was only those who would go to heaven that Christ visited in essence to invest them with the grace that He had just won by His death on the cross.

§ 18. *It was fitting that Christ should have arisen from the dead.*

There are four reasons why it was most fitting for Christ to have arisen from the dead. They are all intimately connected with His relationship to the members of the human race. (1) Christ came to tell all what they must do and believe to be saved. He came to teach faith and morals. A person has true humility when he accepts and lives according to Christ's teachings. Such a one will be rewarded if he remains faithful to the end. This is only another way of saying that he who humbles himself shall be exalted. Christ gave practical expression to his own principle. By His death on the cross He humbled Himself. It was most fitting that He should be exalted. By His resurrection His exaltation became an accomplished fact. (2) In the last chapter, we saw that Christ combined miracles with His teaching. He summarized His teaching in a superlative way by humbling Himself even unto the death on the cross. It was most fitting that according to His pattern of teaching He should also summarize the probative force of His miracles in a superlative way. He did this by rising from the dead. (3) By His resurrection from the dead, Christ gave people the most powerful motive for living according to His teachings. Even though Christ had redeemed the world by His death on the cross, people needed a new motive to use the means of sanctification to the maximum. If Christ had died and had remained dead, a great many would have thought that He had been conquered by death and that death marked the end of His teaching and power. When He arose from the dead, He demonstrated that He had conquered death and that the power of His works is timeless. (4) By rising from the dead, Christ gave a practical demonstration of what those who are faithful to Him can expect in their own existence. People with fallen natures are more easily impressed and moved by concrete things than by abstract ones. It is easier to impress them with a corporal resurrection than with a spiritual elevation. It is easier to get people to work for the latter after they have been promised the former.

§ 19. *At His resurrection from the dead, Christ arose with a glorified body.*

After His death, there was nothing to prevent the glorification of Christ's body. From the first moment of its creation, Christ's soul was glorified, for it always beheld the Beatific Vision. Christ's body was not glorified from the first moment of its existence. Christ had emptied Himself, that is, had divested Himself of His external glory "taking the nature of a slave and being made like unto men. And appearing in the form of man, he humbled himself, becoming obedient to death, even to death on a cross." (Phil. 2:7, 8)

But when Christ had accomplished our redemption, there was no reason why the glory that already had invested Christ's soul should not now also invest His body.

Some heretics have denied the identity of Christ's body before and after His resurrection. Those who hold this error are forced to hold that Christ was guilty of conscious deception. Before His death, He had prophecied that He would arise from the dead. This prophecy could be fulfilled only if His body was the same both before and after death for resurrection means the revivifying of what had been dead. After His resurrection, Christ again wanted His body to be looked upon as the same one that He had during mortal life. This is the only interpretation that can be given to His invitation to St. Thomas to touch His body and His request that He be given something to eat.

§ 20. *It was fitting that Christ should have ascended into heaven after His resurrection from the dead.*

The frequency with which Christ appeared to people after His resurrection was enough to convince them of the fact. If He had appeared only once, some critics would have constructed a good semblance of an argument for not accepting the account. The number of Christ's appearances knocks out this possibility. There are twelve apparitions recorded in the New Testament. There probably were more that have not been recorded.

It was fitting from the point of view of Christ Himself that He should have ascended into heaven. The world in which we live is one in which things are born, live, and then die. They are mortal and corruptible. Christ arose glorious and immortal on Easter Sunday. While it was appropriate that Christ should have shown Himself after He had donned immortality to show men to what heights their lowly bodies could be transformed, it was not appropriate that the immortal Christ should visibly remain among mortal men. The mortal and the immortal, each should have their own proper place.

It was more beneficial to the spiritual life of man that Christ ascend from earth into heaven. God wants man to use his life on earth to reach the goal of seeing Him face to face in heaven. If Christ had remained on earth, it would be difficult to get people to work for heaven. Why work to see God in heaven when we can see Him on earth without working? They would not easily make the distinction of seeing Christ with bodily eyes and of seeing Him face to face in heaven. Christ's presence would be for many an end in itself instead of being a means to an end. While Christ worked miracles and taught in person during His public ministry on earth very few took advantage of His presence to better themselves spiritually. After He departed, He was believed and accepted by peoples from every nation, race, and age in the world.

NOTES

1. *S.T.*, III, 1, 3.
2. *S.T.*, III, 48. 2-4.

3. *S.T.*, III, 50, 1.
4. *In Verrem*, 2, 8, 66.
5. Ricciotti, *The Life of Christ* (Milwaukee: Bruce, 1947), p. 617.
6. *S.T.*, III, 46, 5.
7. Ch. 49, 6.
8. *S.T.*, III, 52, 2.

VIII

Blessed Virgin

§ 1. *The Church teaches that the Blessed Virgin is really and truly the Mother of God.*

The theology of the Blessed Virgin is closely related to that of Jesus Christ. Christological heresies have often meant Mariological ones as well. This is well illustrated by the errors of Nestorius who denied that in Christ there are two natures united in one Person. When he said that these two natures were loosely united only after Christ had been born, he equivalently denied that the Blessed Virgin was the Mother of God. The Council of Ephesus in 431 A.D. condemned Nestorianism saying: "If anyone does not confess that God is truly Emmanuel, and that on this account the Holy Virgin is the Mother of God, for according to the flesh she gave birth to the Word of God become flesh by birth, let him be anathema." (D-113)

Sacred Scripture is also clear on this doctrine. We read that the Archangel Gabriel said to Mary, "The Holy Spirit shall come upon thee and the power of the Most High shall overshadow thee; and therefore the Holy One to be born shall be called the Son of God." (Luke 1:35) And in revealing Christ's birth to the shepherds, the Angel said, " . . . For today in the town of David a Savior has been born to you Who is Christ the Lord." (Luke 2:11) These two passages show that Christ's two natures were joined at the moment of His conception. The Person born to Mary was truly God and consequently she was truly the Mother of God.

The first Christian writer who defends the divine maternity of the Blessed Virgin is St. Ignatius of Antioch (d. 107 A.D.). He first explicitly says that Jesus is God and then says, "He is in truth of the family of David according to the flesh, God's son by the will and power of God, *truly born of a Virgin.*"[1] In the quoted passage and the ones that follow, St. Ignatius refers to the Person of Jesus Christ implying that Christ's actions such as birth and death were performed by the individual and not merely by one of His natures.

§ 2. *By a special privilege of God, the Blessed Virgin was preserved free from the stain of original sin.*

This doctrine was repeated by Pope Sixtus IV in the Fifteenth Century. The most explicit statement of this truth was made by Pope Pius IX in 1854 A.D. He defined, "We declare, pronounce, and define that the doctrine which holds that the most Blessed Virgin Mary at the first instant of her conception by a singular grace and privilege of Almighty God, in virtue of the merits of Christ Jesus, the Savior of the human race, was preserved immaculate from all stain of original sin, has been revealed by God, and on this account must be firmly and constantly believed by all the faithful." (D-1641)

The doctrine of the Immaculate Conception of the Blessed Virgin is not explicitly revealed in Sacred Scripture, but theologians connect three Scriptural passages with it. (1) The *protoevangelium* in which God said to Satan, "I will put enmity between you and the woman, between your seed and her seed." (Gen. 3:15) (2) The archangel said to Mary, "Hail, full of grace, the Lord is with thee." (Luke 1:28) (3) Elizabeth said to her on the occasion of the visitation, "Blessed art thou among women and blessed is the fruit of thy womb." (Luke

1:42) These passages place the Blessed Virgin in a special category completely opposed to the realm of Satan in that of sin. Theologians point out that this could not be done if the Blessed Virgin was not completely free from all sin. Now "freedom from all sin" includes freedom from original sin, and so we can conclude to the fact of Mary's Immaculate Conception. It must be remembered that original sin is a true sin in the one stained with it, for it effectively prevents sanctifying grace from entering the soul.

§ 3. *By a special privilege of God, the Blessed Virgin received as much grace as a human being could receive.*

This proposition embodies the common teaching of theologians (D-1978a). Scriptural evidence supporting this doctrine is found in the passage from St. Luke's Gospel quoted in the last section in which the Archangel said to Mary, "Hail, full of grace." (Luke 1:28) The expression is to be interpreted to mean that Mary's capacity for sanctifying grace was exhausted. Since she is a creature, her capacity for grace was limited. But even with this necessary limitation, she had a great deal more grace than other humans could receive. (This is not to deny the fact that Mary grew in grace constantly.)

Several conclusions flow from the fact that the Blessed Virgin had the fullness of grace. (1) Since a human being has a capacity for grace as soon as it is constituted a human being, the Blessed Virgin received grace from the first moment of her conception. The superlative degree of Mary's grace together with the time that she received it indicates that she received it by virtue of a special privilege of God. (2) The "fullness" of grace in the Blessed Virgin precludes the possibility of any moral defect throughout her life that could lessen the degree of grace in her soul. She was always free from all mortal and venial sin. The Council of Trent defined, "If anyone shall say that a man once justified can sin no more, nor lose grace, and that therefore he who falls and sins was never truly justified; or on the contrary, that throughout his whole life he can avoid all sins, except by a special privilege of God, as the Church holds in regard to the Blessed Virgin, let him be anathema." (D-833) St. Thomas[2] sees in the Blessed Virgin's fullness of grace a confirmation in grace rendering it impossible for her to commit sin of any kind. St. Augustine held that any sin on her part would necessarily reflect on and do a measure of dishonor to her divine Son. His conclusion is the same as that of St. Thomas, who held that the Blessed Virgin was free from all personal sin throughout her life.

§ 4. *Mary, the Mother of Jesus Christ, led a life of perpetual virginity.*

The perpetual virginity of the Blessed Virgin was defined in explicit terms by the Lateran Council of 649 A.D. It said, "If anyone does not properly and truly confess in accord with the holy Fathers, that the holy Mother of God and ever Virgin and immaculate Mary in the earliest of the ages conceived by the Holy Spirit without seed, namely, God the Word Himself specifically and truly . . . and that she incorruptibly bore Him, her virginity remaining indestructible even after His birth, let him be condemned." (D-256) Mary, therefore, was a virgin before, during, and after Christ's birth. (1) In the Messianic prophecy of Isaias to King Achaz, the prophet predicted, "Behold a virgin shall conceive, and bear a son." (Isa. 7:14) The Fathers, in commenting on this verse, say that it proves Mary's virginity before and during Christ's birth. The two verbs "conceive" and "bear" must be ascribed to the same person, namely, the Virgin. (2) In describing the Annunciation, the Evangelist wrote, "The angel Gabriel was sent from God . . . to a virgin . . . and the virgin's name was Mary." (Luke 1:26, 27) When informed that she was chosen to be the Mother of God, Mary inquired, "How shall this happen, since I do not know man?"

(Luke 1:34) An exegesis of Mary's question shows that the virginity implied therein refers to both the past and to the future. It strongly hints at a vow of virginity taken by Mary. (3) St. Thomas shows that there is no contradiction in Mary bringing forth the infant Christ while remaining a virgin. It would have been impossible in the natural order of things but not impossible by divine power.

§ 5. *The Church teaches that after the death of the Blessed Virgin she was assumed into heaven body and soul.*

The dogma of the Assumption of the Blessed Virgin was formally defined by Pope Pius XII in 1950 in these words, "We pronounce, declare, and define that the dogma was revealed by God, that the Immaculate Mother of God, the ever Virgin Mary, after completing her course of life upon earth, was assumed to the glory of heaven both in body and soul. If anyone . . . should dare either to deny this, or voluntarily call into doubt what has been defined by us, he should realize that he has cut himself off entirely from the live and Catholic faith." (D-2331) There is no direct reference to the Assumption of the Blessed Virgin in Sacred Scripture. The definition made by the Church is a good example of how a doctrine implicitly contained in other doctrines is discovered by the work of theologians, brought to maturity, and finally defined by the infallible teaching authority of the Church.

The Church has condemned the opinion that holds that the Blessed Virgin died as the result of original sin. We must hold that her death was a consequence of the simple privation of the praeternatural gift of immortality. There is a close parallel between the reason for her death and the reason for Christ's death. Theologians point out a number of reasons why it was fitting for the Blessed Virgin to arise from the dead in a glorified body and be assumed into heaven. One of these is in consideration of her participation in Christ's work. "As Mary, in her capacity of Mother of the Redeemer, took a most intimate share in the redemptive work of her Son, it was fitting that, on the completion of her earthly life, she should attain to the full fruit of the Redemption, which consists in the glorification of soul and body."[3] Just as her life paralleled Christ's life before death, so it should also parallel Christ's life after death; hence her bodily assumption into heaven.

§ 6. *The Blessed Virgin Mary is entitled to a special veneration of the faithful.*

Veneration may be described as the respectful recognition of another's virtues of good qualities. In the supernatural order, the greatest quality that a person can possess is sanctifying grace. The greater another's sanctity is, the firmer is the basis for venerating him. The Blessed Virgin was endowed with a plenitude of grace from the first moment of her existence. Since she was the recipient of a singular favor from God, she is entitled to special veneration from men.

Honor given to the Blessed Virgin is not honor subtracted from God. When one honors her, he is obviously imitating God who has already honored her. When one venerates the Blessed Virgin, he indirectly honors God Who is the Source of the grace conferred upon her. Veneration due to the Blessed Virgin does not mean that she must be given veneration equal to that given to God. The adoration given to God is called *latria;* that given to the Blessed Virgin is called *hyperdulia;* and that given to the saints is called *dulia.* Pope Innocent XI in 1687 A.D. condemned the opinion that held that praise given to the Blessed Virgin is vain and useless (D-1256). Perhaps the oldest picture of Christian art discovered to date proves the reverence of Christians for the Blessed Virgin. It dates from about 125 A.D. and can be seen in the catacombs of Priscilla in Rome.[4]

We can honor the Blessed Virgin in a variety of ways. Two such ways are by imitating her virtues and by seeking her intercession. Today, God still honors her by granting requests through her intercession. The Church teaches that while we are not obliged to ask the Blessed Virgin to intercede for us with God, it is heresy to hold that asking her intercession is useless.

§ 7. *By her cooperation in the incarnation of Christ, the Blessed Virgin earned the title of "Mediatrix" of grace.*

In the encyclical "Ad Diem" of 1904, Pope St. Piux X said, "As a result of the participation between Mary and Christ in the sorrows and the will, she deserved most worthily to be made the restorer of the lost world, and so the dispenser of all gifts which Jesus procured for us by His death and blood. . . . Since she excels all in sanctity, and by her union with Christ and by her adoption by Christ for the work of man's salvation, she merited for us *de congruo,* as they say, what Christ merited *de condigno,* and is the first minister of the graces to be bestowed." (D-1978a) Since the Blessed Virgin gave the world the Person who would redeem all mankind and merit all grace, she, in a sense, can be said to be the channel of all those graces.

The important role of the Blessed Virgin in the salvation of the world was noted as early as the Second Century. St. Irenaeus draws the parallel between Eve and Mary. He first says that Eve by her disobedience caused the destruction of the human race, so Mary "a virgin" by her obedience became the cause of her own salvation and the salvation of the whole human race.[5] Many writers have expanded on this same parallel between Eve and Mary.

St. Thomas says that Christ is the sole Mediator between God and man and by His death on the cross fully reconciled the two. "But there is nothing to prevent others in a certain way from being mediators between God and man, insofar as they, by preparing or serving, cooperate in uniting men to God."[6] In the role of cooperating with Christ, no one could possibly be given

a closer and, therefore, more important role than His Mother.
The doctrine of the Mediatorship of Mary in no way lessens
the redemptive might of Christ's act of atonement.

NOTES

1. *Ad Smyr,* 1, 2.
2. *S.T.*, III, 27, 5.
3. Ott, *Fundamentals of Catholic Dogma* (St. Louis: Herder, 1954), p. 207.
4. Marucchi, *Manual of Christian Archeology* (Paterson: St. Anthony Guild, 1935), p. 320.
5. *Adv. Haer.*, 3, 22, 4.
6. *S.T.*, III, 26, 1.

IX

Actual Grace

§ 1. *No one can make progress toward his assigned goal with only the natural powers of the fallen state.*

Man's goal is to see God in the life after death. Only God could assign man such a goal; no one can legitimately substitute another in its place. We have already shown that God could have assigned man the goal of seeing Him either by the natural light of reason or face to face. As a matter of fact, God has assigned man only the second of these two ends. It was the only one that God ever intended that man should have. Man retained this goal even after his fall from original innocence.

Everyone who is given a goal must also be given the means to reach it. God did this when He created Adam and Eve. Over and above the powers essential to human nature, Almighty God gave our first parents both praeternatural and supernatural gifts. He endowed them with the supernatural life they needed to reach their supernatural goal. Notice that He gave them supernatural life itself and not merely the means to gain supernatural life. But God also entrusted to Adam the titles to grace that He wished each human being to receive. Then came the tragedy of Eden whereby man lost both praeternatural and supernatural gifts.

Original sin tumbled man from the supernatural plane

down to the natural plane. While it left him with a complete human nature, it stripped from him everything he needed to reach his supernatural goal. He then was capable of operating only on a purely natural plane. It is a self-evident principle that one can do only what he has power to do. In the natural state, man lacked the things he needed to be elevated once more onto the supernatural plane from which he had fallen. His natural powers, his intellect and will, his body and soul, were capable of producing only natural effects.

§ 2. *Actual grace is the transient supernatural influence of God in the soul moving it to an act ordered toward sanctification.*

In theology, the term "justification" means the process of transition whereby one is elevated from the natural plane to the supernatural plane. In it one loses the status of being an enemy of God and receives the status of being an adopted child of God. He who was once in original or mortal sin is now in sanctifying grace. We shall notice distinct stages in this process.

One of its indispensable elements is actual grace. It is obviously important that we have a clear notion of this term. (1) Actual grace is a transient help enabling one to perform a particular act in time. If it is not used when it is given, its power is lost to the person to whom it was given. It cannot be stored up for future use. It is in a sense like electricity which must be used when it is made. (2) This grace is a supernatural influence. It is a quality, a force that completely surpasses any created cause. A natural person does not have it; he cannot work to obtain it; he cannot demand that it be given to him. He cannot receive it from any other created agent. The grace must come from God. (3) Actual grace influences man's intellect and will. It does not supplant the intellect and will in the performance of an act, but it bonds itself to these powers thereby making them a new kind of power. They become supernaturalized powers. We can liken it to the quality of hardness that is given to a piece of steel by the process of annealing. (4) Actual grace is given to enable one to perform a salutary act. This is an act by which one could receive sanctifying grace. Notice that this does not mean that the person will necessarily receive sanctifiying grace from the act.

§ 3. *There are several distinguishable phases in the process of justification.*[1]

The separate phases in the process of justification were topics of bitter theological controversies in the early centuries. We consider them here in sequence. (1) A person must first dispose himself to receive justification. He does this by cooperating with God's grace. Thus he makes a distinct act of the will welcoming the influence of grace. This is a real phase of the process of justification, for without it the process could not even begin. We may liken it to the preparation of soil before a planting is made. (2) When a person has disposed himself, God sends further actual grace. It is a distinct supernatural influence or impetus on the person's intellect and will. This quality bonds itself to the powers of the soul, thereby supernaturalizing them and making them capable of supernatural acts. (3) While the powers of this soul are under the influence of actual grace, the person must make a new decision. He can elect to act in harmony with this influence and perform the act which the grace moves him to perform, or he can reject the salutary influence of grace and refuse to perform the act. Throughout the process, he retains free will. (4) The act that is performed under the influence of actual grace can have several effects. If the entry of sanctifying grace is blocked by the presence of an obstacle, the person does not receive justification, but he can be given new actual graces in view of his morally good act though he has no right to them. If the salutary act be one by which the affection for mortal sin is rejected, then sanctifying grace does enter the soul and the process of justification is completed. If the salutary act is performed by a person who has already been justified, there is an increase of sanctifying grace in the soul. The person is said to receive greater justification and holiness.

§ 4. *The actual grace needed for all phases of the process of justification must be given by God.*

The first part of the proposition states that actual grace is needed in all phases or stages of the process of justification. The Church has branded both Pelagianism and Semi-Pelagianism as heresy. The first held that one does not need actual grace in order to perform the act whereby the process of justification is completed; the second held that God's help is not needed to dispose oneself to receive actual grace. Against these errors, the Council of Carthage in 418 A.D. stated and Pope St. Zozimus approved, "Whoever says that . . . what we are ordered to do through free will, we may be able to accomplish more easily through grace, just as if, even if grace were not given, we could nevertheless fulfill the divine commands without it, though not indeed easily, let him be anathema." (D-105) The Council concludes its statement by couching its teaching on the necessity of grace in Christ's own words, "Without me you can do nothing." (John 15:5)

A person must have God's grace even to dispose himself to receive actual grace. An act is either natural or supernatural. These two things are essentially different, not merely different in degree. Now the act whereby one disposes himself to receive grace is indispensably connected with the actual reception of this grace. In order to merit this classification, it must be on the same plane as the actual reception. They must both be essentially superior to any purely natural act, and therefore, one needs God's supernatural help both to dispose himself to receive actual grace and actually to receive it.

Actual grace comes from God. The purpose of actual grace is to enable one eventually to reach the supernatural goal of seeing God face to face. This goal is essentially superior to any created goal, for it is after a fashion the soul's sharing of God's uncreated nature. There must be a proportion between the means and the end. They must both be on the same plane. Actual grace is and must be a supernatural influence and as such can be given only by God.

§ 5. *All of the actual grace that a person may receive is a free gift of God.*

A gift is free if the giver is in no way compelled to give it and the receiver has no basis to demand that it be given to him. Both of these conditions are present in the granting of actual grace by God to the individual soul. We must conclude, therefore, that this grace is a free gift of God.

God is under no obligation or compulsion to give actual grace. This flows from the fact that He is an infinitely perfect being. There is no one greater than He is who could force Him to do what He does not freely choose to do, for He is the necessarily existent being. All creatures depend on Him for their initial creation and continuation in existence. There is nothing internal to God that can compel Him to give us grace. The only thing that God must do by necessity is to exist as God. This pertains to Himself and not to the acts that He does outside of Himself, that is, in the created universe. It would be wrong to say that God must give us actual grace because He gave us a supernatural goal and justice demands that He also give us the means to reach it. This would be true if God *first* gave us a goal and *then* gave us the means. But this is not the case. The assigning of the goal and the giving of the means was accomplished in a single free act.

In reference to man, actual grace is a free gift, for man has no basis upon which to anchor a demand that it be given to him.

God could bind Himself to give actual grace to one who already enjoys God's special friendship because of the fact that he is in the state of sanctifying grace. By virtue of this divine promise, one in sanctifying grace can say that he has a right to actual grace. But this actual grace is still a free gift of God, for nothing that man can do could compel God to make the promise in the first place.

§ 6. *Actual grace influences the intellect by suggesting salutary thoughts to it.*

The intellect is man's knowing power. It is capable of conceiving ideas, of judging, and of reasoning. Actual grace can influence the mind in all three of these activities. A salutary thought is a great deal more than one which begins and ends in the intellect. The influence of the actual grace that suggests it does not end in the intellect, but spills over into the will and invites the will to act according to the directive that it has received. A person who has a salutary thought also sees that he should not be indifferent to it, for its distinctive feature is that it is geared to action.

There are a number of categories of salutary thoughts that one might receive. We list a few examples of them. Actual grace might suggest a supernatural truth to a person, not merely as an exercise in theological speculation, but as a doctrine that must be accepted and believed in obedience to God's command. It might supply a supernatural motive for doing good such as loving enemies out of love of God. It might invite one to do a particular good work or to say a particular prayer because it is a means of sanctification. It might suggest a plan of mortification in order to remain detached from the allurements of temporal goods. Actual grace can suggest many things necessary to avoid sin. It might point out to one the heinousness of sin and sharply drive home its ugliness. It might show him how to formulate a plan designed to cope with a habit of sin or an occasion of sin. It might bring home to him the loss of supernatural benefits as a consequence of sin.

God can suggest salutary thoughts immediately or mediately. In the first instance, God directly enlightens the mind as He did the minds of the Apostles on Pentecost. In the second, God uses creatures as His instruments of enlightenment. He can and does use such things as a sermon, a book, a person, a picture, a physical misfortune, and the like. But He is the ultimate source of grace, for it ever remains a supernatural influence.

§ 7. *Actual grace influences the will by strengthening it to perform salutary acts.*

The intellect and will are distinct powers of the soul, for they have distinct objects. The object of the intellect is truth, while that of the will is goodness. But intellect and will work as a unit. The will cannot choose unless it has alternatives presented to it by the intellect. The intellect is driven to enrich its store of knowledge by the will. In the last section, it was pointed out that actual grace suggests salutary thoughts to the intellect. Regardless of how many such thoughts there are or how clearly the mind grasps the value of the thing they represent, the intellect cannot choose them, for it is not a choosing power. This choice must be made by the will. And the will cannot choose without God's actual grace.

Actual grace elevates the will to the status of an essentially new and higher power. It makes it a supernatural power enabling it now to do what it was completely incapable of doing, namely, performing supernatural acts. It is in the sense of "elevating the will to an essentially new status" that grace is said to "strengthen" the will. Grace does not boost the natural effort of the will. It is not a quality which wrings maximum power from it.

A salutary thought is different from a salutary act. The first is in the intellect while the second is in the will. It is from the act, not from the thought, that a person is able to receive sanctifying grace, for one receives grace when he chooses God instead of rejecting Him. A salutary act can either be elicited or commanded. An elicited act begins and ends in the will. It does not overflow into external action. Believing and mental prayer are examples of elicited acts. A commanded act is one which begins in the will but which overflows into some external action as walking or speaking. One will receive sanctifying grace from the performance of salutary acts provided there is nothing to block the entry of this grace into the soul.

§ 8. *A person remains free to accept or to reject the influence of actual grace given to enable him to perform a supernatural act.*

In the early centuries, the Pelagians gave excessive prominence to the will by eliminating the need for actual grace in the performance of a salutary act. In more modern times, the pendulum has swung in the opposite direction. Some heretics have held that actual grace takes away free will. Against this opinion, the Council of Trent said, "If anyone shall say that man's free will moved and aroused by God does not cooperate by assenting to God who rouses and calls, whereby it disposes and prepares itself to obtain the grace of justification, and that it cannot dissent, if it wishes, but that like something inanimate it does nothing at all and is merely in a passive state; let him be anathema." (D-814)

The indication of the freedom of the will under the influence of grace lies in the will's manner of acting while not under the influence of grace. Actual grace is a quality which elevates the will thereby making it a supernatural power. It must be emphasized that the will is supernaturalized, not changed. It can do what it did before the advent of grace. But with grace, it does them in a supernatural way provided, of course, that it should choose to accept the influence of this grace. It would not be acting supernaturally if it should choose to reject this influence.

Man's will is free even under the influence of grace as long as it is presented with alternatives of imperfect goodness. While man sojourns on earth everything that is presented to him has some imperfect features about it. The will *must* choose only that good which is complete and universal. It can reject anything else because it sees that it does not measure up to the universal good. The goods presented to the will by salutary thoughts are obviously imperfect. There are several reasons for this statement. If they satisfy a person in one respect but not in another, they are of limited goodness. There cannot be a series of perfect goods in existence. The fact that one can choose a series of the goods represented by salutary thoughts proves that each of them is imperfect.

§ 9. *God wills that all persons reach the goal that He has assigned to them.*

As an infinitely intelligent Being, God has a reason for everything He does and a goal for everything that He creates. It has been pointed out that God could have assigned to the members of the human race the goal of seeing Him by the natural light of reason, but He *de facto* decreed that their goal should be the supernatural goal of seeing Him face to face. This goal for man was not changed when our first parents committed original sin. In 853 A.D., Pope St. Leo IV approved this statement of the Council of Quiersy, "Omnipotent God wishes all men without exception to be saved although not all will be saved. However, that certain ones are saved, is the gift of the one who saves; that certain ones perish, however, is the deserved punishment of those who perish." (D-318)

One who denies that God wills all to be saved must also make other denials. He must deny that Christ died for all men or that God wills that all men should receive the supernatural means necessary for salvation, or that man can use his free will to co-operate with these means. A person who holds any of these positions falls into the error of Calvin or of Jansenius. Calvin held that God predestines some to heaven or to hell regardless of any other consideration. Jansenius said the same thing in a different way. He held that Christ did not die for all men but only for those who would be saved. Against Calvinism, the Council of Trent defined, "If anyone shall say that the grace of justification is attained by those only who are predestined unto life, but that all others, who are called, are called indeed, but do not receive grace, as if they are by divine power predestined to evil: let him be anathema." (D-827) St. Paul anticipated the error of Jansenius when he wrote, "This is good and agreeable in the sight of God our Savior, who wishes all men to be saved and to come to the knowledge of the truth. For there is one God and one Mediator between God and men, himself man, Christ Jesus, who gave himself a ransom for all." (I Tim. 2:3-5)

§ 10. *God gives to everyone who has reached the use of reason enough actual grace to be justified.*

It must always be kept in mind that God wills that all should reach the supernatural goal that He has assigned to them and that Jesus Christ won the actual and sanctifying grace necessary to make this possible. There are several different categories of people who are the recipients of God's grace. We confine ourselves to those persons who have reached the use of reason, that is, those who know right from wrong.

Almighty God actually gives to every person who has reached the use of reason sufficient actual grace to enable him to be justified. But this does not mean that everyone will make use of this grace and actually be justified. Even before justification one has the free will to be able to reject actual grace. The sufficient grace referred to here must be strong enough to enable the individual to keep the Ten Commandments and thereby to avoid committing any mortal sin. It can be said that it is sufficient to overcome any temptation to mortal sin. This conclusion follows from the premise that God does not command impossibilities.

A person who uses the actual grace that God gives him to avoid serious sin is not necessarily justified, for he has not as yet received sanctifying grace. But those who have progressed this far have clearly disposed themselves for the grace of justification. God never fails to cooperate with those who have used the means to dispose themselves. While the persons themselves have not established a right to the grace, they can be certain that God will send it to them. Theologians list the ways that these persons, even though they live in heathen lands might be given the opportunity to cooperate with the new grace and thereby to receive justification.

It is the common opinion of theologians that God does not abandon those who have fallen into mortal sin but that He can and does give them actual graces sufficient to bring about their conversion from sin.

§ 11. *Even a person already in sanctifying grace must receive new actual grace in order to perform salutary acts.*

A clear distinction must be made between actual and sanctifying grace in the process of justification. Even though they have a relationship to each other, their roles are truly distinct and separate. Actual grace is a transient help, while sanctifying grace is permanent habit in the soul. One cannot play the role of the other. Even though a person is already in sanctifying grace, he does not by this fact alone have the supernatural help he needs to perform new salutary acts.

A person with habitual grace in his soul has been made an

adopted child of God. God loves him with a love similar to that love with which He loves Himself. The very existence of sanctifying grace in the soul of a justified person represents a title, a strict right to new actual grace to keep and to increase the sanctifying grace. This person can expect and can count on the actual grace to overcome a temptation to mortal sin and also to perform virtuous acts. God has promised supernatural help to a justified person. Such a person is worthy of God's help and God, being infinitely just, never denies help to one worthy of it. This help is still free, for God was not compelled to promise to give it. It seems reasonable to conclude that the more sanctifying grace one has in his soul, the more lovable he is to God and the more inclined God is to give him more and more actual grace.

A person who lacks justification is an enemy of God. He lacks any basis for expecting that God should give him any actual grace he needs to be justified. If God does help such a person it is because He has mercy on him. This person cannot even lay claim to the supernatural help that would dispose him to receive the actual grace that would enable him to perform salutary acts. God has not promised to help such a person.

§ 12. *Each Sacrament can confer a special title to the actual grace needed to fulfill the end of the Sacrament.*

Each of the seven sacraments has a definite role in the life of the person who receives it. The Council of Florence in 1439 A.D. listed the end or purpose of each Sacrament in the life of the individual or of society (D-695). And since Christ instituted each sacrament to fulfill a special role, He annexed a special actual grace to enable the recipient of the Sacrament to attain the benefit that it was meant to confer. St. Thomas writes, "Now the sacraments are ordained unto certain effects which are necessary in the Christian life. . . . Just as the virtues and gifts confer, in addition to grace commonly so called (sanc-

tifying grace), a certain special perfection ordained to the powers' proper actions, so does sacramental grace confer, over and
above grace commonly so called, and in addition to the virtues
and gifts, a certain divine assistance in obtaining the end of
the sacrament."[2] The student can learn the precise nature of
the actual grace of each sacrament from any textbook on Sacramental Theology.

For how long a period does one receive actual grace from a
sacrament? It depends on the spiritual state of the person. Certain sacraments cannot be repeated, that is, cannot be received
a second time within a fixed period. A person who remains in
sanctifying grace throughout this period retains a title or right
to the actual grace at all times. If the recipient of the sacrament
falls into mortal sin, he loses all right to sacramental grace,
but he will recover the right or title to this grace if he removes
the mortal sin within the period when the sacrament cannot
be repeated. Some theologians are of the opinion that God may
still give some sacramental grace to a person who had received
a sacrament validly but has since fallen into mortal sin. Such a
person would not receive these graces because he had a right
to them but only out of God's mercy for him.

§ 13. *A person can receive actual grace from the performance
of good works.*

The Council of Orange in 529 A.D. said, "The assistance of God
ought to be implored always even by those who have been re-
born and have been healed, that they may arrive at a good end,
or may be able to continue in good work." (D-183) The term
"good works" irrespective of whether or not one receives grace
from them means the observance of the Ten Commandments.
In the concrete, there is no such thing as a morally indifferent
act. It is either good or bad. The Church has condemned the
opinion of those who hold that every act of an unjustified person is bad (D-817).

Each commandment has a positive and a negative phase. Each tells us what to do and what not to do. There is no difficulty in seeing how doing what we are commanded is morally good. But one is not neutral when he chooses to avoid sin. He has made a definite choice to remain loyal to God. The good work that is recommended to us more frequently than any other is prayer. By prayer, one confesses his dependence on God and asks God for what he needs. All prayer is at least implicitly a prayer of petition asking God for what one needs to reach his assigned goal.

Does one always win actual grace by his prayers and other good works? If he already be in sanctifying grace, he will always receive both new sanctifying and actual grace from them. He will merit them, for he already has established a title to them. If he be not in sanctifying grace, he does not win new actual grace in the sense that he can lay strict claim to it by right. But these good works do show that he has a disposition for new actual grace. And God in His love for all will not fail to send new helps to those who have disposed themselves for these helps. These helps are not given to the person in justice but out of mercy.

§ 14. *It is possible for some persons to gain actual grace for others.*

There are numerous passages in Sacred Scriptures which urge that we pray for others. The didactic feature of St. Paul's epistles is very pronounced on this point. "This is why we too have been praying for you unceasingly, since the day we heard this, and asking that you may be filled with knowledge of his will, in all spiritual wisdom and understanding." (Col. 1:9) Again, "I urge, therefore, first of all, that supplications, prayers, intercessions and thanksgiving be made for all men . . . . This is good and agreeable in the sight of God our Savior, who wishes all men to be saved and to come to the knowldege of the truth."

(I Tim. 2:1-4) Finally, "Brethren, pray for us, that the word of the Lord may run and be glorified even as among you." (II Thess. 3:1) When we keep in mind that actual grace is a supernatural enlightening of the mind and strengthening of the will, we see that St. Paul refers to this grace in these passages.

It would be an impossible task to quote here all the passages from the Apostolic Fathers recommending that we pray for others. There are some in every one of St. Ignatius (d. 107) of Antioch's letters. The implication in all of them is that living persons can be given supernatural help or actual grace because of our prayers for them.

Some persons get discouraged because they do not see the "results" of the grace they ask for others. They lose heart because a loved one is not converted from evil ways. This does not necessarily mean that God has not heard those prayers. One in habitual grace gains new grace for himself even when he prays that God give actual grace to another. Actual grace does not compel one to do things against his will. The reason why, for example, one who is the object of prayer is not converted is that he has not cooperated with the grace that God has most probably sent him.

NOTES

1. Pohle Preuss, *Grace Actual and Habitual* (St. Louis: Herder, 1937), p. 147 ff.
2. *S.T.*, III, 62, 2.

X

Sanctifying Grace

§ 1. *The fact that Christ died for all men does not mean that all of them will automatically be saved.*

We saw that the Church condemned the tenet of Jansenism which held that Christ died only for the elect. On the other hand, Pope Vigilius in 543 A.D. anathematized those holding the error that every person condemned to hell, even demons, will eventually be saved (D-211). These two errors have opposites which are evidently the positions that the faithful must accept. Against Jansenism, the Church taught that Christ died to redeem all men. Against Origenism, the Church taught that some persons are not saved. We must believe that Christ won back for all men the title to grace that they had lost by the sin of Adam and Eve, but that not everyone will receive or keep the grace that Christ wanted him to receive or to keep. When a person receives the grace that Christ won on the cross, he is said to be justified or holy. Christ won objective justification for all, but each person must receive subjective justification individually.

Jesus Christ stated that the fact that He died for all does not mean that all will be saved. "Not everyone who says to me, 'Lord, Lord,' shall enter the kingdom of heaven; but he who does the will of my Father in heaven shall enter the kingdom of heaven." (Matt. 7:21) Christ is implying here that definite means must be taken in order for a person *to be saved.*

§ 2. *The Church condemns as error every opinion which holds that man is justified by something external to the soul.*

This proposition does not deal with objective redemption but with subjective justification. A number of heretics have held that Christ's merits can be related to a person in an external fashion and yet render him holy and justified. (1) Some have said that justification consists of the remission of sin and nothing more and that Christ's merits do nothing more than wipe away one's moral faults. This is a negative as well as an external view of justification. (2) It has been also held by heretics that justification consists of a confidence that God will not impute or charge one with his sins. This opinion, of course, denies that sins are taken away in justification. It holds that those sins are still present but covered over or whitewashed. To Luther who proposed it, faith was a blind confidence similar to the definition of hope.[1] It is very different from the definition of the theological virtue of faith traditionally held by the Church. (3) It has been erroneously held that justification consists of obedience to the commandments. Notice that to these people observance of God's law is not a means to an end but is an end in itself. It is similar to the error of Kant who said that sanctity consisted in virtue. (4) An error which was held by certain leaders of the Protestant revolt was that a person is justified by the external favor of God. This is the predestination held by heretics of the Calvinistic persuasion. They said that God selects some persons for justification and salvation regardless of the way these persons use or abuse their free wills.

In all these opinions, justification is obtained through something external to the soul. The Church has anathematized anyone who holds any of them.

§ 3. *The Church teaches that a person is justified, that is, rendered holy, by the infusion of sanctifying grace into his soul.*

The Church says that justification is not external to the soul but is a quality that inheres in the soul. In 1547 A.D., the Council of Trent defined, "If anyone shall say that men are justified either by the sole imputation of the justice of Christ, or by the sole remission of sins, *to the exclusion of grace and charity,* which is poured forth into their hearts by the Holy Spirit and remains in them, or even that the grace by which we are justified is only the favor of God: let him be anathema." (D-821) Justification, therefore, is something internal to the soul.

Jesus Christ brought out the internal character of the grace that causes justification by calling it "life." "He who believes in the Son has everlasting *life*; he who is unbelieving towards the Son shall not see *life*." (John 3:36) "God so loved the world that He gave His only-begotten Son, that those who believe in Him may not perish, but may have *life* everlasting." (John 3:16) To the Samaritan woman at Jacob's Well, Christ said, "The water that I will give him shall become in him a fountain of water, springing up unto *life* everlasting." (John 4:14) To the people of Capharnaum, who had witnessed the multiplication of the loaves and fishes and had heard the promise of the Eucharist, Christ said, "Amen, amen, I say to you, unless you eat the flesh of the Son of Man, and drink his blood, you shall not have *life* in you." (John 6:54) To the lawyer who had recited the contents of the law to Him, Christ said, "Thou hast answered rightly; do this and thou shalt *live*." (Luke 10:28) The last two passages quoted here must be interpreted to mean that the things suggested are the means to the end which is justification. The practices, that is, receiving the Eucharist and keeping the Commandments are not ends in themselves.

§ 4. *New Testament writings besides the Gospels state that justification is accomplished by the infusion of grace.*

St. Paul was the New Testament writer who was most insistent on the role of grace in the sanctification of the individual. Among New Testament writers, he is called the "Doctor of Grace." The Apostle to the Gentiles faithfully reflects Christ's description of grace as being a new life infused into the soul. "He (Jesus) saved us through the bath of regeneration and renewal by the Holy Spirit; whom he has abundantly poured out upon us through Jesus Christ our Savior, in order that, *justified* by his *grace,* we may be heirs in the hope of *life* everlasting." (Titus 3:5-7) "With Christ I am nailed to the cross. It is now no longer I that *live,* but Christ *lives* in me. And the life that I now *live* in the flesh, I *live* in the faith of the Son of God, who loved me and gave himself up for me. I do not cast away the grace of God." (Gal. 2:19-21) To the Romans he wrote, "But now set free from sin and become slaves to God, you have your fruit unto *sanctification,* and as your end, *life* everlasting. For the wages of sin is death, but the gift of God is *life* everlasting in Christ Jesus our Lord." (Rom. 6:22-23) To the Ephesians, St. Paul wrote, "But God, . . . by reason of his very great love wherewith he has loved us even when we were dead by reason of our sins, brought us to *life* together with Christ (by *grace* you have been saved." (Eph. 2:4-5) In a beautiful passage from the same Epistle to the Ephesians, he shows that justification and grace is not external to man but elevates him interiorly. "But be renewed in the spirit of your mind, and put on the new man, which has been created according to God in *justice* and *holiness* of truth." (Eph. 4:23-24) This theme is the great theme that runs through all of St. Paul's epistles. His great message is to tell all men of the wonderful effects that sanctifiying grace works upon its recipients and that in comparison to it everything else pales into insignificance.

§ 5. Sanctifying grace is a permanent quality of the soul.

In the created universe, we find substance and nine accidents. This is true regardless of whether the things are material as a stone or non-material as a soul. A substance is anything that can exist by itself although not necessarily of itself. It need not be a material thing. Matter and substance are not identically the same. A spirit cannot be seen; it has no parts or size or weight and yet it is a substance, for it does not inhere in anything else. An accident, however, is something which must inhere in substance. It is never found by itself. Motion, for example, is an accident, for it inheres in a substance which moves. Thought is also an accident, for it can only exist in a subject that thinks. Size is an accident for the same obvious reason.

A quality is a factor or a power that inheres in a substance. It either helps or hinders that object in reaching its proper goal. It too is clearly an accident. A habit, for example, is a quality. A good habit helps a subject to reach its goal and a bad habit hinders that same subject. There are two kinds of habits that can inhere in a person, namely, operative and entitative habits. (1) An operative habit aids one in acting. It is a fixed tendency to perform an act developed because that act was repeated often in the past. For example, by constant practice, one develops a facility to play the piano. (2) An entitative habit does not give one facility for action, but it does help or hinder the pursuit of a goal. Health, for example, is an entitative habit, for although it does not represent a fixed tendency to perform a particular act, it does aid one in reaching a goal.

There is the same relationship between the soul and sanctifying grace as there is between substance and accident. Of the nine distinguishable accidents that can modify a substance, sanctifying grace is a quality. More particularly yet, it is an entitative habit. It inheres in the soul and fits that soul to reach the goal assigned to it by God, namely, the goal of seeing Him face to face in heaven.

§ 6. *The supernatural life bestowed by the infusion of sanctifying grace is essentially superior to natural life.*

In teaching the people who came to listen to Him, Christ was often handicapped, not by His inability to teach, but by the incapacity of the people to understand. It was difficult for them to grasp abstract ideas. Christ was compelled to use many concrete examples and parables. Even a cursory reading of the Gospels brings this out. In describing the meaning of holiness, Christ does not use the unfamiliar word "grace." He does, however, use the very familiar word "life." The people knew the difference between life and death. The circumstances in which He uses it are very revealing. It tells us a great deal of the nature of grace. He was addressing living individuals and yet He was calling them "dead." The reason is obvious. They lacked sanctifying grace in their souls. Nothing is farther away from life than death; nothing is farther away from death than life. Sanctifying grace, that is, supernatural life, is as far superior to the natural life with which we are born as this natural life is superior to death.

The supernatural life of grace is not an intensification of natural life; it is not the complete unfolding of natural powers or capacities. It is something completely new and wonderful. The difference is not one of degree but of kind. We say that natural and supernatural life are essentially different. No matter how skillfully a block of stone is cut, shaped, and polished into a statue of a lion, it still lacks life. A living animal is essentially superior to its stone likeness. The stone is not half of the living creature. There is an unbridgeable chasm between them; and the stone cannot even begin to cross it in an effort to become like the animal. There is no half-way point between death and life. This gives us some idea of the staggering greatness of sanctifying grace and its wonderful effects on souls.

§ 7. *A person in sanctifying grace has received a share in the life that is proper to God.*

In 1567 A.D., Pope St. Pius V condemned the error which held that, "Justice . . . does not consist in any habitual grace infused in the soul, by which man is adopted into the sonship of God and renewed according to the interior man and made a sharer of the divine nature, so that, thus renewed through the Holy Spirit, he can in turn live well and obey the mandates of God." (D-1042) The same Pontiff on the same occasion also condemned the error which held that "the sublimitation and exaltation of human nature in participation with the divine nature" was natural and not supernatural (D-1021).

There is a fine passage from the Second Epistle of St. Peter on this topic. "For indeed his divine power has granted us all things pertaining to *life* and piety through the knowledge of him who has called us by his own glory and power—through which he has granted us the very great and precious promises, so that through them you may become partakers of the divine nature." (II Peter 1:3-4) A number of the Fathers describe the action of grace in the soul as a "deification" of man.

Two things must be said in describing the effect of grace on the soul of one receiving it whereby he receives a share of the life or nature proper to God. The first is that the grace does not cause one to be absorbed into God in the manner that rain drops are absorbed into a lake. Grace does not make one lose his individuality and creatural status. The second is that the grace that makes one holy is not split off or subtracted from God's holiness. Grace is not a substance which must be divided before it can be shared by another. On the other hand, we have pointed out that this grace is not something external to the soul. A justified person does not have grace *on* his soul but has it *in* his soul. The example often used is the plunging of a piece of cold iron into a heap of red hot coals. The iron takes on the heat and color of the coals while maintaining its own individuality. The heat and color permeate the whole iron. It does more than merely coat the surface of the metal.

§ 8. *Sanctifying grace makes the person who receives it an adopted child of God.*

The doctrine stated in the proposition is clearly contained in documents issued by the Holy See or approved by it. In 1547 A.D., the Council of Trent in describing the effects of grace in the soul taught, " . . . justification of a sinner is given as being a transition from that state in which man is born a child of the first Adam to the state of grace and of the adoption of the sons of God through the second Adam, Jesus Christ." (D-796) Pope Pius XI in 1929 repeated that "Christ redeemed and restored (man) to his supernatural dignity, to be the adopted son of God, yet without the praeternatural privileges by which his body had before been immortal, and his soul just and sound." (D-2212)

St. Paul insists on this effect of grace in many places throughout his letters. " . . . In love, He (God) predestined us to be adopted through Jesus Christ as his sons, according to the purpose of his will, unto the praise of the glory of his grace, with which he has favored us in his beloved Son." (Eph. 1:5) St. John wrote, "Behold what manner of love the Father has bestowed upon us, that we should be called children of God." (John 3:1)

What is implied by adoption? By adoption, a person freely accepts into his own family a child born of other parents, and places that child on a par with his own children. The adopting father erases all difference and distinction that existed between the adopted child and his own offspring. No preference will be shown to his own blood children over the adopted one. That adopted child receives the very name of his new parents and is entitled to equality with the others in the love, privileges, rights, protection, and inheritance of those who received him into their family. When we say that sanctifying grace makes its recipient an adopted child of God, the term "adopted" must be taken as literally as possible. It will not do to take it in the figurative or fanciful sense. God cannot communicate His substance to us, for there can be only one infinite being. But He does communicate His life, beauty, and goodness as far as God can give and man can receive. The benefit is given and received, not as a substance, but as an accident.

§ 9. *God loves the soul in sanctifying grace with a love similar to the love with which He loves Himself.*

"But in all these things we overcome because of him who has loved us." (Rom. 8:37) Each power has its own object. The object of the eye, for example, is light; that of the intellect is truth; that of the will is good. Love is the attraction of the will for a thing apprehended as good, that is, as desirable. Happiness follows closely upon love, for happiness results when the will actually possesses the object seen as good. The degree and quality of the happiness that a rational agent can experience depends on the quality of the goodness rooted in the object and on the intensity with which it can be possessed. This description will help one understand better the love of God for a soul in grace.

As an infinitely perfect being, God is and must be limitlessly good. And as an intelligent being contemplating His own perfections, He must be attracted to what He sees and contemplates. Since the good that God sees in Himself is infinite, the love that God has for Himself and the happiness that results must also be infinite. It is impossible for this happiness to be more intense than it already is.

A soul in sanctifying grace participates in God's nature in the manner already described. It shares in God's life, goodness, and beauty. And when God looks at that soul in grace, He sees one that participates in His own nature. And as a consequence of this, God loves that soul with a love similar to the love with which He loves Himself. Of course, the intensity of this love is not the same in both cases. God loves Himself with infinite intensity. A soul is limited even though it be in grace. It cannot receive, nor can God give it all the love of which God is capable. But this love is essentially superior to the love that the soul can receive from any creature. It is far superior to any love that a pure creature such as an angel can give, for it is a supernatural love.

§ 10. *Sanctifying grace entitles one to share the happiness that is proper to God.*

In a Gospel passage already quoted, Christ said, "He, however, who drinks of the water that I will give him shall never thirst; but the water that I will give him shall become in him a fountain of water, springing up unto life everlasting." (John 4:13-14) It is easy to interpret the figurative details of this verse. In the most explicit form of this passage Christ says that anyone who properly uses the means of sanctifying grace will eventually receive an eternity of happiness (D-809). The Council of Trent in 1547 A.D. defined, "If anyone shall say that the good works of the man justified . . . do not truly merit increase of grace, eternal life, and the attainment of that eternal life if he should die in grace, and also an increase of glory: let him be anathema." (D-842) In these statements we see that man in grace is entitled to one of the notes of the happiness proper to God, namely, its endless duration.

We saw that happiness is engendered by the possession of that which is good and desirable. God is infinitely happy because He enjoys the infinite good. Man cannot be infinitely happy because he has a limited nature with a limited capacity for happiness even though the grace in which he is invested makes him share in God's nature. Save for these necessary limitations, sanctifying grace entitles one to the happiness that is proper to God. Since it is supernatural happiness it is essentially superior to any joy or ecstasy that anyone could experience on earth. The type of good determines the type of happiness. If all the happiness that all men could experience were compressed and concentrated into the lifetime of a single individual, it would still be natural happiness, for it would result from the possession of natural goods. The happiness to which sanctifying grace entitles its recipient is essentially greater and more intense. It is absolutely impossible for anyone on earth to have an adequate notion of it. The best that we can do is to let our imaginations be catapulted to a better notion of it from a consideration of the ecstasy with which we are familiar.

§ 11. *The theological virtues of faith, hope, and charity are infused into the soul with sanctifying grace.*

We have seen that there are two types of habits, namely, entitative and operative habits. An operative habit confers a facility to perform a particular act. An entitative habit does not give a facility for action but it is a quality which helps or hinders one in the pursuit of a goal. The Council of Trent taught, "Man through Jesus Christ, into whom he is ingrafted, receives in the said justification (i. e., reception of sanctifying grace) together with the remission of sins all these gifts infused at the same time: faith, hope, and charity." (D-800) In setting these points down the holy Council implies that while sanctifying grace and charity are concomitant, they are not the same thing. Faith is the acceptance of truths revealed by God motivated by the attribute of His omniscience and truthfulness; hope is trusting in God's promises motivated by His attributes of goodness, power, and fidelity to His promises: charity is loving God above all things because He is infinitely loveable.

Are the virtues of faith, hope, and charity infused with grace operative or entitative habits? They are operative habits. They are qualities which help one to reach the supernatural goal assigned to him by God. Everyone in grace receives these infused virtues or habits regardless of his age. They are even in newly baptized infants.

Must the theological virtues coexist in the soul with grace? Where grace is, there also must charity be. Where charity is, there also must faith and hope be. But the loss of grace and charity does not necessitate the loss of the infused virtues of faith and hope. These two virtues are lost when one commits serious sins directly opposed by the divine attributes which motivate faith and hope.

§ 12. *The moral virtues of prudence, justice, fortitude, and temperance are infused into the soul with sanctifying grace.*

The proposition embodies a doctrine which while not a defined statement yet is more commonly held by theologians. Sacred Scripture attests to the existence of those moral virtues which are called the cardinal virtues. "Or if one loves justice, the fruits of her works are virtues; for she teaches moderation, and prudence, justice, and fortitude." (Wis. 8:7) We saw that the motive behind the practice of the theological virtues was a divine attribute. The purpose of the moral virtues is to regulate the use of creatures insofar as they affect man's relationship to God. Prudence disposes a person to choose the right means that will promote his progress toward his goal; justice inclines one to render to everyone what is his due; fortitude inclines one to overcome the obstacles that hinder progress toward the goal; temperance inclines one to subject the use of temporal goods to the dictates of right reason. Notice that these are infused virtues, and so must not be confused with acquired habits.

St. Thomas[2] shows why it is necessary that moral virtues should be infused into the soul with sanctifying grace. Virtues, not grace, are the proximate principle of action. For example, a man uses only his lips and tongue in speaking but the whole individual is responsible for what is said. Sanctifying grace is an entitative, not an operative habit. A person in grace can increase in grace but must perform supernatural acts to do so. These acts fall into one of the four categories of acts covered by the moral virtues. Grace pertains to being; habits pertain to actions. Since everyone in grace can perform supernatural actions, it follows that everyone in grace must have the moral virtues listed above. The only way that this could be is if the moral virtues are infused into the soul with sanctifying grace and are lost when the grace is lost.

§ 13. *The seven gifts of the Holy Spirit are infused into the soul with sanctifying grace.*

While the doctrine contained in the proposition is not a defined truth, theologians put forth very strong reasons for its acceptance. The Biblical quotation that contains evidence of the existence of the gifts of the Holy Spirit is Isaias 11:2. It lists the gifts as wisdom, understanding, counsel, fortitude, knowledge, piety, and fear of the Lord. These gifts have marked similarities and dissimilarities with the infused virtues already studied. Like the virtues they are qualities infused into the soul.

A gift of the Holy Spirit is a quality which enables a person to be especially receptive to a particular kind of inspiration coming from the Holy Spirit. It disposes one to receive actual grace. Now actual grace is an illumination of the mind and a strengthening of the will moving one to perform a supernatural act. There are different kinds of actual graces in that each is given to enable one to perform particular kinds of acts. All the kinds of actual grace can be said to fall into seven categories. Each gift of the Holy Spirit enables us to be receptive to one of these categories of grace. The gift remains in the soul as long as sanctifying grace remains.

While all impulses from the Holy Spirit help both intellect and will, the individual gifts perfect either intellect or will. Wisdom, understanding, counsel, and knowledge are "gifts" of the intellect. Fortitude, piety, and fear of the Lord are "gifts" of the will.

The difference between virtues and gifts can be illustrated in this way: The theological virtues studied in the last section are like motors which propel a ship through the waters. The gifts of the Holy Spirit are like the sails of a windjammer. Sails do not propel the ship as motors do. They are set to catch the impulsion of the wind. Just as each of the many sails has its own role in the progress of the ship, so each of the seven gifts has its own role in the spiritual progress of the individual.

§ 14. *There is a personal indwelling of the Holy Spirit in the soul of one in sanctifying grace.*

In condemning the errors of Michael du Bay in 1567 A.D. Pope St. Pius V linked the infusion of sanctifying grace into the soul with a special indwelling of the Holy Spirit there (D-1015). There are a number of Scriptural passages quoted to support this doctrine. St. Paul wrote, "Do you not know that you are the temple of God and that the Spirit of God dwells in you?" (I Cor. 3:16) "And hope does not disappoint, because the charity of God is poured forth in our hearts by the Holy Spirit who has been given to us." (Rom. 5:5) "But if the Spirit of him who raised Jesus from the dead dwells in you, then he who raised Jesus Christ from the dead will also bring to life your mortal bodies because of his Spirit who dwells in you." (Rom. 8:11) The letters of St. Ignatius of Antioch (d. 107 A.D.) faithfully echo this doctrine as found in St. Paul's epistles. "Let us perform all our actions with the thought that God is present within us; and then we shall be His temples, and He will be God dwelling with us."[3]

What is the nature of the indwelling of the Holy Spirit in the soul of a justified person? We can safely say that it is a union of some sort. But there are several types of union. It is not a substantial union such as one whereby man's body and soul are immediately joined to form a human person. Nor is it a hypostatic union such as the one whereby Christ's two natures are united in one Person. The first union cannot be destroyed without also destroying the individuality of the person; the second cannot be broken up without a miracle of God. The union of the Holy Spirit with a justified person must, therefore, be an accidental union, for each of the two persons would remain integral if the union should be ended. This indwelling results from a new and special love which permeates the soul. Christ said, "If anyone love me, he will keep my word, and my Father will love him, and we will come to him and make our abode with him." (John 14:23) The passages quoted above refer to the abiding of the Holy Spirit in the soul of a person with grace, because to the Holy Spirit are attributed works of love.

§ 15. *Prudence dictates that definite means should be instituted to distribute grace to men.*

A means is said to be "definite" when it is an unchangeable act circumscribed by indispensable conditions instituted to procure a particular effect. Let us examine these elements separately. (1) The means must be instituted or authorized by the one who assigned the goal. One may not assign a goal without also appointing the means that must be used to reach it. This in turn implies that the same person has authority over both. He may institute the means personally or may authorize another to do so in his place. In either case, the means would have a common source. (2) In order to deserve the label "defi-

nite" the means must have a measure of stability or unchangeableness about them. They admit of no addition, subtraction,
or substitution without the authority of the person who instituted them in the first place. This relatively unchangeable
characteristic greatly facilitates the task of teachers instructing
others how to use them. It also facilitates the task of those who
must learn how to use them. Constantly changing means are a
fruitful source of confusion and eventual disuse even when
the change is made legitimately. We should, therefore, expect
the means of grace to be the same for all peoples and for all ages.
(3) To prevent abuse and even disuse of the means of grace, it is
at least advisable to lay down conditions surrounding their lawful and valid use. These conditions insure that the means will
be used only when they will further one's spiritual welfare.
Instead of complicating matters, the observance of these conditions will result in the more frequent use of the means of grace.

§ 16. *Christ instituted the means by which the fruits of His
passion and death could be channelled to men.*

It was seen that one who institutes the means to an end must
have the authority for doing so. Even from the standpoint of
appropriateness, there are several reasons why Christ should
have personally instituted the means of grace. As God, He assigned to all men the supernatural goal toward which all are
required to move; as Redeemer, He actually won the grace that
would make possible the reaching of this goal; as an Omniscient Being, He knew what means would be morally and
physically possible for men to use; as an Omnipotent Being He
possessed the fullness of power and authority to institute the
means. We shall now see what Christ actually did in this
matter.

The Council of Trent teaches that the means of grace are
the sacraments and good works. Of the first it said, "If anyone
shall say that the *sacraments* of the New Law were not all insti-

tuted by Jesus Christ our Lord, or that there are more or less than seven ... let him be anathema." (D-844) "If anyone shall say that the sacraments of the New Law do not contain the grace which they signify, or that they do not confer that grace on those who do not place an obstacle in the way ... let him be anathema." (D-849) Of the second, the same Council says, "If anyone shall say that the *good works* of the man justified are in such a way gifts of God that they are not also the good merits of him who is justified, or that the one justified by the good works, which are done by him through the grace of God and the merit of Jesus Christ ... *does not truly merit increase of grace* ... let him be anathema." (D-842) We shall see that the "good works" mentioned here include the observance of the Ten Commandments. These Commandments indeed ante-date Christ's appearance on earth, but He instituted them as a means of grace, for He annexed grace to their observance. Only the One who won the grace could do this.

§ 17. *A sacrament has all of the notes necessary to qualify it as a definite means of grace.*

The purpose of this section is to show that if the means of grace are not as effective as they could be, the blame may not be ascribed to the one who instituted them. A sacrament of the New Law is defined as an outward sign instituted by Christ to confer grace efficaciously. (1) All the Sacraments were immediately instituted by Christ. He could have authorized others, such as the Apostles or the Church, to institute them but *de facto* He did not. He Himself determined their essential elements at least in a general way although He left to His Church the task of laying down regulations and prescribing ceremonies surrounding their administration. (2) Christ instituted exactly seven Sacraments. Each one of them is intended to help one to meet a particular kind of a crisis in his life when he stands in special need of divine help. The student can learn the role of each sacrament in the spiritual development of a Catholic from books on Sacramental Theology. (3) In the administration of each sacrament there is a rite perceptible to the senses. This rite consists of a special act usually known as the "matter" joined with a special set of words known as the "form." It is a permanent rite, for it has been used in the Church substantially unchanged for all people from the time of Christ until the present day and will remain unchanged until the end of time. (4) A sacrament confers grace efficaciously. Christ attached the power to confer grace to the rite itself. The efficacy of the sacrament does not depend on the sinlessness of the one who administers it. The only way that a sacrament can be prevented from conferring grace is by a recipient who sets up an obstacle or a barrier to the grace. But this factor does not prevent the sacrament in itself from being an effective means of grace.

§ 18. *Observance of the Ten Commandments is a means of receiving grace for those who do not place an obstacle in its path.*

Each of the Ten Commandments has a positive side bidding us to do a specific thing. The penalty for breaking this positive precept is either a sin and its consequences or the loss of the grace that one could have received. This is a very real penalty. Several conditions are necessary for a person to receive grace from a positive observance of a commandment. The act must be performed by one already in the state of grace. Some writers add the second condition that the agent must have at least a habitual intention of performing the act with a supernatural motive. The acts referred to here can be even the seemingly insignificant acts of one's daily life. It may be recalled that Christ said that the person who gives even a cup of cold water in His name would not lose his reward. St. Paul urged that even such things as eating and drinking be done for the glory of God (Col. 3:17). The positive precept that is urged most repeatedly is the First Commandment bidding us to pray without ceasing. The qualities and ends of prayer as well as the specific and general times when the duty obliges are discussed in textbooks of moral theology.

A recital of the Ten Commandments shows that most of them are worded negatively. They tell us what to avoid. It would be a serious mistake to think that a person who avoids what the Commandments forbid "does nothing." One who avoids sin in reality does something very positive. When one is tempted, he is faced with the alternative of choosing to have God or to reject Him. The fact that one chooses to avoid sin shows that he definitely reaffirms his love for God. If this person already be in grace, his choice wins him new grace. No one comes from a temptation in the same condition as he was before he faced it. He will be either better or worse. If he is in grace, the election to avoid sin is truly a good work in the sense defined by the Council of Trent.

§ 19. *A justified person can merit an increase of sanctifying grace.*

Against the errors of some leaders of the Protestant revolt who held that there are no degrees of holiness or sanctity the Council of Trent defined, "If anyone shall say that justice received is not preserved and also not increased in the sight of God through good works but that those same works are only the fruits and signs of justification received, but not a cause of its increase: let him be anathema." (D-834) Some Scripture passages seem to support this definition of the Church. "Grow in grace and knowledge of our Lord and Savior, Jesus Christ." (II Peter 3:18) "But to each one of us grace was given according to the measure of Christ's bestowal." (Eph. 4:7)

Sanctifying grace is an entitative habit in the soul. It cannot increase quantitatively, for it is not the accident of quantity but of quality.[4] One habit can be greater than another in that its object is greater. Health and beauty, for example, are different entitative habits in that their objects are different. In this respect, one cannot increase in grace, for all grace unites one to God regardless of how much he has. But qualities do admit of degrees of perfection or intensity and in this sense one can increase in grace, for he can lay hold of God with ever increasing fervor. The measure of one's charity or love of God is in direct proportion to the measure of grace he has in his soul.

There are three ways by which one can increase in grace. The first is by frequent use of the means of grace. The second one is by a more thorough preparation to use the means of grace. The third is by using the more "powerful" means of grace. It can be shown that some means of grace are objectively more powerful in bringing about their effect than are others. The Holy Eucharist, for example, is in Itself a more powerful means of grace than any other sacrament.

§ 20. *A person can receive or increase sanctifying grace in his soul only during his life on earth.*

The basis for the truth embodied in this proposition is the Church's teaching on the finality of the particular judgment that one undergoes immediately after death. The Council of Lyons in 1274 A.D. taught that upon being judged at death, the soul of a baptized person goes *immediately* to heaven or to hell, or to purgatory and there receives the reward or punishment that it has deserved. No time is allowed for any change in the sentence. The logical conclusion from this is that after death a soul cannot receive or increase in grace. The Church has anathematized the heresy that holds that all souls including the spirits of demons will eventually go to heaven. St. Paul wrote, "For all of us must be made manifest before the tribunal of Christ, so that each one may receive what he has won through the body, according to his works, whether good or evil." (II Cor. 5:10) When St. Paul says "through the body" he means that one can do good or commit evil only while living on earth.

An increase of grace entitles one to greater reward and happiness in heaven. In general, a person is worthy of reward if he chooses good when he could have chosen evil. There is no room for merit or demerit where there is no freedom of choice. One is not responsible for acts which are not deliberate and free. While one sojourns on earth, he is free to accept or reject. At death, a fixity seizes the will. This does not mean that a person is deprived of free will, for it is natural for the will to be free. After death, a person uses his free will to repeat and to perpetuate the selection he had made at death. He cannot make a new selection. He can no longer choose good instead of evil. It follows that one cannot increase the sanctifying grace in his soul after he has departed this life. The Church has indeed always urged us to pray for the dead. We shall point out how these prayers and suffrages do help the Poor Souls in Purgatory. One must not think—as many Catholics do—that these prayers merit new grace for the faithful departed. Their opportunity to increase in grace ended at death.

§ 21. *A person can receive or increase sanctifying grace only for himself; he cannot receive or increase it for another.*

The Council of Lyons quoted in the last section defined, "The same most holy Roman Church firmly believes and firmly declares that on the day of judgment all men will be brought . . . before the tribunal of Christ to render *an account of their own deeds.*" (D-464) This doctrine is anchored in Sacred Scripture. Christ said, "And they who have done good shall come forth unto resurrection of life; but they who have done evil unto resurrection of judgment." (John 5:29) Again, "For the Son of Man is to come with his angels in the glory of his Father, and then he will render to everyone according to his conduct." (Matt. 16:27) St. Peter wrote, "You invoke as Father him who without respect of persons judges according to each one's works." (I Pet. 1:17) All these passages stress the same theme, namely, that whether one is found worthy of merit or demerit will depend on his own proper actions and not on deeds that others have done in his behalf.

When a person decides to use the means necessary to receive or to increase in grace, he in reality desires or reaffirms his desire to make God the goal of his life. And if one rejects these means, he rejects God as his goal, for grace is indispensable in reaching this goal. Acceptance or rejection requires this exercise of free will. Since one cannot choose for another, neither can he decide to use the means of grace for another. It must be a personal effort. St. Augustine put this in a clear definite way when he wrote, "A man can enter the Church unwillingly; he can approach the altar unwillingly; he can receive the Sacrament unwillingly, but he cannot believe unless he wills it." In this context, the term "believe" implies a great deal more than intellectual assent to truth. It implies choosing God as one's goal in life and then choosing to use the means to reach Him. It also implies that one person cannot receive or increase sanctifying grace for another.

§ 22. *By committing even one mortal sin, one loses all the sanctifying grace he has received.*

Certain leaders of the Protestant revolt propagated the error that once a person receives justification he cannot lose it. The Council of Trent was called upon to set forth the perennial doctrine of the Church on this point. It defined, "If anyone shall say that a man once justified can sin no more, nor lose grace, and that therefore he who falls and sins was never truly justified . . . let him be anathema." (D-833) Christ cautioned His followers that they would have to maintain their loyalty to Him in the face of opposition and added, "He who has persevered to the end will be saved." (Matt. 10:22)

There is nothing in the union of God and the justified person that precludes their separation, that is, the loss of justification for the person. In past sections, it was seen that sanctifying grace is an entitative quality in the soul. A quality can be separated from a substance and still leave the substance or person intact. A person can lose the entitative quality of health and still retain his personality. It is not the same type of separation that takes place when a person dies.

The free will of a person on earth lacks that fixity that characterizes the free will of a person after death. While one is still a wayfarer, he can choose either one of contradictory alternatives. One who is tempted to commit a mortal sin has these alternatives before him. A seriously forbidden object is one which cannot be possessed along with the love of God. In actually choosing this object one rejects God as his goal and substitutes the forbidden object in place of God's love and grace. Even one mortal sin is sufficient to strip completely all sanctifying grace from the soul. The first mortal sin makes the essential difference. Subsequent mortal sins make for an accidental worsening of the soul's spiritual condition with respect to its relationship to its assigned goal.

§ 23. *The sanctifying grace that one loses by mortal sin revives when all mortal sin is removed from the soul.*

While mortal sin causes one to lose all the sanctifying grace he has received, this grace is not irretrievably lost. A person can receive it back again. In the Third Century, Tertullian erroneously held that one could receive the sacrament of Penance only once in his lifetime, and that it was powerless against certain sins.[5] This false opinion was opposed by the teaching of Pope St. Callixtus. The Council of Trent repeated that lost justification may be received anew at any time before death. It stated, "If anyone shall say that he who has fallen after Baptism cannot by the grace of God arise again; or that he cannot recover lost justice, except by faith alone without the sacrament of Penance . . . let him be anathema." (D-839) In the Bull of Jubilee issued in 1924, Pope Pius XI said ". . . For, all who by doing penance carry out the salutary orders of the Apostolic See in the course of the great Jubilee, the same regain anew and receive that abundance of merits and gifts *which they have lost by sinning.*" (D-2193)

The mortal sin that deprives the soul of grace or prevents its re-entry can be removed in one of several ways. First, by making an act of perfect contrition with at least an implicit intention to receive absolution. Second, by receiving valid absolution. One can be validly absolved provided he had perfect or imperfect sorrow for all mortal sins. Third, if one is in good faith, that is, is not conscious of the existence of the mortal sin in his soul, he will receive grace by the reception of any sacrament, even one of the living, provided he had made at least an act of attrition or imperfect contrition. This act of sorrow may be made even after the sacrament was received, provided it was made within the period during which the Sacrament could not be repeated.

One cannot receive grace while in mortal sin. The observance of the Ten Commandments while in mortal sin does not win grace that will revive when the mortal sin is removed.

NOTES

1. For a refutation of Luther's exegesis of St. Paul's doctrine of justification by faith see Prat, *The Theology of St. Paul,* II, 233 ff.
2. *S.T.,* I-II, 63, 3.
3. *Ad Eph.,* 15, 3.
4. *S.T.,* I-II, 112, 4.
5. *De Pudicitia,* ch. 1.

XI

The Church

§ 1. *Jesus Christ founded a Church to distribute to all the fruits of the redemption and thereby to lead all to their supernatural goal.*

It is the purpose of this chapter to show in a brief way how Christ went about insuring that all men could receive the fruits of the redemption. The inquiry should be sub-divided into three parts so that it can be better understood. (1) Our Divine Lord founded a Church. Like any organization or society, this Church has four definite elements that make for a group that can be distinguished from other groups. Christ's Church has features that are peculiarly its own, features that other societies cannot duplicate, nor can she communicate to others. In making a study of this kind, it is imperative, not only to notice what two organizations have in common, but also what they do not have in common. (2) Jesus Christ confided to His Church all the means she needed to sanctify and to save the members of the human race. He entrusted to her the fonts of revelation and all that they contained. He left to His Church the written and unwritten word of God, namely, Sacred Scripture and Sacred Tradition. Extremely important also was His legacy of the seven sacraments and the whole treasury of actual and habitual grace. Paramount among these, of course, is the Holy

Sacrifice of the Mass. (3) Our Divine Lord invested His Church with His own authority to carry out the task appointed to her. In giving her a commission to teach, He endowed her with infallibility in teaching the articles of faith and precepts of morals. In giving her His authority to sanctify, He invested her with power to legislate on those matters designed to promote the spiritual welfare of her members. Authority to legislate is meaningless if it does not also imply the right to punish those who disobey the directives.

§ 2. *Christ's Church is made up of the* people *who are directed by the same* officials *in the use of the same* means *needed to reach the same* goal.

The elements listed in the proposition are those exhibited by any organization or society. They are found in such diverse groups as corporations, civil governments, schools, labor unions, athletic associations, and the like. Christ's Church has them in common with other societies. (1) Human organizations are obviously made up of *people*. It is possible for one person to belong to several different organizations provided there is no conflict on any of the other three elements necessary for a group to function as a distinct unit. (2) The *officials* of an organization are those who have the authority to direct the rank and file of the membership. They may issue legitimate commands requiring the members to act or to refrain from acting in a matter over which they have jurisdiction. Those invested with power are not to use it for their own personal benefit, but for the welfare of the organization at large. (3) The *means* that an organization uses are the instruments, the tools, the facilities and the like that are necessary to attain the objective for which the group was founded. (4) The *goal* is the objective, the purpose, or end of the organization. It is this element that gives an organization its distinctive character.

What justifies us in saying that a particular church was

founded by Christ? Although the above elements are in every society, Christ Himself personally designated and determined the special features of each element in His Church. He did so in a manner that cannot be duplicated by any other organization. It is this fact that allows us to label the Church as Christ's Church. It also enables one to distinguish Christ's Church from any society trying to usurp her authority and prerogatives.

§ 3. *Christ intended that all the* members *of the human race should be members of His Church.*

The first element of any human organization is that it be made up of people. The distinctive feature of Christ's Church is that it must open its doors to all peoples. It must cut across every barrier of time and place to include all races in all ages. This is explicitly stated in the Gospels. Christ said, "All power in heaven and on earth has been given to me. Go, therefore, and make disciples of all nations." (Matt. 28:18-19) "And this gospel of the kingdom shall be preached in the whole world, for a witness to all nations." (Matt. 24:14) In the passages quoted, Christ speaks of "all nations." The term "nation" as used here means a great deal more than a sovereign state. It means whole ethnic groups, such as the Latin, Semitic, or Slav races. Notice that the term "all nations" is used without qualification of any kind, that is, no limitation as to time or place. It must reach out, therefore, to all the peoples of all races living in every age until the end of time.

Christ did not merely invite all peoples to become members of His Church. He went a great deal farther. He explicitly stated that membership in His Church was a matter of strict obligation, not option. His order to be obeyed carried with it a heavy penalty against any who dared to disobey it. "He (Christ) said to them (Apostles), 'Go into the whole world and preach the gospel to every creature. He who believes and is baptized shall be saved, but he who does not believe *shall be condemned.'"* (Mark 16:15-16) Again, "For whoever is ashamed of me and my words, of him will the Son of Man be ashamed when he comes in his glory." (Luke 9:26) The punishment meted out to those who refused the invitation to the marriage feast (Luke 14:16; Matt. 22:2) reiterates the insistence that all enter Christ's Church.

§ 4. *Christ invested the* officials *of His Church with authority to direct the members of the Church toward their assigned goal.*

Authority is the right of an official to be obeyed when he directs the members of a society toward the attainment of the goal of that society. It also empowers the official to punish any subject who disobeys the legitimate commands given to him. On the other hand, an official is obliged to render himself competent to rule prudently. When he issues a command he must aim at improving the status of the group at large, and not at furthering his own glorification.

Evidence of the existence of this element in Christ's Church is explicit. Christ founded a Church in which one man would have a primacy of jurisdiction. He promised Peter, "I say to thee, thou art Peter, and upon this rock I will build my Church and the gates of hell shall not prevail against it. And I will give thee the keys of the kingdom of heaven; and whatever thou shalt bind on earth shall be bound in heaven, and whatever thou shalt loose on earth shall be loosed in heaven." (Matt. 16:16-19) Christ fulfilled His promise to confer a primacy of power on Peter in these words, "Simon, son of John, dost thou love me more than these do? . . . Yes, Lord, thou knowest that I love thee. He (Christ) said to him, 'Feed my lambs . . . Feed my lambs . . . Feed my sheep.'" (John 21:15-17) These passages show that in Christ's Church there would always be one person who is the foundation rock, the keeper of the keys, and the shepherd of the flock. These expressions denote supreme jurisdiction. The authority went with the position of **Primate** and Peter was its first occupant.

We read in the Gospel (Matt. 18:18) that Christ conferred real authority on the other Apostles besides Peter. The successors of the Apostles, namely, the bishops of the Church, succeed to the power Christ gave the Apostles, but they may use it only as the successor of Peter, who possesses a primacy of power, directs them. This is a brief sketch indicating the presence of the second element of a society in the Church, namely, the existence of officials with powers to direct the rank and file members.

§ 5. *Christ appointed definite means which the members of His Church must use to reach their goal.*

Almighty God wants all men to reach a supernatural goal. It is much higher than what man can reach with merely natural powers. God who assigned the goal, also appointed the means needed to reach that goal. Jesus Christ revealed to us that by practicing supernatural religion we can receive the supernatural life needed to reach our assigned goal.

The doctrines of supernatural religion, that is, the means that one must use fall into four categories. (1) *Prayer*: Christ urged prayer by word and by example. He dictated the Lord's Prayer verbatim. (2) *Sacraments*: Christ instituted the sacraments as effective means of grace. *Baptism*: " . . . Unless a man be born again of water and the Spirit, he cannot enter into the kingdom of heaven." (John 3:5) Holy Eucharist: "Unless you eat the flesh of the Son of Man, and drink his blood, you shall not have life in you. He who eats my flesh and drinks my blood has life everlasting." (John 6:54, 55) Penance: "Whose sins you shall forgive, they are forgiven them; and whose sins you shall retain they are retained." (John 20:23) The Church has defined that Christ instituted seven sacraments in all (D-844). (3) *Commandments*: Christ said, "He who has my commandments and keeps them, he it is that loves me . . . and I will love him and manifest myself to him." (John 14:21) Our Lord in this passage is referring principally to the Ten Commandments. (4) *Creed*: Christ insisted that His followers must accept certain truths on faith. "Jesus answered . . . 'This is . . . why I have come into the world, to bear witness to the truth. Everyone who is of the truth hears my voice.'" (John 18:37) The truths referred to here are the ones summarized in the Apostles Creed. The categories listed here constitute the means of salvation. They teach a person how to *pray* as he should, to *worship* as he should, to *act* as he should, and to *believe* as he should.

§ 6. *Christ founded the Church to lead its members to the goal of seeing God face to face in heaven.*

The element that gives an organization its most distinct feature is the goal for which it was founded. It is the note which more than any other sets off a group from other societies. In fact, all the other elements of the organization point to this one. God alone could assign to the members of His Church the goal of seeing Him face to face for He alone could reward a person in this way. Christ had this goal in mind when He said, "For God so loved the world that He gave His only-begotten Son that those who believe in Him may not perish, but may have *life everlasting*." (John 3:16) To the Samaritan woman, Our Divine Lord said, "'But the water that I will give him shall become in him a fountain of water, springing up unto *life everlasting*.'" (John 4:14) Christ concludes His description of the general judgment by saying, "And these (those dying in mortal sin) will go into everlasting punishment, but the just into *everlasting life*." (Matt. 25:46)

The phrase "life everlasting" is Christ's favorite expression for heaven. Since a human being has an intellect and will, he is capable of the happiness that is engendered by knowing truth and possessing good. A person in heaven has a happiness much greater than any that can be experienced on earth, for it is engendered by knowing the highest truth and possessing the highest good in the most direct way possible. That truth and goodness is God Himself. The soul experiences this supernatural happiness forever. To teach all men of all ages what they must do and believe to reach this goal is the task of Christ's Church. No organization can have a higher purpose for existing. No task that man can be given can possibly supersede this one in urgency and importance.

§ 7. *The Church is the real but spiritual continuation of Christ on earth.*

No founder of a human society could identify himself as closely and as completely with that society as Christ identified Himself with His Church. The Catholic Church is not merely a society founded by Christ which has survived to the present day. It is a real but mystical extension of Christ into the future. A person studying the Church would run the risk of drawing false conclusions if he attended only to externals, that is, only to the Church's visible elements. The Church, to be sure, has a human element because it was founded to guide men to their supernatural goal. Its officials on earth are human beings with human frailties. In some ages past, there were even considerable discrepancies between the commands and counsels taught by the Church and the manner in which these directives were observed by the Church's members.

But the Church also has a divine element. In the next few sections, we shall see that the Church is Christ. We do not mean that in the sense that the Church is not made up of individuals or that the members lose their identity when they are initiated into this society. The authority by which the Church rules, the truth that she teaches, the supernatural life that she possesses did not come to her through Christ. They are Christ's. Christ has never relinquished His dominion over these things even when He placed an intermediary between Himself and the individual in His Church. Better than saying that the Church teaches and the Church sanctifies, we should say that Christ teaches and sanctifies through His Church. The phrase expresses more accurately the identity of Christ with the society He founded. A splendid expression of the sameness is recorded in the Acts of the Apostles. Saul, the future St. Paul, was going to Damascus to persecute the Church. On the way, he was blinded by a bright light. Then he heard the voice, " 'Saul, Saul, why dost thou persecute me?' And he said, 'Who art thou, Lord?' And he said, 'I am Jesus whom thou are persecuting.' " (Acts 9:5)

§ 8. *Christ's Church is more than a society of men: it is a living organism.*

In the last section, it was seen that the Church is a continuation of Christ. The two in a sense are one. This oneness is not figurative or metaphorical but is real and objective though spiritual. A living thing is vivified by a single life principle that lets it act as a unity. If Christ is the Church and the Church is Christ there must be a single life principle vivifying both of them. We have it on infallible authority that this common life principle is sanctifying grace. As God, Christ had this life from all eternity; as Man, He had it from the first moment of His conception. The members of the Church receive it with justification. It enables them to share in the life and love proper to God. St. Peter had this common life in mind when he wrote, "He (the Father) has granted us the very great and precious promises, so that through them (grace) you may become partakers of the divine nature." (II Peter 1:4) St. Paul was refering to the first effect of the infusion of grace when he wrote, "It is no longer that I live, but Christ lives in me." (Gal. 2:20) The official documents of the Church contain the same truth.

From what has been said above, we see more clearly why it is erroneous to label the Church merely a society of men. In a human organization, unity is attained by impressing it from without. Although members freely choose to unite, they nevertheless retain their own individual vitality. They do not share in a life which is objectively real and yet common to all of them. How different this is in the case of Christ and the Church! The Council of Trent said that, "Christ Jesus continually infuses His virtue (meaning life and strength) into persons who are justified." (D-809) Merely human societies lack the single life principle common to Christ and to His Church. The members of the Church who are in mortal sin are likened to the dead branches of a tree. They hang on the tree but lack any of its vitality.

§ 9. *Sacred Scripture likens the unity of Christ and His Church to a vine with branches and to a living human body.*

Christ said to His Church, "I am the vine, you are the branches. He who abides in me, and I in him, he bears much fruit: for without me you can do nothing. If anyone does not abide in me, he shall be cast outside as the branch and wither." (John 15:5, 6) Unlike most plants, a grape vine is not compact. Within a year's time, its branches grow considerable distances from the trunk. The shoots are long and thin and yet the plant always exhibits a perfect unity. The fruit that hangs on a particular branch is the product of the whole plant working as a unit. Each part has its own role to play. Injury to one part of the vine affects the health of the whole. The plant is a unity because the same life courses through every part of it. This same life is at once in the roots, in the trunk, in the branches, and in the fruit. The use of this example to describe the unity of Christ with His Church shows that the Church is not an aggregation of disjoined parts but is a single whole.

The expression "Mystical Body" dates from about the Ninth Century. The ideas expressed by it are found in the New Testament and especially in St. Paul's letters. "He (Christ) is before all creatures, and in him all things hold together. Again, he is the head of his body, the Church." (Col. 1:17,18) Then, "Just as in one body we have many members, yet all the members have not the same function, so we, the many, are one body in Christ." (Rom. 12:4, 5) Finally, "And all things he (God) made subject under his (Christ's) feet, and him he gave as head over all the Church, which indeed is his body." (Eph. 1:22) By these expressions, St. Paul precludes the notion that Christ and His Church are distinct entities, separated from each other. They are one in the sense that although the members of the body are in different places and carry out different functions, yet all together they make up a single individual. The same life pulses through the whole body. What happens to one member affects all other members.

§ 10. *The Church is an extension of Christ for she teaches His doctrines, administers His sacraments, functions by His authority, and survives by His strength.*

Christ's role in His Church is much different than that of a leader who founds a republic or establishes an empire. A leader can organize a government and distribute power to subordinates. But he merely reshapes the materials at his disposal. He does not create them. The president of the United States, for example, does not rule by the authority of George Washington, who was the father of this country. But Christ did not merely rearrange the means available to Him. He is the sole source of the Church's vitality. He revealed her doctrines; He instituted her sacraments; He won her grace; He gave her the authority she has, and He prevents her from collapsing when attacked from internal and external foes.

Christ so closely identified Himself with His Church that He made it impossible for anyone to drive a wedge between the two. He made it plain that a person cannot accept Him without also accepting His Church. He said to His Church, "He who hears you, hears me; and he who rejects you, rejects me; and he who rejects me, rejects him who sent me." (Luke 10:16) Special attention must be given to the verbs "listens" and "rejects." They convey a great deal more meaning than "believe" and "disbelieve." One who "listens" to Christ, not only accepts the articles of faith that He teaches, but accepts all that Christ stands for. This means that he believes and does all that Christ wants him to believe and do to save his soul. St. Paul found it difficult in practice to departmentalize the teaching of revelation into faith and morals. To him Christianity was life in Christ. His motto was "For to me to live is Christ and to die is gain." (Phil. 1:21) He shows the unity of a "justified person with Christ when he writes, "For all you who have been baptized into Christ, have put on Christ." (Gal. 3:27)

§ 11. *Christ stamped four marks on His Church enabling one to distinguish it from unauthorized churches.*

The Church is a real but spiritual extension of Christ, for the two have the same supernatural life. Some have pressed this doctrine to erroneous conclusions and have said that Christ's Church must be invisible. They have sought to fortify their position by quoting the Scriptural verse, "The Kingdom of God is within you." This error was held by Gnostics and Montanists in the Second and Third Centuries and is held by certain Protestant groups in modern times.

A mark of the Church is an externalization, a shining forth of one of the Church's four elements as a society. It enables the Church to be recognized as Christ's handiwork. We can say that in a certain sense the four marks are the Church. One must not look upon them as having been stamped on the Church's surface as a rancher places his identifying brand on his own livestock. Christ did not first found His Church and then give her marks. The founding of the Church and the impressing of the marks was one and the same act. It is impossible to separate the four marks from the Church. Since they are the Church's four elements, it follows that in order to destroy the marks one would have to destroy the Church.

While the discussion of the marks of the Church is more extensive in the study of apologetics, it does have a place in a text such as this one. Our interest in them here is that they show the Church to be a visible organization. They enable the honest inquirer to distinguish Christ's Church from any and all spurious societies which claim to teach Christ's doctrines and to function by His authority. On the positive side, these marks guide one to where he will find the truths he must believe and the precepts that he must obey in order to receive the supernatural life.

§ 12. *The Catholic Church alone has the mark of universality.*

The first element of any human organization is people. Christ determined this element and this mark of the Church when He said that she would be found among all races of peoples in all ages. He made it a matter of obligation that all should be members of His Church.

It is necessary to make a historical investigation to determine which Christian Church can legitimately claim a universality of time and place. We must confine ourselves to the briefest sketch and refer the student to an apologetics textbook. In 107 A.D., St. Ignatius of Antioch writing to the Smyrneans— the letter is still extant—wanted to call Christ's Church by a proper name and so called it "the Catholic Church." The term "catholic" means "universal" in Greek. Why did St. Ignatius use this adjective? He did not find it in the New Testament. He used it because already in his day the Church's universality was her most striking characteristic and both Christians and pagans would know what Church it referred to. The repeated use of this same name in the *Martyrium of St. Polycarp* (d. 155 A.D.) proves that the rank and file people called Christ's Church "the Catholic Church." This same extant writing contains the significant line, " . . . and the whole Catholic Church throughout the world."[1]

Toward the end of the Second Century, St. Irenaeus (d. 202 A.D.) was not satisfied with calling Christ's Church "the Catholic Church." He listed the countries to which she had spread. He writes, "The Church . . . although scattered throughout the world carefully preserves the faith. For the Christian communities which have been planted in *Germany* do not believe or hand down anything different, nor do those in *Spain,* nor do those in *Gaul,* nor do those in the *East* (*Asia Minor* and *Palestine*), nor do those in *Egypt,* nor do those in *Libya* (*North Africa*), nor do those which have been established in the central regions of the world (*Italy*)."[2] Evidence dating after the Third Century is abundant. It proves that the Catholic Church alone has had a universality of time and place.

§ 13. *The Catholic Church alone has the mark of Apostolicity.*

The second element of any organization is the authority of the officials who direct the rank and file members. This element is not lacking in Christ's Church, for He endowed Peter and the Apostles with real power. Peter and his successors were given a primacy of jurisdiction. The Apostles and their successors were given limited and subordinated jurisdiction. The mark of apostolicity means that it can be proved that the supreme ruler of the Church is a successor to St. Peter in the primacy. The inquiry entails proving that the line of supreme rulers has been unbroken from Christ down to the present day. It is clearly a historical investigation.

From the works of ante-Nicene writers, it can be shown that St. Peter went to Rome, set up his See there, and was martyred there.[3] Since Christ wanted His Church always to be ruled by one who had a primacy of power, it follows that those who succeed to Peter's See also succeed to Peter's power.[4] St. Cyprian, a bishop himself, said that the bishop of Rome sits in Peter's

Chair, meaning that he too has a primacy of power.[5] We are fortunate in that reliable writers of ancient times have listed the names of the Roman Pontiffs in their extant writings. St. Irenaeus names the twelve popes who ruled the Church from Peter down to about 178 A.D. St. Optatus of Milevis in Numidia lists the 38 popes from Peter to about 366 A.D. St. Augustine lists the 39 popes from Peter to his day toward 400 A.D.[6] Later evidence is so abundant that no serious scholar disputes it. Even Macaulay had to write, "The proudest royal houses are but of yesterday when compared to the line of Supreme Pontiffs. That line we trace in *unbroken* series from the pope who crowned Napoleon in the Nineteenth Century to the pope who crowned Pepin in the Eighth; and far beyond the time of Pepin the august dynasty extends."[7] The Church that has the mark of universality also has the mark of apostolicity.

§ 14. *The Catholic Church alone has the mark of unity.*

The third element of an organization is the set of means that must be used in order to reach the goal. The means that Christ appointed for all men fall into the categories of prayer, sacraments, creed, and commandments. Since these means came from Christ, they must be true. Since they are true, they must be immutable; since they are immutable, they must be indispensable. The mark of unity indicates that the Catholic Church has always used one set of means to reach her goal.

It is easy to show that the means used in the Catholic Church are the same today as they were when she received them from Christ. (1) A collection has been made of all the official pronouncements on faith and morals made by the popes and the general councils of all ages.[8] It facilitates the comparison of the Church's teaching in one age with her teaching in other ages. The actual comparisons justify the conclusion that the Church has always taught a unified body of doctrine. (2) The complete collection of the Church's teachings is too bulky to be used as a teacher's manual. It is more of a reference work. From time to time crisp summaries of Catholic doctrine called catechisms have been drawn up for instruction purposes. A number of the catechisms composed in early centuries are extant today. Some thirty different catechisms were used in Europe during the Middle Ages and have also survived.[9] A comparison of catechisms written in different ages and in different places proves that the Catholic Church has always taught a perfectly uniform set of doctrines. (3) The Church at different times has drawn up or authorized short formulae of faith called creeds. Many of them composed in ancient, medieval, and modern times are available for comparison. They too give us a solid basis for concluding that the Catholic Church has always used the same means appointed by Christ and so can lay claim to the mark of unity.

§ 15. *The Catholic Church alone has the mark of sanctity.*

The fourth element of an organization is the goal or purpose for which the society was founded. This element more than any other one gives a society its distinctive characteristic and sets it apart from other groups. The purpose of Christ's Church is to bring about the sanctification and salvation of her members. It is to lead them to the goal assigned to them by God, namely of seeing Him face to face in heaven. The mark of sanctity is a characteristic of the Church as a whole and not of each individual within the Church. Christ Himself said that in His Church there would be good and bad members, but the good would be in sufficient numbers to justify the conclusion that sanctity is one of the marks.

Christ pointed out several ways by which a person's interior sanctity could be externalized and thereby recognized. They are the practice of the heroic virtues of voluntary poverty, chastity, and obedience out of love of God, and also the willingness to endure persecution and even death for the sake of Christ.

There is a great deal of literary and even some archeological evidence to prove that the Church has always been adorned by groups of religious under vows and practicing the heroic virtues. Much of it dates from the Ante-Nicene era.[10] The oldest evidence of legislation on clerical celibacy dates from the Council of Elvira in Spain held in 295 A.D. There is a vast amount of evidence proving that the Church has had millions of both white and red martyrs. The first are those who undergo ridicule, hatred, loss of social position, false accusation and the like for the sake of Christ. The second are those who shed their blood for the same cause. The ten general persecutions conducted against Catholics by the pagan Roman Emperors were the prototypes of bloody persecutions against Catholics in every age and in almost every country.

§ 16. *The Catholic Church infallibly leads her members to the supernatural goal assigned to them by God.*

Christ's Church derives her name from her four marks of identification and so is called the One, Holy, Catholic, and Roman Church. No other church today has the authorization to teach the doctrines of revelation. When Christ launched His Church she wanted for nothing. She was fully equipped with all the things needed to carry on her task. She would keep all of her equipment and endowments as long as they were needed, that is, until the end of time.

We saw how closely Christ identified Himself with His Church. He said to her, "He who hears you, hears me; and he who rejects you, rejects me." (Luke 10:16) "Go into the whole world and preach the gospel to every creature. He who believes and is baptized shall be saved, but he who does not believe shall be condemned." (Mark 16:15-16) In these passages our Lord is referring to more than preaching intellectual truths. He is referring to the distribution of all the means necessary for salvation. Christ said that anyone who did not accept these truths as the Church taught them and these means as the Church distributed them would be condemned. It is plain from this that if the Church could err in teaching faith and morals, Christ would be responsible for the error. This is impossible, for Christ is God. The Church, therefore, has and must have the endowment of infallibility in order to carry out the work given to her by Christ. The student can learn from an apologetics text what officials cannot err and under what conditions they can exercise the endowment of infallibility.

NOTES

1. Ch. 8.
2. *Adv. Haer.*, 1, 10, 2.
3. Eusebius, *H.E.*, II. 25, 5.
4. Zapelena, *De Ecclesia Christ* (Rome: Gregorian Univ. Press, 1932), p. 125.
5. *Ep. 53 ad Antonium.*
6. For a list of the popes of the first four centuries as found in the writings of St. Irenaeus, St. Optatus, and St. Augustine see Alexander, *College Apologetics* (Chicago: Regnery, 1954), p. 156.
7. Essay on Ranke's History of the Popes.
8. The name of this work is *Enchiridion Symbolorum* compiled by Denzinger, Bannwart, Umberg, Rahner.
9. For the names and dates of many of these catechisms see the introduction to the Catechism of the Council of Trent.
10. Tertullian, *De Exhortatione Castitatis*, ch. 13.

XII

The Last Things

§ 1. *The Church teaches that the death that the members of the human race undergo is a punishment for sin.*

A human being is formed by the substantial union of a soul with a body. Death is the dissolution of this union. The question we ask here is, "Why do human beings die?" The answer must come, not from philosophy or biology, but from theology. In 418 A.D., Pope St. Zozimus approved a statement of the Council of Carthage which said, "Whoever says that Adam, the first man, was made mortal, so that, whether he sinned or whether he did not sin, he would die in body, that is, he would go out of the body, not because of the merit of the sin but by reason of the necessity of nature, let him be anathema." (D-101) This statement is firmly based on Sacred Scripture. God warned Adam and Eve that sin would entail the loss of immortality. "From the tree of the knowledge of good and evil you must not eat; for the day you eat of it, you must die." (Gen. 2:17) St. Paul traces the consequences of Adam's sin. "Through one man sin entered into the world and through sin death, and thus death has passed all men, because all have sinned." (Rom. 5:12)

Man living in the purely natural state, that is, a person destined for a natural goal, could die, but as a matter of fact he never lived in that state. God assigned man a supernatural goal and gave him endowments enabling him to reach it. Among these gifts was immortality. St. Thomas wrote, "If anyone, on account of his fault, be deprived of a gift bestowed on him, the privation of that gift is a punishment of that fault."[1] Applied to this discussion, this statement means that the loss of immortality was caused by sin.

It would be helpful for a better understanding of the discussion if the student would review the doctrine pertaining to the praeternatural gifts as treated in the chapter on man.

§ 2. *A person's particular judgment takes place immediately after his death.*

The truth embodied in this proposition is implied in many statements issued by the Holy See. It is a mortal sin for anyone to refuse to accept it. We read that in ancient times there appeared an error which held that one's particular judgment is postponed until some time after his death. The Catechism of the Council of Trent issued by order of Pope St. Pius V states that everyone will be judged twice. "The first judgment takes place when each one of us departs this life; for then he is instantly placed before the judgment seat of God. This is called the particular judgment." (*Art.* 8) In 1336 A.D., Pope Benedict XII officially taught that the just and the impious receive their sentence from God immediately after their death. This statement implies that the particular judgment also takes place at the same time (D-530). The Christian writers of the early centuries did not treat of the particular judgment as explicitly as they treated of general judgment. They showed that they did believe in it because they held that a person receives his reward or punishment immediately after death.

Reason illumined by faith confirms that it is fitting that the particular judgment should take place without delay after one departs this life. Death ends the period of man's probation. St. Thomas teaches[2] that it would be purposeless to postpone one's particular judgment until sometime after one's death. Then too, there is nothing that could interject itself to force a delay. In human courts delays and postponements are made so that evidence can be assembled, testimony weighed, juries empanelled, and so forth. These factors do not enter the picture to force delays in the case of man's judgment by God.

§ 3. *The verdict of the particular judgment will be based on the deeds of the person's entire lifetime.*

The Creed of Pope St. Leo IX drawn up in 1053 A.D. reads, "He (Christ) will come to judge the living and the dead, and will render to each one *according to his works.*" (D-344) We read in the Apocalypse that the angel sent to the Church at Thyatira quoted the Son of God as follows, "I am he who searches desires and hearts, and I will give to each of you according to your works." (Apoc. 2:23) Numerous statements of the Holy See pertaining to the subject-matter of man's judgment quote the following passage from Sacred Scripture, "For all of us must be made manifest before the tribunal of Christ, so that each one may receive what he has won through the body, according to his works, whether good or evil." (II Cor. 5-10) This passage tells us that judgment would be based on all the acts of one's life on earth.

What is meant by a person's deeds? In the study of moral theology, we learn that in the concrete there is no neutral act. One is responsible for every deliberate and free act which he performs regardless of how insignificant it seems to be. Deliberate acts can be performed by thought, word, deed, or omission.

§ 4. *The verdict rendered after one's particular judgment is final and irrevocable.*

A juridical decision can be revoked in one of two ways. It can be set aside completely or it can be modified. The reason for the change must be sought for in the judge, in the evidence, or in the person judged. Since none of these factors play a part in the particular judgment, it follows that its verdict is irrevocable.[2] (1) A sentence is revocable if after it has been rendered, the judge is found to lack jurisdiction needed to render it. But this is an impossibility in the particular judgment, for God, being the Creator of the Universe, is the Source of all authority. (2) A first judgment can be set aside in favor of a new one if the first one was based on evidence that was incomplete or distorted. New evidence can warrant a new verdict. The verdict of the particular judgment, however, is based on evidence that is exhaustive and weighed correctly, for the Judge is omniscient and all-wise. He cannot misjudge or miscalculate. (3) A judgment is revocable if it is a conditioned one. In this case a temporary decision is rendered and has force only until the condition set by the judge is fulfilled or left unfulfilled by the person who is judged. It is impossible for the verdict of the particular judgment to be a conditional one, for one's period of probation ends at death. After death, the person cannot merit new grace and thereby force a change of sentence for the better; nor can he sin to warrant a change of sentence for the worse. It must be concluded from a consideration of all the factors involved in it that the sentence rendered at the particular judgment is final and irrevocable.

§ 5. *Heaven is the supernatural goal that God has assigned to all persons.*

An intelligent agent always acts with a purpose in mind. The reason why beings of one class can be said to be higher than those of another class is that they have been assigned a higher goal and powers that enable them to attain it. Man is in the highest class of creatures on earth. His goal far surpasses the goal set for non-rational creatures such as plants and animals. A creature's goal can be assigned to it only by its Creator, who also sees to it that it is properly equipped with the means needed to attain the goal. A study of the powers of man is very instructive. It tells us a great deal about the type of goal that God has assigned to him.

The powers that set man apart from all other creatures on earth are his rational powers. He alone has intellect and will. The object of the intellect is truth and the object of the will is goodness. And when he possesses these objectives, he is said to be happy. The student should review the reasons for holding that when man strives after a limited truth or goodness he is unconsciously striving after the being who is unlimited truth and goodness. This unlimited Being is really God. St. Augustine was right when he said, "For Thyself thou hast created us, O God, and our hearts are restless until they rest in Thee." God Himself is the goal assigned to all men.

The Church teaches that our goal is indeed God and the attainment of Him in a supernatural way. The Council of Trent defined, "If anyone shall say that . . . one justified by good works . . . does not truly merit increase of grace, eternal life, and the *attainment of that eternal life* (if he should die in grace), and also an increase of glory: let him be anathema." (D-842) In this pronouncement, the Church, implicitly tells us what our goal is, namely, the attainment of eternal life, and also tells us how to reach it, that is, by the infusion of grace.

§ 6. *Earthly happiness is too limited to constitute man's ultimate goal in life.*

It is impossible for a human being on earth to get an adequate notion of the happiness of heaven. But he can make a platform from which he can catapult his thoughts to get a better understanding of the happiness that St. Paul could only describe in negatives (I Cor. 2:9).

Happiness is the joy engendered by possessing something good or desirable. The good that can produce happiness is either of the material order such as health, wealth, power, or pleasure or of the non-material order such as knowledge. All of the good things that can produce happiness are not of the same value. There are different levels of them, for some can produce more happiness than others. The goods that produce greater happiness for a longer period of time are to be preferred over those that produce less happiness for a shorter period of time.

How can happiness be measured? The greatness of the happiness which a person experiences depends on three factors, namely, the magnitude of the object that produces it; the capacity of the person to possess this good; and the permanence with which the person holds the object. There is great variation in these factors limited on all three counts. None of the goods that he seeks to possess satisfies all the facets of his craving to be happy. If a thing satisfies him in one respect it does not satisfy him in another respect. Wealth, for example, cannot buy health or knowledge or a clear conscience. The fact that man is always seeking happiness is an indication that his capacity for it is never filled while he sojourns on earth. And in all of man's feverish activity to acquire those things that will make him happy, he is secretly conscious that his enjoyment of it must be short-lived, for he must give it up at death. A study of the nature of man's intellect and will proves that the happiness which is the goal of his quest is not of the calibre he experiences on earth.

§ 7. *The happiness of heaven is essentially greater than the happiness of seeing God by the natural light of reason.*

Man's intellect and will are the very powers that enable him to be happy. Since these are man's highest powers, it follows that they were given to him in order that he might pursue the supreme goal assigned to him by God. The object of the intellect is not the knowledge of any particular limited being, but truth in general. The mind's capacity for knowing is not exhausted when it knows individual, finite things. Its object is being or truth in general. The object of man's will is not any particular, limited good, but good in general. These considerations give us some idea of the great capacity for truth and goodness of man's intellect and will.

God does not give great capacities without there being proportionately great things that can fill them. The capacity of the intellect and will is not filled by limited truth and goodness. It can be filled only by the possession of perfect truth and perfect goodness. Since one's ultimate goal must be in harmony with the capacity of its powers, it follows that man's goal is the perfect being whose possession can alone produce perfect happiness.

God alone is the perfect being sufficiently great to satisfy man's craving to be perfectly happy. If God had so wished, He could have assigned man the goal of seeing Him by the natural light of reason. Seeing God in this way would produce a happiness far superior to any aggregate earthly things could produce. Man would then possess the greatest possible good to the limit of his natural capacity. The happiness of heaven is vastly superior to perfect natural beatitude. It is the supernatural happiness of seeing God face to face. The soul in heaven experiences a happiness similar to God's happiness.

§ 8. *The supernatural happiness of heaven is produced by seeing God face to face.*

In the dogmatic constitution issued in 1336 A.D., Pope Benedict XII set down the Church's teaching on the Last Things. Concerning the happiness of heaven he said that the Saints "see the divine essence by intuitive vision, and even face to face, with no mediating creature, serving in the capacity of the object seen, but divine essence immediately revealing itself plainly, clearly, and openly to them . . . the souls . . . are truly blessed and have eternal life and rest." (D-530) Several Scripture texts are usually quoted on this subject. "We see now through a mirror in an obscure manner, but then face to face. Now I know in part, but then I shall know even as I have been known." (I Cor. 13:12) "We know that, when he (God) appears, we shall be like to him, for we shall see him just as he is." (I John 3:2)

The key to the understanding of the happiness of the saints is the expression "face to face." In the last section we saw that if a person could see God by the natural light of reason he would experience a happiness far greater than anything possible on earth. God is essentially supernatural to creatures. A soul seeing God by the natural light of reason would not see God as He is. The vision of God would be heavily veiled and obscured.

How can man see God as He is? It is plain that man's capacity for seeing God must be, not merely expanded, but it must be raised to an essentially higher plane. He must have a capacity for happiness similar to that which God Himself has, for the happiness of the Saints is similar to God's. The only difference is that man's happiness has the necessary limits of being experienced by a creature. Since the soul in heaven sees and enjoys God with absolutely no obstruction, it follows that there can be no happiness greater than this. Not even God in His infinite power could promise or give man a happiness greater than this one.

§ 9. *While everyone in heaven is perfectly happy, some are happier than others.*

The Council of Florence in 1439 A.D. taught that the Saints "are immediately received into heaven and see clearly the one and triune God Himself just as He is, yet according to the diversity of merits, *one more perfectly than another.*" (D-693) Jesus Himself revealed that in heaven some are happier than others when He said, "For the Son of Man is to come with his angels in the glory of his Father, and then he will render to everyone according to his conduct." (Matt. 16:27) The teaching of Sacred Tradition is uniform on this subject. St. Augustine said that while all the Saints shall not be equally happy in heaven, this difference will not cause any pain or jealousy.[3]

A soul in heaven is perfectly happy in the sense that his capacity for happiness is completely filled, but some souls have a greater capacity for happiness than others. The Church teaches that a person's capacity for happiness in heaven is in direct proportion to the sanctifying grace with which he departs this life. St. Thomas describes how the different capacities of souls in heaven result in greater happiness in some than others. "The intellect which has more of the light of glory will see God more perfectly; and he who has more charity will have a greater participation in the light of glory. Where there is greater charity, there is the more desire; and desire in a certain degree makes the one desiring apt and prepared to receive the object desired. Hence he who possesses the more charity, will see God more perfectly, and will be the more beatified, that is, happier."[4] While charity and sanctifying grace are not identically the same, the two are proportioned, and any increase in grace means an increase in charity.

§ 10. *The happiness of the Saints in heaven is everlasting.*

On many occasions, the Church has taught that the happiness of the Saints in heaven is everlasting. The most commonly used expression for heaven is "life everlasting." It appears in all the creeds drawn up by the authority of the Church since ancient times. In the pronouncement of Pope Benedict XII already quoted, we read that those who depart this life without the stain of any sin immediately begin to enjoy the intuitive vision of God and enjoy it from the time of their death until the last judgment and "thence forward forever." (D-530) Our Divine Lord explicitly states that the happiness is unending.

"The just . . . into everlasting life." (Matt. 25:46) Christian
writers teach the same doctrine. It is interesting to note that
while some heretics propounded errors on the nature of heav-
en, none of them denied that it is everlasting.

Not only will a soul in heaven not lose its happiness but it
cannot lose it in spite of the fact that even in heaven man's will
is free. The will's freedom is not taken away when the fixity
seizes it at death. The object of the will is that which is desirable, for the will is a choosing power. It cannot choose an
object which is not in some way desirable. But when an object
is partly undesirable, the intellect can concentrate on its defect
and judge the thing to be undesirable as a whole. The will then
makes the intellect's judgment final and rejects it. In heaven,
the soul sees God as the infinitely desirable being. There is in
Him not the slightest admixture of undesirableness. Once the
soul sees God, it freely chooses to have Him. It cannot possibly
find anything that could lead it to reject Him or to prefer anything else to Him. It has been proved that the soul is immortal.
It must be concluded that the soul's supernatural happiness
in heaven is everlasting.

§ 11. *It seems to be the more common opinion of theologians
and exegetes that the greater number of adult Catholics are
not saved.*

The question of the number of persons who are saved has arrested the attention of theologians of almost every age. Some
of them have expressed their opinion in works that have survived to the present day. While the author has no opinion on
the question, he thinks it interesting to note the opinions of
writers of past centuries.

Theologians and exegetes have expressed their opinion on
the number of those saved in their commentaries on these two
Gospel passages: "Enter by the narrow gate. For wide is the gate
and broad is the way that leads to destruction, and many there

are who enter that way. How narrow the gate and close the way that leads to life! And few there are who find it." (Matt. 7:13) "Many are called but few are chosen." (Matt. 22:14) The Church has not said that these passages prove that most adults are not saved.[5] But St. Jerome, St. Augustine, St. Basil the Great, St. John Chrysostom, St. Ephrem, St. Gregory the Great, St. Anselm, and St. Robert Bellarmine were of the opinion that they are not. Notice that everyone of them is a Doctor of the Church. Suarez, who held the opposite view, admitted that the more common was against him.

On what do these writers base their opinion? The principal reason is that the greater number of Christians live habitually in mortal sin and "as a person lives, so shall he die." It is not common for people who live in sin to die in sanctifying grace and vice versa. Experience has taught parish priests that death-bed conversions are far from easy and are seldom satisfactory.

§ 12. *The person who departs this life in mortal sin goes to hell forever.*

The doctrine of the existence of an eternal punishment for the wicked appears in official documents issued by the Church from early Christian times. In 1245 A.D., the Council of Lyons taught "If anyone without repentence dies in mortal sin, without doubt he is tortured forever by the flames of eternal hell." (D-457) Pope Benedict XII taught, "We declare that according to the common arrangement of God, the souls of those who depart in actual mortal sin immediately after their death descend to hell where they are tortured by infernal punishment." (D-531) Christ said, "It is better for thee to enter into life everlasting lame, than, having two feet, to be cast into the hell of unquenchable fire." (Mark 9:44) Notice how Christ used the term "unquenchable" to balance His use of the term "everlasting." An unusually large number of Scripture passages could be quoted to prove the existence of hell.

Some think that an eternity in hell is too severe a punishment for those who die with one mortal sin on their soul. They have probably lost sight of the true nature of a mortal sin. A person tempted to serious sin has two alternatives before him. They are God and a seriously forbidden object. When one chooses this object he of necessity rejects God, for the two cannot be simultaneously possessed. A mortal sin is, therefore, an act of implicit hatred of God. Even by one mortal sin, a person shows that he does not want God as his ultimate goal in life. St. Thomas pointed out that since the malice of a sin is measured by the dignity of the one offended, mortal sin is in a sense an act of infinite malice.[6] God, being infinitely just, cannot mete out a punishment out of proportion with the magnitude of the crime.

§ 13. *The principal suffering in hell is caused by the loss of God.*

In order to get a clear idea of the principal suffering of the souls in hell we must keep in mind the nature of man's rational powers. Far from losing these powers or having them dulled at death, the soul undergoes a great awakening. For the first time, it sees itself with perfect intuition and clearly grasps its nature, needs, and goal. It realizes that it was made to see the perfect truth and to enjoy the perfect good. It sees with startling clarity that nothing can take God's place as the cause of its happiness. It completely loses all interest in partial goods. By nature, the soul was made to be perfectly happy. It cannot do otherwise than to fling itself at God in order to have its terrible thirst and hunger for happiness completely slaked.

The soul must crave God but the will of the damned soul unalterably persists in its hatred and rejection of God. There endures for all eternity this horrible conflict in the soul between the nature attracted to God but the will obstinately rejecting Him. The resultant frustration and despair produces a suffering and a torture that human words cannot describe, nor can one adequately imagine. Thirst, hunger, and suffocation can transform a person into a raving maniac. Food, drink, and air are the objects of the appetites of man's body. He suffers terribly when he is denied them. The soul's need for God is as far greater as the soul is greater than the body. His supernatural goal is greater than his bodily needs. The suffering caused by the loss of God is as great as it is because it leaves such a great void. The greater the void, the greater the suffering. A person who commits a mortal sin does not reject God as his natural goal but as his supernatural goal. His capacity for happiness was greatly expanded. His capacity for suffering was likewise greatly expanded.

§ 14. *The damned souls in hell are tortured by fire.*

The Athanasian Creed drawn up and approved in the Fourth Century reads, "At His (Christ's) coming all men have to rise again with their bodies and will render an account of their own deeds: and those who have done good will go into life everlasting, but those who have done evil into *eternal fire*." (D-40) Sacred Scripture repeats the fact of fire in hell no less than thirty-eight times. Our Lord in describing the sentence to the reprobates said He would say, "Depart from me, accursed ones, into everlasting fire which was prepared for the devil and his angels." (Matt. 25:41) Several of the Apostolic Fathers contain evidence of belief in hell-fire by the earliest Christians. In the *Martyrium of St. Polycarp,* composed about 155 A.D., we read, "But Polycarp said (to the judge), 'You threaten me with the fire that burns for a time, and is quickly quenched, for you do not know the fire that awaits the wicked in the judgment to come and in everlasting punishment.' "[7]

What is the nature of the fire of hell? There is real difficulty in determining how corporeal fire as we know it on earth can have any effect on disembodied spirits. "There are two currents of opinion on this subject. One, going back to St. Augustine, holds that the fire of Hell exerts only a subjective or moral action upon the soul; the second adopted by St. Thomas, maintains that its action is physically effective."[8] In spite of the fact that they differ as to the mode of action of the fire on the soul, they agree that it is a real, physical fire though a fire which does not have the same properties as the fire of earth.

Theologians discuss why the damned are tortured by a secondary suffering. St. Thomas says that the punishments of hell match the two aspects of a sin. A mortal sin entails a turning away from God and a turning to a forbidden object. The first is punished by the loss of the infinite good, that is God; "insofar as sin turns inordinately to the mutable desirable object, its corresponding punishment is the pain of sense (fire) which is finite."[9]

§ 15. *The Church solemnly teaches the existence of purgatory.*

No notable heresy attacked the existence of Purgatory until the Sixteenth Century when certain leaders of the Protestant revolt denied it. Its existence was not even denied by Wycliffe and Hus. In 1563 A.D., the Council of Trent solemnly taught, "The Catholic Church, instructed by the Holy Spirit, in conformity with the sacred writings and the ancient tradition of the Fathers in sacred councils, and very recently in this ecumenical Synod, has taught that there is a purgatory—the holy Synod commands the bishops that they insist that the sound doctrine of purgatory be believed by the faithful of Christ, be maintained, taught, and everywhere preached." (D-983) Pope Leo X condemned the opinion of Luther that the existence of purgatory cannot be proved from the canonical Scriptures (D-777).

In 1254 A.D., Pope Innocent IV in a reference to purgatory quoted this Scriptural passage, "The work of each will be made manifest, for the day of the Lord will declare it, since the day is to be revealed in fire. The fire will assay the quality of everyone's work; if his work abides which he has built thereon, he will receive reward; if his work burns he will lose his reward, but himself will be saved, yet so as through fire." (I Cor. 3-13:15)

There is evidence in ancient Christian literature on belief in purgatory. "St. Augustine gave a very exact outline of the existence of purgatory which he establishes in I Cor. 3-11:13. He recognized that there is temporal punishment in the next life, by which souls are purified."[10]

§ 16. *In purgatory, souls with only venial sin or temporal punishment due to sin are cleansed before going to heaven.*

To understand why those in venial sin are sent to purgatory and not to hell, it is important that one grasp the nature of a venial sin. The Church teaches that mortal and venial sin are essentially different. They differ, not in degree, but in kind. A mortal sin is a sin in the strict sense of the term, for it strips the soul of sanctifying grace. A venial sin is a sin only by analogy, for it does not strip grace from the soul. The catechism says that venial sin is a slight offense against the law of God. The person who commits it does not reject God in favor of a seriously forbidden object. The choice of a slightly forbidden object is compatible with sanctifying grace. But it is a definite deformity. The Church calls attention to its malice, when she teaches that it is matter for confession. In this life, the debt for venial sin is remitted by satisfaction; in the next, it is remitted by "satispassion."

Every mortal sin implies a turning away from God and toward a forbidden creature. In mortal sin, the turning away from God is complete; in venial sin, there is no turning away from God. By turning away from God, one loses grace and contracts a debt of guilt; by turning toward a creature, he contracts a debt of punishment. These two debts are not extinguished at once. In this life, proper sorrow or absolution can erase the debt of guilt and part of the debt of punishment. If the debt of punishment is not completely erased before death, it must be erased by suffering in purgatory. We can liken a sin to a bodily wound. Different measures can be taken to stop the bleeding, but a scar remains after the wound is closed. The temporal punishment due to sin are the scars that sin leaves after the guilt has been removed.

§ 17. *The principal cause of suffering in purgatory is the soul's delay from seeing God.*

St. Thomas[11] proves that the suffering of purgatory is similar in intensity to that in hell except that those in purgatory do not experience the frustration of the damned. "The least pain of purgatory is greater than the greatest suffering of this life. The more ardently one desires a thing, the greater is the suffering caused by the lack of it. And since the regretful desire with which the holy souls hunger after the supreme God is most ardent . . . it follows that the suffering arising from the delay in attaining it is most intense." The soul's capacity for suffering is greatly increased after death. "Since the whole sensitiveness of the body is rooted in the soul, it follows that a more bitter affliction results from any suffering that directly affects the soul." Both of these causes of suffering are brought together when we say that the terrible suffering of purgatory must be traced to the soul's delay in reaching the goal for which it was created, namely, to see God face to face.

Is there fire in purgatory? There is no official statement on this point; the Scripture passages quoted by some to support belief in it have not been interpreted with uniformity by exegetes. The opinion that there is fire in purgatory is at best a doubtful one.

The suffering of the Poor Souls in Purgatory is not without some consolation. It must be remembered that they have departed this life with sanctifying grace in their souls. And this grace makes its force felt. It engenders a great love of God and an assurance that the soul will eventually see God. The love of God combined with the assurance of seeing Him must create a joy and expectation far beyond any experienced on earth. The Church has branded as heretical the opinion that the souls in purgatory are not sure of salvation (D-778).

§ 18. *The faithful on earth can use the appointed means to shorten the stay of the poor souls in purgatory.*

The person who departs this life in venial sin must have both the debt of guilt and debt of punishment removed from his soul before he can enter heaven. Even after death the debt of guilt can be removed only with an act of sorrow which is an act of love or its equivalent. There is nothing contradictory about a soul already in grace making a new act of love. While this act of love can erase guilt it cannot win new merit for the soul (*Supp. Q.* 7, A.1).

In 1439 A.D., The Council of Florence taught, "So that they (Poor Souls in purgatory) may be released from punishments of this kind, the suffrages of the living faithful are of advantage to them, namely, the sacrifices of the Mass, prayers, and alms-giving, and other works of piety, which are customarily per-formed by the faithful for other faithful according to the insti-tutions of the Church." (D-693) The Church teaches that the indulgences gained by the living on earth can help the Poor Souls in purgatory (D-723a -740a).

St. John Chrysostom has written a very explicit statement on the topic being discussed. "As far as lies within our power, we must help them (Poor Souls), not by tears but by prayers and supplications, by alms and intercessions. It is not without rea-son that these practices have been established, nor is it in vain that in the Sacred Myteries (the Mass) we make a memorial of them that are no more."[12]

Two of the most famous discoveries of Christian archeology

of the Second Century implore the living to pray for the dead. They are the inscription of Pectorius of Autun in Gaul and the inscription of Abercius found at Hieropolis in Asia Minor. The latter says in two of its lines, "Let him who understands these things and grasps their meaning, pray for Abercius." The places where these monuments were found, that is, in widely separated and little known places, shows that it was the universal practice of the Church even in those days to pray for the faithful departed.

§ 19. *The Church teaches that all the dead will arise again with the same bodies that they had during life.*

In 1274 A.D., the Council of Lyons taught, "The same most holy Roman Church firmly believes and firmly declares that on the day of judgment all men will be brought together with their bodies before the tribunal of Christ to render an account of their own deeds." (D-464) The dogma of the resurrection of the body is mentioned in every creed drawn up throughout the Church's history beginning from the Apostles' Creed composed about 100 A.D.

Belief in the resurrection of the body is firmly anchored in Scripture and Tradition. A classic passage is the following, "Now if Christ is preached as risen from the dead, how do some among you say that there is no resurrection of the dead? But if there is no resurrection of the dead, neither has Christ risen; and if Christ has not risen, vain then is our preaching, vain too is your faith." (I Cor. 15:12-14) Several decades after St. Paul wrote his epistle to the Corinthians, Pope St. Clement of Rome dispatched his famous letter to the Christians of the same city. In it he wrote, "Let us consider how the Master continually proves to us that there will be a future resurrection, of which he has made the first fruits, by raising the Lord Jesus Christ from the dead." (Ch. 24)

Why is it fitting that the dead should arise? It is a principle of philosophy that all actions must be traced to the supposite that performed them. A human being is a rational nature or supposite called a person formed by the substantial union of body and soul. Justice demands that everything involved in good or bad should be rewarded or punished. It is necessary, therefore, that the body should share in one's reward or punishment. This would be impossible if the person that performed the acts was not reconstituted by a resurrection from the dead. St. Thomas shows that since it is natural for the soul to be united to the body, it cannot reach its complete perfection without this body. While the souls in heaven are perfectly happy, they are completely happy only joined to their bodies. Since this perfection will not be denied them, there will be a resurrection of the body.

§ 20. *After the resurrection, the bodies of the Saints will have the notes of impassibility, brightness, spirituality, and agility.*

It is defined doctrine that all will arise from the dead with the same bodies they had during life on earth. The qualities of the bodies of the Saints will be patterned after that of Christ after His resurrection. It is theologically certain that they will have characteristics listed in this proposition. St. Paul wrote, "So also with the resurrection of the dead. What is sown in corruption rises in incorruption; what is sown in dishonor rises in glory; what is sown in weakness rises in power; what is sown a natural body rises a spiritual body." (I Cor. 15:43, 44) These are the four qualities of a glorified body. (1) *Impassibility* means that the glorified body will be incapable of suffering and dying. It will be above the need for food and bodily necessities of mortal bodies. St. Paul calls this quality "incorruption." (2) The *brightness* of the glorified body is a radiance like that which Christ exhibited at the transfiguration even before His resurrection. St. Thomas says that all deformities will be made good. The marks of wounds which martyrs endured for Christ will remain to enhance the glory of the body even as the print of the nails and spear remained in the body of the Risen Christ (3) *Spirituality* means that although the glorified body is as material as Christ's was, it will act and behave like a spirit. For example, it will be able to penetrate material substances as Our Lord's Body did when He appeared to the Apostles in the upper room. (4) Agility means that the glorified body will no longer be subject to the limitations of space. It will be able to move from place to place with great speed. The bodies of the wicked, while having agility and spirituality, will not have the qualities of brightness and impassibility.

§ 21. *Jesus Christ in person will conduct the general judgment of all the members of the human race.*

This proposition has three parts. The first is that besides the particular judgment that all undergo individually, there will be a general judgment when all men will be judged; the second is that this judgment is all inclusive, for no human being will be excepted; the third is that Christ will be the judge. The Nicene Creed drawn up in 325 A.D. reads, "We believe . . . in Jesus Christ . . . who was made man, and suffered, and arose again on the third day, and ascended into heaven, and will come to judge the living and the dead." (D-54) The same doctrine in almost the same words was repeated by the Council of Constantinople in 381 A.D. and the Lateran Council of 649 A.D. The expression "living and dead" means all humans without exception, thereby, precluding any humans living on earth after this judgment, hence the label "General Judgment."

Christ described this judgment. "The Son of Man shall come in his majesty, and all the angels with him, then he will sit on the throne of his glory; and before him will be gathered all the nations, and he will separate them one from another."

(Matt. 25:31, 32) He says that charity will be the touchstone for dividing the good from the bad. This is to be expected, for where charity is there also is sanctifying grace.

St. Thomas lists a number of reasons why Christ in Person should conduct the General Judgment. The Saints will go to heaven because they accepted Christ; the wicked are damned because they rejected Him. The Blessed are saved because they believed the truths He revealed, obeyed His precepts of morals, used the Sacraments He instituted, and followed the guidance of the Church He founded. The wicked are condemned because by rejecting Christ's truths, commandments, sacraments, and Church, they rejected Him.

NOTES

1. *S.T.*, II-II, 164, 1.
2. *S.T.*, Suppl., 69, 2.
3. *Enchiridion*, ch. 111.
4. *S.T.*, I, 12, 6.
5. Chitignano, *L'Uomo in Paradiso*, p. 269.
6. *S.T.*, III, 1, 2.
7. Ch. 11, 2.
8. Michel, *The Last Things*, p. 67.
9. *S.T.*, I-II, 87, 4.
10. Cayre, *Manual of Patrology* (Tournai: Desclee & Co., 1936), I, 712.
11. *S.T.*, Suppl., 2, 1.
12. *Hom. In I Cor.*, No. 4.

Epilogue

"Blessed is the man that shall meditate on the law of God day and night." (Ps. 1:3)

The Gospels record three episodes when peculiar questions were put to Christ. In the first, the Jews asked, "Is it lawful to pay tribute to Caesar, or not?" In the second, the lawyer wishing to justify himself asked, "And who is my neighbor?" In the third, Pilate asked, "What is truth?" All these questions had something in common. Not one of them was an honest inquiry. Those who asked the questions were not seeking correct answers to them. The Jews wished to stir up hatred against Christ; the lawyer wanted to justify himself; Pilate's question was really the answer of a sophist who had despaired of finding truth.

The three episodes referred to here are capable of a wider and figurative interpretation. They epitomize the attitude of the world at large toward Christ, toward His teaching, and toward His Church. They are no longer put to Christ in person, for Christ no longer walks the earth in human form. But they are put to His Mystical Body which is the Church. Today, those who ask these questions labor under the same affected ignorance as the Gospel inquirers did. But the Church has not sidestepped those questions. She has answered them for all who have the sincerity to listen and to understand.

The modern contemporaries of those who asked whether or not it was lawful to pay tribute to Caesar are those who ask the Church why she does not have more interest in science, sociology, world affairs, and the rest. They complain that she does not care to improve man's lot in this world. To the first group of inquirers, Christ answered, "Render to Caesar the things that are Caesar's." The same answer is still valid for the modern inquirers. The Church cautions us to be in the world, but not of the world.

The Church has a double answer for the moderns who ask, "And who is my neighbor?" She first answers that it is every human being made to the image and likeness of God. She then repeats that this neighbor must be the object of charity, not cold philanthropy. Moderns have woefully confused these two terms. Those that practice philanthropy instead of charity run the grave risk of falling into the unfortunate position of the pharisee who praying said, "I thank Thee, O Lord, that I am not like the rest of men . . . I give alms twice a week."

When Pilate cynically asked, "What is truth?" he was unwittingly the spokesman for millions of sophists who would populate this planet in the centuries after him. The first generation of these sophists were those who conducted St. Paul to the areopagus to hear his views on truths, but stayed to listen only so long as he said what they wanted to hear. Never has there been so much talk about truth as there is today, and never have there been so few who could define its meaning. It would be a mistake for us here to examine the many new and novel definitions of truth that have appeared in recent decades. This would give their proponents a prominence that they do not deserve.

To the honest inquirer who asks "What is truth?" and "What is wisdom?" the Church points out that in its highest form it is the content of revelation. This is the most noble body of doctrine that has or can arrest the attention of man. This truth rests on the firmest possible certitude and leads one to his loftiest goal.

The Church reminds those who already possess the faith that they must make their faith ripen into realization of the meaning of these truths. Simple faith accepts a truth; realization drives it home. The first has an effect on the intellect; the second has a great effect on the will. Faith changes one's pattern of thinking while realization changes one's pattern of living. The former speaks to the mind; the latter speaks to the heart. In short, Holy Mother Church bids us to follow the advice of the Psalmist who wrote, "Blessed is the man that shall meditate on the law of God day and night. He shall be like a tree which is planted near the running waters, which shall bring forth its fruit in due season." (Ps. 1:3)

BIBLIOGRAPHY

Bibliography

ADAM, KARL. *The Spirit of Catholicism.* Translated by Dom Justin Mc-
Cann. New York: MacMillan, 1941.

ALEXANDER. *College Apologetics.* Chicago: Regnery, 1954.

BUCKLEY. *Man's Last End.* St. Louis: Herder, 1949.

CALLAN-McHUGH. *Catechism of the Council of Trent.* New York: Wagner,
1937.

CAYRE. *Manual of Patrology.* 2 vols. Translated by Howitt. Tournai:
Desclee & Co., 1936.

DENZINGER. *Sources of Catholic Dogma.* Translated by DeFerrari. St.
Louis: Herder, 1957.

GARRIGOU-LAGRANGE. *The One God.* Translated by Dom Bede Rose. St.
Louis: Herder, 1943.

JOURNEL. *Enchiridion Patristicum.* Freiburg, Herder, 1928.

KLEIN. *The Doctrine of the Trinity.* New York: Kenedy, 1940.

MICHEL. *The Last Things.*

MARUCCHI. *Manual of Christian Archeology.* Translated by Vecchierello.
Paterson: St. Anthony Guild, 1935.

OTT. *Fundamentals of Catholic Dogma.* St. Louis: Herder, 1954.

OTTEN. *History of Dogma.* 2 vols. St. Louis: Herder, 1918.

PARENTI. *Dictionary of Dogmatic Theology.* Milwaukee: Bruce, 1951.

PHILLIPS. *Modern Thomistic Philosophy.* 2 vols. London: Burns-Oates,
1934.

POHLE-PREUSS. *Dogmatic Theology.* 12 vols. St. Louis: Herder, 1937.

POPE. *St. Augustine of Hippo.* Westminster: Newman, 1949.

PRAT. *The Theology of St. Paul.* 2 vols. Translated by Stoddard. London:
Burns-Oates, 1942.

QUASTEN. *Patrology.* 3 vols. Westminster: Newman, 1950.

RICCIOTTI. *The Life of Christ.* Milwaukee: Bruce, 1947.

RICCIOTTI. *Paul the Apostle.* Milwaukee: Bruce, 1953.

St. Thomas Aquinas. *Summa Theologica.* 3 vols. Translated by English Dominicans. New York: Benziger. 1947.

Sheeben. *The Mysteries of Christianity.* St. Louis: Herder, 1946.

Smith. *The Teachings of the Catholic Church.* 2 vols. New York: Mac-Millan, 1949.

Studies in Comparative Religion. 5 vols. London: Catholic Truth Society, 1925.

Tixeront. *History of Dogmas.* 3 vols. St. Louis: Herder, 1930.

Wilhelm-Scannell. *Manual of Dogmatic Theology.* 2 vols. London: Kegan-Paul, 1890.

INDEX

Index